P9-CDM-056

Cookson, Catherine

The black velvet gown

DATE DUE		
JUN 1 7 1987	AUG 1 0 1990	
SEP 1 2 1987	FEB 1 3 1991	
SEP 2 8 1987	MAR 1 9 1991	
APR 29 88	JUL 2 1991	
	NOV 9 1991	
SEP 13 88	NOV 1 8 1991	
DEC 7 88	APR 1 1 1992	
NOV 9	MAY 2 1 1992	
FEB 1 3 1990	JUN 1 2 1992	
APR 1 3 1990	JUL 6 1992	
APR 3 0 1990	MAY 1 8 1993	
JUL 2 1990		

X

MYNDERSE LIBRARY

31 FALL STREET

SENECA FALLS, NY 13148

THE
BLACK VELVET
GOWN

A NOVEL BY
CATHERINE COOKSON

SUMMIT BOOKS
New York

This novel is a work of fiction. Names, characters, places and
incidents are either the product of the author's imagination or
are used fictitiously. Any resemblance to actual events or
locales or persons, living or dead, is entirely coincidental.

Copyright ©1984 by Catherine Cookson
All rights reserved
including the right of reproduction
in whole or in part in any form
Published by SUMMIT BOOKS
A Division of Simon & Schuster, Inc.
Simon & Schuster Building
1230 Avenue of the Americas
New York, New York 10020

SUMMIT BOOKS and colophon are trademarks of Simon & Schuster, Inc.
First published in Great Britain in 1984 by William Heinemann Ltd.
Also available in Pocket Books Paperback Edition
Manufactured in the United States of America

1   3   5   7   9   10   8   6   4   2

First American Edition
ISBN 0-671-46788-3

Fic.

MYNDERSE LIBRARY
31 Fall Street
Seneca Falls, New York 13148

Contents

CARROLL COUNTY
PUBLIC LIBRARY
DUST JACKET COLLECTION

PART ONE

The Journey

1

❧❧

The pit shaft would have been in their backyard if the pit rows had had a combined backyard, but they stood one behind the other, separated only by the ash-middens and the new innovation, the wooden-box privies.

The rows had dainty names: Primrose, Cowslip, and Dog Daisy. There were twenty-five cottages to each of the first two rows and thirty-three to the third row, Dog Daisy. The residents in Dog Daisy considered themselves lucky because from their single window in the downstairs room and their similar but smaller one in the upstairs they could view the fells, and on a clear day see the top of the mast of a ship going down the river.

The pit community was like one large family, yet, like a family, separated through marriage. So did the inhabitants of each row combine to gather together and preserve their own interests; until a time of calamity hit them, when, just as would a family at a funeral, so all three rows would group as one.

They were all well aware, even as tiny children, from where calamity sprang. It came out of that hole in the ground: it came out through water or fire, and it didn't even provide some men with the dignity of a funeral, not under the open sky anyway; it buried them, certainly, under mausoleums of stone.

But the latest calamity to strike the rows hadn't come from the mine. It was a strange new calamity, like a fever, but worse. It emptied the stomach both ways and brought water from the pores like tears from the eyes, and had a strange name, they called it cholera.

The scourge had passed now, but there were four men, two women, and three children less in the rows.

Seth Millican had been the first to go; and the one, they whispered, who had brought the disease to the rows. And all because he must visit that man in Gateshead who had taught him his letters.

Pride went before a fall, they said when he had died. He had been an overproud man, had Seth Millican, and not because of the work he could do with his hands and because he set the pace down below at the coal-face, but because he could write his name and read the Bible. But his pride had stretched too far when he refused to let his eldest son and daughter go down below, and the boy ten and the lass nine. No, it had to be working in the fields for them, under God's sky. And he hadn't been shamed into doing it, even after Parson Rainton had told him that God allotted man a certain free time to enjoy the sun and light according to the station in life to which he had been appointed. And it was known far and wide what answer Seth Millican had given to Parson Rainton. "To hell with that idea," he had said. And it was also said that the parson hadn't cursed him in words but in his look, and his look had borne fruit. And it was also said that Seth Millican would now be sorting his ideas out in hell.

Then there was Seth Millican's wife Maria, known as Riah. She had come as an intrusion into the row, for she was the daughter of a fishwife from Shields. And, as everybody knew, such a marriage wasn't a good thing: those who sailed over the land and those who crawled under it could never meet.

But Seth Millican and Maria Riston had met, and married when he was twenty-six and she but sixteen, and in the ten years since they had reared four of the eight children she had given birth to. Such was her stamina.

Unlike many women in the row, Riah still carried herself straight. Her stomach wasn't flabby; her hair still retained its bright auburn shade; her eyes still flashed; and her tongue, it was said, could clip clouts, so sharp was it. And it had sharpened since her man had died, especially when directed towards Bill Norsecott.

Others had turned their eyes on her, but the one who seemed unable to turn them away was Bill Norsecott. And it was this man who was under discussion now in the Millicans' two-roomed earth-floored habitation that was called a house.

Riah stood to the side of the table, one hand on the edge of it, the other spanning her hip. Her head was up and back and held slightly to the side as she looked at her brother-in-law and said, "I've told you, Ted, if Norsecott was the last man on God's earth

4

I wouldn't let him touch the mud trail on me skirt. What you're proposin' in order to provide meself with a roof is for me to take him and his nine bairns on. Ted——" Her face screwed up until the eyes were lost in their large sockets, and now the lips spread away from her teeth as she finished, "Man, there's no room in that pigsty for them lot never mind me and my four. Fifteen of us in that hovel! Oh" – she now shook her head slowly from side to side – "I thought you had a little more respect for me, Ted Millican, than to propose that."

Ted Millican, so unlike his deceased brother in all ways in that he was small in stature and of a poor intelligence, muttered now, "It's either that or the road, Riah. If Seth had died in the pit there might have been a chance of them transferring you down to The Mouldings, but even those have gone to the new men coming in. He didn't die in the pit though, and so there's no chance they'll let you stay here. Brannigan's coming along any time now to tell you to get. That's why I mentioned Bill, in fact." He stumbled on now, "Well, it's like this, I ... I had a word with him and he's willing to take you and...."

Before he could draw breath for the next word, she almost screamed at him, "Willing to take me! Bill Norsecott, that snotty-nosed, dirty, drunken numskull willing to take me. Go on, get out, Ted. Get out afore I lose me temper altogether. ... But wait, let me tell you this: I'm not goin' to wait to be put out, I'm goin', an' back to me people. And if I have nothing else there, I'll have fresh air, for I can tell you now, I've hated every day I've been on the doorstep of this pit, with the mountains of slag getting nearer, an' the middens and the folks an' all. Aye, an' the folks an' all, who had the nerve to look down on my Seth because he wanted to make somethin' of himself and his family. If it hadn't been for the respect I had for him and the kind of man he was, I'd have up and went in the first months of me marriage. And one last thing I'll say to you before you go, Ted. I notice that you and Mary Ellen haven't offered us shelter. There's only two of you and your two lads, and one of them's courting and will soon be gone."

She watched her brother-in-law now hang his head before he said, "'Tisn't that I didn't think of it, Riah, 'tisn't that, but you know Mary Ellen. You and her has never seen eye to eye, and, put under the same roof, there would be hell to pay."

Riah's attitude changing now, she sighed, then said quietly,

"Yes, I know that, Ted. And I feel if it had been left to you things would have been different. But don't worry about us. I'm capable of seeing to me own. I always have and I always will."

The man stood at the open door now and looked into the roadway where the April showers coming over into early May had left puddles in which tiny children splashed their bare feet and cried joyfully in their play, being as yet unconscious of the dark days ahead. "When are you goin'?" he said.

"The morrow, early."

He turned his head as he asked, "What about your bits and pieces? Mary Ellen . . .." He checked himself, then said, "I'd store your bed and things."

There was a cynical note in her voice as she replied, "Yes, I know you would, and Mary Ellen too, but I've thought about me bits and pieces over the last few days. It took money and hard grime to get them and I don't want to give them up, so Arthur Meddle and Kate are going to take them into their place for me. They've hardly anything upstairs except the shaky-down, so they'll be glad to make use of them for a time. And Kate's a clean and careful woman."

His head still turned towards her, he said, "You haven't been idle then?"

"No, Ted, I've never been idle in me life, whether it was workin' with me hands or me head."

"You're a strange lass, Riah. I've never met anyone with as much gumption. If I don't see you again, because I go down at two o'clock an' you'll be away afore noon when I rise, I wish you luck. In all you do, I wish you luck, Riah."

"Thanks, Ted."

She waited until he had taken so many steps from the doorway, and then she went to it and closed it. And now standing with her back to it, she pressed her hands flat against its rough wood, and, her even white teeth coming down sharply on her lower lip, she made a small sound; it was the echo of a groan deep within her. Gumption, he had said she had. She could go back to where she had come from, she had said. If they had nothing else, they would have fresh air, she had said. Her gumption, at this moment, she knew was threaded with fear and she knew exactly the welcome that awaited her when she went back from where she had come; and as for having fresh air, if nothing else, the fresh air she

6

remembered from those far times reeked with the stink of fish.

She brought herself from the door and went towards the fire, and taking up a bucket of small coal that stood on the hearth, she flung its contents on to the back of the grate. As she did so a cloud of dust went up the chimney, but the rest wafted its way over her face. She puffed at it for a moment; then taking a cloth from the brass rod that ran under the wooden mantelpiece, she went to the table and began to wipe it down.

Of a sudden she stopped and, pulling from underneath it a wooden stool, she sat down and, leaning her elbows on the table, she rested her head in her hands. She wanted to pray but she could find no words; and anyway, Seth had always said, God helps those who helps themselves. He used to laugh when he said it because he called it a contradiction: as he said, if you didn't help yourself, then nothing happened and you blamed it on God. She had often wondered what he had talked about with the Methodist man in Gateshead who appeared to be a good Christian, because at bottom Seth hadn't much time for God and His Doings; even the Bible, he said, was just stories thought up and written by men.

She had learned a lot from Seth. He had taught her to use her mind, and he had taught her to read and write, as he had them all. She had been proud of the fact that she was mother to the only children in the three rows who could write their names. This alone had set them all apart. Seth could have taught lots of men in the rows to read and write, but they were afraid in case the pit keeker split on them to the manager, because reading was frowned upon, and, as some of the older men had pointed out forcibly to Seth, it got you nowhere except into trouble with those that provided your livelihood. And after all they had them to consider: you didn't turn round and bite the hand that fed you.

Only two men in the rows had braved the wrath of the owners and the management and sat in of a night with Seth: Arthur Meddle and Jack Troughton. But they'd had to pay for it. They, like Seth, had been put on to poor seams down below, seams that gave more rock than coal and where a twelve hour shift barely brought in three shillings.

Oh, education had to be paid for and paid for dearly. But what filled the head didn't fill the belly, and Seth had always been aware of this. That's why he had prepared for a rainy day. For ten years he had prepared for that rainy day, saving only coppers some

7

weeks, a shilling others. In the first month of their marriage he had told her of his scheme to save, because he didn't always want to work in a mine, and he envisaged buying a little cottage of their own and a piece of land. And she knew that in the first year he had saved one pound fifteen shillings. But strangely, from that time onwards he had never told her how much he put away each week. He was paid once a fortnight and some pay days he had put as little on the table as a single sovereign. He had been sparse in his dealings with a number of things. After the second year of marriage he had never said he loved her, but she took it for granted that he did; nor had he been gentle with her without expecting to be satisfied in return.

He had first seen her when she was fifteen, when, late on a free Saturday afternoon, he had walked along the Shields quay. She had been standing amid a group of fishwives. Her head was bare and she wasn't wearing the usual thick blue flannel voluminous skirt with its white apron in front, nor the cross-over body shawl, but she was in a blouse dress, the top layer of the skirt taken back and pinned under her buttocks, and she had a yellow patterned neckerchief over her shoulders. The skirt came just below her calves, and she had clogs on her feet. He said it was her eyes that he noticed first. He said he spotted the intelligence in them when they first looked at him.

From that day he had come to the quay on a Sunday and any free Saturday night he had; and on his sixth visit he spoke to her. "Hello," he said. "Hello," she said.

"You are a fisherman's daughter?" he said.

"Yes," she said.

"You don't look like one," he said.

"Oh, what did you expect me to look like? Cod, salmon or smoked fresh herring?"

He hadn't laughed but said, "You know what I mean." And that had caused her to be silent.

It was on that day that her mother said, "Who was that pit lout you were talking to?" And she had asked, "How do you know he's a pit lout?" And her mother's answer had been, "You can tell, the coal's got into his veins. There's blue marks on his brow. Have nothing to do with him," she had warned her. "There's plenty of fisher lads for your choosing. If you feel ripe the sooner you look among them the better."

8

Odd; she had never liked her mother; but she had loved her father. He had put out to sea one day with her two brothers when she was ten years old and they were never seen again. Three boats were lost that day, two from North Shields and one from the South side.

She'd also had a strong dislike for the smell of fish, and she wondered why that was because she had been reared on it. She had been forced to eat so much fish that her stomach had revolted; cod in particular made her retch. At times when this happened her mother would say she took after her grandfather for it was known that he was a landsman and finicky, besides which he was a square-head Swede, and had hair so fair that it was as rare among their own men as a woman's bare backside.

Her first-born, David, took after the square-head, for he too had hair and skin that stood out markedly from the children about the doors; and, working in the fields as he did, his hair became even more bleached by the sun, and, unlike that of many of his age down the mine, was not matted with coal-dust or running with head-lice.

That was another thing that Seth had been particular about: everybody had to wash all over on a Friday night, summer and winter alike. He himself washed his upper parts every day and his water couldn't be used again. But on a Friday night he saw that the children one after another went into the tin bath, and she herself followed them; then he, last of all, washed himself straight down.

She had come to like the ritual on the Friday nights. It added to the feeling that her family were different. The only time the routine was broken was when Seth lay on the plank bed in the corner of the room waiting for the hearse to come and take him away. He had died only that morning; but he was to have the honour of being ridden to his grave in a hearse. That honour wasn't awarded to the poor very often unless there was a great whip round to pay for an undertaker. But in the case of the cholera the authorities transported all the bodies to the graveyard in a hearse.

She sighed deeply now, then rose to her feet. It was on half-past six; the children would be in from the fields shortly. Johnny, seven, and Maggie, six, had been stone picking on Bateman's farm for the past two weeks. It was hard work for bairns from eight in

9

the morning till six at night. And then there was the mile walk there, and back. But sixpence a week was sixpence a week and not to be sneezed at. David who was working near Gateshead Fell, brick carrying for the men who were putting up houses, was getting three shillings a week. And Biddy who was a year younger was working in Mrs Bateman's kitchen for a full one and six a week and her food. Five and sixpence from four of them was nothing to what they could have earned down the mine. But she had been with Seth all the way in being determined that none of her bairns should go below if she could help it.

But now they would all lose their jobs because there wasn't a house to be let within miles, and no farm mistress would take her on with the addition of four youngsters. She had even made a suggestion to Mrs Bateman, and the farmer's wife had laughed at her, saying, "If I had a pigsty, missis, I could let it for rent. Anyway, what use could I put four of them to? Things are bad; we can hardly sell our stuff in the market at times. And it's your lot that causes it, with their strikes. Strikes. My word! I know what I would do with them; gaol them; shoot them."

She hadn't answered the woman, for what answer could she give to gaol them, shoot them?

But as regards rent: that was a point nobody but herself knew about, for she could pay the rent on any cottage, and all because of Seth's little hoard. . . . But what was she talking about, terming it little? Eighteen pounds, fifteen shillings was a small fortune. It was odd when she came to think about it. Seth had known he was dying, yet he never mentioned the money or where it was hidden. She had known for a long time it was behind one of the bricks in the fireplace. But most of them were loose, and she had never attempted to pry because, being sharp-eyed and sharp-witted like he was, he would have known, and that would have caused a difference between them, and she had never wanted that.

Although during the past years the warm feeling she had for him had dwindled and its place had been taken by respect, they still lived a peaceful and comparatively happy life; at least so she had told herself, especially when she'd had to clamp down on the inner feelings and unrest that rampaged about the stomach at times, those times when a little gentleness, a touch of the hand on her hair, or her cheek, or his arm thrown over her in the night would have sufficed to soothe the unrest within her. But he wasn't a man like that, so life had gone on from day to day.

Bridget was the first to come home. She was known as Biddy. She was tall for her nine years and was of the same colouring as her mother. Her hair might have had a brighter sheen, but her eyes were the same brown, and her height promised that she would grow taller than her mother. All her movements spoke of liveliness, the way she lifted her feet, the turn of her head, her lips that opened to laugh easily and often at something she herself had said, because she was of a quick wit. "Hello, Ma," she said.

"Hello, hinny," said Riah.

"She let me keep the slippers. But then they wouldn't hold much water, would they?" She now stuck her fingers through the holes in the house slippers. "I nearly said, 'Thank you very much, missis, you can pass them on to the next one,' but I thought I'd better not."

"I should think better not. You shouldn't be cheeky."

"I'm tired, Ma." The brightness went out of the child's voice for a moment, and her mother said to her, "Well, sit yourself down then. There's some broth ready."

The girl sat down on a cracket near the fire; then turning her head to her mother, she said, "She was like the prophet from the Bible, Ma. She spoke of nothing else but doom because we are leavin'. I don't think she wanted to lose me."

"No, she wouldn't, because you can work as good as anyone twice your age. Of course, she wouldn't."

"You know what she said, Ma?"

"No. What did she say?" Riah was putting some wooden bowls on the table.

"She said we were all too big for our boots, and you would find your mistake out she said, bein' able to write your name wouldn't peel any taties. . . . She can't write, Ma. None of them can, not even the master; he counts up the cans of milk with straws in a jar." Her face now broke into a broad smile and she bent forward, her arms hugging her waist, as she said, "You know what I did the day, Ma?"

"No. What did you do?"

"Well, when she sent me over to get the milk, I stuck in six more straws."

It was a long time since Riah had laughed, but she turned and leant her buttocks against the side of the table and, like her daughter, she also leant forward and with her arms around her waist, too, she laughed until the tears came into her eyes. Then not knowing whether she was laughing or crying, she went swiftly to her daughter and sat down beside her on another cracket, and, taking her hands, gripped them tightly as she said, "We'll be all right. We'll be all right. As long as we can laugh we'll be all right. Oh dear me!" She shook her head. "What a fuss there'll be when she tries to find the other six pails of milk."

"I thought of that, Ma." Biddy's face was wet. "And I could see the missis skittering around blaming everybody for drinking them; and then it might dawn on them that the cows couldn't give all that much extra in one day, and then they would start to think."

Riah now nodded her head and bit on her lip, "Yes, and who would they think about?" she said.

As they were laughing the door opened, and when the boy came into the room and dropped his bait tin and cap on to the table his mother rose and, looking at him, said one word, "Well?"

He answered quietly, "He didn't mind. He said I was a fool, 'cos there's another twenty to step into me shoes."

"They wouldn't work like you."

"Yes, they would." He moved his head slowly. "When you're hungry you'll work twice as hard, and most of them are hungry."

She turned away as if ashamed of depriving him of his work. But quickly she was confronting him again, her voice harsh as she said, "We've got to get out of here. There's no other way. Anyway, you said yourself you would be glad to get away because it was killing work."

"I know. I know." He nodded at her now, his tone soothing. "But I'm just afraid I won't get another job, for I wouldn't be able to fish, 'cos you know I can hardly stand going over in the ferry let alone go out to sea."

"Nobody'll expect you to fish; there'll be plenty of other work in Shields. There's chemical works there, and there's Cookson's glass works, blacking factories and nail making places. When I was a young lass the place was alive with factories and there'll be many more now. Then of course there's the boat building. Oh, there'll be heaps to choose from, more than around here. This place is a dead end."

"But where'll we live?"

12

She paused and half turned from him before she said, "Well, we'll stay at your granny's for a time, and then we'll get a house."

"Me granny doesn't like us."

Riah turned and looked at her daughter now and drew in a deep breath before saying to her, "That's as may be, but when people are in a fix she's all right that way; I mean, she'll help. Anyway, it'll just be for a day or two till I can look round. And as your da always said, education's starting there, people are looking ahead. There's Sunday Schools an' things."

"We can beat anybody from Sunday Schools." Biddy now glanced at her brother as she added, "We could beat them at Sunday School, couldn't we, Davey?"

The boy didn't answer; he was looking at his mother. "Have we any money to carry on with?" he asked her.

"Yes" – she nodded – "we have money to carry on with." She hadn't told them what she had found in the bag behind the loose bricks, the fourteenth one she had taken out of the fire breast, because she was of the opinion that no matter how much children were told to hold their tongues, they let things slip out, particularly if they thought they were rich, and eighteen pounds fifteen shillings would have spelt a great fortune to them at this moment.

The boy waited, his eyes narrowed towards her as if he was expecting her to go on, but she turned towards the fire and opening the door of the round oven she took out an earthenware dish which she carried to the table and there ladled out two bowlsful of soup, saying as she did so, and at the same time jerking her head towards the bucket at the end of the room, "Wash your hands. And then after your meal you'd better go down to the burn and starting bringing up the water for the bath."

"'Tisn't Friday." Biddy was now seated at the table, spoon in hand and half-way to her mouth, and her mother answered, "No, it isn't Friday, and I doubt if there'll be any more Fridays for a long time. We'll have to see how it goes."

"Will we have to wash in the river at Shields?" There was a twinkle in Biddy's eye and her mother slapped her face gently with the back of her hand, saying, "You'll have to put up with worse things than that afore you're much older, girl."

Presently she looked towards the narrow window and said, "The others are late. They are likely waiting for Paddy's cart,"

Davey said as he sat down at the table. "He sometimes gives them a lift."

Presently, speaking as if to herself, Biddy said, "They get tired, especially Maggie. Her back aches. It isn't right . . . 'tisn't . . . ."

"Now don't you start on that, girl; there's nobody knows better than me that it isn't right. But what would you have, her go down the pit?"

"Aw, Ma."

"Never mind, aw Ma. Get on with your dinner. That tongue of yours is too sharp by far."

As she finished speaking the door opened and the two younger children came in. Johnny, aged seven, was a replica of his father, dark haired, dark eyed, slightly built, whereas the girl was a different colour from any of the others. Her hair was brown, her eyes green and her skin, even under the dust and dirt, showed up in patches to be deeply cream tinted. It was the boy who spoke first. His voice was bright like his sister Biddy's, and he said, "I told him, Ma. He didn't like it, but he said there were others to fill our place."

Riah made no reply to this but said, "Clean yourselves," and nodded towards the pail before going to the oven once more and taking out the dish.

Not until the children were all seated did she herself sit at the table. Although Davey and Biddy soon emptied their bowls, they wouldn't ask for more until all had finished, and they both watched their mother spooning the soup slowly into her mouth and noticing the difficulty at times she seemed to have in swallowing it. They weren't given bread with their soup; this would come as a sort of extra after it with pig's fat or dripping.

Riah knew they were waiting patiently for her to finish. The two younger ones too had golloped up their meal and were now scraping round their bowls. She wanted to talk to them but she couldn't find the words. She wanted to say to them, You'll never know life more hard from this day on. But that would be throwing reflections back on their father as if he hadn't given them all he could. True, he had worked for them and had saved and fed and clothed them better than the majority of those in the rows; but it wasn't best as she saw it, her best saw a cleaner, brighter side of life. Not less hard working. No. She was prepared to work all the days of her life as she had done since she was four years old – her

14

mother had seen to that – but she wanted something different for the result of her labour and the labours of her children. Oh yes, particularly she wanted something different for them, and at this moment she wanted to say to them, I'm going to see that you get it. But she felt too full and it was almost with a feeling of horror she knew she was about to cry. And not one of her children had ever witnessed her crying; what crying she had done in her life had been in the dead of night when those about her were in deep sleep and dulled with the labour of the day, or mazed with ale or gin. She had only experienced the latter up till she was sixteen, for if Seth had ever touched strong drink there wouldn't have been anything in the bag behind the brick in the mantelshelf. But nevertheless she had often cried in the deep of the night during the last ten years. Sometimes she had wondered what she was crying for: something missing? something she had lost? something that she wanted? She didn't know, she only knew it was a relief to cry. But never, never had she cried in front of her children. They looked upon her as someone strong with no weakness.

She got up hastily from the table, saying, "Take a slice of bread each," and pointed to the cupboard as she walked past it and on to the steep ladder that led to the attic room above. And there, she held her hand tightly over her mouth, saying to herself, "No. Not now, not now. For God's sake, woman, not now." And at this she began tearing clothes from the old chest and putting them into bundles.

2

❧❧

The children were standing outside, each dressed as if for a winter expedition, for they were wearing all the clothes they possessed, it being easier for them to be carried that way; besides, they each had to hump two bundles, one holding a piece of bedding, a blanket or a patch quilt, the other, in addition to mug, plate and spoon, odd items of kitchen utensils.

Riah stood in the bare room and looked about her for a moment and her last unspoken words to herself were, May I never have to live in your like again. Then she stooped and with an effort lifted up a large roll of bedding in one hand and a canvas bag in the other, the contents of which jingled together as she moved out through the doorway. She had asked herself two or three times since last night why she was determined to take such things as a kettle and pans and she could give herself no answer, only that she didn't mind the Meddles using her furniture, but cooking utensils were a different thing.

The sun was shining, the road was dry. They had to pass down the whole length of the row to gain the coach road where they hoped to pick up the carrier cart. But their departure seemed to have been awaited and there was hardly a doorway that wasn't open and a woman standing in it and often her man by her side, his bait tin in his hand, ready to go on his shift but staying long enough to see the Millicans take to the road and feeling not a little satisfaction in the sight, for hadn't they foretold this: Millican had always been above himself. Any man who wasted his time on reading and writing was a fool. What good did it do you? Got you thrown out into the gutter in most cases. It was a wonder that Millican had lasted so long. He wouldn't have done if he hadn't been considered one of the best workers on the face and a man who set the pace. And this opinion itself was enough to make his fellow-men turn against him.

Well, there they went, was the opinion of most; but not of all, for now and again a voice would say, "Good luck, lass," and Riah would turn to the speaker and say, "Ta. Thanks."

Then at the bottom of the road she came face to face with Bill Norsecott. He had come round the corner of the row and when he saw her had stopped dead almost blocking her path, and he muttered through his coal-grimed lips, "Might be bloody well glad of an offer afore you're finished, Mrs Millican . . . ma'am."

"That might be so, Mr Norsecott" – her chin was up – "but you can take it firmly that I'd be hard put afore even thinking about taking an offer from you. Rock bottom I'd be, and I'm far from that. Good-day to you."

"And to hell with you."

The children were moving on, but Davey stopped and turned towards the man, and Riah had to nudge him forward with her knee, saying, "Go on. Go on."

At the coach road they all dropped their bundles down on to the grass verge and the younger children were for sitting down beside them, but Riah said harshly, "Don't do that. Them's your Sunday clothes, on top, remember."

And so they all stood silently now looking along the dusty road that curved downhill to a hamlet in the dip, and the silence was broken by Biddy saying, "I would have died if we had gone into the Norsecotts' house." And to this Riah said tartly, "Be quiet. Save your breath to cool your porridge." Which censure Biddy took, as usual, to mean she was talking too much. But she repeated to herself and emphatically, "I would. I would. Dirty, snotty-nosed lot."

They had to wait a half-hour for the cart, and just as they espied it in the distance coming over the hill, the men from the pit, their ten hour shift at an end, passed them in straggling groups. Most of them looked towards them; few had anything to say. But Arthur Meddle and two other men from Primrose Row stopped, and Arthur said, "Ready for the road, lass?" And Riah answered, "Yes, Arthur. Ready for the road."

The two men almost simultaneously now said, "Good luck, lass." And one went on to add, "Nobody could blame you for

17

makin' the choice. By God, no. Nobody could blame you. We wish you well. More than us do an' all; we all wish you well."

"Thank you." The cart drew up in front of them and Arthur Meddle said, "I won't give any of you a hoist, lass, seein' me being so mucky and you all dressed up nicely. You look a credit, you do that, you look a credit. Goodbye then. Goodbye."

Paddy McCabe, the carter, looked at Riah with a grin on his face, saying, "You've filled me up. This lot's going to cost you, lass."

"I can pay. I can pay."

"Oh, I know you can. I wasn't meanin' nowt. Would you like to sit up front along o' me? They're all settled in the back there, snug." He jerked his head to where the children were sitting amidst the bundles, their hands already gripping the sides of the cart, and she said, "Thank you. I'd be obliged."

And so they set off on the six miles to Shields. But before they had travelled half the distance they were joined by another five customers, so causing the children to have to sit on the bundles, which brought their bodies well up above the sides of the cart, and as the road was potholed, this made for dangerous travel and brought from them cries of "Eeh!" and "Oh!" which made the elders in the cart laugh.

By the time they reached Shields market, their stomachs were well shaken up. But they all felt merry and it showed in their faces as once more they lifted their bundles then said, "Goodbye," to Paddy McCabe and his cart. And Paddy wished them, "Good luck;" at the same time adding words that filled Riah with apprehension, for he said, "Shouldn't surprise me, missis, to see you takin' the journey back some day, an' not too long ahead, for things is bad around here, especially where you said you were going. Fish is goin' rotten in piles along there, they say."

She said nothing to this but marched off, pushing the children before her, while she herself rocked from side to side with the weight of the awkward bundles she was carrying.

They went down the cobbled slope to the quay, where tall sailing boats were lined as close as herrings in a crate. Then leaving the quay, she led the way now between a morass of rotting boats, rusted anchors and chains piled in places four foot high. Then some distance along they mounted a bank and found themselves walking between whitewashed cottages. And presently she saw the end of Low Street where she had been born and had played for a little while and worked for a longer while and had hoped, as she had also done on leaving the pit village today, that she would never set eyes on it again. But she had, although at long intervals.

It was three years since she was last here. Seth had brought them down one bright Sunday in the summer of twenty-nine. Their reception on that day had not been cold, yet it had not been effusive. The visit had gone off as well as it had because within a few minutes of being in the house she had slipped a shilling into her mother's hand. It had made all the difference. What would her mother say now if she told her that she had eighteen pounds dangling in a bag between her breasts? Oh, she'd surely be all over her. But she wasn't going to know about that money. That was for setting them up in a new home. As long as she stayed with her mother, she would work for their keep. At least this was what she had imagined until she reached the door, and the first person to greet her was her mother.

Dilly Riston was fifty years old. Her back was stooped with rheumatics, her fingers were misshapen with the same complaint. As she would tell you, what could you expect? because she had handled cold fish from she was three years old. She looked like a woman well into her sixties, except that her eyes were clear and glinted with hard knowledge of life. It was she who spoke first: "In the name of God!" she said. "What are you doin' here?" Then her eyes scanned the four small figures standing behind Riah, and she added, "The lot of yous."

"Seth died of the cholera. They wouldn't let us stay. I'm going to look for a house." Her tone softened now, it had a plea in it: "I . . . I thought you might put us up for a few days."

"Put you up? God in heaven! you don't know what you're askin'. Put you up? You could never be put up here. Come in and see for yourself." She stood aside, and Riah hesitated before dropping her burdens down on to the shingled road; then slowly she squeezed past her mother and entered the room that had once been so familiar to her. And there she saw three small children, two sitting on a mat before a low fire and one very young one in a basket to the side of it. A young woman was standing near the table that was set underneath the small square window. She had been chopping on a board, but her hands stopped at their work and she now stared at Riah. And Riah blinked her eyes for a moment because she could hardly recognize her elder sister. It was all of five years since she had seen her, when her husband Henry Fuller had got himself a job in Jarrow village; his work was that of a boat-builder. She'd had three children then round about Johnny's and Maggie's age, but here were another three, one a recent delivery by the looks of it. She said quietly, "Hello, Ada."

It was some seconds before Ada answered, "Hello." Then, as if about to greet Riah she walked towards her, saying, "What's brought you?" but when Dilly repeated, "Seth died of the cholera," she seemed to rear back from her sister.

"'Tis all right," Riah said quickly; "it was some weeks gone, it's all over."

"'Tis never over, the cholera."

"And look at this lot." It was her mother's voice now and she was pointing out into the road as she addressed her elder daughter. "She's brought the four of them." And now shuffling towards Riah, she said, "Where d'you intend to put them up?"

"I've just told you, haven't I? I thought you might. . . ."

"Now look here, don't take that tone with me: not in the door a second but playing the high and mighty. Well, you can see how we're fixed. Besides those three" – she pointed – "there's another three on the beach, raking up, and Henry besides."

Not out of real concern for Henry but simply for something to say to quieten the atmosphere, Riah looked at Ada and said, "Is he out of work?"

Ada didn't get a chance to answer because her mother yelled, "Out of work! Is anybody in work here? Where you been? Haven't you heard of the strike at the Hilda pit? Been on weeks now. They are bloody maniacs. Didn't know when they were well off. Wanting to start unions, and them getting four shillings for a seven hour stint; then goin' and rioting and smashing up the pit. Where've you been? Oh, but I suppose your pit was working, so you shut your eyes and close your ears. You've had it easy, madam, you don't know you're born. This place is dead. The town is dead. They started burying it after Waterloo, and now they've nearly filled it in. Out of work? she says." She tossed her head. "The fishing's dead, but that's all we've got to live on, fish, fish, fish. If I'm forced to eat another mouthful of salmon I'll spew."

"What about the factories?" Riah said and as she spoke she looked out through the open door to the children now grouped about it. She made no signal for them to come in, but she saw young Maggie jump at the sound of her mother's strident voice yelling, "Factories, you say. They're sleepin' out to pick up a job in them. Anyway, when fishing's been your life, who wants to go standin' in a factory, blackin', bricks, pottery, glass, what have you? 'Tisn't for fishermen. We'll have a repeat of the big strike with our lot an' all, you mark my words, because it isn't only the fishermen, it's the deep sea 'uns as well. There'll be a repeat, you'll see, and they'll bring in the dragoons again and the cavalry. My God Almighty. I've seen it all, but never as bad as this." Her voice had lessened for a moment, but now it resumed its almost screeching tone as she cried, "And now you land with four of them! You must be mad. And from what I hear the pits inland are crying out for bairns. You mightn't have a man to go down but he looks big enough. And the lass an' all." She had pointed from Davey to Biddy.

Now it was Riah's voice that almost seemed to raise the low roof of the cottage as she cried, "I've told you afore, Ma, an' I'll tell you again, none of mine are going down below. And they won't starve either, I'll see to that. I'll get work, I've got a pair of hands on me."

"Don't be so bloody soft, girl; we've all got pairs of hands, even mine." She held up her twisted fingers. "I could still gut, if it was any use guttin'. Look you." She advanced on Riah, and now her fingers forming into a fist, she punched at her daughter's arm, saying, "You don't know you're born. You never have. I don't know where in the name of God you come from, but from the minute you could open your mouth I knew it wasn't from my side. And although you've passed the colouring on to that one" – she pointed to Davey – "you've got the Swede inside of you. He was a skunk and he skunked off and left me mother with six of us, and every now and again his mark comes up either inside or out. So now let me put it plain to you, miss or missis, there's no work hereabouts; and there's no habitation either because the bloody sea captains are buyin' up the property and lettin' 'em out at rents only the foreigners can pay. And there's plenty of them kickin' about."

The mother and daughter glared at each other for a moment; then Riah, with a catch in her voice, said, "Well, thank you for your welcome, Ma," and, turning, made towards the door, pushing the children aside and pointing towards their bundles to indicate that they pick them up.

Ada followed them out of the cottage, and standing near her sister, she whispered, "She's right, Riah, she's right; there's no work. But . . . but where are you goin'?"

"I don't know. But don't worry; I'll find a place."

"Have you got any money?"

"Enough to get by on."

"Well, look" – Ada puller her to a stop – "there's Mrs Carr, she's at the very far end of the street. They're not fishers, they're river men, one's on the keels, the rest do the trips to London Town and often they're gone for a week or more. When the house is clear she takes lodgers. Go along there and see if she'll take you. If not, I don't know what you're going to do."

Neither did Riah. But she patted Ada's arm, saying, "Thanks, lass. I'll find something. And let me say, I'm sorry you're landed in this plight with me ma."

"There was nothing else for it. It was last year they went on strike for a better deal and now they're a thousand times worse off than ever they were afore. I'm weary, Riah, utterly weary. She gets you down."

"I know that, Ada. I'm sorry."

"Well, go on. Let me know."

"I will." As Riah turned away, Ada, casting her eyes over the burdened children, said, "You've got a nice little crew, healthy lookin'."

Riah smiled at her and nodded and once more ushered her crew before her, and they went on down the long street to the end.

Mrs Carr turned out to be a young old woman. Riah guessed she must be as old as her mother, but was as spritely as someone half her age.

"Oh," she said. "Well now, four bairns and you. Well now. Well now. 'Twill be the floor for two of you, I'm afraid, 'cos our Harold will be back in the night after his keeling. But himself and Bob and Mickie started the London trip last night. God keep them safe and quiet the waters. Come in. Come in."

The little room was clean and packed with relics of the sea and foreign voyages. Cheap bric-a-brac were nailed to the walls side by side with ships' brasses, and in one corner there actually hung, from close to the low ceiling, an anchor, its iron burnished like a piece of brass.

"Now sit yourselves down if you can." She pointed to the children, then to a form that ran at an angle to the fireplace. "Throw your bundles in the corner. And you, missis, take this seat. It's himself's; he's not here so you can sit in it, but he'd kick the backside out of anybody that went near it if he was about the house."

Thankfully Riah sat down and her whole body slumped in weariness as she looked at the vibrant old woman, and when this business-like lady said, "'Tis sixpence a night I charge with a bowl of broth afore sleep and one to set you on the road; and the bairns we'll say half price. What about it?"

Riah merely inclined her head in acceptance while she thought, My, this is the business to be in. She must have acquired a small fortune over the years. By! should she stay here a week, that would take all of ten and sixpence, besides buying their food. And the rapid totalling in her head told her she wouldn't see anything of a pound at the end of it. She also told herself that she must look sharp and find work, not only for herself but for them all.

The old lady now said, "What's brought you here, may I ask?"

And so Riah told her, and as she did so, she watched the wrinkled face stretch until the lined lips formed an elongated, "Oh," before they emitted the word, "Riston. Oh, Dilly Riston's a bitter pill. Always was, always will be. Oh" – she pointed now – "I remember you. Yes I do. I remember you as a youngster, although I never had anything to do with anyone along that end. Fighting, drinking, bashin' lot. But I'll say this for them, they're the crowd to have behind you when you're in a tight jam, and there was some tight jams here last year. Oh aye. Oh aye. Our men made a stand. Three pounds, that's all they got for a trip to London and back, and when they asked for four, God Almighty! all hell was let loose. By lass, you should have been here then. Do you know, a warship was sent here. That didn't help; skull and hair flew. You should have seen it. Two blokes, blacklegs, signed on for less than the four pounds, and God, they nearly lynched them. Eeh! the things that go on in this town, nobody would believe. As our Hal said, he's a joker you know, but he said, 'Why shanghai the blokes for the navy to go across the sea and fight wars when there are ready-made ones here?'"

She turned her attention on to the children now who were sitting wide-eyed staring at her, and she said, "You hungry, bairns?" And it was Biddy who answered for them, saying, "Yes, please, missis, we're all hungry." She glanced at her mother now but Riah didn't chastise her. And the old woman said, "Well, it's many a day since I lodged bairns so I'll give you a treat. I'll make some griddle, eh? Take off your coats and things. And look" – she turned to Riah – "that's your room" – she pointed – "there's two beds in there, one of them's for our Hal."

"You mean . . . he'll be sleepin' . . .?"

"Aw, missis, Hal wouldn't interfere with you. But . . . but if you feel so nickety-pickety about it, he'll go up in the roof for the night. He's been up there afore." She motioned with her head to a hatch set in the low ceiling, then added, "You can't straighten up but as I've said to him, when you're asleep you lie flat."

"Thank you."

"You're welcome, missis, you're welcome."

In the room, Riah pushed the door closed for a moment and looked about her. There was scarcely room to move between the beds and they had to stack their bundles one on top of the other in the corner. The patched covers on the beds looked rumpled and she doubted if the bedding would be clean underneath. But anyway, it was a shelter.

The children had all dropped on to the edge of the bed. They sat in a row all tired and dismal looking, and she, lowering herself down on to a wooden structure opposite, held out her hands to them, saying, "I know you're tired but I want you to change your things: get into your working clothes. We'll go out and look around; there's a lot of daylight left."

"Ma."

"Yes, Davey?"

"I wouldn't like to live here long."

"We'll have to take what we can get for the time being, we can't pick and choose. It's not worse than what we've left."

"It's the smell."

"Well, you had that an' all back there."

"It was different somehow."

"Yes, Ma, it was different," Biddy put in now. And Johnny, as if taking his cue from his brother and sister, piped up, "I'm going to be sick."

"You're not going to be sick. Now stop it, all of you." She looked from one to the other. "We're going out, and we're going to try and find work. And as soon as I get a job, even if you get nothing, I'll get a house and we'll settle down to a new life. It's going to be all right, you'll see. Now get up and get yourselves changed."

As they obeyed her, she thought: a new life of drudgery. It had been that for the last ten years, but then she had had a man behind her. A man was necessary. Without a man your life was like a ship without a captain: there was mutiny on all sides, and within you too, deep within you.

She looked down on the two low wooden-base beds. ... The old woman had taken it for granted that her son would sleep in this room tonight with her. Of course the children would be here, but that wouldn't matter to some men. Her thoughts swung back, but as if reluctantly now, and she almost muttered them aloud, "The family needs a man to steer it." But before the words had time to evaporate she was attacking them, "You going soft, Maria Millican, out of your mind? You've had one man and that's enough for you. Get about it. Get outside and see what's doing."

For a week she saw what was doing, and that was mostly nothing. She herself was offered three jobs during that period but they were all in bars, and her presence wasn't required until seven o'clock at night; and she had recalled enough of the river front to know what happens to a woman, if not in the bars, then when she tried to leave and walk along the apparently deserted streets close to midnight.

Biddy could have been set on in the blacking factory, but when Riah saw the conditions under which the children worked, the sight of them running around like little black imps, and when she caught here and there the gist of their conversation, she said, "You're not going in there." And to this Biddy said in protest, "Ma, it's three shillings a week." And Riah answered, "I wouldn't care if it was thirty-three."

At the beginning of the second week Davey got work. It was on the waterfront, but he was paid in fish.

Then there was the matter of a house. In the lower end they were

25

asking two shillings a week for a rat-infested room. If the house had two or more rooms it was used as a lodging house with four to six sleepers in a room. Some of the beds were used both by day and by night. Further into the town, where the respectable quarter began, they were asking as much as four shillings a week for two rooms downstairs, and four and six for an upper apartment because this had a let into the roof. Still, houses were hard to come by here, and twice she was refused one because she hadn't a man to support her: as the agent said, he understood their plight, but once in it was getting them out again if she couldn't pay the rent. When she assured him she could, and for weeks ahead, he wanted to know how she intended to do this, as she had admitted she and the children were not in work. She was wise enough not to tell him of her little store, because she couldn't trust anyone, and especially not this agent, who looked a mean man.

They were now into June and the day was hot when, footsore, she led Biddy, Johnny, and Maggie back to the house. And there Mrs Carr greeted them with a friendliness that had been absent during the last few days. "You look hot," she said. "I've just got a bucket of water from the tap." She pointed to a bucket standing near the table. "Help yourselves. And I've got a bit of news that could be of help."

Uninvited, Riah sat down on a cracket and said, "Yes?"

"Well, I was in the market this mornin' an' who should I run across but Steve Procket. He was with our Arthur at the pit way out beyond Gateshead. Well, what do you think? He's left the pit and gone back to his old job in Jarrow as a chips."

"Chips?"

"Aye, chips. Shipbuilding you know. Chips."

"Oh!"

"Well, I said to him, how was our Arthur, 'cos it's months since I've seen hilt or hair of him, and what d'you think he told me?" She waited a moment, but when Riah remained silent, she went on, "Winnie's in a bad way, that's his wife ... our Arthur's. A weakling she's been for years; couldn't carry bairns, you know. Well, Arthur got a woman to see to things, but she only stayed three days as it's back of beyond, lonely as hell. It was the pit keeker's cottage, a good one, but way out, he said; that's why he couldn't stand it either. If you wanted a drink you had to take the cart into the town an' shank it back at night. Anyway, the long and short of it is, our Arthur needs somebody there, an' so when he told me that I thought of you. There's four good rooms in the house, but what's more there's outbuildings and a barn almost twice the size of the house running alongside. Would you like to give it a try?"

Riah stared at the old woman; then she looked at the children, her eyes resting on Biddy, and Biddy said, "It'll be in the country, Ma."

Yes, it would be in the country. She was tired and weary to her inmost bone with walking and worrying, and Biddy's words, "It'll be in the country, Ma," brought a picture before her mind of a rural scene. She saw the cottage and the outhouses, she saw the children racing down the field to the river, she saw herself, white apron on, her blue striped blouse open at the neck, her hair combed back from her forehead and she was looking up into the sky and smiling.

Mrs Carr's voice blotted out the picture saying, "Well, there it is. I thought it would give you a chance."

She was on her feet now, her voice rapid: "Oh, it will, Mrs Carr, thank you. Yes, thank you. Where did you say it was?"

"Fuller's Moor, beyond Fellburn. Rowan Cottage."

"Oh, yes, I know that way, at least yon side of Fellburn. We'll start first thing in the morning. Oh, thank you, Mrs Carr. Thank you."

"You're welcome. I'm sure he'll be glad to see you."

The brightness going from her face and voice now, she said, "What if he's already got somebody?"

"I doubt it. Steve only came back two weeks ago. Anyway, that's a risk you'll have to take, but I'm sure it'll be all right. And even if he has somebody, he'd put you up in the barn until you got settled. He's a kind lad is our Arthur. And it's in the country an' the bairns'll love it." She looked at the children. "They've never taken to the quayside, have they? Your lad doesn't like the smell of the fish. Funny that; I can't stand the sight of grass, not big clumps anyway. We're all made different. Thanks be to God for it, I say."

Riah nodded to her, then went quickly towards the other room. And there she looked at her family who had preceded her. They were sitting in a tight row on the bed, their faces bright, and Biddy as usual was the spokesman. "Eeh! Ma, the country," she said. "Should I run and tell our Davey?"

"Yes, do that, hinny."

Biddy was at the door and was about to open it when she turned and, looking at her mother, she said, "Shouldn't wonder but he'll tip the fish all back into the river when I tell him."

"Go on with you." Riah was laughing as her daughter ran out, pulling the door behind her. She often said, "Thank God for Biddy." She knew she was the brightest of the four, and being so she should have loved her more than the rest and she felt guilty when she knew that she didn't. But there was one she loved the best, and that was her son David. He might not have the wit of Biddy, but for her there was a light that shone out of him. She only had to look at him and her throat became tight with emotion that went beyond maternal love.

3

It was half past ten when they left the cart to the south of
Gateshead Fell. She didn't know the part at all, but Mrs Carr had
said that Fuller's Moor was nothing but a good walk from the top
end of Gateshead Fell.

When she stopped a couple of workmen and asked the way, the
men looked at each other, and one of them said, "Fuller's Moor?
By, you're a tidy step from there, missis."

"How far?" she asked.

"Oh!" The men again exchanged glances; then the other man
spoke, saying, "Well, go straight on and you'll come to The Stag.
Now turn off down there, and I should say ... Oh" – he shook
his head – "it's a good four miles from there."

Four miles could be nothing to her or perhaps Davey or Biddy,
but the two youngsters tired easily. "Is there a carrier that way?"
she asked.

The men seemed to think about it. "Aye, when I come to think
of it," one said, "there's one leaves round here eight in the mornin'
and goes by there in a roundabout way to Chester-le-Street and
Durham, an' comes back 'bout four in the afternoon." Then he
added, "But that won't be much help to you, missis. Still" –
he smiled – "it's a fine day, doesn't look like rain, in fact we've
never had any for two weeks now so the roads should be nice and
hard."

She thanked them and was about to turn away when she asked,
"Are there any villages on the way?"

"Well, no, not what you call villages," one of the men said.
"Hamlets, two, Brookdip and Rowdip, a few houses and a blacksmith's in Rowdip."

"Well, you ain't got no horse, so you won't need that." This
caused both men to laugh and the children to titter but it found

no answering mirth in herself. She nodded at them, thanked them again and went on. . . .

It was near noon when they reached The Stag Inn and Johnny and Maggie were already trailing their feet.

Once they left the main road there was one thing that Riah noticed and Biddy exclaimed on, "It's bonny country, Ma, isn't it?"

"Yes," she said as she looked from one side to the other of the bridle-path on which they were walking, and it seemed to her that the gently rising ground dotted here and there with belts of woodland must go on forever.

"My toes are hurting, Ma. They're skinned."

She took off Johnny's boot. Sure enough the middle joints of two of his toes were red raw. "Oh," she said softly, "you should have mentioned them afore. How long have they been like this?"

"Some way, Ma."

She clicked her tongue. "Sit down, all of you and we'll have something to eat."

"Ma" – Davey was pointing – "there's a beck down there."

"A beck?" They were all on their feet again and standing near Davey looking down to where a narrow stream could be seen through some low shrubland.

"Oh, come on!" Riah sounded like a child herself, and she picked Johnny up in her arms and, calling to the others, "Bring the stuff," she scrambled down through the bushes to where the land levelled out into a green sward alongside the stream.

Riah was to remember the next hour for a long, long time. It seemed like a foretaste of heaven. They made a fire and they fried bacon, and as it sizzled its aroma was like perfume to their nostrils, and Davey, with unusual humour, said dryly, "If only we had thought to bring some fish along, Ma, we could have fried them an' all," whereupon they all fell against each other with their laughing.

After the meal, like the children she, too, took off her boots and stockings and plodged in the stream. They sprayed water on her and she sprayed water on them, and later, when she had to call a halt and they had to gather up their things again, Biddy, looking about her, said quietly, "Wouldn't it be nice, Ma, if we could stay here forever?" And she answered, "Well, we will be just further along the road." . . .

They were all walking very slowly as they made their way up the slight incline out of the hamlet of Brookdip. There were five buildings in the dip; one was the church and the biggest house, which was next to it, looked like the vicarage. Who inhabited the other three she didn't stop to enquire. Two miles back in the hamlet of Rowdip there had been about twelve houses altogether but they were scattered, two being farmhouses, and one a smaller manor.

The few people they had encountered on the road, all had looked at them with interest but no one had stopped and questioned them. It was, Riah thought, perhaps not an unusual sight to see a woman and four children hugging bundles along the highway. And that could be true, and folks didn't want to become involved with people in her situation.

They'd had two further stops since they'd played by the stream, but they hadn't been so merry, not merry at all, for now Maggie's heels were skinned and Biddy had stopped talking, which was a sure sign that she was very tired, and to Davey's face had returned that apprehensive look which told her that he was worrying about something.

They had come to a small kind of crossroads and didn't know which way to go when they saw a man driving a flat cart coming towards them. As he approached nearer, Riah noticed that he sat high above the horse. It was the way his seat was placed: the cart looked like a converted brake, but there were no seats in the back, just sacks of something. He pulled up the horse and looked down at them, and she was the first to speak. She said, "Could you tell me, please, the way to Rowan Cottage?"

He didn't answer immediately but looked from her to the four children, then over her head and down the road from which they had come as if he expected someone else to appear; then, still not speaking, he turned round and pointed along the road by which he had come, saying abruptly, "Half a mile back."

"Thank you." She stared at him a moment longer. He was a brusque man, not friendly. Again she said, "Thank you." Then she walked away, and the children followed. She had gone some distance when Biddy muttered, "He hasn't gone on, Ma, he's sitting looking at us."

"Take no heed."

The half-mile turned out to be a long half-mile before they saw the cottage, but the sight of it seemed to make them forget their sore feet. When they reached the gate, they all stood huddled together leaning over it, looking towards the side of the house.

The front door faced a yard. It was a fine big yard, and opposite were the outhouses that Mrs Carr had described. Riah was smiling inside. There was plenty of room; she would settle here and gladly, oh yes. She thrust open the gate and, her step quickening, she marched across the yard and to the front door and she knocked upon it. When there was no answer she turned and looked at the children, saying, "He's likely at work and his wife in bed poorly," and she nodded at them.

It was Davey who, standing behind the others, turned his head towards the window. Taking two steps to the side, he stood in front of it; then with his face close to the pane, he cried, "*Ma!*" His voice was high. "*'Tis empty, empty.*"

She almost jumped to his side and stared through the window. They were looking into a room. On the far wall was a fireplace with dead ashes in the grate. Now she moved quickly to the other side of the door and, looking into another room, saw that that too was empty. She turned and leant her back against the wall and muttered thickly, "My God. There's nobody here." She stared down at Davey.

"I don't want to go back, Ma." She turned her eyes now on to Maggie whose face was crumpled up on the verge of tears, and, pulling herself from the wall, she took in a deep breath, squared her shoulders and said, "Well, we're not going back, not the night anyway. Let's go and see what's in the stables."

They found the two stables dirty, the floor covered with horse muck and dank straw. The barn wasn't much better, but at its end was a narrow platform and on it were two broken bales of straw. She looked up and could see the sky where the tiles were off the barn roof. Fortunately, the straw was at the other end.

"We'll sleep up there the night," she said. "Come the morning I'll think of something."

But what was she going to think of in the morning? Return to Shields? Never. Never in this world. As terrible as the thought of the workhouse was she would rather take them there, yet at the same time knowing that she never would as long as she had money in her pocket. That was the only bright spot on the horizon at the moment, she had money in her pocket, or literally between her breasts. She started to bustle now, urging them, "Put the packages up there" – she pointed – "to the dry end of the platform. We'll make a fire in the yard. We've still got some milk left and there's bound to be a well." . . .

It was about half an hour later when she was boiling up the water that the children had brought from a rill that ran at the bottom of the field adjoining the cottage – there was no well – that she heard the words, "Whoa! there," and turned her head sharply towards the gate. She had been so preoccupied with what she was doing that the cart seemed to have dropped there out of thin air.

She stood up, rubbing her hands down the sides of her skirt, and looked to where the man who had directed them a little earlier sat staring towards them; but by his side now was an old woman. It was she who beckoned her forward; and when she reached the gate, the woman said, "You arrived then?"

Riah blinked, then muttered, "Aye, yes."

"Where's your man?"

"My man?"

"Aye, that's what I said. You're not daft or stupid, are you? Your man, who's for the mine."

"I . . . I think you've made a mistake."

The two people on the cart exchanged glances. Then the old woman, her voice not so sharp now, said, "You're not with your man? Then why are you here at the cottage?"

"I . . . I understood I was coming to look after Mr Carr's wife who's ill. His mother sent me."

The two pairs of eyes were staring into hers. Then the old woman gave a shrill laugh as she said, "Well, did you ever. Well I've got to tell you, missis, that Winnie Carr's been dead and buried this past week, so she's beyond your help. An' I should guess, too, you're more in need of it than she is at the moment."

"But Mr Carr?"

Again the two on the cart exchanged glances, and once more it was the old woman who spoke, "Oh, he had a piece in to look after his wife, but like the others afore her, the place got on her nerves. Townsfolk can't stand looking at the sky, there's too much of it." She again laughed her shrill laugh, then ended, "He had taken to her so when she made back for the town he went with her, and a man called McAllister is being set on at the mine and bringing his family out here the morrow. Six of them I understand. That's so, Tol?" She turned to the man at her side, and he inclined his head towards her. "Where you from?"

She paused a moment thinking, Where was she from? Shields? Fellburn? Beyond Gateshead? She said, "From South Shields, lately."

"You've come all that way the day?"

"Yes." She saw the man turn his head away and look towards his horse. The old woman moved her head to the side and said, "I see you're bedding down here for the night."

"Yes."

"Well, there's no harm in that. But come the morrow, it would be wise to be on your way early, 'cos I understand they're an Irish lot that are comin' in, and perhaps you know what they're like, scum of the earth an' fighters. . . . You're a widow then, are you?" She looked at the four children who were standing further back in the yard.

"Yes."

"And you're lookin' for a housekeeper's job?"

"Well, yes." She was going to add, or a house, when the old woman put in, "You'll be hard set to find one with a tribe of four at your heels. Yet your two eldest could be in work."

Before either of them could speak again the man said softly, "Fanny, time's gettin' on." And she answered, "Aye, yes, all right, Tol. 'Tis kind of you it is; sorry I've kept you. Goodbye, missis, and good luck." She nodded at her and the man said, "Gee-up! there," and the cart moved forward leaving Riah standing looking after them.

She wanted to cry. Stop it. Stop it. It was no time for crying. Oh my God! What was it a time for? Praying, aye; but then she wasn't much good at praying. Planning was what she must do, and the immediate plan was to get them to bed; although it was still daylight they were all dog-tired. But she must get them up at sunrise the morrow morning and they must be on their way before that family came in. She wanted no rows, no barraging, because Davey, she admitted to herself, wasn't a boy to seek a fight, he was a peaceful lad, thoughtful. Now if he'd had Biddy's nature, he would go in with fists flailing to anyone twice his size, she was sure of that.

It was Biddy who, sometime later when they were crossing the yard to bring the last of the pans in and to stamp out the fire, said, "We"ll have to make it back the morrow then, Ma?"

"Yes, hinny."

"Where do you think we'll settle, Ma?"

She stopped by the edge of the fire and she looked across it and over the gate into the thicket at yon side of the road, and her mind at this moment seemed as closed against thought as the low shrub woodland did against entry.

"I don't know, lass," she said. "I don't know, and that's God's truth."

Breaking the short silence that had ensued, Biddy said softly, "Something will turn up, Ma. Something always does. It'll have to, 'cos we've got to be settled somewhere, haven't we?"

Riah looked down at her daughter and said, "Yes, we've got to settle somewhere." Then her mind squeezed out the question, But where? Where?

She received the answer the following morning.

The sun was well up before she roused the children; and when they struggled down from the platform they were still bleary-eyed and tired from the previous day's tramping.

She had a fire going in the yard and she cooked the last of the fat bacon and dipped the remaining pieces of bread in the fat. Then she put a can of water on the fire, and when it was boiling they washed the greasy breakfast down with mugs of it. The meal over, she sent them down to the rill to sluice their faces and hands; then she herself followed them and did the same. Afterwards she combed their hair, then saw to her own.

They were ready, the bundles in their hands, the yard left as they had found it, when the cart appeared at the gate again, and they all stared towards it as if it was an apparition, for there sat the man and the old woman as they had done last evening, except now they were facing the other way. It was the old woman who called to her again, saying, "Here a minute!"

Riah did not look at the children as she said to them, "Stay where you are," before she walked forward. And now she was looking up at the old woman who surprised her by saying, "Can you cook?"

She hesitated before, her chin jerking slightly, she said, "I've been doing it for years."

"Aye, frying-pan stuff likely. But can you make a good dinner?"

Her voice slightly terse, she said, "I've been told I've made many a one."

"Well, tastes differ an' that remains to be seen, but it's like this. I might be able to get you a place. I'm not promisin', mind, I'll have to talk to him, that's if I can get a word in and he doesn't shout me down every time I raise the subject. But look. Stay put for the next hour or so an' if the news is to your good, Tol here" – she turned and inclined her head towards the man – "he'll come back and pick you up." She now looked fully at her companion and, to Riah's ears, her tone seeming to soften considerably, she added, "You will do that, Tol, won't you?" and he replied, "I'll do it, but I can't promise you to be back straight on the hour."

"Well, as they don't seem to be going any place in particular I don't suppose she'll mind waitin' a couple."

She was looking down at Riah again and she said, "Is that so?" And Riah said, "What are you proposing?"

The old woman now bristled and she repeated the word as if it was foreign to her, "Pro ... posin', she says." She was looking over her shoulder towards the man again and thumbing back towards Riah. "Proposin'. I'm only tryin' to get you set up in a good place, that's if he'll take the youngsters. Proposin'! Carry on, Tol." She lifted her hand in an imperious movement now as if she was ordering a servant, and the cart moved off. But as it did so, the man turned his head and looked behind the old woman, and although his expression hadn't altered the movement of his head conveyed to Riah a message which could have been, Take no notice, she means well.

She stood where she was and watched the cart until it disappeared from view at the end of the long narrow lane; then she turned into the yard again.

"What is it, Ma? What did she want?"

She looked at Biddy. "I don't know," she said, "but it seems as if there might be a job in the offing. What it is ... well, you know as much about it as I do. She's a queer old lady."

"The man seemed nice."

36

She looked at Davey, and nodded at him, saying, "Yes, he did, when he could get a word in, although he didn't seem inclined for much talk. Well, we can sit down again. I'll tell you what, leave your bundles inside the barn door and go on down to the stream and have a bit pledge."

"I don't want to. I'd rather stay here, Ma," said Biddy.

"Me an' all." Davey came to her side. The two younger ones said nothing but they, too, came closer to her and held on to her skirt. She looked down on them lovingly; then she said, softly, "I'll tell you what you can do. You two get into your Sunday frocks" – she indicated the girls – "and Davey, you can put on your good trousers, an' I'll see to Johnny, because if we've got to go and see whoever this is what wants a cook or some such, we should look tidy."

"What about you, Ma? You look lovely in your blue blouse. Will you put it on?"

"Oh." She hesitated as she looked down on Biddy. Her blue blouse was special. Seth had bought her the material as a surprise present. He had thrown the parcel on to the table one Saturday night and there was this length of blue cotton with a tiny pink flower here and there as a pattern. She had spent hours making the blouse and she hadn't worn it more than half a dozen times since. She had thought of it as a garment for occasions and there hadn't been many occasions in her life that warranted its wearing. But now, here might be an occasion, and she smiled broadly as she said, "Aye, I'll put it on."

Excitement ran high now as they all went into the barn to change their clothes; then they were ready and stood at the gate waiting. . . .

They waited and they waited, the minutes dragging.

"How long is it now, Ma?" said Johnny.

"Oh," she considered, "well over an hour, I would say."

"If he doesn't come at all, will we have to change back?" Biddy smoothed down her short coat with both hands and reluctantly Riah answered, "Yes, I'm afraid so."

Her reply seemed to cause the children to go limp, for now Johnny and Maggie leant against the bars of the gate, only to be brought upright by Riah saying firmly, "Stand straight, the gate's green with mould, you'll mark yourselves."

As she finished speaking Davey let out a cry that almost verged

37

on a shout: "He's coming, Ma!" Then he clapped his hand over his mouth and ran towards her. And once again they were standing all close together.

And that was the picture of them that Tol Briston held in his mind for a long time: the woman with the auburn hair topped by a black straw hat, her deep brown eyes holding an anxious greeting, her wide mouth partly open, her whole expression seeming to hold a plea for good news; and the children now differently dressed, all clean and tidy, their faces bright, but the two elder ones reflecting something of their mother's look.

After pulling the horse to a stop, he smiled, a slow smile that warmed his thin face, and there came a twinkling light into his dark eyes, and his lips were showing a set of short big white teeth. His chin, like his nose, jutted out from his face and might tend to suggest a rigidness of character, but at this moment his expression could have been termed merry, and his tone definitely held a jolly note as he said, "Up with you, the lot of yous."

Grabbing up the bundles, the children made for the back of the cart. But Riah didn't move. Looking up at Tol, she said, "Is it settled?"

"Oh" – the smile slid from his face – "that I can't tell; it will lie atween you and Mr Miller. Fanny's got you an interview, that's all I can say. But having got that far, it's like a pistol to his head; she could walk out."

Riah couldn't quite follow his meaning, but she turned to where her bundles had lain, only to see that Davey had them already on the back of the cart, and when she made to follow him, Tol Briston said, "You could be seated here if you so like." He edged a little along the wooden seat, and when, after a moment's hesitation, she put her foot on the hub of the wheel, he thrust out his hand and she clasped it; then perched high beside him and looking straight ahead, she began the journey that was to set the seal on her life.

The entry to Moor House was through two unimposing iron gates, both of them thrust back with their bottom bars bedded firmly in weeds and dead grass. The drive was short, not more than fifty yards, and it curved to an open area that was almost as long as the drive itself; but unlike the roughness of the drive, this was paved with larged stone slabs, most of them, like the gates, cemented with grass. The house took up about half the width of the forecourt and the word that came into Riah's mind at the sight of it was higgledy-piggledy, because it looked as if a large cottage had been stuck either side of a three storey medium-sized house. Beyond the forecourt was a yard bordered on two sides by what looked like a stable and a barn.

Tol had brought the cart to a stop opposite the front door and there, almost filling it, stood the old woman. The children were slow to get out of the cart until her voice came at them in a hiss, saying, "Well, come on! Put a move on, you all." And when they had done her bidding she looked them over and said, "Oh, you're tidy. That's good." Her gaze now on Riah, she surveyed her from her black straw hat down to her black boots; then she said, "Come on in the lot of yous." And with that she almost pulled them one after the other over the low step and into a hallway. But before she closed the door she leant forward and called quietly towards the cart, "Thanks, Tol. See you later then."

Now she was crossing the hall, saying in a whisper, "Come this way."

The first impression that Riah got of Moor House was that it needed a good clean up: there was no shine on the hall floor surrounding the carpet, and the pieces of furniture dotting the walls showed plain evidence of dust.

The old woman, who Riah noticed now was limping badly, pushed open the door at the end of the hall, saying, "Go in there and sit yourselves down until I get him."

Pressing the children before her, Riah entered a long room. Although this, too, showed it could do with a good clean, it was evidently used, for a big couch whose upholstery had once been yellow and now was a dirty faded grey in parts showed tumbled cushions at its head, and between the two tall windows stood a desk littered with papers and books, looking as if someone had thrown them on it from a distance, so mixed up were they.

Silently she stopped the children sitting on the couch and directed them to a long backless upholstered seat set at right angles to the fireplace which showed a pile of ashes in which were buried half-burnt logs.

Seating herself on the edge of a chair opposite the children, she smoothed her skirt over her knees, opened the two buttons of her three-quarter length serge coat in order that her bright blue blouse should be in evidence and show her proposed employer that she was neat and tidy. Finally, she tucked her hair swiftly behind her ears, felt that her hat was absolutely straight on her head, then joined her hands on her lap and waited.

A minute was a long time to wait when four pairs of eyes were staring questioningly at you. But when five minutes passed and the children began to move restlessly on the seat, she unclasped her hands and with a raised finger cautioned them to silence; then her hand became transfixed by the sound of a voice coming from the far end of the room. For the first time she noticed that there was a door in the side wall and the voice was coming from there. It was somewhat muffled, yet the words were still clear: "No, Fanny. No. 'Tis blackmail. That's all it is, blackmail. I've told you, *no*."

"An' I've told you, Mr Miller, an' for the last time, I can't make the journeys no more. If it wasn't for Tol I wouldn't be here now. And he's riskin' somethin', cartin' me mornin' and night. If them up at The Heights get wind of it, he could be for the push. An' look at me leg, it's as big as me body. Now, you either take her an' her tribe on or you're left alone to fend for yourself, 'cos nobody in their right senses'll come here an' look after this place for what you have to offer them."

"Is that my fault, Fanny? Is it? Is it?"

"Yes, it is. In a way, yes it is, 'cos come quarter time you've enough money for books, beer, and baccy."

"Oh, leave me my breath. What else have I to live for?"

"Oh, Mr Miller, don't make me say it again."

The man's voice now fell to almost a mutter as he said, "And don't make me say it again, Fanny. What good am I in the outside world? I've tried it, haven't I?"

"I can't understand you. I can't, Mr Miller."

"Well, that's a pity, Fanny. That's a pity. I thought you were the only one who could. But about this woman. You say she's got four children? My God! And you think I'll take on a woman with four children? For fifteen years I tried to knock sense into the. . . ."

"Oh, shut up, will you? Shut up. I've heard your whinin' until

40

I'm sick of it. Now, you're seein' this woman or I walk out, not this evenin' after I've made your meal, but now, along of her an' her tribe. Now I say to you, you've got no other option. No, you haven't, Mr Miller. No, you haven't."

There followed a long silence during which the children, wide-eyed and open-mouthed, stared at Riah while she, her head turned slightly, kept her eyes fixed on the door at the far end of the room. Then the voices began again.

"What are they?"

"They're two lads and two lasses."

"How old?"

"Well, I think the boy seems about twelve and the youngest, I should say, five or six. The two lads you could set clearin' on outside. They've likely been used to work. As for the lasses, well, this house could do with a couple of lasses to help muck it out."

"What's she like?"

"Pleasant, youngish, capable looking."

There followed another silence; and then the man's voice, which held a deep plea in it now, said, "Oh, Fanny, you don't know what you're asking. You really don't know what you're asking me to do."

"Don't be silly, Mr Miller. Go on ... go on, have a look at them."

The few minutes seemed a long time before the door opened and a man entered the room.

The four children turned their heads towards him, and it was to them he looked first, not at Riah. When he did look at her he was about two yards from her. She had risen to her feet and they surveyed each other like combatants before a battle. She saw that he was a man in his mid-forties, perhaps nearing fifty, she would say. He had a round face and fair hair with a slight bald patch on the top of his head. He was of medium height and, although not fat, was inclined to thickness. After having listened to his voice, she had expected a tall, very imposing figure; the man before her appeared like a gentle creature, rather shy. In fact, she couldn't remember ever seeing anyone quite like him at all. She hadn't come across many gentry with whom to compare him, but she would have said he belonged to that class.

When he said hesitantly, "You ... you're wanting a position?" she answered, "Yes, sir."

41

"You ... you are a widow?"

"Yes, sir."

"Your children, can they work?" He turned now and his eyes rested on Davey, and she said, "Yes. Yes, sir. My son David, he's comin' up eleven and he's been workin' in the fields for the past three years. And Bridget" – she inclined her head – "she's very good at housework. She is coming up ten. She too has been working for the past three years." What made her utter the next words she never knew, but she said, "An' they're both learned; they can read and write, sir."

His head came quickly round to her as he said, "Indeed. Indeed. . . . What was your husband?"

"He was a miner, sir."

His eyebrows moved slightly upwards. "A miner? A coal miner?"

"Yes, sir."

"And your children ... can read and write? Did they go to school?"

"No, sir. My husband taught them."

His eyebrows moved further upwards and he said, "Your husband taught them? And he was a miner? And he could read and write? May I ask who taught him?"

"A Methodist man in Gateshead, sir."

"Oh. Oh. What is your name?"

"Mrs Millican, sir. Maria Millican."

"Well, Mrs Millican, I must be plain with you. I'm a man of very poor means. And I couldn't afford to engage you and your children at the wage you would likely require. Mrs Briggs has four shillings a week and her food. You, I am sure, would not consider that enough for your services and those of your family."

Four shillings for the lot of them. It was nothing, but at the present moment if he had suggested that she worked for their board and lodgings only she would have accepted. She said quickly, "I would be pleased to accept your offer, sir."

"You would?" He half turned from her, one shoulder moving as if with the twitch; then, looking at her again, he said, "It is nothing."

"I'll ... I'll be grateful for it at the present, sir, and we would do our best to serve you well."

She was surprised to see him sit down in a chair and, resting his

42

elbow on the table, lean his head on his hand; then, after a moment
during which they all stood staring at him, he rose and, without
first looking at them, he turned from them, saying, "See Fanny;
she'll tell you what to do." And he walked up the room again and
through the door, and as it closed on him the other door opened
and the old woman hobbled in, her face bright, her lips pursed and
her hands beckoning them towards her.

When they reached her all in a bunch, she said, "'Tis done then.
Come." And with that she led them back into the hall, through
a heavy oak door into a stone passage, through another door and
into the kitchen.

Riah took in three things immediately about the kitchen: it
was very big; it was cluttered and dirty; the barred fire of the
iron cooking stove had a hob attached to its top bar.

"Sit yourselves down" – Fanny pointed to the table – "and I'll
make you a drink. Would you like tea?"

"Tea?" Riah muttered the word and Fanny said, "Aye, tea, real
tea. He gets it in Newcastle but it comes from China. It's the one
luxury in this house. But I'm not partial to it meself; too scenty
like." And then she went on, "Well now, you're all set, and it's
up to you."

"Where will we sleep?"

As Riah slapped Biddy's arm gently for asking the question
Fanny nodded at her and in a broad toothless smile she said,
"Practical one you are, aren't you? Well then, I'll answer you.
There's a hayloft outside. But better than that, along at the low
end" – she motioned with her head to a door leading off by the
side of a dresser – "there's half a dozen rooms along there that
haven't been slept in for many a long year. But they are like Paddy's
market, full up with this, that an' the other. Anyway, it'll be one
of your first jobs to clear one of them and get settled for the night.
But first I'll make you a drop of tea and then I'll take you round.
It's a hoppity-hoppity house; you've got to get used to goin' up
a step an' down a step that you didn't know was there. That's
what's worn me legs out over the past ten years. I never meant to
take this on, you know." She was nodding at Riah now as she
poured some boiling water into a cream china teapot which was
stained brown around the lid. "You see, me old man was gardener
here for years, an' his father afore him. That was when there was
only the house standing, this middle one, an' it was of no size as

these houses go, just ten main rooms. But there was about thirty acres of land then, but now it's down to three. The odd bits on the sides were built by Mr Miller's father when he was young. I always says that the builder must have been drunk at the time, but my old man said it was to get the levels of the ground as it slopes away at the side like. Anyway, now they amount to twenty-five rooms altogether, an' that's not countin' larders and cellars an' the like. An' how many does he use ... Mr Miller? Two mostly; one if he got his own way, 'cos he lives in the library room most of his time an' sleeps in it more often than not on the couch. He'll be found dead in there one of these days, I tell him. Eeh, by!" She now poured a small amount of milk into six cups she had brought from a cupboard; then as she filled them with the black tea she added, "I never thought I'd bring it off, not really, 'cos he's agen people: never sees anybody but Parson Weeks and Miss Hobson from The Heights, or when he goes once a quarter into Newcastle to pick up his allowance. And more often than not those times he can hardly walk back from the coach road. But then on quarter days Tol keeps a look out for the coach and generally picks him up from it. I don't know what we'd do without Tol. He keeps us stocked up with wood and he drops the milk in most mornings except when the weather's very bad an' he can't get through."

"Tol ... it's a funny name."

Riah looked warningly at Biddy, but again the old woman smiled as she said, "Aye, I suppose it is."

"What's his second name?"

"Briston, Tol Briston.... Is there anything more you'd like to know, miss, or would you like to wait and ask him?" She was laughing down on Biddy now, and Biddy lowered her head as her mother said, "I'm sorry she speaks out of turn."

"Oh, I wouldn't give you tuppence for any bairn that didn't speak out of turn. Anyway, you'll all likely see a bit of Tol if you see nobody else here, for as I've said visitors are few an' far between here now, not like it once was. Anyway, Tol's the nearest neighbour. His cottage is in Fuller's Dip and the cottage is called The Dip." She bent towards Biddy again, saying, "That's a funny name an' all, isn't it, for a cottage, The Dip? Don't ask me how it came by it 'cos I couldn't tell you. Nor could my old man, and he was born in the hamlet. He used to say it was a natural name 'cos the cottage was in a hollow: an' it was Tol's father's, an' his

44

afore him. All forest men. The grandfather bought an' built on a bit of freehold land with stones from an old stone ruin and timber from an old ship, lugged from the river . . . . Would you like some more tea?"

All the children spoke at once, saying, "Yes, please," which caused Fanny to nod down at Riah, saying, "Well they have manners anyway."

"I like to think they were brought up proper."

A few minutes later Fanny said, "Well now, finish your drink and let's away for an inspection trip." And on this they immediately rose from the table and stood waiting while they looked at her as she put a hand to one side of her face and muttered as if to herself, "Now where shall I start?" Then turning fully to Riah, she said, "I've got no need to point out that this is the kitchen an' here you'll find all the things necessary for cooking except perhaps the stuff to cook with. Meals are pretty sparse 'cos I've had to stretch his shillin's. But there's one thing there's plenty of, an' that's fruit. The orchard's all overrun, but it's there for the pickin', goin' rotten most of it." Her eyes scanned the children now as she said, "You can eat to your heart's content an' be up all night with the gripes." And with this she turned away laughing as she added, "Come on; we'll start this way."

She now led them through the door to the side of the dresser and they found themselves tightly packed in another stone passage from which led three doors. She pushed them open one after the other, saying, "Coalhouse, pantry an' meat store," adding, "That hasn't seen a carcass for years. An' lastly, wine cellar. As you can see" – she moved to one side to let them glimpse in – "the racks are full of bottles. Unfortunately, they're all empty. But there was a time, my old man's father used to tell me, when there was as many as five hundred bottles on those shelves. But them days are gone."

She now opened another door, giving them a warning as she did so: "Mind, there's a step down."

When they had all stepped down, Riah saw that they were in another small hall with stairs leading up from the middle as in the main hall.

Fanny now pushed open another four doors leading off the hall and saying as she did so, "This was old Mrs Miller's sitting-room. In fact, this was her end of the house, 'cos she kept to herself, I understand, the last years of her life. You see, I wasn't here then.

It was Lizzie Watson who was the previous housekeeper. I've always lived in the hamlet. Still do. I like me own fireside. That's what annoys him" – she jerked her head backwards – "I wouldn't live in. Ten hours a day's enough for anybody, especially when there's nobody to open your mouth to. 'Cos there's days when you'd fancy he'd gone dumb.... Well, that was his mother's room. Never seen a duster for months I can tell you. Well, I can't get round to it, can I?"

As Riah shook her head she thought, Never seen a duster for months? Years would be nearer the truth. What a pity the moths had gone into the upholstery; it must have been such a nice suite at one time.

They followed the old woman into the next room which was a small dining-room; then to a music-room where a spinet stood in the corner. It had a fretwork front and the silk behind it had dropped away here and there. As Riah followed their guide up the stairs to the four rooms above and saw that their condition was much the same as those down below she kept repeating to herself: What a shame. What a shame.

When they were once more back in the kitchen Fanny led them through the door opposite to that next to the dresser and into a set of rooms much the same as those they had left. And when again they returned to the kitchen there was only the main house to go through. And now Fanny faced them, saying, "Well you've seen the hall and the drawing-room and now I'll show you the dining-room, but he hardly ever eats there. He mostly eats off a tray in his library room, except when the parson comes. Then I used to knock up a meal for them and they sat down to it properly. There's one thing we'd better not do and that's go near his library room. You can see that later on, but" – she lifted her hand and wagged a finger at Riah – "don't, on the peril of your life, try to straighten up anythin' in there. You'll think on first sight that a great wind had been through it, but he seems to know where everything is. Anyway, I'll take you up above and show you his bedroom. There's another four up there, but they've never been used for years. And the attic above. Oh God alive! the attic. I shouldn't be surprised if some of the old clothes don't come walking down the stairs one of these days, so alive will they be. I've only been up there a couple of times. That was when I first came and I hinted at him that a lot of the stuff could be cut down for frocks and things

46

for needy people in the village, and one of them was meself, 'cos some of the material was fine, the women's things. And there was men's toggery made up of fine worsted and serges. But you know, he nearly went down me throat. It's the only time he's ever gone for me. He told me those things were to be left alone and kindly not bring up the subject again. Oh, he played the master that day all right. Other times he talks like a lost lad. And if I say, what shall I do about this, that, and the other, he'll say, do what you think best, Fanny. You do what you think best. But about those clothes, oh my! So don't think, lass, when you go up there that you will be able to cut anything up for the bairns 'cos that's one thing he's firm on. Why? Don't ask me, I don't know. My man used to say it was just a quirk 'cos he had lived alone so long and the clothes were kind of memories he was hanging on to."

"Has he always lived alone here?"

"No, just for the last fifteen years. Well, not that long. He came back fifteen years gone and it's ten years ago now since his father died. And Lizzie Watson, as I said, was the housekeeper and she went shortly after. And that's how I came in. It was my man who asked me to help out. Just for a week or two, he said; then it went into years. He was always going to leave, my man was, because he was seventy-six and bent double with gardening, and he left all right when he dropped down dead near the rose patch, three years gone. Oh aye, he left all right. And I was left here on me own with young Mr Miller, 'cos that's what he was called when his father was alive and they never got on, his father an' him. Different as chalk from cheese. Used to ride every day, his father did; drunk as a noodle most times; an' gambled like somebody who had lost his brains. That's where the money went. But young Mr Miller was a different kettle of fish. Books seemed to be his weakness. Of course it's brandy now an' all, but in those days it was just books, 'cos he went to this college in Oxford. And then he went teaching. Then something happened. I don't know what, but one day he lands home and decided to stay. And that was funny 'cos when he were at the school in Oxford, he rarely came home for the holidays. His mother used to go there an' stay with him. They were fond of each other. They must have been, 'cos when he came home that time for good they used to wander about the moors and lanes together. I've seen them meself, hand in hand as if he was a young lad or like a couple courtin'. Perhaps it was to make up to her, kind

47

of, for Lizzie Wat ... son." Her voice trailed away as she glanced quickly at the children. "Well, there you are. Let's get out and see the garden, or what was a garden, an' then I'll show you the kitchen ropes. And that'll be that."

Tol Briston stood in the kitchen looking across the table to where Riah was expertly dissecting a rabbit. She had split it down the middle with a chopper and was now snipping off the limbs, and he watched her hands for a few moments before saying, "You're settled in then?"

She lifted her eyes to him and then smiled as she said, "Yes, thanks be to God. I really can't believe it because this time yesterday I was at the bottom of despair."

His eyes were again concentrated on her hands as he said, "It isn't much of a job, as jobs go, I mean what he offers, but you won't find him any trouble. You'll be your own boss, so to speak, as long as you keep the children out of his way. That's the main thing."

"Oh, I will. I will." She nodded at him. "Mrs Briggs has told me."

He lifted his eyes to her face now as he said, "I'll ... I'll drop your milk in by every day an' a load of wood once a month. He ... he doesn't buy much coal. But I meself, I find I like a wood fire better than a coal one. But you bein' from a mining village, I ... I suppose you're used to coal."

"Yes. Yes, I've been used to coal. But ... but I'll manage with wood all right. Oh yes, I'll manage, never fear." Her smile was wide, her eyes were bright.

"That's good then," he said.

He watched her now salt each piece of rabbit before dropping it into a brown earthenware dish, and when she put the lid on the dish he said, "You'll miss an onion and a turnip and such for it."

"What?" She brought her head up quickly towards him, then nodded: "Oh, yes, yes. But Davey is going to get a patch ready, and come next spring we should have vegetables."

"You feel settled then?"

48

Her hands became still on the table and she stared at him as she said, her voice a little above a whisper, "I hope so. Oh, I hope so."

A slow smile spread over his face, and he nodded his head twice before saying, "That's good. It's good when one feels settled. And ... and if you want any help any time just ask."

"I will. Thank you very much."

"Seeing we're your nearest neighbours, you ... you must meet me sister."

"Your ... your sister?"

"Yes, I live with me sister."

"I would like that."

The door opened at the far end of the kitchen and Fanny entered. She was dressed for the road, and her voice was quiet and held a note of sadness as she said, "I never thought he'd be so touched at me goin'. He's given me that. ... Look." She held out her hand. "Isn't it beautiful? 'Tis a brooch. 'Twas his mother's." There were tears in her eyes now and she swallowed deeply before repeating, "Never thought he'd be so touched. An' to give me that. Why, 'tis worth somethin'. Look, Tol."

He picked up the brooch that was made up of three ivy leaves, their stems twisted, and in the centre of each leaf was a small stone. He looked at her a long time before he said, "I think it's gold, Fanny. And the stones, they could be good ones. You'll have to guard that."

"I will, I will, Tol. I will. An' to think he's given it to me when he could have sold it for good money likely. But gold or no, good stones or no, I'll not sell it."

"Oh, no, no, don't sell it. You mustn't do that." There was a shocked note in Tol's voice.

The old woman shook her head, then turned to Riah, saying, "Well, I'm off, lass. It's all yours now, but Tol here will tell me how you go on. An' afore the bad weather sets in he might drop me over for a day to visit you."

"I'd like that." Riah came round the table and took Fanny's hand, saying, "I'll ... I'll never be able to thank you for what you've done for me and my family. If ... if I owned anythin' as precious as that brooch at this minute I'd give it to you. Such is my gratitude to you."

"'Twas nothin'. 'Twas nothin'. If I've done you a good turn,

49

you've done me one an' all. And don't forget what I told you about the rabbit." Her tone had changed now to its usual matter of factness, and, pointing to the oven, she said, "Put it in the bottom an' leave it for the night; it'll be as tender as a day old chick the morning: and let him have it round about twelve o'clock. And don't forget what I told you about the suet pudding. He likes it crusty on top, the harder the better, and plenty of dripping in the gravy. Well, I showed you."

"Yes, thank you very much."

She made for the door now that Tol was holding open for her; yet seeming reluctant to go, she turned again and, looking at Riah, she said, "And don't forget, six o'clock for his cheese and bread, and the fruit cut up in a dish, and the molasses on it, not sugar mind, the molasses. An' keep the bairns out of his way."

"I'll remember."

There was a tightness in Riah's throat: she could sense the feelings of the old woman who, in spite of her desire to be free of the burden of work and the travelling at her age, was reluctant to leave, perhaps not the house, but its master.

She stood alone in the yard and watched the cart being driven from it and onto the gravel, then down the drive. When it was out of sight she still remained standing. And when she eventually turned about she did not go immediately towards the kitchen door, but her eyes went from the one building to the other that hemmed in the yard on two sides; then she looked along the length of the back part of the house. Like the front, it too looked higgledy-piggledy, yet there rose in her the most odd desire, and she only just stopped herself from throwing out her arms in a wide gesture of embrace as, her thoughts tumbling over one another, she spoke to it, saying, "I'll take care of you. I'll bring you back to what you were. I'll make you shine, and him comfortable. Oh, yes, I'll make him comfortable. And the work here will be like giving each of the bairns a trade." And she almost skipped towards the kitchen door now and inside began preparing her new master's evening meal. . . .

It was half an hour later when, balancing the tray against her waist with one hand, she tapped on the library door. She did it softly at first; then when she received no command to enter she knocked more firmly, and when this brought a kind of smothered grunt, she opened the door and entered the room.

She saw that he was sitting before another cluttered desk, one forearm resting on it, his body leaning over it, and he continued to write while she stood wavering as to where she should place the tray.

He did not alter his position or raise his head, but his hand, still holding the pen, jerked outwards and pointed to the corner of the table as he said, "Put it there."

Slowly, she placed the tray on the top of a bundle of papers and books; but seeing that its position was uneven and that the bowl of fruit might slide, she tentatively put her hand under the tray with the intention of moving the papers when his voice came at her, saying, "Don't touch those; just leave it."

She did as she was bid, but could not help but put her hand out to arrest the progress of the sliding bowl, and this caused him to sigh. Quickly now, he put down the pen, leant back in his chair, then still without looking at her he said, "Are you settled in?"

"Yes, yes, thank you, sir."

"Fanny has told you everything?"

"Yes, yes, sir."

"Good."

Once he began to write, she turned and made for the door; and she had just opened it when he said, "I . . . I hope you understand I don't want to be troubled by your children."

There was a space of a second before she said, "I understand, sir. You won't be troubled."

Again he said, "Good." And she went out and closed the door. But there she stood for a moment and drew in a sharp breath before hurrying across the hall, through the kitchen and the door that led into the east wing of the house, where she had set Biddy and Maggie the task of dusting and cleaning two of the bedrooms which entailed putting the mattresses out to air in the sun and brushing the threadbare carpets.

When she came upon them, they were both sitting on the edge of a bed, and to begin with she laughingly said, "I've caught you then, have I, dodging the column?"

"Eeh, I'm tired, Ma." She looked at her six-year-old daughter. Then putting her hand on the child's dark brown hair she stroked it back from the sweating brow, saying, "Yes, I bet you are, hinny, but" – she looked about her – "I can see you've done a good job. I suppose you've done all the work while Biddy there's been sitting watching you." At this they all laughed softly together, and Biddy said seriously, "Ma. I wonder how long it is since this house had a clean out? It'll take ages to get all the muck out of this carpet." She stamped her foot on it. "And look, there's cobwebs hanging in the corners. We couldn't reach them. You'll have to have a brush, a long brush to get at them."

"All in good time." Riah pushed them apart and sat down between them; then putting her arms about them, she looked first at one and then at the other as she said, "Do you think you're going to like it here?"

"Oh, aye, Ma." Biddy nodded her head while young Maggie just smiled.

"Well now." Riah's face became serious, as was her voice as she spoke slowly but distinctly, saying, "All right then. And I think so too. But there's one thing that you must remember, both of you. Now listen. You've got to keep out of the master's way. Whenever you see him coming, scoot! It seems that he can't stand bairns. So remember." She stopped and, again looking from one to the other, she asked, "What have you got to remember?"

"To keep out of his way."

Riah now turned her glance from Biddy to Maggie, and the little girl said, "To keep out of the master's way, Ma."

"Will you do that?"

They both nodded, and with this she said, "Well, come on. You can finish for the day. It's been a day and a half, hasn't it? And you Biddy, go to the garden and tell the boys to come in. But tell them to do it quietly. And you can tell them what I've just told you. Everything depends upon them keeping out of the master's way."

"I'll tell them, Ma."

When Biddy made to run from her, Riah thrust out her hand and grabbed the collar of her dress, saying, "And don't scamper. Learn to walk."

When Biddy walked away but not without first sighing, Maggie, looking up at her mother, said, "Will we never be able to scamper again, Ma?" And Riah, pressing the child to her side, laughed down on her as she answered, "Yes, of course you will. Every now and again we'll go out into the fields and we'll all scamper and have a bit carry-on. What about that, eh?"

And as she walked her youngest daughter from the room she thought, Yes, they'll have to scamper; and I'll have to arrange a time when they can be free and play a bit, because all bairns should play a bit.

4

It was the week before Christmas. For days now the ground had been frozen hard and the boys couldn't do anything outside. This morning, they were over in the stables, lime-washing the walls. They had been there for the past three hours and Riah was about to take them a drink of hot broth. She had on her old coat and a woollen head shawl, and now she tucked a tin bowl into each of her pockets, picked up the lidded can and, opening the kitchen door, she went out. The sharpness of the air caught at her breath, and she was glad when she entered the stable for in comparison it felt warm. The two boys turned from their task and Johnny said, "Ma, I'm near froze."

"You should wear your mittens," she said, and the boy replied, "They get all messed up and sticky."

"Well, that's your look out. Come and have this drop of broth."

After laying down his brush, Davey came and stood by the manger where his mother had laid the bowls, and he smiled at her and asked, "How does it look?" She turned to the wall. "Good," she said. "Good. And it smells fresh."

"But not the fresh smell of horses. An' you know what, Ma?"

"No. What?" Riah watched her son take a drink of the hot broth before he answered: "I wish the master had a horse an' trap; anyway, just a horse. It would be lovely if he had a horse."

"That's a hope; he can barely manage to feed us, never mind a horse."

"Funny that, I think, Ma, a gentleman an' no money."

"Well, he's got some, as I've told you, but it's very little, and it takes him all his time to eke it out."

Davey laughed now and he poked his face towards her, saying, "He didn't eke it out yesterday, did he, Ma?"

She pulled a prim face at him, trying to suppress her smile

54

as she said, "No, perhaps not. Anyway, come on, finish your broth, I've got to get back. I've got work to do, I can't play about."

"Oh, Ma." Johnny looked up at her, his dark eyes twinkling as he said, "I'd rather play about in the house."

She cuffed his ear gently, saying, "Yes, I know you would, you lazy lump." And although she looked tenderly down on her younger son she knew that there was some truth in her last words, for if Johnny could get out of working he would. He still wanted to play as if he was a bairn, but he'd had his eighth birthday last month. Yet wasn't he still a bairn? Weren't they all bairns? Except perhaps Davey. She let her eyes linger on her son. He was dressed in his oldest clothes, the cap was covering his fair hair and there was dirt on his cheeks, but nothing could hide his beauty, nor dull the brightness of his blue eyes. He was so good to look on, and during the last months he seemed to have put on inches. His body was slim and straight, and at times the sight of him pained her and she couldn't imagine he had come out of her and Seth. She was on her way out when Johnny's words stopped her, for in a loud whisper he called to her, "I saw the master this morning, Ma."

Swinging round, her expression dark, she demanded, "Now I've told you. Where were you?"

It was Davey who answered, saying, "It's all right, Ma, it's all right. We were crossing the yard and nosey here turned towards the house" – he pushed his brother – "and he said he saw the master watchin' us from the drawing-room window as we cleaned the steps."

"Did you see him?"

"No. I told nosey here to keep on with his work and not turn round."

She took a step towards Johnny as she said, "You're sure you saw him at the drawing-room window that early on?"

"Aye, Ma. And he wasn't dressed like, not for the day, he had his robe on."

She stared at the boys for a moment; then muttering, "Well, well," she turned about and went hurrying out across the yard and into the kitchen again. And there she slowly took off her head shawl and coat, thinking as she did so, It must have been around nine, and hardly light enough for him to see anything.

She was smiling to herself as she now poured herself out some broth: he must be looking at the children on the sly; and on top of what happened yesterday.

It was only the second trip he had made to the city since she had come into the house, and it was, she knew, to visit his solicitor and collect his allowance. His return had brought a number of surprises because, whereas the first time he had returned Tol had had to help him down from the cart and into the house, this time he had got down himself, and after thanking Tol he had turned about and walked to the front door. Not that he had returned sober, he'd had a small load on that had affected his walking slightly, but nevertheless he hadn't been drunk. And he was hardly in the house when he had rung the bell for her. It was the drawing-room bell, and he had been sitting before the fire, his hands extended to the flames, when she entered the room. But he hadn't turned to her until she stood to the side of the fireplace and said, "You rang, sir?" And then it was some seconds before he said, "I did, I did, Maria, I did ring for you. It is very cold out today."

"Yes, sir, it is very cold," she had replied.

"Newcastle is packed with people. I was glad to get home."

"I'm . . . I'm sure you were, sir," she said.

"The shops in the city are very gay, Maria."

"Are they, sir?"

"Yes, yes indeed, they are." He still wasn't looking at her. He still had his hands extended to the fire. Then he went on, "They made me wish I was a rich man, or a highwayman." Now he slanted his gaze towards her and for the first time in their acquaintance she saw that there was a twinkle in his eye, and she returned it with a smile, saying, "I don't think you'd make a very good highwayman, sir."

"No, perhaps not." He straightened up now and, resting his hands on his knees, he ended, "I don't think I'd make a very good anything. In fact I know it. I'm proof of it, aren't I?" He turned his gaze fully towards her now, and she looked at him but didn't answer. Men got maudlin when they had drink in them; he would never have talked like this if he had been sober; in fact, it was the longest conversation they'd ever had. The first time she had seen him on his return from Newcastle he had tried to do a dance in the hall, but he hadn't spoken to her, and the next morning he had gone down to the river and plunged in. He had often gone into the river earlier on, and even on the hottest days the water was inclined to be cold, as she herself knew for when she had taken the bairns down she sat on the bank and dangled her feet in the water.

Then he had surprised her by handing her two sovereigns, saying brusquely, "Take these. They are to get extra for the table and such during the holidays. Spend it sparingly because there's no more where that came from." And with a slight touch of humour he added, "You'd better hold it tight in your fist because I might ask for it back tomorrow, you never know, because by then the spirit will have evaporated and I shall be back to normal. But ... but as I am not yet normal—" He turned about and grabbed at a long coloured paper bag that was lying on the couch to his hand and, thrusting it towards her, he said, "For your brood. Only mind" – he now wagged his finger at her – "don't take it as a breakthrough; I don't want to see them. Keep them out of my way. You understand?"

"Yes, sir." Her voice was soft. "And thank you. Thank you most kindly for remembering them."

He was on his feet when he almost barked at her, "I didn't remember them, I ... I was just thinking back." And turning, he staggered up the room and out of the far door leaving her still standing holding the two sovereigns in one hand and a fancy coloured bag in the other. There were tears in her eyes when she reached the kitchen.

The children had been seated round the table doing their nightly half hour of reading, which she insisted upon, and she stood looking at them for a while before she opened the bag. Then one after the other she drew out four long multi-coloured twists of candy sugar, and the children's astonishment came as one large gasp, and slowly she handed one twist to each of them, saying, "The master bought them for you in Newcastle."

As usual it was Biddy who was the first to speak. "He never did," she said. And her mother, looking at her, smiled as she said in a strained voice, "He did."

The four children had stared at the twisted columns in awe, but when Johnny bit deep into his, his mother cried at him, "Now don't think you're going to go through that all at once. Break it in three and make it last. Look at the length of them! I've never seen such long ones afore, nor any as bonny."

"Ma, will this mean we can go and thank him?" Biddy said, only to shrink back in her chair immediately as her mother almost pounced on her, crying low, "No, it doesn't, madam! You make a move in that direction and I'll skin you alive. Do you hear? Things are just the same: he doesn't want to see you; he's not going to be pestered."

But undaunted by her mother's attitude, Biddy muttered, "Pestered? We keep miles from him. I did a bunk into the bushes the other day when I saw him coming down the drive."

"Well, keep on doing bunks, and don't you dare go near him. I'm warning you." Then her voice softening, Riah looked from one to the other of her children and said, "You like being here, don't you?" And immediately Johnny and Maggie nodded their heads. But Davey and Biddy said nothing which caused her to bark at Biddy, "Well!"

"We don't see many people, only Tol."

"She's right, Ma" – Davey's face was solemn – "we don't, we don't see many people."

She sat slowly down at the head of the table, her two hands on it, one still doubled, and, her voice slow, she said, "We've got a roof over our heads; we are well fed; plain, but well fed; you've got beds like you've never had in your life afore; you're healthy. What more can you want?"

Their answer came into her mind: A bit of jollification, a bit of fun, young people to mix with; a fair now and again. Seth used to take them to the fair at holiday times, but there were no holidays kept here. She understood how they were feeling.

Slowly she unfolded her fist and slid the back of her hand towards the centre of the table showing them the two sovereigns and, her voice still slow but quiet, she said, "He gave me these, so we could have a bit of jollification at Christmas. We'll all go into Fellburn, perhaps into Gateshead Fell an' all, and" – she ended – "we'll buy up the town." And as she watched their faces brighten and their bodies become animated, she thought, I'll have to ask him for a full day off.

Sometimes Riah felt that she had known Tol Briston all her life. He had become a friend, a friend in a million as she put it to herself.

Nothing was too much trouble for him. He would bring messages from the village, or even do an errand in the town when he had to go in there to help the other outside men from The Heights bring in fodder. He delivered the milk and wood as if it was part of his duty. He had also brought Fanny over twice during the past month, and that had been a treat for both of them, and listening to the old woman she had learned a lot more about her master and his early days in the house. Of course, she realized the old woman's knowledge had come second-hand through her husband, but nevertheless it rang true. And the more she heard the more she realized how her solitary master had loved his mother. But what Fanny didn't know and so couldn't tell her was what had brought this man home and made him into a recluse, because something must have happened to bring a highly learned and presentable man, as he must at one time have been and still could be if he smartened himself up, back to this house to hide away, as it seemed, from human companionship. A broken love affair, most likely. But would that make him detest children?

Anyway, tomorrow was Christmas Eve, and here they were all going into Gateshead Fell to buy Christmas fare.

She'd had her work cut out these past three days to keep her brood from screaming and yelling at the prospect. She had made them keep their voices down but she couldn't stop them from running. Wherever they went they wanted to run. And now here they were, all being piled into the cart, muffled up in their Sunday clothes and the woolly hats and scarves she and Biddy had knitted during the winter evenings.

She felt happy as she had never felt in her life as Tol finally helped her up into her seat; then taking his place at her side, he cried, "Gee-up! there."

They had left the yard and were crossing the drive when Biddy tugged at the back of her coat, and she turned and looked down at her daughter who whispered, "The master, he's at the landing window."

She experienced a quick inclination to turn her head and look towards the house, but she kept her gaze on Biddy as she said, "Keep your eyes down and behave yourself." Then when she turned round, Tol, his gaze fixed ahead, said, "He must be coming round."

"Oh, I don't think so. He never comes near them."

59

"Oh, time's young yet, time's young yet. An' there's one thing, you've made a change in him: I saw him walking the other day and he was quite spruced up, shaven and a coat on that for once looked as if he hadn't slept in it."

She laughed gently now as she said, "I see to his clothes on the quiet, press them and starch his cravats and such."

"You've been a blessin' to him. Fanny did her best, God knows, but at her best that wasn't much even on her good days. She was never given to housework an' such, was Fanny. Her own cottage is like Paddy's market, but she's happy in it, and content, and that's the main thing. Some people can be too clean."

"You think so?" Her voice had risen at the end of the words into a question because she felt he was censoring her. Then he said, "Yes, in a way, when it brings no comfort. Now your kind of cleanness brings comfort, but there are some that would prevent a cinder falling from the fire if it were possible because it would alter the arrangement of the coal."

She laughed to herself as she thought: So that's it, it's his sister.

She had met Annie Briston only four times altogether. She was a woman in her mid-thirties, but she looked much older. She had a pleasant face and voice and, being Tol's sister, Riah had thought she would take to her straightaway, but somehow she hadn't.

When she herself was in Fanny's company, so free was her own chatter that she often smiled to herself, thinking, People won't have far to look to know where Biddy comes from. But with Annie Briston, she found herself being merely polite, correctly polite. During their first two meetings the woman had acted quite friendly, but on the latter two there had been a change in her attitude. She had talked a lot about Tol. Told how she had left good service to come home and take care of him after their mother had died eight years ago. Yesterday, in their last meeting, she had given her two clouty dolls as Christmas surprises for the girls and a wooden cradle which had been made by Tol for Maggie's doll. She had also remarked, as if in passing, how she would miss Tol when he got married and went to live in Rowdip.

Her first reaction to this news had been one of surprise. But then she had asked herself, why should she be surprised? It was a wonder that a presentable man, such as Tol, had gone so long without a wife, and she hoped the one he had chosen would be worthy of him, for he was a good man. She herself would miss him, and not only for his fetching and carrying.

She said now, "Before I forget, I must wish you good luck for the future."

He tugged on the right-hand rein, guiding the horse round a bend in the road, then said, "Careful, careful," before casting a glance at her and saying, "What have you got to wish me good luck for in the future?"

"Well, your ... your wedding."

"Weddin'?" He pulled sharply on the reins again; then swivelled his body towards her, saying, "What weddin'?"

"Oh!" She knew her colour had risen, and now she muttered, "Well, perhaps I misunderstood her, your sister. She gave me the impression you were going to be married, and ... and might move away."

He was staring at her and she at him, but he didn't speak, at least not until he was once more looking ahead, when he said, his voice almost a growl, "I'm not gettin' married."

"I'm sorry. I must have made a mistake."

"You made no mistake." His tone was flat. "When I think of gettin' married I'll tell you."

"Oh, there's no need." She felt annoyed both with his sister and at the attitude he was taking towards her now, and she added, "It has nothing to do with me. I only spoke out of politeness."

"Yes, I know you did." His tone had altered again. "But Annie had no right to give you that impression."

She was still feeling annoyance as she answered, "Well, I should imagine it isn't something that a body would say if they hadn't something to go on."

"She has nothing to go on, except that I sometimes visit this family in Rowdip. Betty is the daughter, but she's just coming up nineteen. I've taken her to the fair and the races, things like that. There's not much fun down in Rowdip. And her parents are elderly. But her mother and my mother were friends for years and I've known Betty since she was a baby. Talkin' of getting married, I should have been a married man for many years now. I was courtin' a girl when my mother died. It was then Annie came home for the funeral and decided to stay. I couldn't do anything about it, that was her home. Well, my future wife didn't see eye to eye with Annie, I mean living in the same house – three rooms and a scullery are not big enough to hold two women – and so she gave me her answer to it all by finding a better man."

"I'm sorry."

"Oh, as things have turned out, I'm not. It's odd" – his voice was light now – "queer in a way, how things work themselves out and how your mind accepts the changes, how little things of no account at the time become of vast importance. My dad used to say, all encounters lead to big battles, and he was right. You can apply that to anything."

Now changing the subject abruptly he lifted his whip and pointed, saying, "Look at that sky. I haven't travelled at all, but I doubt if there's any place in the world where you'll find skies like here. The fire in that sun, you would think, should warm the earth, yet the sky is so vast and the horizons so long, so deep, that its flame is a mere candlelight by the time it touches us."

Her head was turned fully towards him and she said softly, "That was lovely."

"What was?" He glanced at her.

"What you said."

His head swung round fully towards her. "What I said? You mean about the sun an' that?"

"Yes, it's like something I read in a book."

Again his eyes were fixed ahead and it was sometime before he spoke; and then, his voice low, he said, "Aye, they tell me that you can read. And not only you, but the bairns an' all. That's amazing. And here's me a fully grown man, an' I can't write me own name. Yet me head's full of words an' thoughts that colour me thinkin'."

She was bending towards him now, her voice low. "I'll learn you, Tol," she said. "I never thought about putting it to you, but I'll learn you."

"Oh, it would never do. It would never work. What use would it be to me now?" he muttered.

"Good gracious!" she said, a note of indignation in her voice. "You're young; you . . . you could have forty years to go, and think of all you could learn in forty years through reading. Why, even in the last few months when I've had time to meself at night I've improved. I could write a letter now as good as Biddy. I'm sure I could."

"Biddy can write a letter?"

"Yes, oh yes. Biddy's clever. I think she's going to be the only

62

clever one among them. They can all read and write, an' they know their numbers, but Biddy thinks, she tries to work things out." Her voice had been low, and he turned towards her now, his own voice as low and a smile on his face as he said, "I think she's a bit special, is Biddy. She'll go places."

She sat back, and when she spoke it was as if she was asking a question of someone who wasn't there: "Where?" she said. "Where? What chance has she here, but to sweep and clean all her life?"

As if Biddy had heard her name mentioned her head came between them now from where she was standing in the cart and, her voice high, she said, "You know something, Ma? You know what I'm gona buy when I get into Gateshead Fell?"

"No, I don't know what you're going to buy. What?"

"A bundle of pipe cleaners."

"A bundle of pipe cleaners? Whatever for?"

"To give as a present to the master."

"Don't be silly, child, the master doesn't smoke."

"I know that, but he should. It'll soothe him like it used to do me da, and when he sees them it'll put the idea into his head."

She now looked from one to the other as her mother and Tol exchanged glances before bursting out laughing. And when she, also laughing, now sat down in the cart, Davey, shaking his head at her, said, "You know, at times I think you're up the pole, our Biddy." And in answer she nodded at him brightly, saying, "Yes, I know. But from up there you can see more of what's going on."

Now they were all laughing. Biddy knew that the two younger ones didn't know what they were laughing about, but she knew: they were all laughing because they were joyful. Everybody was joyful. It was Christmas; they were going into Gateshead Fell; they had money to spend and their ma looked beautiful; so everything was joyful, so joyful, like bells ringing all the time on a Sunday morning. Joyful.

5

Today was Christmas Day and tomorrow, Boxing Day, she'd be twenty-seven years old. And she'd been aware of Christmases since she was four years old, but she had never known a one like this, full of excitement, yet peaceful. Yesterday, Christmas Eve, they'd had three callers, counting Tol, that was. The other two had been Parson Weeks and a stranger, a correctly dressed woman who looked like a lady, but turned out to be only a lady's maid. Of course, that was still something. She was from the big house called The Heights that lay a good mile beyond the village, which, she now knew from Tol, was owned and lived in by the Gullmington family.

Miss Hobson, she had also learned, was lady's maid to the present master's mother, a grand person well into her seventies. She also learned that Miss Hobson's first post had been in this very house, and not as a lady's maid but as a trainee parlour-maid when she was fourteen. She was twenty-six years old when she went as head parlour-maid to The Heights, and she had remained as such for fifteen years until Madam Gullmington, having lost her maid, chose her to fill the vacancy. But at least once a year she made it her business to come and see Mr Percival, for as she said she had seen him a few minutes after he was born, and had always retained a soft spot for him.

Riah had wanted to put questions to her regarding her master. But Miss Hobson was so prim and her manner so correct that Riah felt in a way she was in the presence of one of the gentry themselves, and she was wise enough to know that one didn't put questions to the gentry.

Of her own accord she had set a tray, using the best cups from the cabinet in the dining-room, and she had warmed the pot before mashing the tea, and when she took it into the drawing-room where Mr Miller was sitting talking to his visitor, she knew that he was surprised at her gesture, but not annoyed. She knew that Miss Hobson, too, was surprised, likely because she had set the tray correctly, but she wouldn't have been able to do so if she hadn't found in the back of the dresser drawer the book called *Household Management*. It covered almost everything that was required in the running of a large establishment, from making blacking for the horses' hooves and the ingredients that went into their mash, to attending to the mistress's wants before retirement. There were a number of pages at the back of the book full of do's and don'ts, and one of the don'ts was: Never make the mistake of offering a visitor pastries or cakes with a cup of tea if they should call before three o'clock in the afternoon. It went on to state that it should be noted that the best tea service did not carry plates, merely cups and saucers. Furthermore, should you be required to offer your guests any sweetmeats, see that they were of a delicate and light quality. A footnote to this statement reminded the reader that it was only the common people who made a meal of sandwiches, buns, and pastry.

In parts she had found the book very amusing; in fact, it had become like a joke book, especially when Biddy read it aloud to them, which she often did for her reading exercise, and she accompanied her reading with mimicry, causing them all to laugh so loudly Riah had often to quieten them, while her own face was wet with tears of laughter.

One thing had disappointed her about Miss Hobson's visit: the lady's maid had made no reference to the change she saw in the house, and she must have noticed that it was different.

Then Parson Weeks had come. He was a very dominant man was Parson Weeks, and he had stayed over an hour, and had spent it in the library with the master. And when he was about to take his leave he had spoken to her, saying, "Will I be seeing you all at church tomorrow morning?" And after a moment's hesitation she had said, "I should like to send the children, sir, but I'm afraid I wouldn't be able to attend myself."

"Well, send the children," he had said.

Again she had hesitated before saying, "Well, if the weather holds and it doesn't snow, sir."

"Oh, the weather will hold," he replied airily; "and the walk will do them good. You send them, ma'am. You send them."

"Yes, sir."

"And every Sunday after. Do you hear?"

"Yes, sir."

Percival Miller had been standing near during this conversation, but he had said nothing, just stood apart, his hands behind his back, his head bowed slightly, his gaze directed towards his shoes. Riah glanced at him before turning away. It was as if he were affected by even the mention of the children. . . .

But here it was, Christmas morning. The children had gone to church and they hadn't to walk the mile or so there and the mile back because Tol, like the good friend that he was, had come and taken them. She had a fire blazing in the drawing-room and one in the dining-room, and in this room she had set the table in style, as she put it, even to putting a trail of holly on the stiffly starched white cloth. It was a round dining table and she had covered the whole of it, not just the end as she usually did on a Sunday which was the only time he used the dining-room; the rest of the week he had his meals served on a tray in the library. She often wondered at what time he left that room at night and went to bed. Some nights he didn't leave it for she would find the bed hadn't been slept in. These were the mornings when she'd come downstairs again with his tray of tea and find him asleep on the couch with books strewn by the side of it. That's all he seemed to live for, books. She felt sorry for him, deeply sorry. She wished she could do something for him to lift him out of this despondency that he seemed to be in. And she knew the full meaning of that word because it came in *Pilgrim's Progress* and Seth had read that to them.

She had placed two glasses on the table, one for wine and one for water, and in front of them she had put the bottle of wine that was their Christmas surprise to him. But she wondered if he would remark on it.

She looked around the room. Everything was ready. The meal was waiting to be served. She knew he had just come back from his walk. He had taken to going for a brisk walk these past few weeks, sometimes being out for half a day at a time.

There was a large hall mirror at the end of the dining-room and she stood in front of it for a moment and smoothed back her hair from her brow. She did not wear a cap; she hadn't one, and he hadn't insisted on it. But today she was wearing her Sunday frock and over it a large white apron. As she smoothed the apron down over her hips she told herself she would do; then she hurried out of the room and made her way to the kitchen, there to be greeted by the children. They had already taken off their outdoor things and they crowded round her, all talking at once.

She silenced them, saying, "One at a time! One at a time! Now what was it like?" She looked at Davey and he said, "It was very nice, Ma, and the singing was nice."

"And the church was decorated," said Biddy. "And oh, Ma, it was lovely. And there was a shelter, like a stable with straw and donkeys, and, oh Ma—" Biddy's lips began to tremble and Maggie put in now, "There was a cradle like mine, Ma, like Tol made me, only mine was better."

"Ma—" It was Davey speaking, and his voice seemed to silence the others and he looked at her for a moment before he went on, "We saw him."

"The master?"

"Aye, close up. He . . . he was walking along the road, and Tol stopped the cart and spoke to him."

"What did he say?"

"Tol? Oh, he talked about the weather an' if it was going to snow."

"What did the master say?"

"Oh, he agreed with Tol, an' he said it could happen any time."

"Ma—" Riah turned her attention to Biddy again, and Biddy said, "He looked at us."

"He did?"

"Aye, one after the other. It was funny the way he looked at us, like. . . ."

"Like what?"

"Oh, I don't know. Not nasty, not as if he didn't like us. I don't know how he looked. Anyway, it was just for a minute, and then he walked off." Riah stared at the children for a moment, then said, "Well, go on now, go in the other room, and don't make a lot of noise. The fire's on, the table's set, and I'll be in with your dinner in a few minutes."

"Oh! pork" – Johnny was hopping from one leg to the other – "an' roast taties."

"Go on, greedy guts!" She pushed him and the others towards the door, then busied herself getting the meat out of the oven.

She had just completed setting the large tray with three vege-table dishes and the gravy tureen and a meat dish, on which lay slices of pork trimmed with the choice of roast rabbit separated by his favourite baked dumplings, when one of the ten brass bells arranged above the kitchen door tinkled. Almost staggering under the weight of the tray, she left the kitchen.

Outside the dining-room door she placed the tray down on a side table, pushed open the door, then entered the room.

He was sitting by the fire and he did not speak as she arranged the dishes on the table, but he watched her. When she was finished and had turned and looked at him, saying, "I hope you enjoy your meal, sir," he continued to stare at her for a moment; then turning his gaze back to the table, he said, "The wine. That was thoughtful of you, Maria, but you should not have wasted the housekeeping money on such."

Her chin moved slightly as she said, "I didn't use the house-keeping money, sir; it is my ... our present to you for your kindness to us."

She watched his eyes widen as he rose from the chair to go to the table; and there, sitting down, he lifted up the bottle and looked at it, saying softly, "It is a good wine. May I ask what you paid for it?"

She hesitated for a moment before she said, "One and nine-pence, sir."

When he replaced the bottle on the table his hand remained on it and he repeated, "One and ninepence. Almost half of what I give you for your week's wages. You are very kind, and ... and I thank you, Maria. What is more" – he now looked fully at her – "my thanks are also overdue for the way you have kept the house. It hasn't been like this for many, many years; you have brought comfort back into it."

The colour, she knew, was rushing over her face and she stam-mered slightly as she said, "I ... I ... I'm glad you find it so, sir."

"I do. I do."

When a silence fell between them she looked at the table and said hastily, "Your dinner will be getting cold. Will I ... serve it out for you?" And he answered, "No. No, thank you; I ... I can see to it. Thank you very much." It was a note of dismissal and she was about to turn away when he said softly, "You have a fine looking family, Maria."

68

Her colour deepened still further as she smiled widely at him. "Thank you, sir," she said. "I'm glad you find them so."

He was reaching out to fork a piece of rabbit as he spoke again, saying, "Why is your elder boy so fair, and the others dark?"

"He takes after his grandfather, sir, who came from Sweden."

"Oh. Oh, is that the reason? He's a fine looking boy. They are fine looking children."

She said again, "Thank you, sir." And when he said no more she turned hastily about and left the room. But in the hall she joined her hands and pressed them tightly against the nape of her neck. He was going to recognize the children, soon they'd be able to move about freely. Whatever thing he had against children as a whole was disappearing; she could feel it. Oh, what a lovely Christmas this was. And it wasn't near ended, because this afternoon, Tol had promised to drop in and have tea with the children.... Tol. She closed her eyes for a moment and a slow smile spread over her face, only to be wiped off quickly and for her whole body to jerk as an inner voice cried, None of that now! None of that! And Seth hardly cold; and Tol a younger man; and you with four bairns. Have sense, woman, have sense. Don't spoil things.

As if answering the voice, she said, "No, no; I mustn't spoil things. I'll take what is offered and be thankful." And on this she started hurriedly towards the kitchen.

6

❧❧

The winter had been long and hard. Yet, on looking back, it had passed quickly; she'd had so much to do. Every room in the house had been cleaned from floor to ceiling. Where it was possible she had washed curtains and bedspreads. She had also carefully darned worn fabrics, using a box of coloured silks she had found in a drawer in Mrs Miller's room. The lady had evidently spent a lot of her time doing tapestry for there was much evidence of it in chair-back covers and seats.

At night, when she went to bed, very often too tired to sleep, she would lie awake going over and over the activities of the day, especially of those days or evenings when Tol had come for his lesson. He was progressing nicely and could now not only write his own name and address, but could spell over fifty words of two syllables. His progress hadn't been due so much to herself, and to his own adaptability, but to Biddy, who had now read right through the Bible, and not only that, but was able to memorize and quote passages. So bright did she appear at times that Riah thought she was getting a bit above herself and so had to check her in no small voice, at such times as when she read pieces from the Newcastle weekly paper that Tol picked up for the master, and which Mr Miller usually threw in the wastepaper basket the day after arrival.

Since Christmas the master had seemed more relaxed. Sometimes he would talk to her when she took in his meals, asking her questions about her early life.

Yesterday she had asked leave to go into Gateshead Fell, saying she wanted to do a little shopping for the children. She didn't state the exact nature of the shopping, which was to go to the second-hand stall, the equivalent to Paddy's market in the city, and there pick up some old clothes that she could cut down for trousers for the boys and dresses for the girls, for now their clothes were getting very threadbare.

So here she was, making the journey alone, for she knew if she had brought the girls with her they would hold her up wanting to see this an' that in the market.

She had to walk the mile to the coach road and from there she took the cart into the town.

Once in the market she too had the desire to wander around the stalls; but this she curbed and made straight for the clothes pile. There was an assortment of garments on a trestle table, but the kind she was looking for were thrown here and there on the ground, which fortunately was dry. She wasn't the only one on the same errand and at one stage she had a gentleman's tail-cot almost wrenched from her hands. But as she had already seen it transformed into a pair of knickerbockers for Davey, who was growing so fast that the two pairs he possessed were not only thin in the seat but now well above his knees, she hung on to it fiercely.

When she finally left the stall her two canvas bags held two cotton dresses, a voluminous serge skirt which would eventually provide her with a dress, two men's corduroy coats, both lined and padded which was an asset, and the swallowtail-coat.

Before leaving the market she treated herself to a plate of hot peas, and afterwards, after waiting an hour and a half by the side of the road, she mounted the cart for home. She felt so pleased with her purchases and her day's outing that somewhere inside herself she was humming.

She hadn't told Tol where she was going so he hadn't made an effort to meet her. She had of late made as few requests of him as possible. If he did anything for them it must be, as she thought, off his own bat. In fact, at times of late she had been a little reserved with him, not laughing as freely as she used to do, and she knew he was puzzled by it. But, as she told herself, it was her only safeguard, even though it was a poor one.

Although she had shared the clothing between her two bags she was finding them heavy and when she reached the old toll gate that was no longer in use, having been transferred to the main coach road, she sat down on a low dry stone wall, behind which was a bank of trees bordering a woodland walk. This was the beginning of the Gullmingtons' estate and the woodlands that came under Tol's care.

There was also a grassy drive on this side of the wall, and this was bordered on its other side by another wood, and half a mile along this drive lay Tol's cottage where the two woods spread out to make what was known as Fuller's Dip.

Riah now narrowed her eyes to take in the distant figure walking down the drive in the shadow of the trees. It was still some distance away when she recognized Annie Briston. The coming meeting didn't fill her with any pleasure for she knew that, unfortunately, Annie had come to resent her; and she wasn't unaware of the reason. But up till now they had continued to be civil to each other.

Annie Briston was of medium height. She was of a delicate appearance and one would have imagined her voice would have complemented her features, but, unfortunately, it was in sharp contrast, its tone mostly ranging between peevishness and a stridency which indicated temper; and it was the latter that came over in her first approach to Riah as she said, "Well, you seem loaded up. Been out begging again?"

It would appear that Riah had been pushed from the wall, so quickly did she jump to her feet; and now her voice almost matching that of Annie Briston she said, "What do you mean, Miss Briston, out begging again? I've never begged in me life."

"Well, I must be misinformed, because from what I hear you begged hard enough from Old Fanny Briggs."

Riah stared at her. This was an open attack, no subtlety. It was as if they had met every day and were continuing a row of some sort. So she spoke plainly now, saying, "What are you getting at, Miss Briston? Why are you taking this attitude towards me?"

"You know well enough why I'm taking this attitude. You've caused nothing but trouble since you settled yourself into Moor House."

Trouble? What trouble had she caused up at the house? She never saw anyone to fight with except the master and Tol, and the parson, and that one visit from the lady's maid from The Heights. What was she meaning, causing trouble? She repeated her last thoughts, saying, "What do you mean, causing trouble?"

"You know what I mean all right. You've got our Tol not knowing whether he's coming or going. Running back and forward like an errand boy with your wood and your milk and lifting your bairns to church, twice on a Sunday now. Then learning him to read and write. Who do you think you are anyway?"

Riah, drawing herself up and assuming a dignity she was far from feeling at the moment because she felt that she wanted to take her hand and slap this woman's face for her, said, "Your brother has always delivered the milk an' the wood. As for taking the children to church and Sunday school, he did it at the parson's bidding. The only thing me and my family have done for him is teach him his letters."

"Yes, and disturb his peace thereby."

"How can that disturb his peace, woman?"

"Because it's putting ideas into his head. He's no longer just satisfied being a forester, and he's wastin' time, his master's time, and it'll be found out. What's more there's things to do around the cottage. But whereas at one time he used to be outside mendin', now he's sittin', his nose stuck in bairns' books. It's pathetic like, he's making himself a laughing-stock."

"Do you want to know something, Miss Briston?" Riah didn't wait for an answer but went on, "I think the only laughing-stock in your household is you. What I'm just finding out must be already well known, that you're an embittered old spinster an' that you're afraid of losing your bread support, because then you would have to go out and work for yourself like many a one better than you has had to do."

For a moment it would appear that Annie Briston was lost for words; then, her mouth puckering, and almost spluttering, she cried, "Oh, you! You'll come to a bad end. I've seen your like afore. You'll come to a bad end. You mark my words."

"And you'll try to see I do, won't you? But let me tell you something, miss, I'll be here when you're gone. Yes, I will. I'll be here when you're gone."

"Ooooh!" It was a long-drawn-out sound, and they glared at each other as if it would take very little to make them spring. Then Annie Briston flounced around and walked back up the way she had come, and Riah sat down on the wall again because she was trembling. Oh, that woman! She was jealous, madly jealous. Well, there was one thing sure, whatever came of her association with Tol – and at times, and more often now, she was longing for it to ripen – she would never be able to share his house with that piece in it. Oh no. He'd have to make a choice. And what could he do? His hands were tied. Something like this would have to happen to spoil the day, wouldn't it? Life never went smoothly for long. Out here in the wilds you would have thought it would be impossible to come across an adversary like Annie Briston. There were so few people in this neighbourhood, yet one of them had to be a bitch of a woman like her, because that's what she was, a bitch.

The last word had not died in her mind when she gave a cry and sprang from the wall as a voice behind her said, "I'm sorry to disturb you, but this is the lowest part and I usually get over here."

She turned and in amazement saw her master making his way in between the branches of the two trees, and when he reached the wall she watched him vault it with an agility she would not have given him credit for. And when he was standing looking at her he said, "I arrived almost at the same time as your late companion did." She saw his shoulders lift, and the shrug told her that he had witnessed her meeting with Annie Briston and heard every word of it. But he made no further reference to it; instead, he looked down at the bundles placed against the wall and asked, "What have we here? You certainly have done some shopping." As he went to lift one up, she said, "No, I'll carry them, sir."

"You carry one and I the other. Come." He walked away and she followed, a step behind him.

Presently he turned to her and asked, "What have you been buying?"

"Clothes . . . I got some articles second-hand to remake for the children; their . . . their things are getting rather threadbare."

He stopped and stared at her for a moment before he said, "Paddy's market stuff?"

She was surprised that he knew about Paddy's market, but she was quick to deny the association, saying, "No, no, not like that, sir; they are from a proper clothes stall in the market."

"But worn stuff, second-hand . . . dirty."

Her head moved from side to side before she answered, "I mean to wash them before I alter them."

They were walking on again and had travelled some distance before he spoke again, "You don't know who's been wearing these things," he said; "they could belong to anybody . . . scum."

In defence she now answered, "They are gentlemen's clothing and ladies', padded and lined and of good material."

Again they walked on in silence, and it wasn't until the gates of the house came in view that he said, "So I understand you've been teaching Tol to read and write?"

"Yes, sir; but only in the evenings when my work is done." She didn't want him to think she was using any of his time.

"Of course. Of course." He was nodding at her now. "Why couldn't he have asked me to teach him?"

"I don't think it would have entered his head, sir. Anyway, it was me that proffered."

"Did you know I used to be a teacher?"

"No, sir?" There was a note of surprise in her voice, and he glanced at her slowly with a smile on his face now, as he said, "Oh yes; I was a teacher, for many years, but I had a fancy name, I was a tutor, and my pupils were young men in the university."

She remained silent.

They had almost reached the front of the house where he would enter by the front door leaving her to go round to the kitchen door, when he stopped once again and, looking at her squarely, he spoke, and his words actually made her drop her bag to the ground: "I shall take it upon myself to instruct your children," he said; "it is not enough that they should be able to read and write. If at their age they have got this far, then it is only fair that their knowledge be extended. I shall take them for two hours each morning. See they come to the library at nine." And on this he turned from her, his departure being as abrupt as his voice, and went in the front entrance.

It was a good half-minute before she lifted the two bags and then almost scurried towards the kitchen, bursting to tell her news to Biddy. Why only to Biddy? she asked herself. And the answer she got was, Biddy would likely be the only one of the four to welcome this, as she saw it, utterly fantastic change of front in the master.

It was dark when a knock came on the kitchen door, and when Maggie opened it she cried, "It's Tol! It's Tol, Ma." Tol had made himself a favourite with the children, and they now crowded round him, all talking at once, until Davey, dashing to the settle, took up the large swallow-tail coat and, putting it on, strutted round the table, causing roars of laughter.

"Was that what you went in for?" Tol looked from the bundle of old clothes lying to the side of the fireplace to Riah, and she answered softly, "Yes. It's the only way I can keep them decent. But after I've unpicked them I'll wash them before making them up again." He nodded at her; then turned to Biddy, saying now, "What's that you say?"

"I said, what do you think, the master's going to make us go to school."

"School? Where? There's none hereabouts."

"Oh, it's a long way; we'll have to take the coach."

Tol glanced down at Johnny who now doubled up at his own joke. But then Davey, taking off the coat, said flatly, "He's going to do us here, two hours every morning. How will I get the garden done? There's so much to do outside."

"That a fact?" Tol was asking the question of Riah now, and she nodded as she said, "Yes; a surprising fact, the last thing in the world I expected to hear. But it's marvellous, don't you think? I mean" – she looked around her brood and her face softened – "to get the chance of being educated by a man like him, because he's very learned."

"Aye" – Tol nodded at her – "there's no doubt about that. I should imagine that's half of his trouble."

"Trouble?"

"Well, I mean, just shutting himself up in the room there. You can get too much of a good thing, anything." He now turned half from her, saying under his breath, "Can you step outside a minute?" And she, looking from him first to Davey and then to Biddy, said to them, "Get on with the unpicking. And mind, do it carefully, don't tear the stuff." Then taking a shawl from the back of the door, she put it around her shoulders and followed Tol into the yard.

She had closed the kitchen door behind her and now stood blinking in the light from his lantern which he had left at the door, and before he could speak, she said, "I know what you're going to say."

"Aye, well then, it doesn't need any lead up to. I'm ... I'm sorry, but ... but that's our Annie, she causes more trouble than enough. Always has done, I think, since the day she was born. But ... but

76

what I want to say to you, Riah, is, not to take any notice of her. She's always been like that, always wanting to rule the roost. To tell you the truth, I don't know what to do about her. Our Mary would take her off me hands for a time but there's her man Robbie, and he can't stand the sight of her."

"You have another sister?" There was a note of surprise in her voice and he said, "Oh, yes, she's Annie's twin, Mary, and she's as different as chalk from cheese. There was eight years between them and me and I suppose" – he gave a short laugh – "because I came late in me mother's life, she left me upbringing to the pair of them. Mary was always kind and gentle, but Annie, she had to boss the show or know the reason why. I used to give her most of her own way just to keep the peace; not any more though. But what I wanted to say to you was, I'm sorry if she upset you."

"Well" – she laughed softly now – "if she upset me, I certainly upset her."

"Aye, by all accounts you did that." He too chuckled, then said, "I suppose she told you I was neglecting me duties and the house?"

"Something to that effect."

"It isn't the first time I've heard that and for different reasons. Anyway—" He stepped closer to her and looked down on her and, his voice coming deeper from his throat, he said, "I wouldn't like anything to spoil what's atween us, Riah."

The gulp she gave in her throat was audible and the desire just to fall against him and feel the closeness of him was almost overpowering. And when, his voice still low, he said, "The way I'm placed I cannot say what I want to do, but I think you know what's in me mind," her body trembled with the thought, Let him kiss me, just once, just this once.

But then what would happen? What would come of it? With his sister lording it in the cottage, there would be no hope for them setting up a home there. And don't let her forget she had four bairns to bring up and, what was more, she was living like a lady in this house, practically her own boss, more content and happy than she'd ever been in her life before. So no, no kissing. Don't light up your pipe near a haystack in the height of summer.

She was surprised at the matter of fact tone she was able to assume as she said, "It's all right, Tol. I understand. Just let things go on as they are. But I'll . . . I'll tell you this, I'm . . . I'm grateful for your friendship."

77

When he took her hand in both of his, in spite of herself, she nearly allowed the haystack to ignite; but at that moment the door behind was pulled open and Davey said hastily, "The drawing-room bell's ringing, Ma."

"All right. All right." And she pushed him back into the room before saying to Tol, "I'll have to go. But don't worry. It's all right; everything will pan out."

"Aye, aye. Good-night, Riah."

"Good-night, Tol."

In the kitchen, she said, "How many times?"

"Just the once, Ma."

She now hurried up the room, through the passage and into the hall, meaning to make her way straight to the drawing-room. But there he was, standing at the foot of the stairs holding a lamp in his hand, and without any preamble he said to her, "Bring the other lamp," and pointed to the pink globe lamp standing on a table to the side of the front door. Mystified, she picked up the lamp and followed him up the stairs.

For a moment she imagined he was making for his bedroom, but he passed all the doors on the landing and went to the very end of it, then round the corner into a narrow passage and began to mount the attic stairs.

She hadn't been in the attics more than three times in the months she had been here because, adding to what Fanny had told her, her master had said formally at the beginning of her service, "I don't wish you to disturb anything in the attics." So when she had come up here all she had glimpsed were a number of cedar trunks at one end and, standing down the middle where the roof was highest, two long wardrobes, each with four sections, and their ornamental tops were stacked against the attic walls. She knew that both held an assortment of clothes: the first one was a gentleman's wardrobe, the second one a lady's. And her glimpses into both of them had shown that all the garments were arranged neatly on hangers and that each hanger also carried a bag of scented herbs. And she had said to herself, so much for Fanny saying everything was moth-eaten.

When he put his lamp down on one of the trunks she did the same, then stood waiting while he slowly walked to the wardrobe that was at the far end of the attic. Opening the door to the first compartment, he pulled out the top tray, revealing a number of silk shirts. Lifting one up by the collar, he shook it out, then handed it to her, saying, "Would you be able to make shirts out of these for the boys?"

Holding the beautiful soft material in both her hands now, her words spluttered over it as she muttered, "But 'tis silk, sir. Much too good. It's not . . . practical like."

"They have a change of clothes on a Sunday, haven't they?"

"Yes, sir."

"Then, make them Sunday shirts. You'll find something for weekdays in that trunk there." He pointed to one of the trunks. And now he opened another compartment. Taking down a suit, the trousers of which were clipped to the bottom rail of the hanger, he said, "That's a rough tweed; that should make them workaday clothes. And this one" – the next one he picked was a fine blue gaberdine – "could match the silk shirt for Sunday."

"But, sir."

He stopped on the point of opening another door and repeated, "But sir, what?" His voice had an edge to it as if what he was doing was against the grain.

In pulling open the next wardrobe door to disclose a row of dresses, his voice softening, he said, "These belonged to my mother. She wasn't a woman for frills and furbelows. Her day dresses were inclined to be plain and her evening dresses the same, with one exception." He now put his hand to the end of the rail and took from it a long black velvet gown. The neck was square, the sleeves were short. The bodice was gusseted into the waist, from which the skirt fell in three tiers. The only ornament on it was a faded pink silk rose hanging by its stem from a vent at the waistline. As he held it up there emanated from it a perfume as faded as the rose yet, at the same time, pungent.

"It was my mother's favourite," he said. "Although she had many other evening gowns she always returned to this; but she only wore it on special occasions. She had beautiful skin; it enhanced it."

"It's lovely," Riah said softly.

"Yes, I think so too." He turned to her now, the dress still held in his hand. "I often come up here and look at it. It recalls many memories."

He hung the dress back in the corner of the wardrobe; then, pushing the other garments here and there, he brought down two at once, saying, "These were her morning dresses. They're print, aren't they?" He held one out for her to feel, and she said, "Yes, sir; and lovely print if I may say so."

"You may say so."

She stiffened slightly as she thought, That's the second time he's mimed me. And it isn't that I'm talkin' cheap; many people say words like, If I may say so.

"Well then, take these" – he pushed the dresses into her arms – "and the suits and the shirts and get to work on them. But before you do that, throw that dirty rubbish out that you bought today. God knows who had them on last."

Throw them out? She certainly wouldn't do any such thing. She'd wash them and unpick them and when she'd had time to sew them, he wouldn't recognize them on the children. Anyway, she needed clothes herself. She would get a skirt, a couple of petticoats and a blouse out of them. Throw them out indeed!

"Did you hear what I said?" He had picked up both lamps now, and she turned her head over the bundle of clothes that lay across her arms and, looking at him, she said slowly, "Yes, sir. I heard what you said."

"Good."

She was going to move down the room but stopped as she searched for words with which to thank him and which he wouldn't mime or mimic, and what she said was, "I'm grateful for your kindness, sir."

"You're welcome. Being able to help in this way, I shall not now feel under such an obligation to you."

"Oh." Her precise manner fled and she turned squarely to him, where he was standing, his face illuminated from the lamps, and in the second that she stared at him she was made aware once more of the great loneliness that lay, not only in his eyes, but in the drooping of his mouth and the slackness of his shoulders. There was no spring in him. The only thing in him that had any urgency was his voice. And she said rapidly, "Oh, sir, you needn't be beholden to me; the boot's on the other foot. What would have happened to us if you hadn't taken us in that night, God alone knows. And my children have never been so happy, nor so healthy, nor, may I add, so well housed in their lives. Oh, sir, the boot's on the other foot."

Well, she felt he had plenty with which to come back at her from that little speech. However, he didn't come back at her, not in the way she expected, but with words that surprised her, for he said, "You're a good woman, Riah. I almost said a good girl, because sometimes you don't look or act much older than your daughter."

"Oh. Oh . . . oh, sir."

"Oh, sir."

There he was, mimicking her again. This was a new line he was taking. She would have to laugh at it. And this is what she did. Then she turned from him and walked the length of the attic and down the narrow stairs; and he followed her, holding the lamps high.

When they reached the hall she turned to him and smiled but said nothing more; then hurried towards the kitchen to display her new-found treasures to the children, recalling, as she did so, his face as she had seen it in the light of the two lamps, and she thought, If only he didn't look so sad. I wish I could do something for him to lighten his days.

But perhaps when he got to teaching the children it would make a difference. Yes, yes, perhaps it would.

7

It was past high summer; the ground was hard, the grass was yellowing. Riah had now been in Mr Miller's service for fifteen months, and it was difficult now to remember that she had ever lived anywhere else. This shining house seemed to be her own. And it was shining, for Biddy and Maggie took as much pride in it as she did. But once it had been bottomed there was less work to do in it, and for some weeks now Biddy had been out helping the boys picking fruit, clearing brushland ready for more planting in the autumn. No one would recognize the garden from what it had been when they first came here. The drive was grass free, the hedges bordering parts of the garden were clipped, that is all except the great yew hedge that had, at one time, divided the kitchen garden from that which was laid out in beds and walks and whose top had been cut into the shape of birds. There was little the boys could do about this hedge other than clip it as far as a short ladder would reach.

Except for a piece of land that had once been a games lawn and which was now more like a hayfield, the whole garden was in order, and the credit for its rejuvenation could not be given alone to Davey and Johnny, for Tol had, at the beginning, done a lot of the rough work, and she herself and the girls, too, had gone out of an evening and helped. This was after Davey had complained that he would never get through his work if he had to knock off for two hours of book learning in the morning.

Davey wasn't at all taken with book learning, not like the other three, and Riah was sorry about this for the master seemed to have taken a special interest in Davey and seemed bent on his learning. She had wished more than once of late that Davey and Biddy could have changed places, at least in their minds, because Biddy's wits were needle sharp and her mind like a sponge for soaking up things, whereas Davey seemed to have great difficulty in remembering his lessons. And sometimes she didn't wonder at it, especially those about gods and goddesses; they would bemuse anybody. But the master insisted that these were part of the lessons, besides history and geography.

And of all the things on God's earth to make them learn was this Latin. For what good was a Latin language going to be to her bairns? And what was more, not only did the master insist on the two hours in the morning but they had to do an hour in the evening after their day's work was done. He had even come into the kitchen once or twice with the idea, she imagined, of catching them out.

She supposed she should be grateful for all this attention her children were getting from such an educated man. She was. Oh she was. And if they had all taken it alike, she would have had no question in her own mind about it. But in some way it seemed to be souring Davey. He got sulky at times and he went for Biddy. Not that Biddy couldn't hold her own with him, or two or three like him, but he had never done it before. She supposed it was because he realized that she could take in things that were an absolute puzzle to him.

She was making it her business to sit with Davey at night and try to help him, and therefore she knew she herself was learning. Not that she could see it was going to do her any good.

But these were things, she told herself, that she could control: they were all in a day's work, part of bringing up a family; in a very odd way, she had to admit, but nevertheless, bringing them up, and in a style she had never imagined possible. But there was this other thing in her life, this private thing, this thing that was a want in her, a hot urge which she knew there was little hope of alleviating because Tol had surprised her one might by making it clear to her that he was in a forked stick and he could see no possible way of getting out. So therefore he couldn't, as it were, speak his mind to her. His sister, it seemed, had taken on a kind of illness that put her to bed at times, and at such times she wasn't capable of looking after either him or the house. So he had his hands full, and that was why, he said, he couldn't slip round as often as he might. Did she understand?

Yes, she had said, she understood, while at the same time feeling sick.

He still brought the milk and the wood, but he did not always take the children on the cart to church on Sunday. And naturally he no longer came at night to learn his letters and his tables.

She had, as it were, had it out with herself that she must stop thinking in his direction, for even if he had spoken what could have come of it? If the bell hadn't rung from the drawing-room that night and they had come together just with a kiss where would it have gone from there? She knew where it would have gone. Anyway, it hadn't happened, and it was just as well, because what you never had you never missed. ... Oh! that was a damn silly saying. Look at the things she hadn't had in her life and yet was aware of missing them: a decent house of her own; decent clothes for the bairns ... and herself; food, just a little out of the ordinary, a taste of the fancy meats she had seen in the shops in Gateshead Fell; a long ride on a coach to a distant town, past Newcastle, away, away somewhere, perhaps London where the King lived ... What you never had you never missed! How did these sayings originate?

She was standing at the stone sink under the kitchen window. There were two jars of flowers on the kitchen window-sill and lace curtains to the side. She had got these from the store cupboard and cut them down. She liked prettying places up. The whole house was pretty. The sad thing about it, nobody saw it but themselves and the parson. Fanny had told her there used to be a lot of callers at one time but that he had been rude to them, and so now he was left to himself. It was odd: to look at him you wouldn't think he was that kind of a man, a man who would be rude to people; but he had only to open his mouth at times and his words cut like a cleaving knife. She had heard them used on Davey. He bawled at him in the library at times. Yet she knew he was very fond of him. Oh yes, she had sensed that from the very beginning.

She lifted her head now from where she was peeling apples for a pie, and her hands became still and the apple peeling snapped before she had reached the end. She always tried to take off the peeling whole; it gave her a feeling of satisfaction somehow. But her gaze had become focused on where the master and Davey were entering the yard. The master had his hand on Davey's shoulder. It was such a nice picture that it brought a lump to her throat and she leant her head further towards the pane to watch their progress. They had stopped now opposite the stable door and the

84

master had his two hands on Davey's shoulders and he was bending down towards the boy's bent head. He seemed to be talking to him earnestly. Then she watched the master take his hands from her son's shoulders and ruffle his hair before pushing him gently towards the stable.

She swallowed deeply as she thought, What a pity he's not married and has children of his own. He'd been different altogether since he had taken up with the children. He was made for children. Poor man. What age was he now? Nearing fifty, she would say; she didn't know for sure. What a pity some of the spinsters who were sitting in their drawing-rooms wasting their time in needlework or at best in visiting and at parties hadn't come along here and forced his hand in some way or another.

She finished peeling the apples, put them into the pastry cases ready waiting, dribbled some honey over the top of them, covered this with more pastry and trimmed the top with cut out pastry leaves, after which, she brushed the tarts with milk and put them in the oven. This done, she washed her hands; then went out of the kitchen, across the yard and into the barn.

The barn was used mostly for stacking wood and it had a chopping block at one end of it, and on this Davey was slowly splitting small logs. When he saw her approaching he stuck the hatchet in the log and said, "Is it time to knock off, Ma?"

"It's nearing six. You can go and tell the others in a minute. By the way, what was the master talking to you about?"

He turned from her now but he didn't answer her, just kicked against the chopping block with the toe of his boot; and so, going to him, she turned him about, saying, "What was it?"

"Oh" – he tossed his head impatiently – "about learning. Wanted to know what I want to be later on."

"Yes?" She looked at him. "And what did you say to that?"

"I . . . I told him I wanted to drive a coach."

He raised his head now and, a puzzled expression on his face, he said, "He got angry, Ma. He said, couldn't I think any further than that? Well Ma, what further is there? Ma—" he put out his hand towards her now and she caught it and gently soothed it between her own as he appealed to her, saying, "I can't take in all this. And what good is it anyway? I'm not like our Biddy. She likes it. But . . . but Ma, I just can't understand half of what he's saying to me about them myths an' that Latin. What do I want with Latin,

Ma? I can read and write and I can count up as well as the next, better than most, you know I can. But I can't remember all those names in the Illyard thing he keeps yapping on about. Our Biddy says they are just fairy stories. Well, that's for lasses, Ma. What do I want with fairy stories or the like?"

"They're not fairy stories, Davey" – her voice was soft and gentle – "they're a kind of history. At least that's how I see it, ancient. It came about afore Jesus, afore the Bible like."

"I thought nothing came about afore the Bible, Ma, and the Garden of Eden."

She closed her eyes now, saying, "Oh Davey, don't get me as bamboozled as yourself. Look, leave what you're doing; go and fetch the others. Your tea'll be ready by the time you get back. See that they wash well under the pump first." She now leant towards him and smiled as she ended, "I'm as bamboozled as you are, I've got to admit, about the things he wants to learn us. Anyway, we'll put our heads together after tea and see what we can make out of the day's lesson, eh?"

He didn't smile back at her and say, "Right Ma;" instead, he turned from her and went out of the barn, leaving her standing gazing after him and thinking again, Oh, if only Biddy and him could change places. God has a funny way of dealing out brains.

They were all seated round the table when a knock came on the kitchen door; and when Biddy opened it, she cried, "Oh! Hello, Tol." Then turning her head, she called, "'Tis Tol, Ma."

Riah got to her feet and, her voice polite sounding, she said, "Hello there, Tol." And he answered, "Hello, there. You all busy?" And he looked from one to the other.

"Doing our lessons." It was Biddy coming to the fore again. "Do you want to sit in, Tol? I'm on Latin; but t'others are still learning their English." She laughed at her brothers and sister.

"Latin?" He screwed up his face at Biddy; then looked at Riah, and she nodded at him, saying, "Yes, it's Latin now."

"Good God! He's gona make a scholar out of her."

"Here, take a seat, Tol." Riah had pulled a chair to the end of

86

the table where he could sit between Davey and Biddy. And she asked now, "Have you eaten?" And he said, "At dinner-time; yes, I had a bite."

"Haven't you been home?"

"No; I'm just on me way. But" – he looked up at her – "I put Annie on the coach this morning for me sister Mary's. She's lost her man, you know. Annie thought she'd better go an' stay with her for a few days."

"Oh, yes, yes. So . . . so you're looking after yourself; and I bet you've had very little the day. Could you do with some cold mutton and apple pie?"

"Could I do with some cold mutton and apple pie!" He was looking round the children now, and they were all laughing, Davey included. "Did you hear what your mother said? Could I do with some cold mutton and apple pie? What would you say?" And together they all shouted, "Aye!" then added, "He could do with some cold mutton and apple pie, Ma."

Amid much laughter she set down a plate of neck chops before him and to the side a shive of bread and butter. As he ate the children all watched him, and after chewing a couple of mouthfuls, he put down his knife and fork and gulped as he said, "Get on with your lessons, 'cos if you don't I'll feel that I'm in a menagerie an' you've come to see me eat."

"I don't want to get on with me lessons."

Tol turned to Davey. "You don't?" he said.

"No."

"He hates lessons."

Tol turned his attention to Biddy now, saying, "And you don't?"

"No, I don't. It's like a holiday from work every mornin'. Do you want to hear me talk Latin?"

Tol glanced up now at Riah where she was standing with her hand on Davey's shoulder, and he grinned widely at her before looking at Biddy again and saying, "Yes, yes, I'd like to hear you talk Latin; not that I'll understand a word of it."

"I could learn you. . . . No, the master says nobody can learn anybody, they can teach you an' it's you who learns. Do you understand?"

"Yes, Miss Schoolma'am. Yes, I understand." There was more laughter now as Tol nodded his head in jack-in-the-box fashion, as a simpleton might.

"Well, listen ... now listen, this is Latin, Tol. Am ... mo ... me ... am matrem."

"Well, well!" Tol showed exaggerated astonishment as he gazed at the beaming face of Biddy, who now said, "It means, I love my mother." And her eyes flashed up to Riah whose lips were pressed tight together to suppress her laughter.

"Do you want to hear some more?"

"I can't wait."

"Oh, you!" She tossed her head, recognizing Tol's sarcasm, but she went on, "Add ... erbem ... ayo utt ... parnem ... aymam." She gulped as she finished, then stated triumphantly, "That means, I am going to the city to buy some bread."

"*You ain't!*"

"Don't make fun, Tol. The master said nobody can be learned unless they know Latin."

"And the master says you don't pronounce it properly."

Anger showing in her face, Biddy turned towards Davey, and she pursed her lips for a moment before she retorted, "Well, that's better than not being able to pronounce anything at all, not even English."

"Now, now, now! Get on with your work, madam, and not so much of that cheek. Davey will pronounce his words all in good time."

"What have you got to learn tonight?" said Tol, trying to throw oil on the troubled waters flowing across the table. But it was Johnny who answered now, saying, with a wide grin, "A story from an ee-pick."

"Oh, and what might it be about?"

"Oh." Johnny shook his head, then slanted his eyes towards Biddy as he said, "Oh, funny names, about men fightin' and turnin' boats into rocks an' things."

And now Biddy, preening herself with her knowledge, supplied the details in her own way, saying, "It's this, U ... lissees," only to be stopped by Davey saying, "You've got it wrong. That's how you said it this mornin' an' he said it was wrong."

"Who's he? The bull's uncle?" Riah's tone held a deep reprimand as she looked down on her beloved son, and Davey, his chin jerking, said, "The master." Then returning to his protest, he looked up at his mother, saying, "Well he did. He said she pronounced the names all wrong."

88

"I like that!" put in Biddy. "But anyway, I remember them, an' the stories. An' that's something you don't, thick skull."

"Enough! Enough! Either tell Tol the story or get yourself up and away to bed."

Biddy nipped on her bottom lip before she turned to Tol, saying, "Well, this man had been tramping a long time round about in wars and things and he comes across a friend, and they have a meal and the friend puts him in a boat and sends him off home with presents. But the sailors know there's something afoot and they put him on an island when he's asleep. But when they got home they were met by U ... lisses's enemy called Neptune who ruled the sea, and he was mad at what they had done and he hit their vessel with his pronged fork and turned it into a rock."

"It's a daft story." The quiet comment came from Maggie and caused everybody to explode again, including the teller and Davey. And Tol, patting the dark brown head of the little girl, said, "And I think I'm with you there, Maggie. It does sound a bit daft to me. But then, 'tis but a tale, and you learn words through it, so I suppose it's of some good after all."

Maggie again caused a renewal of laughter when, looking up at Tol, she said, "I like Baa! Baa! black sheep, better." And at this Biddy and Johnny started to chime;

> Baa! Baa! black sheep,
> Have you any wool?
> Yes, sir. Yes, sir,
> Three bags full:
> One for the Master,
> And one for the Maid,
> And one for Maggie Millican
> Who lives up the lane.

The two younger children now threw themselves about with laughter; and Riah, looking at her son whose face was straight, wondered for a moment why, if he didn't take to the hard bits of learning, he couldn't enjoy the simple bits. In a way she was getting worried about Davey.

She said briskly, "Now come on, all of you's, away to bed with you. And no noise, mind, no carry on."

One after the other they kissed her and said good-night to Tol before gathering up their books and scrambling from the room.

The kitchen to themselves, there was silence between them, and Riah was aware of the embarrassment on both sides. And when Tol stood up and made ready to go, she said, "You've got to get back then?"

"Aye, there's odds and ends to do, but it's nice calling in." He looked at her, asking now, "How are you getting on?"

"Oh, as usual. Me days are full, I keep busy, and the master's very kindly given me some of his parents' clothes to cut down for the children."

"My, my! I should say you're honoured there, because Fanny was often after pieces from the attic, but he warned her off and in no small voice, so she tells me."

"I think the company of the children has changed him."

"Definitely. Definitely. I came across him going through the woods the other day, and he walked along of me and talked amiably. He seems a different man, lighter in himself. Yes, there's no doubt about it, the bairns have made a difference to him, and he to them, because you've got to admit, it isn't every day working-class bairns are educated. Now, is it?"

"No, you're right there, Tol. I'm grateful. Oh yes, I'm grateful. Except——" She now rubbed one palm against the other before she continued, "I'm . . . I'm a bit worried about Davey. He doesn't take to the lessons like the others, and what's more, he's got this thing about horses, working with horses. He's disappointed there's not a horse here. But I've told him the master can't afford one. And he angered him the day, so he says, when he told him he wanted to drive a coach."

"Is that what he wants to do?"

"It seems so."

"Well, his education would be wasted if that's as far as he wants to go. And I can see Mr Miller's point of view. At the same time I understand Davey's, because all I wanted to do when I was a lad was to go to sea. But," he said smiling at her now, "from what I hear of the life sailors have, it's a good job I didn't have me wish."

She nodded. "You're right there," she said; "I've seen a bit of it when the ships docked in the Tyne. It's a brutal life, and it breaks some. You don't get that kind of cruelty in the woods."

90

"Oh—" he turned his head to the side and nodded slowly as he commented, "the woods have their own cruelty, animal to animal. 'Tis amazing what you see. Even trees in winter suddenly decide to snap a branch and you're lucky if you get away alive. Then there's man's cruelty." His face became stiff now. "The master's thinking of trapping the woods."

"You mean mantraps?" Her voice was a whisper.

"Aye, just that. I can't keep me eyes on a thousand acres, and I must admit I close me eyes when the locals are just after the rabbits. But when it comes to the birds, well, I've warned them on the quiet, and that's all I can do."

"I think that's cruel, traps of any kind for animals, but when it's for men ... eeh!" She now whipped a towel from the brass rod and, going to the table, she rubbed it vigorously, muttering as she did so: "There's so much cruelty. I heard tell through the paper of two men being hung for sheep stealing."

"Well, it's a serious offence that; they know what to expect when they go in for it."

"Yes, but hung. I could understand in a way them gibbeting that Mr Joblin for murdering the mine manager, but for stealing sheep they could have been transported."

"If it was meself, I'd plump for hanging."

When she looked at him he was smiling, and she stopped her rubbing and sighed; then folding the cloth into a square, she said, "When are you expecting your sister back?"

"I'm not sure, a week, perhaps a fortnight. The only thing I'm sure of is that she'll be back."

She looked up at him. His eyes were waiting for her, and he added, "Life's not easy. It seems that few people can do what they wish."

As she stared back at him, the words came into her mouth, but stuck there, for how could she say, "You've got a week, perhaps a fortnight to do what you wish. Why don't you speak? Why don't you come round here now and take me in your arms? It would be some sort of compensation to both of us." But she couldn't say that, the risk would be too great. She guessed though that he knew what she wished, it must be written all over her face. Yet he wouldn't take the risk either, for he, like herself, knew that their arms had only to entwine, and that would be that, for they were both starved of the same thing. And she was also aware that the ensuing result was in both their minds, perhaps more so in hers, because what if she was to have another bairn? And she fell easily. Oh yes, she fell easily.

"I'd better be on me way now, Riah."

"Yes, yes."

"Is there anything you want doing, outside I mean?"

"No. No, thank you. The boys are managin' fine."

"Yes, it's amazing the difference they've made in that garden, them bits of lads. Well, I'll be off then." He still stood, and she said, "Yes. Good-night then."

"Good-night, Riah."

He picked up his cap from the knob of the chair and went towards the door, and there he turned, and again he said, "Good-night, Riah." And she answered once more, "Good-night, Tol."

Going to the fireplace, she put the towel back on the rod, then turned its ends into a corkscrew as she muttered bitterly, "Why has he to come?" And after a moment she released her hold on the towel and watched it unscrew itself, and with it the tenseness went out of her body; then leaning her head against the wooden mantel, she muttered, "That's that. That's final. He'll never have a better chance and he didn't take it. So that's final. I'll think no more of him."

The four children were seated at the table in the library, the two boys at one side, the two girls at the other. Percival Miller sat at the top end and, holding his hand to his head, he said, "Your accents are atrocious. Do you know that? Atrocious."

They gazed at him in silence, until Johnny caused a diversion. Aiming to be a peacemaker, he said, "Do you want us to read from me book?"

"Oh, my God!" The master now gave Johnny his full attention. "By 'us', I suppose you mean 'me', boy? And tell me, where was your tongue when you said, uss?"

Johnny looked for help across to Biddy, and Biddy, hoping to be unobserved, sat back in her chair and under cover of rubbing her nose with her forefinger, pointed to her mouth; and Johnny, quick to take her advice, said brightly, "In me mouth, sir."

"Which part of your mouth? And perhaps your sister will help you to answer this too. When you said, uss, where was your tongue?"

Johnny remained silent, his round bright eyes staring at the man who appeared like God to him; and after a moment, Percival Miller slowly turned his gaze on Biddy, saying, "Well, you've done your excavation, and where, tell me, was your tongue when you said, uss?"

Her head gave him an almost imperceivable wag as she said, "Sticking to me bottom teeth, sir."

"Yes, exactly. Sticking to your bottom teeth and pushing your jaw out. All of you say, uss."

So they all said, "Uss," their faces showing different forms of contortion and so causing the word to emerge in different ways. After the fifth attempt their pronunciations still varied widely, and it was Biddy as usual who came in for censure and caused another diversion, because after she had been asked to pronounce the word by herself, he bawled at her, "It is not 'arse', you happen to be sitting on that."

An explosion of laughter brought the other three bodies wagging; even Davey had his head bent over the table and his hand pressed tightly across his mouth; and more surprising still, their master had a deep twinkle in his eye, as he said, "Your exaggeration of 'us' will, I have no doubt in the years to come, cause more comment than the raw pronunciation of these, your brothers and sister. You are well set, madam, to becoming a Mrs Malaprop, I think. We must go into that later." Now his voice rose and with it his hand and he brought his ruler down on the table close to the fingers of Maggie's left hand, while her right one jerked away from her face as he cried, "Leave your nose alone, girl! Doesn't your mother give you a handkerchief? That is a disgusting habit of yours."

As the tears spurted to the child's eyes, he continued, "None of that now. None of that." Then after a moment of staring at her bowed head, he said, "Anyway, your primitiveness has given me a further lead. Tomorrow you will learn what Lord Chesterfield thinks of people who pick their noses. Now to return to fundamentals. Johnny and Maggie, you will do these sums," and he passed them a piece of paper. "You may make use of the abacus. And you two" – nodding to Biddy and Davey – "you will render me speechless with admiration while listening to your reading."

And so it went on for the next hour, until it was time for them to get back to their work, when he dismissed Johnny and the two girls; but to Davey he said, "I want to talk to you. Stay where you are."

When they were alone together, he did not immediately begin to talk but, leaning back in his chair, his hands covering the large knobs on the arms, he stared at the boy, whose eyes were cast down and head was slightly bent forward.

The sun from a mullioned window had turned the boy's hair almost to silver and Percival Miller gazed on it for some minutes before he said softly, "You are not a dullard, David, so why don't you try harder at your lessons?"

Davey raised his head and his eyes were still cast down as he said, "They ... they don't interest me, sir. I ... I mean I don't seem inclined that way."

"What way are you inclined?" Percival Miller was now sitting on the edge of his seat, his forearms on the table, his hands joined tightly together, and he entreated the boy, "Tell me. Tell me."

Davey now turned his gaze fully and frankly on his master as he said, "I've told you, sir, I ... I just want to be with horses, drive horses, or something like that."

Their faces were only a few inches from each other.

It was some seconds before Davey blinked and, as if coming out of a trance, he drew his head back on his shoulders and straightened up; and as he did so, his master caught his hand and said, "If I promised to buy you a horse ... well, say a pony, will you promise to pay attention to your work, and ...?"

"You'd get me a pony, sir? Really?" The boy's face became alight. "For me own? Really mine?"

"Yes, yes, really yours."

"Oh! sir. Yes, yes, I'll try. Oh, yes I will, I'll try. I'll pay attention. An' ... an'—" His mouth opened and closed twice before he brought out, "There's the remains of an old trap beyond the summer-house, sir. A dog cart it was, sir. I could fix it, I'm sure I could. I could fix it. Yes, sir." He was nodding his head now, his face showing his joy. "Yes, sir, I'll try. Oh, yes, I'll try."

They were both standing now and Percival Miller still retained the boy's hand; and now he laid his other hand on top of it and said, "That is a promise?"

"Yes, sir. I promise. Oh, thank you, sir. Thank you, thank you very much." And Davey withdrew his hand from the warm grasp and backed three steps away before turning and, almost at a run, left the library.

Bursting into the kitchen, he startled Riah by shouting, "Ma! Ma! What do you think?"

She dried her hands of blood from a hare that she was cutting up, and her face too was bright as she looked at her son and said, "I don't know. Tell me. Tell me."

"The master, he's ... he's gona get me a horse ... a pony. He's promised. That's if I stick into me lessons. An' I will, Ma. I will. But just think – an' it's going to be mine, not his; he said it'll be mine – a pony, Ma."

She pulled a chair towards him and sat down, and she said quietly, "He really said that?"

"Yes, yes, he did."

Her face became serious as she put her hand up and gripped the boy's arm, saying, "Well, I hope you appreciate the sacrifice he'll be making, because, you know, he's got very little money. And you know what happens on quarter day with his books and baccy and beer."

"Yes, Ma, I know." And Davey's face lost some of its brightness as he said, "Do you think he'll have to go without all those?"

"Yes, I can't see any other way he can do it. And you know, if it wasn't for what you grow in the garden and the fruit, and the eggs we're getting from the hens now, and such like we would not live as we do. He's hard put to pay me the four shillings a week that he does, so Davey" – she gripped both his arms now – "you'll have to do as you promised and stick in because that'll please him more than enough. All he thinks about is learnin'."

"I will, Ma. I will."

"Go on then, get on with your work." And after the boy ran out of the kitchen she stood and watched him flying across the yard as if he had wings to his feet, and she felt troubled, for deep within her she knew that her son, unlike her elder daughter, hadn't it in him to pay more attention to learning than he was already doing.

95

Davey was one of those who would always work better with his hands than with his brain. And she returned to chopping up the hare, thinking it was a great pity the master was so set on education that he could think of nothing else.

8

The man seemed to be a changed being. Yesterday he had actually played ball with the children in the yard there. She couldn't believe her eyes. And then for the past week he had been coming into the kitchen to talk to her. He had sat in the chair and their conversation had ranged over all things. He treated her as an equal. Yesterday, they had even discussed how strange it was, this thing called coincidence. Had it been a coincidence that she had arrived at Rowan Cottage, hoping to look after another man's wife? Had it been coincidence that Tol and Fanny had come across her? Had it been coincidence that she had come here with her four children? Didn't she think life was planned? And when she had agreed with him, saying, "Yes, God has strange ways of working," only then had he contradicted her and very sharply, saying, that God had nothing to do with it. There was a power, yes, that shaped their lives but it had nothing to do with a God who was supposed to be a person sitting up there in the clouds on a throne.

He had gone on and on about this, and she had become a little shocked, but had made herself remember that he wasn't as other men. Being learned like he was, he was bound to think differently. And that he did think differently, she had been made aware before this, because she had heard him arguing with Parson Weeks. But Parson Weeks, although dominant when it came to church-going, was a tolerant man. Likely, because he enjoyed his ale.

And then last evening, when the children were all standing round the pump getting the grime off themselves, he had come through the kitchen and stood at the door watching them. And when he had muttered, "Beautiful. Beautiful," she had felt so sad for him. Here was a man who, behind all his odd ways, was starved of a family. He would have made a wonderful father. In that moment she had felt drawn to him. She had wanted to put her arms about him and bring his head to her breast, as a mother might . . . or perhaps not as a mother might. And this had jerked her mind back to Tol.

She had seen Tol twice during the last week and his manner hadn't changed; in fact, she thought, if anything, it had become a little cool. He hadn't stayed to chat with her, and in a way she had been thankful for this. So, she had made up her mind about Tol, and she faced the fact that if he had cared for her enough, he would have made it known when he had the opportunity. He liked her. Oh yes, she knew that, but liking and loving were two different things. . . .

It was later that evening when the children had gone to bed and she was clearing up for the night and preparing for the following morning by setting the table for breakfast, that the kitchen door opened and her master appeared. He began with an apology. Standing a few feet from her, he asked, "Am I intruding?"

"Not at all, sir. Not at all. Would you like to sit down?" She felt he wanted to talk, but he refused the offer of the seat and walked to the fire and, looking down into it, he said, "I think we understand each other, Riah, don't we?" And after a moment's hesitation she said softly, "Yes, sir."

"You're an intelligent woman. Even from your background you must know the ways of the world and that what appears right to some people is vastly wrong to others."

Again she said softly, "Yes, sir."

Another silence followed before he turned to her and said, "Well then, come along upstairs, I want to give you something."

After a moment's hesitation she followed him as he led the way up into the attic once again. And when he opened the wardrobe door and took down the black velvet gown her mouth fell into a gape, for now, holding it with both hands, he put it up in front of her, saying, "As I told you, this was my mother's favourite gown, and I love it because I loved her. In some ways you remind me of her, you're the same build and" – he paused – "you have the same kind heart, an understanding of human nature and its strange twists, turns and foibles. . . . There take it, it is yours."

As he let loose of the garment, it fell over her joined hands, and the softness and the weight of it seemed to flow through her, and when he said, "Go down and put it on. Then come into the drawing-room; and we shall drink to this occasion," she was unable to utter a word, and it was he who took the lamp and led the way down the stairs. . . .

In her bedroom, she sat on the edge of the bed and looked at the gown now lying across the foot of it. Her heart was thumping against her ribs as if she was a young girl about to go to her first man. As she chastised herself saying, "Well, you knew what was coming; and face it, woman, you need him as much as he needs you." Then her eyes travelled to the door and across the corridor to the children's rooms. What would they think? Well, they needn't know. Oh, Biddy with that uncanny way of hers would be bound to sense something. She was like a weathercock, that one, where emotions were concerned. Well, what did it matter? In a way, their livelihood as well as her own depended on her pleasing this man, and it would be no hardship. No, it wouldn't.

She rose abruptly to her feet and, stripping off her workaday clothes, she sponged her face and hands, telling herself that she needn't worry about being clean as, fortunately, she'd had a wash down last night. But when the time came for her to step into the gown she held it up in front of her and as if it were embodying its previous owner, she said, "I'll be as kind to your son as you were."

The gown, she found, was a little tight under the arms and around the waist, but, nevertheless, she managed to fasten the myriad hooks that went down each side of the gown from the oxter to the hips. She found this kind of fastening very strange, but it left the back and front of the gown plain, and when she swung the little mirror on the dressing-table backwards and forwards she was amazed at what it revealed. She moved the lamp to get a better view and couldn't believe that this dress had so transformed her. She took a comb through her hair, softening it above the ears, bringing a quiff down on to her brow and, finally, pinning the bun at the back lower down on her neck. This done, she looked at her hands. They were red, the nails were broken. Then her gaze travelled to her feet. She was wearing house slippers, but there was a small heel on them. Anyway, the dress covered them almost to the toes. It dipped slightly at the back and trailed on the floor, which indicated that his mother had been an inch or so taller than herself.

Now she was ready to go. She picked up the lamp, but with one hand on the door handle she gripped it and closed her eyes tightly, and the words that came into her mind were, Goodbye Tol. . . .

99

MYNDERSE LIBRARY
31 Fall Street
Seneca Falls, New York 13148

He was sitting in a chair to the side of the fire when she entered the drawing-room, and he stood up immediately but did not move towards her. His mouth slightly open, he gazed at her as she walked slowly up the room. She had put the lamp on the table before he moved and, now taking her hand, he courteously led her to the seat at the other side of the fireplace. But still he didn't speak. Then he turned from her and, going to a side table, he lifted a bottle and poured two glasses of wine, and as he handed one to her he said, "The last of the cellar, but none of it before has been drunk on such an occasion and to such a beautiful woman."

She was hot from her brow to her feet. When he held up his glass, she did likewise and sipped at the wine. It tasted like whisky, only better. Now he was seated opposite to her, but on the edge of his chair, and, leaning towards her, he said, "I think this is the strangest night of my life, Riah. You are my mother sitting there as she once sat, but you are many things besides. There are so many different ways of loving, different kinds of love. Do you know that, Riah?"

She found no need to answer and he went on, "I have only ever loved one woman and that was my mother. But it wouldn't be hard, I think, to love you. Why are we made like this, Riah? So complex that we are given the faculty to love yet we are afraid of exercising it, and we dissipate it in other ways that very rarely bring us joy. We didn't ask to be made as we are. Do you understand me, Riah?"

She did and she didn't; and she again had the feeling he wasn't needing an answer, he just wanted to talk; and so once more she sipped from her glass, and he went on, "I can't imagine what my life was like before you and the children came into it. I look back to those long years spent with Fanny shuffling here and there, garrulous, slovenly, yet, in a way, a friend ... well, the only one I had. And then one night she comes and tells me she is leaving. It seemed the end of life, my way of life. When she told me there was a woman and four children to take her place, I fought her. I thought, Oh no. It was as if the gods were laughing at me and throwing me back into my early years when I longed for children, and longed to be a father figure, but without having to resort to a woman to bear them. But what I dreaded has turned out to be a wonderful experience. You have given me life again. Do you

MYNDERSE LIBRARY
31 Fall Street
Seneca Falls, New York 13148

know that, Riah? With your generous warm heart and your under-standing, you have given me life again, and a family."

He lay back in the chair now and sat looking at her, until all of a sudden he rose to his feet and came towards her. Taking her hand, he brought it to his lips; then drawing her gently upwards, he said, "Thank you, Riah. Thank you. You and your family will always be my concern, especially David. You understand that? I do so want David to be as a son. I want to see him become someone." He smiled gently as he added, "I'm talking like a father who has failed in life and longs to see his son achieve his ambitions. . . . Now go to your bed, Riah. Go to your bed."

The last was a whisper and, like someone in a dream, she picked up the lamp, then turned from him and walked with slow step out of the room, across the hall, and, skirting the kitchen, she took the side door into the east wing and to her room.

Once inside, the lamp almost fell to the floor as she put it on the corner of the dressing-table. Quickly righting it, she sat down on the stool. She had thought it would take place in his bedroom, but he had said, "Go to your bed." And he knew where her bedroom was, for he had one day made a tour of this end of the house and had seen where the children slept and she too.

The unfastening of the dress took longer than the fastening. Her fingers, she told herself, were all thumbs. But when at last it dropped to the floor, she picked it gently up and hung it in the wardrobe, and just before she closed the door she stroked its soft texture with the back of her hand.

She usually slept in her chemise with her nightdress over it for warmth, but tonight she took off the chemise; and she did not put on her calico nightdress, but a long bodice petticoat that she had made out of the lining from one of the dresses he had given her for the children. One last thing she did before getting into bed was to leave the door slightly ajar.

And now she was lying waiting, the lamp turned low on the bedside table, her hair in two plaits lying on top of the counter-pane, her hands joined tightly under her breasts; and her body, she knew, was ready. . . .

The travelling clock which she had taken from another bed-room told her that it was half an hour since she had got into bed. Well, she told herself, perhaps he was shy. Hadn't he said he had never loved any woman but his mother. Yes, but that didn't mean he hadn't had one. Good Lord! Young men of his standing went in for that kind of thing in a big way. Perhaps he was having a bath. Of course, he wasn't! he wouldn't bath in cold water and Davey and Johnny always carried the hot water up for his bath. . . .

When the clock said she had been lying for a full hour and ten minutes, she slowly swung her legs out of the bed and sat on the edge of it. What did it mean? Was he getting drunk before he came? That was another silly thought. That wine, he had said, was the last in the cellar, but he meant in the bottle and tomorrow, if he bought that pony for Davey, he wouldn't be able to afford any wine at all. What was keeping him?

When the clock said ten past eleven she lay down again. There was now threading the urges in her body a feeling of humiliation. What, she asked herself, was he playing at? Two hours now she had been lying here. What did he mean? Getting her all worked up like this, and then not coming. Go to your bed, he had said. That was plain enough, wasn't it? And the look on his face. There had been love there, or some kind of feeling anyway. But what was that he had said about wanting children but without having to go to a woman. . . . Oh that was just his complicated way of talking.

She didn't know what time it was when she turned her face into the pillow to smother her sobbing, but when she woke up she was amazed to find the lamp on the last flicker; it had burned down to the wick.

She stumbled out of bed and, her eyes squinting at the clock on the little mantelpiece, she saw to her amazement it stood at a quarter to five.

Why? Why?

"You got a headache, Ma?"

"What?" Riah turned from the stove with the porridge pan in her hand, and looking at Biddy, she said again, "What?"

"I said, you got a headache, Ma?"

"Yes, a bit of one."

"You didn't sleep?"

"No. No, I didn't sleep very well."

"I wish I didn't sleep so much; it's a waste of time."

"Eat your porridge."

"I could sleep all day." No one commented on Johnny's remark, but Riah looked at the two younger children who were sleepy-eyed and she said sharply, "Get on with your breakfast, it's nearly seven o'clock." Then she looked at Davey. His plate was clean and he asked brightly, "Can I have another, Ma?"

Once more she brought the porridge pan to the table, thinking as she did so that she knew what had sharpened her son's appetite: the prospect of the pony was oozing out all over him like happy vapour, because today the master was going into Newcastle to collect his allowance and bring back the promised pony. But if the master's promises to her son were anything like the promises to herself, she would have a surly and disappointed boy on her hands tonight. But no, he would bring back the pony all right because he wouldn't want to lose favour in the children's eyes, especially Davey's, for he was obviously very taken with the boy.

But how was she going to face him this morning? Had he been laughing at her? Having her on? Getting her all dressed up just for his amusement? She couldn't think so, for he wasn't an unkind man. But what kind of a man was he to leave her lying there like that for hours waiting? . . . Oh, she didn't know. She only knew that she was shaking inside at the thought of coming face to face with him.

But she needn't have worried. An hour later when she took his breakfast into the morning-room he was dressed and ready for his trip into Newcastle, and he greeted her brightly, so brightly that, after placing the tea-tray on the table to his side, she remained leaning forward as she looked at his face because she was amazed to see that he looked happy.

"It's a lovely morning, Riah, don't you think?"

She didn't answer him, and he stopped in the act of unfolding his napkin and his eyes narrowed as he asked, "You're not well?"

"I'm . . . I'm all right, sir. I've just got a bit of a headache."

"Oh, then you must get outside and walk. You're too much in the house, you know Riah. Anyway, here I am all ready to gallop into town to buy a horse." He actually laughed out loud, then added, "Well, a small horse, a pony. I'm as excited as David is at

103

the prospect of that animal joining the household. Do you know that, Riah?"

"Yes, sir."

He now picked up his knife and fork but did not use them on the plate of bacon in front of him, but standing the cutlery on its end, he stared down at the table and more to himself than to her said, "It signifies so much this day: a new lease of life, and ... and you have given it to me, Riah. You have in a way given me a son." He turned his face towards her now, and for a moment she thought, He's not right in the head. Given him a son, indeed! Davey was no more his son today than he was yesterday. And look at him, all smiles, after last night working me up like that, then leaving me high and dry.

"Tell David I want to see him before I go off. Will you?"

"Yes. Aye, yes."

In the hall she stood for a moment thinking, he's gone a bit funny. It sounded different last night when he talked of them all as his family, but not now when he was singling out Davey as his son. She wasn't going to like this; she knew she wasn't. Davey was hers; she was father and mother to him, and that's how she wanted things to remain. And anyway, he was deluding himself if he thought he was going to make a scholar out of Davey. ... Now if it had been Biddy.

She knew that Davey had started to scythe the bottom field and she could have sent Biddy for him but she went to the garden herself, down by the long hedge to where he had just started at the top corner and she called to him, "Davey! Davey!" And he laid down the scythe and ran towards her.

"Yes, Ma?"

"The ... the master wants to see you before he goes into town."

She watched his face light up, but without a word he ran from her and up the garden towards the house.

She had been in the kitchen a few minutes when he came into it, his face still beaming.

"'Twas about the pony, Ma. He ... he asked me what colour I preferred. Fancy. Eeh!" He shook his head. "I can't believe it. And I will try. I've told him. I'll do everything he says." And he made a face now as he added, "I'll even take note of bright Biddy. I asked him how he was gona get it back, and he said he'd get Robbie Howel, the carrier, to trot it alongside his horse, and I'd have to be at the crossroads around three and pick it up, I mean lead him back, because he himself won't be back till nearly four on the coach. Oh, Ma, I'm excited. An' Ma. . . ."

"Yes, Davey?" Her face was straight and her voice flat.

"He's kind, isn't he? the master, kind. If only" – he grimaced now – "he didn't want to stick so much into me head."

As she watched him run from the kitchen she felt slightly sick, but she couldn't tell why. She should be happy for her son because she had never before seen him so bright, and because of the pony he would try to work hard at his lessons, she knew that. But why wasn't she happy? Was it because there was still the great want in her body and that she couldn't understand the business of last night? She didn't know.

At half past one Davey was sluicing himself under the pump and when, later, he came into the kitchen, his hair plastered down, Biddy, entering the room from the far door, called to him, "What you getting ready so soon for?"

"Well, it will take nearly half an hour to get to the crossroads."

"Well" – she looked at the clock – "you'll still have nearly an hour to wait."

She had a duster in one hand; holding one end of it, she kept pulling it through the half closed fist of her other hand as she said, "I wonder what it will be like, the colour and that? You told him brown, didn't you?"

"Well, I said it really didn't matter, but I liked brown."

"What are you going to call it?"

"I don't know. I'll have to see if it's a he or a she," at which they both burst out laughing. Then coming quickly round the table, he looked appealingly into her face as he said, "You'll help me, Biddy, won't you? I mean with the learnin'. It's those myth things I can't remember, the names like. I'm not good at remembering names, well, not made-up names like that, that don't sound like any we've heard afore. You know what I mean?"

She nodded at him, her eyes shining as she leant towards him and whispered, "After we go upstairs afore me ma comes up, she's nearly an hour down here or more, and I never can get straight to sleep so I'll come into your room and learn you ... teach you." She had stretched the last two words, and now their foreheads touched for a second and again they were laughing.

She watched him run to the corner of the mantelpiece and take down the comb and pull it through his hair. He had lovely hair. He looked lovely altogether, did Davey. She always liked looking at him, even if at times she didn't like his ways. He had a face like some of the figures in the books in the little room off the library. There were special books in there that held paintings. She often glimpsed through them when dusting. She always took a long time to dust that room. She brought her elbows tight into her sides at the thought that she wished she could be like the master and sit reading all day.

"Where's Ma?" He was still combing his hair.

"She's up in the attic, sorting things out. The master says she can have some of the underwear from the trunks. Oh, it's lovely stuff, Davey. I could have stayed up there all day going through the boxes, but she wouldn't let me." She paused now and, her face becoming thoughtful, she added, "Ma's not herself the day. Is she worried about something, do you know, Davey?"

He shook his head, saying, "No, not that I would know of anyway. She seemed the same to me, except she said she had a headache."

Biddy turned from him, muttering, "'Tisn't only a headache, she's had headaches afore. It's funny like. ... Where you going?"

"To say goodbye; tell her I'm goin'."

When Davey reached the attic, he saw his mother kneeling on the floor in front of a trunk with a number of garments scattered around her. He walked cautiously down the middle of the room – he didn't know why but he didn't like this part of the house – and when she turned and looked up at him he said, "I'm just off, Ma."

"Is it that time?" She rose to her feet.

"Well, I'm a bit early." He smiled at her, and she put her hands on his head, saying, "Your hair's wet."

"Aye." He grinned sheepishly at her now as he made one of his rare jokes: "I felt I wanted to be spruced so when me pony saw me he would know ... I was a good little lad."

She smiled at him now but she didn't laugh. A good little lad,

106

he said. He didn't consider himself a lad; he was coming up twelve and could be taken for fourteen any day. He was tall and straight and so good to look upon. Often, when looking at him, she wondered how she had come to give birth to such a precious thing as this son. She loved all her children, oh yes, she would defend openly to her last breath that she loved them equally, all the while knowing in her heart that this one she held very special. She put her arms out now and pulled him to her and held him tightly for a moment. The unexpected embrace left them both embarrassed, and when he stepped back from her, his eyelids were blinking rapidly.

They weren't a demonstrative family; it was unusual for them to hug each other. And so, remembering the conversation he'd had a few minutes earlier with Biddy, he asked tentatively, "You . . . you all right, Ma?"

"Oh, yes, yes."

"You're not bad or anything?"

"Bad?" She now gave a short laugh as she said, "Have you ever known me to be bad? Bad tempered, yes." She pulled a face at him, and at this he shook his head and said, "No, Ma, you're never bad tempered. Cross a little at times" – he smiled – "but never bad tempered."

"Go on, get yourself off," she said, only to halt him as he turned and cause him to laugh outright now as she said, "See if you can pick up a sword and some armour on the way, and you can come riding back into the yard like one of them knights you've been readin' about of late."

"Oh aye, Ma, that'd be the thing. An' it would please the master. By, that would."

Listening to him clattering down the stairs, she thought, That pony's going to alter his life.

It was turned half-past four when Davey came back. They were all in the kitchen: Johnny, Maggie, Biddy, and Riah. The children were excited, and she'd just cut them shives of bread to be eaten before going along the road to meet their brother. But unexpectedly the kitchen door opened and there he stood, his shoulders stooped, his face blank, his lips pressed tight.

No one spoke as he came up to the table, and it was at his mother he looked as he said, "It wasn't there. Mr Howel laughed."

"Laughed?" The word was just a whisper from Riah, and Davey nodded as he said, "Aye, he laughed and said, 'Shanks's pony is all you'll get out of Mr Percival Miller.'" He paused; then his lips trembled as he added, "He said if he knew anything the day, the master wouldn't even be able to use Shanks's pony, it would be Tol Briston's cart as usual."

Slowly Riah walked round the table, but when she went to put her hand on her son's shoulder he shrugged himself away and, his voice almost falsetto, he cried, "I'll get changed an' about me work. An' that's all I'm gona do. Do you hear, Ma? That's all I'm gona do, me work. He knows what he can do with his learnin'. And I'll tell him that. Aye, I will. That's all he thinks about, learning. Well, to hell with his learnin', an' him. An' him."

And he dashed from the room, leaving them all looking at each other for some seconds, until Biddy muttered, "There must be a reason, Ma." Then the girl almost jumped back in surprise as her mother turned, bawling at her, "Yes! there must be a reason and we all know the reason, an' it'll come rollin' in that door in a very short time. Get back to your work, the lot of you. I'll deal with this. Yes, by God! I'll deal with this. Go on!" She scattered them with a wave of her arm. And when she had the kitchen to herself, she stood beating her fist rhythmically on the chopping board, oblivious of the cut vegetables jumping like puppets on to the table and then on to the floor, and all the while her head jerked rapidly as if with a tick as she repeated Biddy's words, "There must be a reason. There must be a reason." And she stared towards the door as if awaiting the entry of a drunken husband.

It was almost an hour later when Percival Miller entered the house. He stood in the hall, his head lowered for some moments before looking first one way and then the other, and finally up the stairs; then he turned and went into the drawing-room and there he pulled on the bell-rope hanging down by the side of the fire-place.

He must have waited a full three minutes before Riah put in an appearance. She opened the door slowly and she entered the room slowly, her step flat and firm, only to be brought to a halt as she looked to where he was standing solid and sober, his face wearing an expression she hadn't seen on it before.

Slowly he approached her, stopping an arm's length from her and saying, "Where is he?"

Her reply was soft as she said, "Scything in the field, sir."

"Oh, Riah." He half turned from her; then once again looking into her face he said, "I had to force myself to come home."

"What happened, sir?"

"It's a long story, you wouldn't understand. I don't know whether I understand it myself or not. I only know that I was informed by my solicitors that a good half of the shares that provide me with my allowance, as pitiable as it is, have declined sharply in value. Whereas I usually get between twenty-four and twenty-six pounds a quarter, I was given only twelve today, and that to last for three months; and what then?" He spread out his hands, then doubled them into fists before beating them together and adding, "What could I do? I . . . I did not stop at my usual inn because I knew how the boy would be feeling. How did he take it?"

She swallowed deeply and the concern was in her voice as she said, "Badly, I'm afraid, sir. But oh, I'm glad there was a reason, a good reason. Biddy said there would be."

"Huh!" There was a sarcastic note in his voice now as he said, "I must thank Biddy for having faith in me, while you thought, and doubtless David did too, that I would come rolling back or prostrate on the cart."

"Well, sir. . . ."

"Oh, I know, I know." He swung round, his hand flapping now. "David hasn't got his pony. But we all stand to lose; I don't know how I'm going to go on."

It came to her as she watched him pacing up and down at the far end of the room that he was still capable of earning money by his brains, and she dared to voice this. "Have you ever thought about tutoring, like, young gentlemen, sir?" she said.

He became still in his pacing, his back to her, and it was several seconds before he swung round and faced her, saying slowly now, "Yes, Riah, I have often thought of tutoring young gentlemen. Oh yes, yes. I have often thought about that, but I have refrained from taking the matter further. You understand?"

No, she didn't, so she remained silent. "I must go and explain to the boy," he said.

"Should I go and fetch him, sir?"

"No, no; I'd rather do it on my own."

He had taken off his overcoat and his hat in the hall, and she now watched him pulling at his cravat as he went towards the front door. When she herself reached the door she saw him crossing the gravelled drive to where the path led into the shrubbery, his step now almost on the point of a run. And as she watched him she recalled Davey's attitude of a short while ago, and this caused her to hurry through the kitchen, then across the yard and into the garden. There her step slowed, and she was halted by Johnny who was humping a basketful of weeds when he called, "You looking for Maggie, Ma? She's down by the greenhouse."

"No, no, I'm going to see Davey."

"He's in a bad temper, Ma, slashing at the grass like nobody's business. He chased me, he did."

"Go and empty your basket," she said.

She had reached the high yew hedge when she heard the master's voice, it was coming from the other side of the hedge and she was stopped by the note of pleading in it as he was saying, "David, David, try to understand. It didn't lie with me, it wasn't my fault. Oh, David. ...."

"Don't! Don't!"

Riah's face suddenly stretched and then when Davey's voice came again, louder now, crying, "Stop it! Stop it! Leave go of me. Leave off!" her feet didn't seem to touch the ground as she started to race along by the hedge. But almost simultaneously with her son yelling, "Stop it, man. Leave go. Stop it!" an agonized scream brought her to a shuddering halt.

Her shoulders hunched almost up to her ears, she didn't move until she heard the words, "Oh my God! My God!" She didn't know who had uttered them, but once more she was running, and when she rounded the hedge she stopped in horrified amazement at the sight before her. There, standing with the scythe still in his hand, was her son, and lying on the ground, with blood gushing from his forearm and his hip, lay the master. She watched Davey fling the scythe from him before dashing to her.

Gripping hold of her dress, he cried, "Ma! Ma! I didn't mean it; I just tried to stop him. He would keep holding me. He would keep holding me. Oh, Ma. Ma."

"Oh, Almighty God!" It came as a soft groan from her mouth.

The man on the ground was writhing as if in agony. His hands were now dripping with blood where he was trying to stop the flow from his arm, but for the life of her she seemed unable to move towards him, until Davey, clinging to her, cried, "What'll I do, Ma? What'll I do?"

What would he do? She stared at him, and she almost screamed aloud herself as she saw him hanging from a gibbet; for if that man on the ground died, that's what would happen to her son. Gripping him by the shoulder, she cried at him, "Go and get Tol. Find him! Find him!" But as Davey made to dart from her she brought him to a jerking standstill again and under her breath she whispered, "Don't tell him you did it. Tell him . . . tell him, the master's happened an accident. Just tell him that."

When she released her hold on the boy he didn't now dart away but stumbled like a youth who had taken his first long swill of ale. And now she moved towards her master who was lying on his side gasping, and he turned his head up to her and in a weak voice said, "Fetch . . . fetch the doctor." But not until his head fell limply to the side was she galvanized into life. Flying now from the field, she screamed, "Johnny! Johnny! Johnny! You, Maggie!"

It was Maggie who came in sight first and she bawled at her, "Run to the house. Tell Biddy to bring sheets. The master's had an accident. Quick! Quick!"

After staring at her mother a second or two, Maggie turned and flew up the garden; and as she did so, Johnny passed her carrying his empty basket, and when Riah yelled at him, "Here! Here!" he too came running to her.

Grabbing the basket from him, she yelled, "You can run, can't you? You can run?"

"Aye, Ma. Aye, Ma, I can run. I'm a good runner."

"Well, run to the village, to the parson, and ask him to send somebody on a horse for the doctor."

Johnny turned from her, about to run, then stopped and said,

"I've got to tell the doctor ... I mean, tell the parson to tell the doctor? Is our Davey bad?"

"No. Tell them it's the master. He's had an accident. He's badly cut."

"What with, Ma?"

"*Will you go?*"

He went, running as only the young can run. And now she herself turned and ran back round the end of the hedge and into the field.

Her master was just as she had left him, only the dried grass round about his hip was now soaked in blood. Kneeling by his side, she reluctantly put her fingers into the blood covered slit in his coat and shirt and tugged at them, then gasped as she saw the size of the wound, and all the while she was muttering, "Oh, my God! Oh, my God!"

Gripping his arm between her hands now, she tried to press the ends of the wound together in order to stop the flow of blood, but to no avail. In desperation she stood up and screamed, "Biddy! Biddy!" And as if in answer to her cry, Biddy and Maggie came stumbling round the hedge both carrying sheets. Running towards them, she pulled the top sheet from Biddy's arms and began tearing at it frantically, crying as she did so, "Tear them up! Tear them up in strips!"

When she had finished winding the roughly torn strips of the linen round his arm, she pulled his now unconscious body on to his side, and she herself almost fainted as she saw the size of the gash in his trousers and his small clothes. Again her hands delved into the blood-soaked material and wrenched it apart. Then, rapidly folding a large piece of sheeting, she put it over where she thought the wound was, before strapping it up again with the long strips the girls were handing to her.

"What happened, Ma?"

"Be quiet! Be quiet!" She pushed Biddy aside.

"Where's our Davey, Ma?" There was a trembling note in Biddy's voice and her mother who was about to tell her again to shut up simply muttered, "Gone for Tol."

"Oh, Tol. Aye, Tol'll know what to do. Oh Ma, all the blood."

"Shut up! girl. Shut up!" But then her tone changing, she said, "He's ... he's comin' round."

Percival Miller emitted a long deep groan. When he opened his eyes and saw Riah looking down on him, he murmured, "Oh, Riah. Riah."

Once he had spoken she felt anger rising in her, and she wanted to yell at him, "You've brought this on yourself, wanting to play the father, because you're incapable of being a father." Yes. Aye, that was it, he was one of them who couldn't take a woman. My God! Why hadn't it struck her before. What had he tried to do to Davey to make the lad react like he had done? *Hold* him, Davey had said; but after all, that didn't warrant him almost killing the man; it was the disappointment over the pony that had put the lad in a rage. And yes, he had been in a rage. She had never seen him like that before. But oh God! What was to be the outcome of it? Once again she was seeing her son hanging on a gibbet, for who would believe that these wounds were accidental. The justice had just to question a boy like Davey and the truth would be blurted out. He couldn't talk falsehoods, could Davey. Biddy, yes; Biddy could sell her soul in a like situation, or if it was to save someone's skin. But Davey wasn't made in the same mould; he would have neither the determination nor the ability to face up to authority.

"Riah."

She looked down into the grey face and the dark eyes that seemed to have sunk deeper into their sockets and she said slowly, "Help is coming."

"Riah." His good arm came out towards her but she shrank from it, and from the look in her eyes he closed his own.

The blood had stopped oozing through the linen on his arm, but it continued to spread over the pads and bandage on his thigh and she became sick at the sight of it.

Tol didn't arrive by way of the hedge; from the main road, he had cut across the fields which were part of the Gullmingtons' estate and jumped the fence, and so he came into the field by the top way. Standing by her side and looking down at the prostrate figure, who once again seemed to have lost consciousness, he said, "My God! How did this happen? I couldn't get anything out of Davey."

"It . . . it was an accident."

"Have you sent for the doctor?"

"Yes, Johnny went."

"Johnny?" He turned and looked at her.

"I sent him to the parsonage and told him to tell Parson; he'd ride for him. Where's Davey, Tol?"

"I don't know. He wouldn't come back with me; the boy's frightened. What really did happen?"

She shook her head. "I'll ... I'll explain later. We've got to get him into the house."

"Yes, yes" – his tone was urgent – "we should put him on a door."

"A door?" She shook her head. "We haven't a door."

"There's a big wheelbarrow, Tol."

He turned and looked down on Biddy, saying, "Aye. Aye. Where is it?"

She ran from him, and he, at a run, followed her. A couple of minutes later he was back pushing the barrow. It was grimy but dry, and Riah, after flinging the last sheet over it, stood at one side of the master while Tol stood at the other, and she followed his directions when he said, "Grip my hand under his shoulder blades, and the same under his thighs." Then he called, "Keep the barrow steady, Biddy."

Once they had laid the blood-soaked man in the barrow, Tol commanded, "Support his leg, Riah. Keep it straight. And you, Biddy, keep his arm on his chest." And when they had obeyed him he bent and gripped the handles and, like this, he pulled the barrow backwards out of the stubbly field until he got on to the garden path, and then he went forward to the house.

At the front door he said, "You'll have to help me carry him in. Do you think you can manage it?"

Riah made no answer; but bending, she did as before and joined her hands to his. And when they had stumbled into the hall, he said, "Where now? We can't get him upstairs," and she gasped, "The drawing-room, the drawing-room couch."

After they had laid him on the couch, Tol looked at his hands and coat; then glancing at Riah, he murmured, "I ... I don't think it will be any use cleaning up until the doctor gets here. He's bound to want help."

She did not confirm this and he, looking at her closely, said, "You're all in. Sit yourself down. Biddy, can you make your ma a cup of tea?"

For answer Biddy scrambled from the room, taking Maggie with her.

In the kitchen, Biddy thrust the kettle into the heart of the fire, and as she did so, Maggie said, "Will he die, Biddy?" And Biddy glanced at her, saying, "I hope not, Maggie, 'cos if he does, we will an' all."

"We'll die?" There was a frightened note in the child's voice, and Biddy answered, "Not like that, not graveyard dying; only we'll have to leave here."

"Oh, I wouldn't like that, Biddy. I like it here."

"You're not the only one. Fetch the cups."

"Biddy" – Maggie had run to the window – "'tis a trap coming into the yard."

Looking out of the window, Biddy saw the end of the trap disappearing on to the drive and she said, "'Twill be the doctor. Ma won't want tea now."

They had carried the kitchen table into the drawing-room; Tol, Riah, and the doctor had managed it between them. Parson Weeks hadn't offered his assistance; his thoughts were on less mundane things as he sat by the side of this learned gentleman, as he had always thought of Percival Miller.

They stretched the injured man out on the table and Doctor Pritchard made no comment until he had unwrapped the rough-sheeting bandages and pad from Percival Miller's thigh, and then he exclaimed, "Good gracious! Good gracious! How did he come by this?" Then he leant over the patient and in a high voice as if Percival was deaf, he cried, "How did you come by this?"

Percival Miller simply stared straight back at him, but did not attempt to reply; and the doctor turned to Riah, saying, "Have you any spirits in the house?"

"No, sir."

"No? Well, that's strange, no spirits in this house." Again he looked down on the patient and, his voice still high, he said, "This is not going to be pleasant; you'll have to hang on. Some extent of stitching to be done here, mostly on your hip, and I can't tell about the tendons. Just have to sew you up and trust to luck." He now turned and looked towards Tol, saying, "You hang on to that arm, will you? I'll start on the other one. And Parson, can you hold his legs?"

"Oh, oh, I don't think I'd be any use at that."

"Hell's flames, man! all you've got to do is to grip his ankles. Oh, away . . . . Woman!" He beckoned to Riah now. "Press down on his legs, will you? Just to save him rolling off the table."

As Riah made to grip her master's ankles, Tol said quietly, "Here, you hang on to his arm. I'll see to those." And when they exchanged places, the doctor said, "His arm will be more trouble than his legs in a minute. But have it your own way. Well, let's get at it."

As Tol watched the needle being jabbed into the flesh and listened to the groans and saw the agonizing pain on Mr Miller's face, he thought to himself, a horse doctor would do it kinder.

The arm sewn up and bandaged, the doctor prepared to start on the hip. He soaked some padding into a liquid and almost dangled it before the patient's face as he called down to him, "This is going to bite a bit. Get set."

When the soaked padding hit the raw flesh, Percival let out a cry almost resembling that of a vixen in the night, and then he closed his eyes and lapsed into unconsciousness, and at this the doctor cried, "That's good. That's good. Now we can get on with it." And he probed for quite some time before he stuck the needle in one side of the open wound and pulled it up through the other with as much gentleness, Tol again thought, as his sister used on a bodkin when progging old rags through hessian to make a mat.

At last the operating finished and Riah, almost on the point of collapsing herself, brought a bowl of clean water and a towel for the doctor to wash his hands. When this was done, he turned to her and in a quiet aside, he said, "You're sure there's no spirits in the house . . . no wine or anything?"

"Yes, sir; I'm sure."

"I understood from the boy that he had just come back from the city." He jerked his head towards the table and the prone figure.

"That was right, sir" – Riah's tone was stiff – "but he brought no wine or spirits with him; nor yet had he taken any."

The doctor looked hard at the woman before him; then he said, "Indeed! Indeed!" before turning to the parson, standing now with his eyes cast downward, and saying, "Well, I'm ready, if you

116

are." He then looked towards Tol who was gathering up the bloodstained strips of linen from the floor and added, "You staying the night here?"

Tol hesitated, and then said, "I suppose someone should in case he moves. But sir, don't you think he would be better moved on to a bed of some sort?"

"No, I don't; the less he is moved, the less likelihood of his bleeding again. He's lost all he can I should say. I'll be back in the morning."

Without further words he went out, the parson going hurriedly after him.

No sooner had they left the room than Riah, going to Tol, said, "They can't find him. They've been lookin' for him. He's not in the garden anywhere."

As if he were patting her Tol put his hand out towards her and said quietly, "Don't worry. I've got an idea where he'll be. Likely in my outhouse. Anyway, I'll slip back there now before it gets too dark, and I'll bring him over. Never fear. In the meantime, rest yourself; you look all in."

She nodded but made no reply; but after he had left the room she sat down in the chair near the fire and turned her head away from the table and the death-like figure lying there. Her mind was full of recrimination. He had wanted to play the father; and look where it had got him; look where it had got all of them. He had changed their lives when he had given them shelter, but now he had changed them again, for whether he lived or died this place, she told herself, could afford them no more shelter. Only the fact that he was utterly helpless prevented her from going upstairs and bundling their things together and taking them on the road once more.

At this point her thinking was stopped by a question. Would Tol let them take to the road again, or would he offer them shelter? But were he to do that, could she take it, knowing that she would have to share it with his sister? She didn't know. She only knew she was so tired, so wrought up and so frightened at the consequences that might fall on Davey. And besides this, she was ashamed, ashamed that she had waited for a man to come to her last night, when there hadn't been a man to come to her.

*

117

It was more than an hour and a half later when Tol returned; but without Davey. And when she gasped, "You haven't found him?" he put in quietly, "It's all right. It's all right. He's safe enough."

"Where is he?"

"In my cottage."

"Why didn't he come with you?"

At this he looked towards the still figure on the table and said slowly, "He won't come back here any more, Riah. He swears on that. He told me he did it, but why, he didn't say. Perhaps you'll tell me."

Her hand was tight on her throat and she swallowed deeply a number of times before she said, "The master had promised him a pony. Then he . . . he didn't get it, and Davey was upset."

"Good God! he didn't do that just because he was upset over a pony?"

"Well, I . . . I don't know. The master must have got hold of him. Tried to hold him, Davey said. He's sort of become possessive like of him."

Tol stared at her for a long moment before he said, "Oh." Then after a pause, he added, "Nevertheless, he shouldn't have struck out like that. No, no."

"What'll happen to him? He must come back."

"He won't; no, he won't come back. But don't worry; he can stay with me for as long as he likes. And . . . and I've had an idea. Up at the house, they're wantin' a young stable lad; they've taken on another three horses and the work's heavy. The youngsters are riding now. I could get him set on there, I'm pretty sure. And from what I gather he seems crazy to work with horses."

"Yes, yes" – she nodded her head slowly – "he's crazy to work with horses. Oh yes" – she repeated her words – "he's crazy to work with horses." Then bowing her head, she burst into body-shaking sobs, and when she felt his arms about her, she leant against him, muttering, "Oh, Tol. Oh, Tol. What's to become of us?"

He said nothing, just looked over her head as he stroked her hair with one hand while pressing her tightly to him with the other.

When her crying eased, he led her to the couch that had been pushed to one side, and having pressed her down on to it, he sat beside her and, taking her hands, he whispered, "Don't worry about that." Then looking towards the table, he said, "He didn't give the lad away. He must care about him. About all of you, particularly you. I was getting the idea he might be more than fond of you. . . ."

At this her manner changed and, leaning towards him and her voice a low hiss now, she brought a look of surprise to his face as she said, "Well, your idea is as far out as the moon from the earth, see, because he's no man, he's not natural. That's why he liked Davey. Said he wanted to be a father to him. Father, huh! He wants bairns but can't take a woman." As if she knew she'd gone too far she clapped her hand over her mouth and bowed her head; but in a moment he brought it upwards again as he said, "It comes as no real news to me, Riah; I guessed there must be something like that for a man like him to hide himself away an' to be so against bairns, then take yours as he did. I'm sorry for him, Riah."

"*What!* "

"Oh yes" – he nodded slowly at her – "I can say that again, I'm sorry for him. I think he's been putting up a fight for many a long day, but when somebody as bonny lookin' as Davey was thrust afore his eyes, it was too much for him. There are men like him; it isn't unknown. No, no, it isn't unknown. There's one in the village now. Lived with his mother for years, then got friendly with another fellow from Gateshead. 'Twas then Parson Weeks wouldn't let him in the church."

She stared at him now in hostility as she said, "You talk as if you were on their side."

He smiled softly at her now as he said, "You've told me you've had eight bairns, yet you're a very innocent woman, Riah. You don't know much about life, do you, an' what goes on, although you were brought up in the town. People get the impression that we're all numskulls, we in the country. My! My! The gentry live in the country, you know, half the year, and if you knew what went on in some of these big houses round about, it would raise your scalp. He's" – he nodded his head again towards the table – "an innocent compared with some men. Well, the boss, Mr Anthony, he may not be like his father or his grandfather but he has a good try at times. But his grandfather who died some twenty years ago, and I remember seeing him, he was frisky to the end, but in his heyday, he never allowed one of his men to be married unless he first tried the bride. Oh . . . oh, don't look so shocked, Riah. Mr

Anthony's father died in the hunting field one morning after carousing all night with a bevy of ladies he and his pals had brought from the town. His wife, madam, is still alive and kickin', she's coming up eighty. She lives in the west wing and still rules the roost. Oh" – he smiled quietly – "there's lots of things happen in the country, Riah. Havin' said that, I know this business has come as a shock to you and I don't know what the outcome of it's gona be. But whatever it is, my dear" – he stroked her hand now between his – "don't worry. Things will pan out. They always do if you wait long enough, things pan out. Now look, go and see the bairns off to bed then settle yourself down for the night. I'll be all right."

"No" – she shook her head – "I'll take me turn."

"Nonsense. I'm a light sleeper. I'll sleep on here" – he patted the couch – "and I'm only a hand width away from him, and if he stirs I'll hear him."

"You sure?"

"I'm sure." He rose to his feet, pulling her upwards, but he did not attempt to kiss her, and at this particular moment it didn't seem to matter because, in a way now, she felt safe. When she left here she knew where they would go, Annie Briston or no Annie Briston.

9

They had brought a single bed down into the drawing-room and
Percival Miller had been lying on it for three weeks; and today,
on Doctor Pritchard's suggestion, he had attempted, for the first
time, to walk, with disastrous results, for he fell on to his side and
had to be helped by the doctor back on to the bed. But the doctor's
voice was cheerful and reassuring as he did so: "Oh, that's usual,
don't worry," he said, "I'll send you a crutch along. That'll help
you in the meantime. But the wound has healed marvellously. A
good job done, although I say it myself."

"I can't bend my hip, not even when I'm lying here." The words
were full of bitterness, and the doctor replied, "That's natural too.
Even if you hadn't had such an injury, lying on your back all this
time would stiffen your limbs. Make yourself move about in the
bed, that'll help. Anyway, it's up to you now."

"What is up to me? Whether I walk or not?"

"Yes, yes, just that, whether you walk or not. But there's
nothing to stop you if you persevere. The sinews weren't cut, for
which you can be thankful. It's as well you were such a ham-fist
at scything, for if you had swung it with any force it would likely
have gone right through you. So you've got that to be thankful
for. Well now, I must be off. By the way" – he put his hand into
his breast pocket and pulled out a folded sheet of paper – "that's
my bill. I'll leave it there." He laid it on a side table, then added,
"I'll collect it next time I come, which should be towards the end
of the week. Now keep trying, that's a good fellow, keep trying.
Good-day."

During all this Riah had been standing some distance away from
the bed, and now Percival turned his face towards her, crying,
"Did you ever hear the like?"

"Yes," she said, "and he's right."

"What do you mean, he's right?"

"You've got to make an effort ... you'll just have to make an effort."

"Just have to?"

"Yes, I said, just have to, because you're soon to be on your own, I'm goin'."

She watched him press himself upwards with his good arm, then half lean out of the bed; and, his face screwed up as if in inquiry, he said, "What did you say?"

"You heard what I said, sir. I'm goin'. Me and the bairns, we're goin'."

"You mean, you're walking out and leaving me here helpless like this?"

"You can get Fanny back, or someone from the village. There are two girls down there back from place I've heard."

She watched him flop back on to the pillows, but his head was still turned towards her as he said, "You would leave me at the mercy of old Fanny, or some half-wit of a girl from the village? You would do that?"

"Yes, I would."

"Why?"

"Oh!" She tossed her head. "Do you need to ask? You know why, because I cannot bear to be near you. Have I to say it? You're not natural, you're ... you're dirty." Following the last word her lips had puckered, but now they sprang apart and she actually jumped as he flung his good leg over the side of the bed and, bringing himself upright, he screamed at her, "Don't you dare apply that word to me, woman! Do you hear? Never! Never say such a thing again. What I felt for your son was good. I would never have hurt him."

Her courage coming back, she now yelled, "I've only your word for that."

He looked from side to side as if he wanted to get his hand on something to throw at her; then of a sudden his body went limp, his shoulders slumped, his head drooped on to his chest; and he stayed like that for some moments before he said, "Woman ... woman, I'll never be able to make you understand, or anyone else for that matter. I was deluded into thinking that you did. I loved the boy. I still do, in spite of what he did to me. I loved him as I might have done a son."

He now slowly raised his head upwards and his voice took on the same tone that it did when he was talking to the children: "There are all kinds of love, Riah," he said. "Whoever gave us our beings . . . our feelings, didn't cut us all to the same pattern; here and there he diverged. In the main it was directed that a man should simply love a woman, but then something was left out of a few of us, or, as I like to think, added to our mentality; and we could not only love a woman, but love our own kind. As I think I've already told you, I've never loved any woman other than my mother, but at times I've thought I could love you, Riah. Yes, yes, I've said this before, so don't look like that. But again my pattern was cut differently. My love has never flown to a man in all his gross coarseness, but to the being he was in all purity before his maleness swamped all sensitivity in him. I have always loved beauty in whatever form it takes." He paused, then shook his head slowly as he said, "You do not understand, do you?"

No, she didn't understand. Yet she was wild at herself that some part of her was now feeling sorry for him and was thinking, if only he wasn't what he was, because she had liked him so much and had been willing to like him more.

If he had come to her that night she wore the black velvet gown, this awful business might never have happened, everything would have been changed, been normal like. But as he had said, he wasn't that kind of a man.

A thought stabbed her like a sharp knife now: That's what he had given her the gown for, sort of payment for Davey. *My God! Yes, yes*, when she came to think of it. He had imagined she had understood the whole situation and he had paid her for her son with his mother's black velvet gown. He may not, as he'd said, have harmed him, but he had in a way meant to take him over, not only with all this education, but as a parent, and eventually she, being a comparatively ignorant woman, would have been completely ousted from her son's life. She seemed to rear up as she said, "Well, understanding or no understanding, it's as I said, we're goin'."

"*No, you're not, Riah.*" His voice had changed, the patient schoolmaster tone was replaced by a slow definite firm statement.

"You can't stop me."

"Oh, yes I can." He now hitched himself to an easier position on the side of the bed before he spoke again, and he continued in the same tone as he went on, "You attempt to leave me and I'll immediately inform the justices that your son attacked me, and you know what the result of that would be."

Yes, yes, she knew what the result of that would be only too well, but she thrust the thought aside as she cried back at him, "If you did that he has only to say that he was defending himself, and there's good, honest, God-fearing men among the justices."

"There may be, but it would be his word against mine and defending himself against what? I had promised him a pony and because of my reduced circumstances was unable to fulfil my promise. My solicitor will bear this out. Also, there is no smirch against my name: I am known as a scholastic recluse and come of a very good family, what you, Riah, would call a God-fearing family. More so, I left no trace of my weakness in Oxford." His voice changed a little now and became more grim as he said, "I fought my weakness there. As the Bible would put it, I flew temptation, and therefore, I do not consider myself unclean or dirty as you suggest."

He now attempted to stand upright, then hopped on one foot and eased himself back into bed while she stood staring fixedly at him, her hands clenched in front of her waist, her lips pressed tight. When he had settled against the pillows he let out a long slow breath before he said, "Your boy has been with Tol, so Tol told me, and has started this week at The Heights. It's a good beginning; he wanted horses, he'll have his fill of them up there. But how long he remains there rests entirely with you, Riah."

She seemed to have to drag the words up from her stomach and her voice cracked as she said, "If, as you say, you cared so much for him, you ... you couldn't do anything to hurt him, not like ... well...."

"Not like having him transported or sent to the House of Correction?" He was looking towards her now, and he said, "Oh, yes, I could ... and I would go to any lengths in order to keep you here ... and the children.... Oh! Oh!" – he lifted his hand – "You needn't worry about them being contaminated, my eyes don't see them, my feelings are not touched by them at all. The two younger ones I see as grubby little urchins, even when they are clean. As for Biddy, I sometimes think it's a pity she wasn't born male, because what good is the knowledge that she soaks up like a sponge going to be to her? If she marries one of her own kind she'll despise him and there's no hope of her every marrying her mental equal. But whether I continue to coach her or not, she will learn for herself. She has the grounding on which to build and she is of the type that will use it. I don't envy her her life. So you need not worry about the other three sparrows, Riah. But return to David's future. It all depends upon you, because should you leave me and go to Tol, and it is to him you would go, because he feels for you, I've known this for some time, then I will do exactly as I say. I swear to you, Riah, on your God, I will do exactly as I say. . . ."

She didn't know how she reached the kitchen and when she got there she didn't know for how long she sat staring into the fire, nor how many times her mind had repeated, Yes, he would, he'd do it. She could still see the look in his eyes as she'd backed from him and fled from the room.

What kind of a man was he anyway? She didn't see him as an ordinary human being, but part pitiable creature, someone who needed comfort, mothering, loving, and part devil, cold calculating. The opposing natures couldn't fit any other person she had met in her life before. They were two extremes, but they fitted him all right. And so she was stuck here. No Tol, no security . . . no love, no easing of the want in her that could go on for years. She had lost her son. Yes, she knew she had lost him as sure as . . . as if he had been transported, because each time they had met since that fateful day he seemed to be more distant. And the night before he had gone to take up his new post he had said to her, "You're not gona stay with him, are you, Ma?" And she had said, "No. As soon as he can walk I'm coming down here to Tol's." Then not knowing how to put her next words to him, she had begun, "There's . . . there's something that you must . . . well, you must do, you must be careful of . . . you mustn't ever give a hint that . . . well, the master . . . you know what I mean, that the master liked you, because if you did people would put two and two together and come up with the wrong thing. And . . . and if his name was smirched he'd likely . . . well——" She did not know what made her say the next words, but she said them, "he'd likely turn on you, just to protect himself and his name and you could be up before the justice."

Davey had hung his head as he muttered, "I know, Ma. I know. And there's another thing. I'm sorry I did it. But he wanted to fondle me like. I don't suppose I'd've minded if I'd got the pony, but I was so disappointed. And anyway, I thought he was drunk...."

She had stared at him in amazement as her mind repeated his words, I don't suppose I'd've minded if I'd got the pony. She hadn't heard wrong, that's what he had said; in plain words he would have accepted the master's attitude towards him, as long as he gave him what he wanted. It came to her that she didn't know what went on in her son's head, but she refused to dwell on it, except to allow herself to think, He doesn't know what he's saying.

She was brought out of her reverie by the far door in the kitchen opening, and Biddy came running towards her, crying, "Master's on the floor in the drawing-room an' he can't get up. I was passing and I peeped in the door. He ... he was thumping the floor with his fist."

Riah had risen to her feet, and now she turned her head away from her daughter's penetrating stare, closed her eyes tightly for a moment, then hurried up the room, across the hall and into the drawing-room, but once inside the door she paused a moment and looked to where Percival was thrusting out his good arm in an effort to reach the end of the couch, but when his hand slid down its silk-padded side she saw his head bow almost to his knees.

It was when Biddy's voice, almost in a whimper came from behind her, saying, "Aren't you going to help him, Ma?" that she spun round and, gripping her by the shoulders, thrust her out of the room, then banged the door behind her without saying a word.

Slowly now she went forward and stood by his side, and as if she was chastising an errant child, she said, "What's all this, then? Making a big effort?"

He looked up at her and said, "Just that. But on this occasion I don't want your help, I can manage."

She made no reply to this but, bending down, she cupped her hand under his good arm and in no gentle fashion she hauled him upwards, and when he toppled and fell against her, she was forced to put her arm around him and guide him, hopping, on to the couch, where he sat for a moment, his body sagged, a picture of utter dejection. But when he straightened himself up and laid his head back, his voice did not represent the picture given off by his body because his tone was curt now as he said, "Sit down, Riah."

"I have no time for sittin', sir."

126

"Well, stand if you will, but the situation must be made plain. Whether you like it or not, and apparently you don't, you are to continue looking after me and this house, and when later on I gain my full strength and I'm able to hobble, I shall take up the tuition of the children.... Don't say it, woman." He thrust out his hand, the fingers spread wide. "Again whether you like it or not, your children will be given an education not only for their own good, but to give me some kind of an aim, to help me go on living for the time that I might have left to me. And you will consider this in part payment for your services for, from now on, if my finances remain as they are, there will have be, what is called, a tightening of belts all round. There may be times when you may not get your wage, this will be the quarter day when I decide to indulge my other weakness which, by the way, I am missing sorely at the present moment. Well, having made this statement, I want to say this." He paused here and, his tone changing, he went on, "If we have to share this roof, Riah, don't show me your enmity as you have done these past days. You're such a kindly person at heart. I have longed for a sympathetic word from you. Do you know that? Well, you might never find it in your heart to give me one, but at least let us be civil to each other."

Riah now sat down on the end of the large wing-chair that was set at right angles to the couch, and she brought her fingers tightly across her mouth to stop the flow of tears that threatened to engulf her, and after a moment she said, "How can you act like this one minute, sir, while just a while ago you threatened to send my boy before the justices, knowing full well the consequences of that?"

"I cannot expect you to understand the complexities of human nature ... my human nature, Riah, but I would only go to those lengths if you deserted me, because then I would have nothing, nothing at all. You came into my life, as I've said, under protest; your children were thrust upon me; but now they are here and you're here, I cannot bear to think of the days, and perhaps the years ahead, without your presence, and theirs. In fact, I know that I couldn't face the future as I lived it before you came. I might as well tell you, more than once I have questioned my feelings for you. It isn't only the comfort you have brought me, the change you have made in the house; it isn't only that you have revived my interest in teaching; it is something that, even I who have always prided myself on being able to explain anything away through my reasoning cannot do so in your case."

When the silence fell between them and she found she could not break it, not even by rising from the chair, she was grateful when his voice came at her as a mutter now, "Would you like to make me a cup of tea, Riah? Please. Very strong."

She rose and as she went to pass him he put out his hand and caught hers. The contact made her want to jerk her flesh from his, but she left it within his weak grasp, and she was forced to look down on his face as he said, again in that kindly helpless way she had come to know so well, "I was going to bring you a present of some coffee back that day. I thought I'd give you a treat. Now I have to ask you if we have enough tea to even last the month out?"

While drawing her hand from his now she said, "It'll do."

As she walked down the room she found that her legs were shaking, and so, after closing the drawing-room door behind her, she did not walk across the hall but she stood to the side and leant her back against the panelling, and muttered, "Dear, dear God. What's going to be the end of it?"

She didn't see Tol for three days. He hadn't called in when he left the milk in the yard in the morning, and so she guessed that his sister had returned. Of course, he hadn't expected her to stay away as long as she had done, but he'd had word from his elder sister through the stage coachman and she had wanted to know if he would mind if Annie stayed with her for a while. He had smiled broadly as he said, "I penned a note back, printed like you showed me. It took me some time but I did it and said, no, she could stay as long as she liked."

That was a week ago.

It was Tol, too, who had told her about the girls in the village who were looking for a place in service, and she did not ask herself why he was concerning himself with her affairs, for she knew he was trying to pave the way for her leaving when the time was ripe.

Well, the time was ripe, but there'd be no harvest of it; yet she still asked herself why he hadn't put in an appearance. . . .

Then there he was, striding across the yard, Johnny hanging on one hand and Maggie on the other. As he came through the kitchen door he pushed them off, saying, "Shoo!" And they ran back into the yard, imitating the cackle of chickens.

"Hello, there," he said.

"Hello, Tol. . . . You all right?"

"Couldn't be better."

She looked into his face and saw that he was very pleased with himself and she smiled slowly and said, "Something good happened?"

"I'll say. Look. From our Mary. She must have got someone to pen it."

He now pulled from his pocket the crumpled envelope and, taking out a single sheet of paper, he handed it to her, and she read the few scrawling words,

Dear Tol,
    I hope you don't mind but Annie wants to stay with me for a time. She is company and has taken to the town life and is very cheerful for me. I hope you don't mind.
        Your loving sister,
        Mary.

She raised her eyes to his and he said, "Our Annie cheerful for anybody. Can you believe it? And she's taken to the town life. I'd like to bet she's got some fellow in her eye. She was disappointed in love, you know; that's what made her bitter. Well, well." His smile widened and, catching hold of her hands, he said, "The road's clear, Riah. You see, the road's clear."

"Sit down, Tol." He still held her hand as he said, "What's the matter? Something more happened?"

She tugged her hands from his and said again, "Sit down, Tol." And when he sat down she went round the table and sat opposite to him; then looking straight into his face, she said, "I . . . I know what you want to say, Tol. But it can't be."

"What do you mean, it can't be? You know how I feel about you, and . . . and I think I know how you feel about me. Am I right?"

She bowed her head, then said, "Aye, yes, you're right. But still" – her head jerked up again – "it can't be."

"Why? What's to stop us?" He turned his face now towards the end of the room and said, "It'll be all right, Riah. Either of those lasses from the village will be glad to come for a couple of bob a week. He could have them both for what he's paying you. And you could slip back and see they didn't shirk."

"Tol—" Her voice was little above a whisper now as she went on, "I can't leave here. I can't leave him. For as long as he's here, I'll have to stay."

When his chair had scraped back on the stone floor she looked up at him. He was standing now, bending across the table towards her, asking, "What is it? What's happened? He can't hold you. He's got nothin' on you."

"Oh, yes he has, Tol. He's got Davey on me. He threatened, and he means every word of it, that if I leave him he'll take the matter to the justices. He's got proof of attack, hasn't he?"

"No. No." Tol's voice was high now. "He told me he had been swinging the scythe himself."

"Was the doctor there when he told you?"

"No."

"Then it's only his word against yours, like it is against Davey's. And what chance has either of you against, as he himself said, a gentleman who is known to be a schol ... astic re ... cluse." She stumbled over the words, then repeated them, "Scholastic recluse, and whose family was highly thought of in these parts."

"Highly thought of, be damned! His mother had religion on the brain, and his father.... From what Fanny's old man says, they hardly spoke to each other in years, him at one side of the house, her at t'other. His side was where you and the bairns are now. They were odd, the lot of them. There's other things that people remember an' all about them, when they lived up in The Heights."

Her face stretched now as she said, "They lived up in The Heights? His family?"

"Yes, yes. This was just a sort of cottage at one time, a kind of dower-house. Of course it's some years back, near a hundred I should say, but nevertheless that's where they came from. And all the land around here was theirs, at least until they sold out to the Gullmingtons round sixty years ago."

"That seems to make it worse."

"How do you make that out?"

"Well, he is gentry. No matter how queer his family have been, he's gentry. And what chance would my word, or my lad's, or even yours, have against him?"

Tol gripped the edge of the table with his fists and ground his teeth together for a moment before he said, "Aye, you're right in a way, but there's one thing, they'll want to know why he's kept quiet so long."

'Oh" – she jerked her chin – "he'll get over that, he could say that he was suffering from shock or some such, his memory had gone. Oh, he could say anything and he'd be believed."

He narrowed his eyes at her now and, his voice thick, he said, "And you're willin' to let it go at that and stay on here? . . . Riah—" He leant across to grip her hand, but she moved away shaking her head, and now he barked, "Woman! I want to marry you. I've waited long enough. I don't know how I've managed. You're ready for it as much as meself. Don't let's beat about the bush, we're both grown-up beings and we want each other. Riah." His voice sank now. "God! woman, you know how I feel. And it isn't only that, it's . . . I like the bairns, and we could be happy in the cottage. I'd build you on a kitchen. And the roof space would take a bed for the lasses. Riah, I've got it all worked out."

"Tol!" The tone in which she said his name carried such finality that he straightened up and stood with his eyes closed for a minute while his head bowed towards his chest; and after a pause, she went on, "He knows about us, and he's not for it."

"Not for it be damned!" He was rearing upwards now, his face red, his whole attitude showing such anger as she had never imagined him capable of. His name she had imagined at first had stood for tolerance; but she learnt it wasn't short for anything, he had been christened after his father and he had been a Tol, as his father before him, and both men had tended the toll gates, and their christian name had become lost in their craft.

"I'll go in to him."

She sprang round the table, her arms spread wide blocking his way up the room, and she cried at him, "No! no! It would be useless, and I can't stand much more."

The raw anger was still in his face as he ground out now, "Neither can I, Riah. And if this is your last word and you're givin' in to him, then hear mine. I'm not gona wait for you until he pegs out or softens. I'm a man and I have me needs, an' I need you, but if I can't get you, then I'll have to find somebody to take your place. *Do you understand me?*"

She swallowed deeply in her throat before she said, "Yes, Tol, I understand you, and I wish you luck in your choice. Perhaps it's for the best after all, because although, as you said, my need might be as great as yours, I'd want to be picked for something else besides. Good-night to you, Tol."

She watched his Adam's apple jerk up and down, and then his mouth open and close a number of times as if ramming back the words that were bent on spewing out, before he turned from her and marched out of the room.

After a moment she herself moved. She went slowly through the passage, into the east wing, across the small hall and up the stairs and along the corridor into her own room. Still with the same slow step she crossed to the wardrobe and, opening the door, she took down the black velvet gown and, gripping the front by the shoulders, she wrenched her arms apart, so ripping the garment down to the waist. Then gripping the pleated band, she again flung her arms wide. But her efforts now did not succeed in splitting the skirt, and so, flinging the gown to the floor, she stood on one side of it and, bending down, she wrenched at the material until of a sudden the buckram waistband gave way and with a soft swishing sound the front of the skirt split down to its hem. Not satisfied with this, she followed the same procedure with the back of the gown: first the bodice, then the skirt. When she was finished the sweat was running freely down her face, but there was no water coming from her eyes. This done, she kicked the torn remnants into a bundle and, stooping, she gathered them up, and retraced her steps, but quickly now, back to the kitchen.

Biddy was in the room and she gaped at her mother making towards the fire, saying, "What you doing, Ma? What you doing?"

Riah didn't answer her for a moment but she took the poker and pushed the red cinders to one side, then she flung the first piece of the gown on to the blazing embers. That done, she turned and looked at her daughter, saying now, "You ask what I'm doing, Biddy? I'm burnin' me folly. Remember that. Keep this picture in your mind until you're grown up and remember that your mother one night burned pieces of a velvet gown in the kitchen fire."

"Oh, Ma. Ma." The tears sprang from the child's eyes and she muttered, "That was the gown the master gave you, and ... and you said you'd put it on sometime and let me see you. Ma, what's the matter with you?"

Not until the last piece of velvet was on the fire and the room was filling with smoke and the smell of the burning material was making them sneeze did Riah answer her daughter's question; and then, as if it had just been asked of her, she replied, "I'm coming to me senses, lass. I'm coming to me senses." ...

Later that night when she took the tray of soup into her master, he said, "I smelt burning, Riah." And she answered briefly, "You would."

He looked at her slightly perplexed and asked quietly, "What were you burning?" And she said, "Just your mother's gown."

She looked at him long enough to see his expression change from surprise to pain, and she was going out of the door when she heard him murmur, "Oh, Riah. Riah." And the sadness with which he uttered her name sounded like the cry of a night bird that she often heard coming from the wood. It held a lost sound. The bird's cry had always affected her, sometimes causing her to get out of bed and close the window, for there were some sounds that carried messages that the understanding couldn't grasp.

PART TWO

✤✤

The Time Between

1

❧❧

Dear Boy,

You are now come to an age capable of reflection, and I hope you will do, what however few people at your age do, exert it, for your own sake, in the search of truth and sound knowledge. I will confess (for I am not unwilling to discover my secrets to you) that it is not many years since I have presumed to reflect for myself. Till sixteen or seventeen I had no reflection; and for many years after that, I made no use of what I had. I adopted the notions of the books I read, or the company I kept, without examining whether they are just or not; and I rather chose to run the risk of easy error, than to take time and trouble of investigating truth. Thus, partly from laziness, partly from dissipation, and partly from the *mauvaise honte* of rejecting fashionable notions, I was (as I since found) hurried away by prejudices, instead of being guided by reason; and quietly cherished error, instead of seeking for truth. But since I have taken the trouble of reasoning for myself, and have had the courage to own that I do so, you cannot imagine how much my notions of things are altered, and in how different a light I now see them, from that in which I formally viewed them through the deceitful medium of prejudice or authority. Nay, I may possibly still retain many errors, which, from long habit, have perhaps grown into real opinions; for it is very difficult to distinguish habits, early acquired and long entertained, from the result of our reason and reflection.

My first prejudice (for I do not mention the prejudices of boys and women, such as hobgoblins, ghosts, dreams, spill-

137

ing salt, et cetera) was my classical enthusiasm, which I received from the books I read, and the masters who explained them to me. I was convinced there had been no common sense nor common honesty in the world for these last fifteen hundred years; but that they were totally extinguished with the ancient Greek and Roman governments. Homer and Virgil could have no faults, because they were ancient; Milton and Tasso could have no merit, because they were modern. And I could almost have said, with regard to the ancients, what Cicero, very absurdly and unbecomingly for a philosopher, says with regard to Plato, *Cum quo errare malim quam cum aliis recte sentire*.

The ruler slapped the table. The man with the lined face and white hair hanging over his ears leant towards the tall young girl sitting to his right hand side and slowly he said, "At last! That's better. But your French accent remains atrocious, Biddy." And he deviated again. "You have learned that often 'a' is pronounced 'ah' when you're speaking in your own tongue, even if your brother hasn't." He looked now to where twelve-year-old Johnny was staring at him wide-eyed. "Both he and Maggie" – his eyes now turned on to the eleven-year-old girl whose green eyes were laughing at him – "who will still say bass ... kit to the end of her days. Well, there might be an excuse for them, but there is none for you." He had again turned his attention to Biddy, and she, looking at him calmly, said, "I can speak it as good as many of the young ladies about, I bet."
"Say that again."
"What?"
Now his voice rose and he cried at her, "Say that again."
"I can speak it as *good* as many of the young ladies about, I bet. Oh" – she lifted her head – "I can speak it as *well* as any of the young ladies...." She was stopped from continuing by his finger pointing at her as he cried, "You can omit the last two words. Sometimes I think I am wasting my time with you and that I have been wasting it over the past years."
"Yes, sometimes I think you have, and, as you say, still are."
"Miss, have I to remind you again about forgetting yourself?"
"Well, you will keep on."
She smiled a small secret smile as she watched him close his eyes

and bow his head, and she knew him well enough to know that he wasn't vexed with her but was really amused at the exchange. Words from the colloquial part of her mind would daily fight with the world of words her master would insist on instilling into her, and he enjoyed a see-saw with her. And she enjoyed it too. The two hours had grown into three, and she looked forward to them; as she also did to her homework at night, although she knew that this annoyed her mother who would have her sewing and patching or mat-making.

She particularly liked the present phase in her learning. She felt pride in herself that she had reached a good way into the second volume of *Lord Chesterfield's Letters To His Son*, because what that man said was sensible, although it had taken quite some time to get used to the print because all the "s"s looked like "f"s; and she knew she had learned more through reading these letters than she had done through Voltaire, although she liked Voltaire. But he seemed a bit airy-fairy. This man Chesterfield was more down to earth. Still, she knew she didn't hold with lots of things he said for he thought women never grew up, not really, they were always children at heart, just made to prattle, they couldn't reason or be sensible. Well, she didn't agree with that, but she had to admit he was right in lots of other things. And he was funny at times, especially the bit he wrote to his son about picking his nose. She had laughed about that.

She used to read bits out to her ma at night, but not so much of late, for, for no reason whatever, her ma would stop her in the middle of a letter and say, "That's enough." And only last week her ma had said to her, "I think you're getting beyond yourself with this learning."

She had looked puzzled and said, "Why! Ma, I thought you liked me learning." But her ma had come back at her, saying, "What'll be the end of it? It'll just divide you from the other two, and me an' all."

"Oh, Ma, don't be silly," she had said; "as if anything could do that. It's only a kind of game, Ma, me learning. I find it easy, and ... and I like it, I mean reading and such."

"You speak differently already."

"Oh, no, I don't, Ma," she had protested loudly.

"Yes, you do," her mother said. "You mightn't notice it but I do."

She didn't mean to speak differently, but he – her eyes flicked towards him – was always on about her sounding her "g"s at the end of words and turning her "a"s into "ah"s when speaking and opening her mouth instead of speaking all words through the front of her mouth.

"Pay attention, you're dreaming again. Continue."

She took up the book and went on.

"Whereas now, without any extraordinary effort of genius, I have discovered, that nature was the same three thousand years ago, as it is at present; that men were but men then as well as now; that modes and customs vary often, but that human nature is always the same. And I can no more suppose, that men were better, braver or wiser, fifteen hundred or two thousand years ago, than I can suppose that the animals or vegetables were better then, than they are now. I dare to assert too, in defiance of the favourers of the ancients, that Homer's Hero, Achilles, was both a brute and a scoundrel, and consequently an improper character for the Hero of an Epic Poem; he had so little regard for his country, that he would not act in defence of it, because he had quarrelled with Agamemnon. . . ."

She stopped here and half rose from her chair and, looking towards her master, she said, "What is it? Have you got that pain again, sir?"

Percival was sitting back in the chair now, his eyes closed, one forearm held tightly under his ribs, and without speaking he turned his head and nodded towards the shelf of the large breakfront bookcase that stood against one wall and on which was a small opaque-coloured glass bottle. As she grabbed it up, she called to Maggie, "Run into the drawing-room and bring the carafe." Then looking at Johnny who was standing by the table now, she added quietly, "Go and tell Ma."

A minute or so later when Riah entered the room, she saw that Biddy was holding the glass of water to his mouth, and she went quickly up to her and said, "How many did you give him?"

"Just one, Ma."

"Give me the bottle here."

Biddy handed her the bottle and Riah shook out another pill and put it to his blue lips, and after he had swallowed it she spoke without looking at Biddy again, saying, "Go and turn the bed down and bring a hot shelf from the oven, and take them with you."

After a moment when the pain eased, Percival opened his eyes and looked up at her and, a half-smile on his lips, he muttered, "That was short and anything but sweet. Could I lie down, do you think?"

"Yes, come along." She helped him up from his chair and from the room and into the drawing-room where he had been sleeping for the past four years because Doctor Pritchard had done such a good job on his leg that he had little movement from the hip; nor could he straighten out his left arm, and the flexibility of his fingers in that hand had become restricted.

Like a wife who might be attending to her husband, she helped him off with his outer things, but when it came to his small clothes, she slipped his nightshirt over his head and, like a modest and virtuous woman might have done, he drew his short clothes down from his legs under the cover of the gown. Then sitting on the edge of the bed, he eased himself into it. When he lay back on the pillows he closed his eyes for a moment before saying, "It would happen today when I have callers coming."

It was the day when the clerk to his solicitors brought his allowance, which had fortunately resumed its previous standard two years ago and so enabled him to have his little luxury of wine and tobacco and she to have more provisions for the table.

The clerk was a talkative man and from him she had learned that the master's allowance would die with him and go into a religious trust. This was a stipulation his mother had made in her will, but she had been unable to do anything about the house because that had been the property of his father and was without mortgage for neither Mr Miller nor his father had been allowed to raise a mortgage on it, a stipulation made by Mr Percival's grandfather. And the clerk had informed her further that even if it had been open to mortgage Mr Percival would have been no better off, worse in fact; for his father would undoubtedly have mortgaged the place up to the hilt, and the interest would have had to be found.

For relatives, she understood, he had two cousins: one lived in

Somerset, and the other was in America. The one abroad was a man in his seventies and the one in England was a spinster lady of uncertain age. That was how the clerk had put it.

When Riah tried to think back over the past four years her memory became blurred. Everything was clear up till then, she could have practically told herself every thought that had been in her head, even to the night when Tol had gone from the kitchen and out of her life and she had burnt the black velvet gown. But from then, for months ahead, the vision of her days was blurred.

She couldn't recall when her attitude towards her master had softened and they had begun to talk, she in monosyllables at first, just listening to him; then glimpsing faintly an understanding of this odd man. Nor could she tell the exact time when pity took over. They said that pity was akin to love, but her pity hadn't reached that stage and never would, but it had picked up a deep kindliness towards him and concern for him. And so life, on the surface, went forward on an even keel, except that there was another current flowing rapidly in the depths below, and over the years it had aimed to wash Tol out of her mind, but without complete success.

It was only six months after their parting that she heard he was to be married to a girl from the village, and she twelve years younger than him. She was one of the two that he had suggested should take up a position in this house. Yet the marriage didn't come off. What happened, she didn't know. It wasn't because of Annie. She hadn't returned, having surprised everybody, even her sister Mary, by getting herself married, and to a man with his own business, that of a pork butcher. She had certainly gone up in the world. Tol had gone to the wedding. All this she had gathered from Fanny whom she saw at rare intervals. But she had never as much as clapped eyes on Tol for over two years now, for he had stopped leaving the milk, having one morning told Johnny that in future he must go and collect it from the farm. The farm lay almost two miles away and so she arranged that the boy go only every other day. But in the real bad weather she went herself and was glad of the walk and also to exchange a word with Mrs Pratt, the farmer's wife.

There had been times of late when she hungered for company. She had the children ... and him, but there was a great gulf between the talk that she exchanged with the children and that which she exchanged with him; it was something in the middle that she was missing, and she knew what it was, the conversation that would flow between her and an ordinary man or woman.

She felt vexed at times that she couldn't talk with Biddy as with somebody ordinary. Biddy was her daughter and fast growing into a young woman. She was fourteen, coming up fifteen, but was developing quickly and was tall for her age. She was thin but she was strong with it. But Biddy's conversation always tended towards things that she was learning and the repeating of things he had said. She had been thinking more and more of late that this standard of education wasn't a good thing for her daughter, in fact, she had become worried over it. Here was the girl spending the main part of her days now outside digging, weeding, and planting, because since Davey had left the work had been too much for Johnny, and she had trained Maggie into the housework, and so Biddy had taken over the garden. But that wasn't as spruce as it should be. Well, it couldn't be, could it, with him taking up three hours of her time in the morning, and also that of the younger ones. And it was in the morning that you got the best work out of people, because as the day waned so did their strength and inclination. She knew it from how she felt herself.

When he had lengthened the two hours of tutoring to three, she had pointed this out to him, and he had laughed at her, saying, "You're quite right. But what applies to the body applies to the mind also." And on that day he had said to her, "I have often wondered why I was born at all; yet lately I seem to have had the answer. I was sent to bring enlightment to the daughter of one Riah Millican. Yet at the same time I ask, why had she to be born a daughter? For what will she be able to do with a brain like hers. Yet she might suddenly up and blossom into some great personage."

And to this she had replied, "Oh, don't talk nonsense." Such was the feeling between them that she could say that to him without him taking offence as he would have done before the change had come about.

She did not think it strange that he never mentioned Davey's name to her. His going from the house was like a death that neither of them wanted to recall. But she did recall that if she had cried at all during those first months after the accident, it was for loss of her son.

Davey had a half-day's leave once a fortnight. It began on a Sunday at two o'clock and ended at seven in the summer and lasted from twelve to five in the winter. And on his first two leaves she had gone to Tol's to see him; but under the changed circumstances she couldn't go there again. Then when she could bear his loss no more, she sent Biddy down to tell him to come up through the back way and she would meet him on the west side of the house.

At the first meeting she had put her arms around her son and held him close, and he had laid his head on her breast and clung to her. But it hadn't happened after that; in fact, they barely touched hands. If the weather was fine they walked the fields. If it was raining or storming they went into the small barn at the end of the courtyard; and there Biddy would bring them a pot of tea and some scones.

At first it was only when she mentioned his work did his face ever show any sign of liveliness. There were eight hunters and four hacks in the stables and five dogs running around. He spoke with awe of Mr Mottram who was the coachman and Mr Lowther who was the groom, and the four stable boys under them, two apparently young men.

But as time went on his tongue loosened and he talked of the household. There were so many in it he couldn't begin to count them. When asked what the mistress was like he replied he had never seen her; and that was after he had been there ten months. He had seen the master and the young sirs and sometimes the daughters of the house when they went out riding, but their horses were seen to by the two older stable boys; the younger ones seemed to do nothing but muck out. Yet this was all her son appeared to want to do.

In the changed appearance of her family since the accident the change in her son was the most noticeable. He was nearing sixteen now and he was no longer slight but had thickened out; he had seemed to grow broader instead of taller; his hair was still silver fair, but his features had altered; his skin, from having a fine delicate softness about it, had reddened. But the most striking difference, in her eyes, was his features. He no longer appeared beautiful. Sometimes as she sat in the barn staring at him she thought she only imagined this yet she knew that it was no imagination, and at such times she was made to wonder what the master would think of the boy now for there was no resemblance between the one who had attacked him with a scythe and this thick-set youth who was no longer beautiful. But she could find no name in her mind with which to describe how her son looked, except perhaps, blunt. His cheeks seemed to have fattened out; his face had taken on a squareness. Perhaps this was how his grandfather, the Swede had looked. Perhaps all Swedes were beautiful when they were young. But he was still young, merely a boy. Yet no, his voice had broken and was that of a man. His talk, too, was that of the stable. Oh, if only. . . . Again her mind was exchanging him with Biddy, because if he'd had her brain he would have been able to put it to some use, whereas, as far as she could make out, it was going to cripple her daughter.

"Sit down, Riah."

It wasn't an unusual request. She pulled a chair up to the bedside and sat down, and he lay looking at her for a few moments before he said, "I'll slip away one of these days. You know that, don't you? Like that." He snapped his fingers. "Here one minute, gone the next."

"Don't talk silly."

"And don't you talk silly." His voice had an edge to it now. "You know as well as I do what's going to happen, and I want to talk to you about it. What are you going to do when I'm gone?"

"What I did afore, take to the road and find another job."

"How much money have you got saved?"

"Oh! Oh!"

He smiled weakly at her. "You never spend anything. You haven't bought a new stitch for the children or yourself, except boots, in years now. In the main you've had your four shillings a week, apart from the time when it was reduced to two, so you must have a little pile."

Yes, she had a little pile. She had saved forty pounds of her wages; then added to that there had been the shilling a week for the first two years from Davey. He had brought the sums intact to her each half-year; but in the meantime she had given him tuppence on each of his Sunday visits. But in the third year his wage had gone up by another shilling a week and so his pocket money had risen to fourpence. The fourth year it had remained the same, but next year he would get a sixpence rise. Altogether she had had thirteen pounds from him. In all she had over seventy pounds including the money that Seth had hidden in the fireplace. So she was well set. But he, lying there, didn't know anything about that first nest-egg, and so she said to him, "I've around fifty pounds."

"Fifty pounds. My! My! That's good. Well, Riah, I'm afraid that you're going to need it, because when I die your life is going to change somewhat."

"I know that; and you needn't worry, I'm prepared."

"You are?"

"Yes. So don't lie there frettin' about that."

"I do fret about that. I fret about you. Do you believe me?"

She didn't answer and he said, "There is a subject that has long been taboo between us, Riah, but I must bring it to the fore again, because I know my time is running out."

"*Please*. Please, don't. There're two questions to be answered there, and I say no to both of them. You can live a long time yet if you take care and take your pills when you should, regular like. As for the other, it's buried."

"It may be for you, Riah, but it's never been that way for me; so I have nobody to exhume. It is here with me all the time."

She got to her feet, thrusting the chair back as she exclaimed, "Now I told you."

"Riah, sit down, please."

Such was the note of pleading in his voice that after a moment's hesitation she sat down again. He remained lying still with his eyes closed as he said, "I want to ask one last request of you; and it is a last request, I'll never ask anything of you again. I want to see David, just once more."

"*No. No.*"

"Don't say it like that, Riah." He still had his eyes closed, but now his fingers began to pick at the thread-worn silk of the

146

padded eiderdown and he went on, "I don't mean you to bring him here, not inside. I ... I just want to glimpse him from the window."

She bowed her head and rested her hand on the edge of the bed before she said, "I've got to tell you, he ... he doesn't look like he used to."

"No?" He opened his eyes and turned his head towards her.

"No. He's changed."

"In what way?"

"I ... I can't explain it. Yes, I can. He's not ... well, beautiful any more, not like he used to be as a boy. You would only be disappointed."

"Never."

"I say you would, because...."

When she didn't go on he said, "Well?"

"Because I myself am disappointed."

"In what way?"

"In different ways. He's changed. He's no longer the Davey that I knew, he's rougher."

"Well, of course he would be, working with four stable hands: their minds must become like the backside of their horses, unpleasant."

"He's not like that. He's not unpleasant, just ... just different."

"As you say, just different. Nevertheless, I would like you to arrange this one thing for me."

"I ... I can't." She was on her feet again.

"Why? You see him on his leave days. You have your meeting in the stable."

"How did you know that?" She paused. "Our Biddy ... she had no right. I'll...."

"You'll do nothing of the sort, Riah, unless you want to distress me, for Biddy, besides having a brain, has a heart. Oh, if I'd only more time to see the finished Biddy. I'm telling you this, Riah, Biddy has more understanding than you. She is but a girl, a child in years, but her mind is away, away above yours and all your class."

Her lips trembled as she looked at him. He could still be viciously hurtful, could this man. Her and all her class. It made her feel like scum, and she said so: "You talk as if we were scum."

"That wasn't my intention, but because your kind have been

147

deprived of education your minds have not learned how to function, how to reason. Only when people can do this can they understand fully the pain that they are not suffering, the hardships that they are not enduring and the quirks of nature that, thankfully, they are not burdened with. People of lesser minds, through their ignorance, condemn. If your daughter ever condemns anybody it won't be through ignorance or superstition." He lifted his head upwards now, saying, "If I'm not mistaken, that's the front door bell. It will be my visitors."

Hurriedly and gladly, she turned from him and when she opened the front door it was to admit three gentlemen: the usual clerk, and two other men. The third man was differently dressed and it was apparent from the start that he was also a superior of the other two, for there was a cutting edge to his voice as he said, "I'm Mr Butler, of Butler and Morgan. Please announce me to your master."

She took his hat and coat while the other two men divested themselves of theirs; then going to the drawing-room door, she opened it and without any announcement she allowed them in; then closed the door after them.

It had been usual for her, when admitting the clerk, to say, "Mr Tate, sir, to see you." But that man had, as she put it to herself, got her goat. What, she wondered when she went back to the kitchen, was this all about? He had no money to leave, nor anything else that she knew of: the house and furniture would be claimed by the cousins. She pictured the spinster lady storming into the house and finding fault with everything. As she set the tray for refreshments she thought to herself, I'll make it me business to go into the town next week and see what kind of jobs go on market day. It was no use her going to the parson to ask him if he knew of any such position that would fill her needs, because since the rift with Tol there had been no lift for the children to church on a Sunday, and in the winter they had often returned frozen and wet to the skin. And so she had dared to keep them away from church. And strangely, this stand of hers had pleased the master, but had, for a time, caused a rift between him and the parson, for he refused to use his authority to force her to send the children to church and Bible school in the afternoon whatever the weather.

The solicitor and his clerks did not stay long, not more than half an hour, and when in the hall they stood ready for departure Mr

Butler looked at her through narrowed eyes and, shaking his head, he said, "Dear, dear." She did not know what to make of this; but then as he went out of the front door she thought she had the explanation when he turned to her and said, "When it happens, send immediately for the doctor, and then he will get word to me."

She watched them mount the shabby looking coach, and after they had disappeared down the drive she went indoors and stood looking towards the drawing-room. Was it really as bad as all that? She would put the question to the doctor when he next came. . . .

The following day when Doctor Pritchard called, she did put the question to him as she was seeing him out of the front door. "Is he in danger of going?" she asked. And looking at her straight in the face, he replied, "Any minute, and has been over the past two years. That being so, he could go on for another two, if you tend him as you're doing. Keep worry from him, and – who knows? – he might see you out." He smiled, a brown-tooth smile.

She had never liked the doctor: his teeth were decayed, his cravat and coat were always snuff-matted, and at times he smelt strongly of spirits. And it was said that he wouldn't be paid in either pig meat or fowl by the common people; if they hadn't a sixpence they got short shrift.

It was a fortnight later on a Sunday afternoon. The October sun was thin; the air too was thin and sharp. There was no wind, a stillness everywhere. It was, as Biddy put it to herself, a real Sunday. Sundays she always considered were funny days: you hadn't to work on a Sunday; you hadn't to read anything but the Bible on a Sunday, although she did; you had to go to church on a Sunday, which she didn't; it was an extra kind of sin for a man to get drunk on a Sunday, yet, and this was an odd thing, it was no sin for couples to roll in the grass, or to cuddle and kiss behind the hedges on a Sunday. Funny that. She would have thought there would be more sinning in that than getting drunk, or reading other than the Bible.

The master had laughed when she voiced her opinion on this matter. She liked to make him laugh. She wished she could make him happy. He had never been happy since the accident, not really, and that was all through their Davey, because, as far as she understood it, the master wanted to act like a dad and make a fuss of him and he didn't like it. She had tried to talk about it to her ma, but her ma had shut her up quick. It was as if she had sworn or used bad words or something, the way she had gone for her that time.

She had never been fond of her brother, and with the years she had grown less fond. But the master had told her himself this morning that there was only one thing he wanted and that was to glimpse their Davey again. And he'd asked her help. She didn't know what she should do. Herself, she couldn't see any harm in it; but why he should want to see their Davey the Lord only knew.

She couldn't understand her mother's attitude towards the master, not really, because he was a kind man. He'd been kind to all of them. She should say he had. Look how he had taught them, particularly her. She couldn't imagine what she would have been like if he hadn't taken time to teach her . . . all empty inside, because her mind would have had nothing to work on, whereas now, she felt learned, and she considered she knew things that nobody else did. Not that she'd brag about them, but she felt sure there was not a girl in the village or in the city itself of her own age who could rattle off things like she did, so therefore she was very grateful to the master. And yes, she would, she would do as he asked. When her mother went to meet their Davey today, she would get the master through the kitchen and along the corridor and to the window at the far end that looked on to the stables and the little barn.

And so she told him.

"Thank you, Biddy," he said. "About what time does he arrive?"

"Round half past two."

He smiled wanly at her as he mimicked, "Round half-past two." He had stressed the round. And she answered his smile with a wider one as she, aiming to imitate his voice in return, said, "About har . . . f-par . . . st two."

"You're a good girl, Biddy. What a pity I shall not be here to see the flowering of you."

"Oh, you could be here a long time, sir, if you took care."

"What did I tell you about speaking the truth?"

Her lids fluttered and she looked downwards as she said, "You've also pointed out that diplomacy is made up of white lies and that it's often kinder to use it."

"Yes, yes indeed, that's true. Do you know something, Biddy?"

"No, sir."

"I think that you will be the only one who will really miss me when I'm gone."

"Oh, no," she was quick to retort now; "we'll all miss you, sir. We'll all miss you, me ma and all of us."

"*Me ma.*" He shook his head; then smiling he said, "I doubt, Biddy, whether *me ma* ... will."

"Oh yes, she will, sir. She's always telling us not to worry you, and to do what we're told, and how lucky we are to have been taught by you."

"She has?"

"Yes, she has."

"Well, I am pleased to hear that. Yes, yes, indeed I am." He paused for a long moment while looking at her; then he said, "Has your mother talked to you about David and me?"

Her eyelids fluttered again and she said, "No, no; not much."

"Have you ever felt afraid of me, Biddy?"

Her eyes sprang wide and her voice registered a higher note as she answered, "Afraid of you, sir? No, never. I couldn't imagine anybody being afraid of you ... well, I mean, not when they got to know you." Her smile was soft as she went on, "I've never been afraid of you, not even when you used to bellow at me because of my 'a's and 's's and colloquial sayings."

She felt happy when she saw his body shake slightly as if he was laughing inwardly, and she knew he was laughing when he said, "Remember the day when you cheeked me because I was reprimanding you all for saying 'us this and us that', and you stood up and said, 'Well, usses is fed up to the teeth'?"

Her laughter filled the room: she screwed up her eyes and, her arms hugging her waist, she rocked herself for a moment, then said, "Eeh! yes." And he mocked her again, saying, "*Eeh! yes.* Well that's an improvement. At one time you would have said, Eeh! aye."

She became silent, and he too, and they looked at each other; then on an impulse she bent towards him and, putting her hands round his shoulders, she kissed him on the cheek before turning and scampering from the room.

He lay motionless for a full minute; then slowly he turned his head on the pillow and for the first time since he had stood by his mother's grave did he allow tears to roll down his face.

It was with difficulty she had got him through the kitchen and into the passage. He seemed to have no strength in his legs, not even in his good one, and she put her arm round his waist and said, "Lean on me. It isn't far now and I've put a chair there."

The passage led into the small hall before going on again to the end of the house. It was narrow and they could hardly walk abreast. There was a small sitting-room went off it and she said, "There's a couch in there. Wouldn't you like to lie down and I'll tell you when . . .?"

"No, no. I'll go to the chair." He nodded to where the chair was set sideways to the wall and opposite the end window, and when she had him seated he closed his eyes, and it seemed for a moment that he was unable to get his breath.

She looked at him in concern. His face had changed colour: it looked grey and seemed to accentuate the whiteness of the hair about his ears. She placed her hand on the back of his head where his hair was straggling over the collar of his dressing-gown and she thought, I'll clip that when I get him back to bed. It looks raggledy. I wonder me ma hasn't done it before now. And at the thought of her mother she felt a little tremor, not of fear, but of apprehension go through her. What if she should find out? Anyway, she'd have him back in the room and tucked up before she returned from setting Davey on his way again.

"They wouldn't have come, would they?" he said softly.

"No, no; the door's open; she usually closes it, me ma."

"Then what happens?"

"Well" – she paused – "after a bit she comes over and gets a tray of tea and things."

"How long does he usually stay?"

"Oh, not very long. If the weather's fine, they dander . . . I mean they walk round the fields, but sometimes he doesn't stay long; that's when he wants to go into the town. But if it's like the day, chilly, he stays longer in the barn. Oh!" – she put her hand on his shoulder – "here they come."

He leant slightly forward, saying, "Where?"

"Oh, you'll see them in a minute, they're coming through the passage. I wouldn't get too near the window in case me ma turns. . . ."

He took no heed of this, but, his face almost touching the pane, he waited. Presently, there came into his view a tallish woman and a youth walking by her side. At the sight of him, he felt a stab of pain go through his heart, but it was not caused by the disease from which he was suffering, nor was it connected with the love he had once had, and still felt he had, for the boy David, but the figure he was looking at now was that of no boy. He could not imagine that that bulky form had ever been slim. True, the figure might be exaggerated by the corduroy jacket, but there was no covering except the cap to exaggerate the head which seemed to be so much larger than he remembered it.

The pair were half across the yard and as yet he had only seen the profile of the youth. Then the head was turned in the direction of the house, and now he saw the face in full view and the sight sharpened the pain in his breast, and his head made almost imperceivable movements as if keeping time to the monosyllables *no! no!* that his brain was repeating. As he gazed at this once beautiful boy, who had rapidly been enveloped by rough young manhood, disappearing into the barn he did not see Riah turn, as if drawn by some force, and look across the yard and directly to the window. But Biddy saw her and almost roughly she jerked her master back into his seat. Yet she wasn't greatly perturbed that her ma had espied them for she knew that the master wasn't long for the top, and surely she wouldn't begrudge him this; although again, for the life of her, she told herself, she couldn't see what attraction Davey had ever held for a man like the master.

"Come on," she said gently. "Come on."

When he didn't move, she bent towards him and looked in his face. His eyes were closed, and she shook his shoulder gently, saying, "Master, come on. Come on; you've got to get back to bed or me ma'll be on us." She put both her arms under his oxters now and helped him to rise; then slowly led him back to the kitchen. But there he had to sit down a moment to gain enough strength for the journey to the drawing-room.

It was five minutes later when she had him settled in the bed, and she put her fingers to his brow and stroked his hair back as she looked at his closed eyes, saying anxiously, "You feeling worse?"

"No." He opened his eyes and looked at her as he added, "It would be impossible, Biddy, to feel worse."

There was something in his look that pierced her. It went right down through her ribs into her stomach and seemed to twist her guts. This was the description she gave herself when in after years she tried to describe the weird pain it caused in her. At the moment the pain was such that she had the desire to throw herself alongside him on the bed and cuddle him, stroke his white weary face and tell him that she loved him, and that no matter what had happened that day between him and Davey, although she didn't know the rights of it she didn't blame him because nothing he could do would be bad.

"Don't, don't, my dear Biddy," he said. "Please don't cry." He put out his hand and gently brought his fingers over both her cheeks as he said, "I am grateful to you for your tears, always remember that; and also, my dear Biddy, remember that love has as many facets as a bursting star. Will you remember that? Love has as many facets as a bursting star."

She gulped audibly in her throat, then said, "Yes, I'll remember that: love has as many facets as a bursting star." Then in a practical way she said, "Lie you still and I'll make you a pot of tea."

When the breath caught in his throat his hand delayed her; then after a moment he said, "Before you go, hand me my writing board and the ink."

After she had placed the board across his knees and the ink on the side table, she hastily left the room, and in the hall she took up the bottom of her pinny and dried her eyes. She was still rubbing at her face when she entered the kitchen but she stopped dead inside the door for there was her mother about to lift the tray to take to the barn. But she too had stopped, and what she said was, "By! madam, I'll deal with you later." And on that she picked up the tray and went out. . . .

It was about an hour and a half later when they met again, and whereas previously Biddy had known that her mother was mad at her for what she had done, she had imagined in the time between she would have cooled down a bit; but she saw now to her surprise that her mother was in a real temper. "I could knock your head off your body this very minute. That's what I could do," she said. "You think you know everything, don't you, you with your learnin'?"

"Ma, he just wanted to see...."

"I know who he just wanted to see. And he shouldn't have seen him. You're an interfering little busybody." Riah now gripped Biddy's shoulders and attempted to shake them, but Biddy, her face flushing red, dragged herself away from her mother's grip and yelled back at her, "I wanted to show him a little kindness and a little gratitude, 'cos you don't. And he's dying and he's lonely, and all he wanted to do was to have a look at our Davey for the last time. But God knows why, because he's nothing to look at, he's nothing but a big gormless lout."

The blow across her face sent her reeling. She stumbled backwards, lost her balance and fell, her head coming in contact with the end of the settle, and she lay huddled for a moment not knowing where she was, only that her mother's hands were on her, pulling her upwards, and that her voice was rattling in her ears but not with remorse, for she was saying, "You've been asking for that for a long time; you're getting too big for your boots. And you say anything like that again about our Davey...."

It seemed that her brother's name cleared Biddy's head for, blinking rapidly against the sting of tears raining from her eyes and her breath coming in gasps, she once again pulled herself from her mother's hold and, going round to the other side of the table she leant on it and, as if in the last few moments she had grown up into a woman, she gazed at her mother before saying thickly, "Don't ... don't you ever hit me again, Ma, for doing nothing wrong, for if you do I'll ... yes I will, I'll hit you back, because I'm not going to be treated like the others, like numskulls knocked about, so don't start that on me. You haven't up till now, so don't start. As for our Davey, I'll say it again, and you can do what you like, throw me out, but he is, he is a big lout, brainless. Always was and always will be. Your lovely son, you've always loved him better than any of us, and I've known it. Johnny or Maggie don't know it yet, but they soon will, 'cos you only live for the odd Sunday. There ... there I'm telling you."

Standing with her back to the fire, Riah wasn't aware of the heat fanning her hips, for she was feeling dead cold inside. This girl, this. . . . What was she? She was no longer a girl, she had just upbraided her as a woman might. But this child, for she was still her child, was her daughter and when all was said and done she was very proud of her. And oh God, she was right, she hadn't loved her or any of them like she had loved her first-born. And she was right, too, about the change in her son. But he was not a lout. No, she wouldn't have that. He was not a lout. He could read and write and count; he was strong and healthy and holding down a good job, one he would rise in; he was no lout. She could put a future name to her son, he'd be a good working man, but she couldn't put a name to her daughter. Her eyes narrowed as she looked at her. One side of her face was scarlet, the other a deep creamy white. She was beautiful now, as Davey had been beautiful, but would she change too? Yet if she did, she would still have that mind of hers, that character that had made her take a stand and say what she had done. Was there any girl of fourteen alive who would dare to say she would strike her mother back if she raised her hand to her? What she should do now was go round that table and wipe the floor with her. That's what her own mother would have done to her. But then, she had never been like Biddy, and she doubted if her own mother would have attempted to flail her; with her tongue yes, but not with her hands. She turned from her and took up her usual stance when in despair; she leant her forearm on the high mantelpiece and dropped her head on to it.

The silence began to ring loudly in Biddy's ears as she stared at her mother through her misted eyes, and she was asking herself now how she had dared to say all that. She wasn't regretting what she had said about their Davey, oh no, but that she had dared to say she would hit her mother. What had come over her? Is this what learning did for you? If it was, did she wish she had never been taught anything? No, no. Her fist beat a silent tattoo on the table and again she said to herself, Oh no.

The silence was broken by Maggie coming running into the kitchen, crying, "Ma! what do you think? There's been a coach hold-up."

Slowly Riah turned from the fireplace and she stroked her throat twice with her finger and thumb before she said, "Where did you hear that?"

"Sammy Piggot from the village. He was out walking with his

big sister and they stopped me and Johnny and they told us; the highwayman took the ladies' necklaces and rings."

When her mother made no comment on this, but walked to the cupboard and began to take plates down from the shelf, the girl looked at Biddy, saying brightly now, "When I grow up I'm going to have a necklace. I'm going to save up and get one from the tinker. He has lovely necklaces. Would you like a necklace, Biddy?"

Biddy patted her sister's head twice, then turned about and went out of the room; and Maggie, going up to her mother, said, "Ma, has our Biddy got the toothache? Her face is all red." And Riah answered, "Yes, yes, she has the toothache," adding to herself, And I've got the heartache. One as painful as his. And I wish I could die of it an' all and be finished with all this.

2

Percival died six days later at eight o'clock on the Saturday morning.

"It's a strange time to die," said Doctor Pritchard, "eight o'clock on a Saturday morning. They usually go around three in the morning, for the body is low at that time; or on towards midnight. But eight o'clock is a very odd time." He hadn't had anyone that he could remember dying at eight o'clock in the morning.

His attitude to the death shocked Riah. It was as if he were talking about an ordinary happening, like the coach arriving on time, or them being snowed up at Christmas.

Inside, she felt greatly upset, much more so than she had imagined she would be when he went. She had taken his breakfast in. She had made the porridge thin, almost like gruel, so it would slip down, as he hadn't been eating at all these last few days. But he hadn't touched any breakfast. With a weak wave of his hand he had pushed the tray away, directing that she put it on one side; and then he had pointed to the chair. After she had sat down by the bed he had said to her, "It's going to be a fine day, Riah." And she had answered, "Yes, the air's nippy, but the sun's comin' up." And then he had said, "You'll have to make your mind up about something very shortly, Riah. I don't know how you'll do it. I . . . I know how I'd want you to do it, but then I am making no more requests." She had looked at him blankly as she had said, "I don't quite follow you."

"No," he had said, "but you soon will. And yet I doubt if you'll understand me any more then, likely less. Yes, likely less." And then his voice halting, he had said, "Be kind to Biddy. She needs you, at . . . at least now. If you let her go she'll never come back. You . . . you made a mistake when you struck her."

Her eyes had widened at this. He must have noticed the mark

on Biddy's face, yet he had never spoken of it, at least not to her, and she wondered if Biddy had told him. But no, the girl was not like that, she wasn't one to beg sympathy, to create trouble.

He had then gasped for breath before he had managed to say, "If things had been different, we would have been different, you and I, Riah. Anyway, that is in the past and something that could never have happened because we weren't different. Or perhaps we were different, I cannot make out at this stage. Anyway I am not going to say I am sorry that I have, in a way, chained you to me over these past years. You think you have missed out a lot not having had Tol. Well, there's a large question there. There's one thing certain: in your sacrifice you can feel a certain satisfaction that you have given your other three children a new start in life, for no one of them will lose out by what he has learned during these past years." Then he had closed his eyes tightly before saying, "I am very tired, Riah; the pain has been with me all night, not sharp, sort of damped down, just waiting to escape."

"Will you take some more pills?" she had said.

"No, thank you, Riah. I am past pills now." Then he had said, "Can I see Biddy for a moment?"

"Yes, yes." She had risen quickly and hurried from the room, but went no further from the hall, calling, "Biddy! You, Biddy!"

When Biddy came running her mother had pointed towards the door and she went into the room and stood by the bed and there he had taken her hand and, looking at her, had smiled faintly as he said, "I don't know where I'm going, Biddy, as I don't believe in Heaven or Hell, but my spirit must find a place somewhere. Wherever it goes, I would ask the gods to let it watch over you, and to let me continue to indulge in the sin of pride in having stirred your mind to reason and awareness. Promise me something, Biddy, promise me that you will never stop reading; if it is only for five minutes a day you will read. It will prepare you. For what, I don't know. A governess perhaps or a mistress. Oh yes! you would make a delightful mistress, Biddy. However, learn ... remember the lines of wisdom you were taught: you can only learn by recognizing your ... ignorance." As his voice trailed away she had done what she had done once before, she had bent over him and kissed him; and had then run choking from the room. And Riah had resumed her seat; and she too was unable to speak; and when, twenty minutes later, the chiming clock struck eight, he had given a little start. It was, she thought, as if he had jumped off a step, and then he lay still. She had bowed her head and wept as she hadn't done in many a long day, even as she thought, my God, he would have educated her up to nothing else but some man's mistress.

Strangely, the funeral was well attended. There was even a representative from The Heights. Mr Gullmington was away but his eldest son Stephen followed the hearse in his carriage. Also, the lady's maid had come, but she didn't follow the hearse, because women never did; but she had looked at him before he was screwed down; then she had left; and she hadn't spoken a word.

Several men from the village came too; and the solicitor and his clerks; and the doctor; and two strange gentlemen who had come all the way from Oxford and who had stayed overnight in Newcastle. One was a learned man with Professor to his name. They were both men in their sixties.

After the funeral she had laid some refreshments and ale in the kitchen for the pallbearers and the men from the village, and better class meats in the dining-room for the solicitor, the doctor, and the parson. Mr Stephen Gullmington had not returned to the house; neither had the two gentlemen from Oxford. There had been another man attended the funeral but had not returned to the house. This was Tol.

The doctor and the parson both stayed to hear the reading of the will. This was done in the library. Riah had expected the spinster cousin to arrive for the funeral, but the solicitor had told her the lady was indisposed and of such an age that it was impossible for her to travel. However, he had added, what remained was of no concern to her.

This had indicated to Riah that the property and household goods would therefore go to the cousin in America. Anyway, she would soon know, for here she was sitting facing the three men. The solicitor had opened the parchment.

"This won't take long," he said; then very slowly he began to read the formal opening as in all wills. Riah listened to his voice droning: "I Percival Ringmore Miller of Moor House in the County of Durham do hereby. . . ."

She felt tired. She wondered why she was sitting here. She wished he would get on with it because she had such a lot to do. Most of their things were packed yesterday and she had to go into Gateshead Fell first thing in the morning to see the farmer and his wife. The farmer had half promised her a cottage when he learned she had three lively workers, but it would all depend upon how his wife took to her. One part of her was thanking God they would have a place to go to, another was asking Him why He had to separate her from her son, and seemingly finally this time, for with the miles that would now be between them there was little hope of them seeing each other, except at rare intervals.

"I leave the freehold property of Moor House together with its three acres of land and all contents of the house in trust with my solicitor to Maria Millican until either (1) she remarries or (2) she dies. The property will then pass absolutely to Bridget Millican, the eldest daughter of Maria Millican. On relinquishing the trust through marriage Maria Millican must no longer reside in or on the property."

Here the solicitor paused and glanced up at the stupefied face of Riah before going on:

"I am sorry I am unable to leave money with which to maintain the property, but Maria Millican, being an enterprising woman, will no doubt find a way to meet the small expense that it entails. Lastly, no mortgage may be taken out on the property during the continuation of the trust and while Maria Millican remains in residence there.

"Signed this day, the twenty-sixth of October, eighteen hundred and thirty seven.
Percival Ringmore Miller."

The three men now stared at Riah, but she had eyes only for the solicitor, and he, who was very rarely surprised by anything he experienced in the legal profession, was almost stunned when the fortunate woman sprang up from her chair and, glaring at him, cried, "Even in death he would prevent me leaving here and marrying. It isn't fair."

"Woman" – he himself was on his feet – "don't you realize that you are the most fortunate of human beings at this moment. You have been left this splendid house which is not in any way encumbered, and the like of which, if you lived a thousand years, you in your position could never hope to own. But now you can enjoy it and its beautiful furniture and you grumble at the conditions your late master has laid down. Well, all I can say is, he must have had very good reasons for the provisions he made."

"Yes, yes, indeed." The parson was nodding at her; but the doctor said nothing, he only held his head on one side while he gazed at her, his lips pursed, and it was he now who spoke to her, saying, "Did he prevent you from marrying before, Riah?"

"Yes, he did."

"How? You are a free woman."

"You don't understand."

"No, I don't. Nor do these gentlemen either." He looked first at the solicitor and then at the parson. "We would like an explanation."

Now she surprised them by barking at them, "You can like all you can, but you won't get one, not from me. It was a private matter. And——" she now poked her head towards the parson, sitting with a most shocked expression, as she cried, "I wasn't his mistress . . . never!"

"I am very glad to hear it," said the parson, now rising; and the doctor put in, "And surprised."

"Yes, I thought you would be." She bounced her head furiously at him. She had never liked him.

"Don't you realize your good fortune, Mrs Millican?" the solicitor broke in, his voice quiet and serious. And it seemed that all the fight began to seep out of her, and she passed her lips tightly one over the other and licked round them with her tongue before she said, "In a way it's surprising, sir, but the price I've got to pay for it is equally surprising."

"Well, as I have learned, everything in life must be paid for. In one way or another it has its price, perhaps not immediately on the nail, but somewhere along life's road it exacts its toll. Now I must take my leave." He turned to the doctor, saying, "I'd like a word with you, and you, Parson." And at that, they all walked out of the room after inclining their heads towards her. And there she was, left in this room which was lined from floor to ceiling with books. And as she slowly gazed around it, it dawned upon her that they were all hers now, all these books, everything in this room, everything in this house, and the two sections on both sides of it, and for the first time the enormity of the gift came as a shock to her and she flopped down on a chair and, her head bent, she asked herself why she had gone off the handle like that. It had been unseemly, to say the least. And in front of the doctor. She had no feeling for either the solicitor or the parson, but she disliked the doctor, because he sensed too much. She had always had the feeling he had his own ideas about the master's accident, especially after he had tried to quiz her about Davey's going to The Heights. It was as if he already knew the reason. Yet how could he because Davey had kept his mouth shut. She was sure of that; he had been too afraid of his own skin. Oh, why was she thinking like that about Davey? She was getting as bad as Biddy. *Biddy.* This place would be hers if she herself went into a marriage. But that would never happen because who would she marry? Tol? No, not Tol now. Yet, who knew, that might come about now that she was free. *Free,* did she say? She was more firmly tied than ever.

Why had he done it, making her pay for his own disability? It was vindictive. He need not have bothered to leave her anything and she could have walked out and made a life for herself. She supposed she could still do it. But if she did that, she knew that Biddy would stay behind. Oh yes, Biddy would stay in this house, simply because he had wished it. And yet how would she manage to keep it going? She would have much less chance than herself. Now that was a problem.

She stood up and walked slowly into the hall. She had things to think about. Of course she could live for a time on what she had saved, but it wouldn't last forever. The only way she could keep things going would be if the others went out to work: Biddy, and Maggie when she was a year or so older, and that together with what she got from Davey would enable her to manage. That would leave only Johnny here, but between them they could see to the place both inside and out, for there would be no nursing to do and no fancy meals to make.

Now she must go and tell the others. . . . But not all. That bit about Biddy coming into the place if she herself should leave could wait because the girl had enough big ideas in her head, without imagining when she would one day be mistress of this house.

*

The children reacted joyfully to the news, Johnny and Maggie jabbering their delight; only Biddy remained silent, but the glow on her face told Riah she was not really overcome with the news, and was likely thinking what a splendid man the master had been. And this made her want to show him up in a different light. "I haven't got this house without paying for it," she said.

"Paying for it, Ma?" piped in Maggie. And she nodded towards her as she answered, "Yes, my dear, paying for it. The price is that I haven't got to marry, ever, if I want to stay here and make a home for you."

"Were you thinking about marrying, Ma?" The quiet question came from Biddy, and Riah almost barked at her, "Yes, I was, my girl. Yes! I was."

"But Tol's got a woman, Ma."

Her young son was sitting next to her on the form as he spoke and she sprung up so quickly that it tipped, causing him almost to slide off the end of it, and she cried at him, "Who said anything about Tol Briston? There are more fish in the sea than have ever been caught."

She turned quickly from the table. What on earth was the matter with her? Why was she acting like this? She had never been like this with her children. Oh, If she only had a friend, someone she could go to. Some adult.

She thought of her family in Shields and shook her head. Oh, no, not them. Any anyway, if they knew of her good fortune they would be round like locusts thinking she had come into money, and seeing the size of this place, they wouldn't be past wanting to share it. Well, would that be a bad thing, because she was going to have a lonely life of it if she was left here solely with Johnny. She shook her head at herself. She would have to think of something, do something.

"Did he leave you any money, Ma?"

Again it was Biddy speaking, and Riah turned on her and, more quietly now, she said, "No, he had no money to leave; his allowance goes into some kind of charity. It's up to us, if we want to stay here, to work for the place, and so you, Biddy, and you, Maggie, when you're a bit older, will have to go into service of some sort."

"Service, Ma?" Maggie screwed up her eyes at her mother. "What can I do in service?"

"You can be trained like your brother Davey but in the pantries

164

or kitchen in a big house, unless, of course, you'd like to go and work in the blacking factory or foundry and such."

The girl was puzzled by her mother's tone and she drew her hand over her dark hair, saying, "I wouldn't like to go into a blacking factory, Ma."

"You'll go where you're sent."

"What about me, Ma?"

She looked at Johnny, then said quietly, "There's the garden to see to; I need a man here of some sort." She forced a smile to her face to emphasize the compliment but, the boy's face sullen, he said, "I'd rather go out, Ma."

"You'll go where you're sent an' all, and do what you're told without any backchat. And that goes for you too." And she inclined her head now towards Biddy who was looking up at her in a quietly penetrating way. And it was as if in this moment her daughter had become her enemy, whereas she should be finding her a comfort and able to talk to her because Biddy was sensible and older than her years. She knew she couldn't because there stood between them the man who had trained her to think and who, in the same way, had put a lock and chain on her own life. Whatever pity she'd had for him was now swamped under a feeling of resentment, that touched on her daughter too, and she thought, She's got to get into service, and soon, for as long as she's in the house, he's here, and I can't bear it. Books, books, books, I'd like to burn the lot. People are right, the gentry are right, the working class shouldn't be allowed to handle them, they're disturbers, trouble makers. Why had she to go and marry a man who could write his name? . . . . It had all stemmed from that.

3

"Davey said they were wantin' a laundry hand up at the house and I told him to ask for a place for you, and he's done it."

"*In* a *laundry, Ma?* But I don't know anything about laundries."

"Well, you'll soon find out. You'll be trained."

"I don't think I'll like that, Ma."

"It isn't what you like, it's what you've got to do."

"I don't think the master would have been pleased."

"Shut up! girl."

"I won't shut up, Ma. I don't want to go into a laundry. I could go to a nursery and teach children their letters and. . . ."

"And who's gona take you on in a nursery around here, a girl of fifteen, no training behind her? What are you going to do? Go up to the lady of the house and say, Can I tutor your children, ma'am? Because I've been learnin' for the past five years. You should consider yourself damn lucky you've been kept at home this long. You've let that learnin' go to your head, girl, and the quicker you forget it the better."

"I'll not forget it, Ma, and . . . and I'll make use of it. Yes, I will."

"Tell me, where?"

"Ma." Biddy's lips trembled and there were tears in her voice as she said, "I don't want to go into a laundry, not up at the big house. I won't know what to do."

Riah's voice came soft now as she replied, "It'll be all right. They'll show you. Everybody's got to start and it's the only post that's open, and you'll get a shilling a week for the first year and everything found, and it's a nice uniform, Davey said, and the same time off as him, and he'll be there to keep an eye on you."

Now the atmosphere changed at lightning speed as Biddy cried, "I don't want our Davey to keep an eye on me; he can't keep an eye on himself. Him! gormless."

"*Now*, girl, I'm warning you. You know what happened when you attacked your brother afore with your tongue."

"Yes, I know, Ma. But don't let it happen again, 'cos I told you then, and I tell you now, don't let it happen again."

"Oh, my God!" Riah turned away. "To think it should have come to this, to be threatened by my own flesh and blood."

"I'm not threatening you, Ma, I'm only telling you I won't be hit. I can't stand being hit. It ... it does something to me, I ... I want to strike out. It was the same when we were playing and Davey used to punch me, I always punched him back. I ... I can't stand being pushed about."

"Well, let me tell you, girl" – Riah was facing her again – "you'll be pushed about afore you get very far through this life. I'm warnin' you. Now get yourself upstairs and get your things together, for the morrow mornin' I'm taking you up to The Heights."

"*The morrow, Ma?*"

"Yes, the morrow."

As Riah marched out of the library Biddy put her fingers on her eyeballs and pressed them tightly, telling herself that she mustn't cry; she had been crying a lot since the master had gone. The next moment she looked about her quite wildly. His papers, all his writings, what would happen to them? Would her mother put them in the fire? It was just possible she would.

She had started sorting his papers from the drawers in the library a couple of days ago. He had been writing a history all about the philosophers. He had talked to her about it. The very last time, a few weeks before he died, he had told her about Rousseau, who wasn't for Voltaire and his philosophy, and how he had been a man who had the courage of his own convictions, although he was born poor, and lost his mother and father, and wasn't recognized in his own time, not until after he was dead, and then he was made into a great man whom others took a pattern from, both poets and philosophers. The master had said they would later start to read his book called *Confessions*, for it was very enlightening. She had been looking forward to this because she wondered if she was going to like the writings of a man who didn't like Voltaire; and she had spoken of this to the master but he had assured her and she remembered she had laughed at him. Why, she didn't know, for he had said nothing that could have evoked laughter. But it was like that: she often laughed at him for no reason, and he seemed to like it, not like Lord Chesterfield, who seemed dead set against laughter, describing it only as the outlet of fools.

She hadn't known he wrote poetry too.

Eeh! If her mother came across some of his writings she would surely burn them, especially that one about their Davey. She would get that and keep it; perhaps she would take it away with her. Nobody would know. He must have written it that Sunday when she had brought him back to bed and he asked for his writing materials.

She had brought all his papers from the two bureaux in the drawing-room. The bed was no longer there and the room was much as it had been before it became a bedroom.

Kneeling down on the floor, she sorted among the papers she had arranged in piles until she came to the one she was looking for; then sitting back, her legs curled under her, she read it again.

> So does the eye mislead the brain;
> So does insanity its power gain;
> So does the heart dictate the urge;
> So does desire all reason purge;
> So does man look upon his kind,
> And with love drives out of mind his mind.
> So did I see David as a boy
> And today what four years did destroy,
> And as my tears make a pool
> I will by dying drown a fool.

She gulped in her throat; then moved her head from side to side before slowly folding the piece of paper and pushing it down the front of her print dress.

Hastily now, she gathered all the papers together until there was six piles, and having tied them up she pushed them well back into the bottom of the cupboard that ran under the bookshelves.

Next, she made a choice of four books which she meant to take with her. One was by Sir Richard Steele and Joseph Addison. They were all essays and very interesting. The master had been particularly fond of this book. The second was the first volume of *Lord Chesterfield's Letters To His Son*. The third was Voltaire's

Candide. And the fourth book, seemingly thought-years removed from the others, was *A Book Of Fables And Fairy Tales*.

She was about to leave the library with the four books held close to her breast when she stopped and looked back down along the room towards the table where she had sat, she felt, for as long as she could remember. And five years was a long time to remember.

She had promised herself one day to reckon up the hours she had spent in learning. If only they'd had another year together, she knew she would have become very fluent with her Latin and French. Nevertheless, he had recently praised her progress. Oh, she missed him. Her eyes ranged about the room. Every part of it held his presence; yet he was gone; but where? He had said there was no Heaven or Hell and no Purgatory, the place where Catholics believed they were sent to before they were sorted out. Then where was he? He had once said to her that when you died you went back into a power, and if you could believe this then you would return again, be born again.

The day before he died he had said something very strange to her. She had thought about it last night in bed and it had frightened her a little. What he had said was, "If you are ever faced with a great obstacle, or decision, Biddy, ask me what to do." Well, how could she ask him if he was dead? It had made her feel creepy.

She looked towards his chair and whispered softly, "Goodbye, Master, and thank you. Your work won't go to waste, it won't. I won't let it. No matter what happens, I won't let it."

PART THREE

The Laundry

1

❦❦

They started off from the house just as it was getting light. When she had kissed Johnny and Maggie, Biddy had only just prevented herself from joining them in a bout of weeping.

She carried in her hand just a bundle of underclothes for she had been told that was all that would be necessary; but nevertheless the bundle was heavy, for in the middle of the garments she had placed the four books. Her mother had gone for her, crying at her, "When do you think you'll have time to read that stuff?" And she had answered pertly, "I suppose they'll let you breathe some time in the day."

It was two miles to The Heights, that's if you took the byroads, it was much longer by the coach road. She had on her Sunday frock and her best hat, coat and boots. She looked, she told herself, as if she were going some place special; but where was she going? Into a laundry. She had no idea of the work it would entail, only that it would be hard and that it was the commonest employment a girl could be put to in a house of the gentry.

As they walked her mother talked spasmodically, telling her how she must behave; also, that everything at first would be very strange.

Biddy was paying little attention to the advice because she had a lump in her throat and all she wanted to do was cry. Most of the time she walked with her eyes cast down, partly in misery and partly to avoid the potholes over which there were thin films of ice for she knew that if she stepped into one and messed up her boots her mother would rave at her. She didn't know what had happened to her mother lately. She could remember the time when they had laughed together. But that time seemed far back now.

On the sound of cart wheels crunching on the rough road, she lifted her head and saw coming towards her a familiar horse and

173

cart. Glancing at her mother, she knew that she had already seen its driver and his companion.

When they stood to the side of the road to let the cart pass Tol drew the horse to a standstill and, looking down at them, he said, "Well, hello there. You're out early."

As Riah answered briefly, "Yes, yes, we are," she looked past him to the young woman sitting at his side; but he made no effort to introduce his companion, only said, "Where are you off to then?"

Biddy lowered her head as she heard her mother reply tartly, "Well, I thought you would have known. News flies around here quicker than birds."

There was a pause before Tol replied, "Well, it appears I don't know everything, only that you've had a bit of luck, Riah. And I was glad to hear it, very glad."

"Thank you." Her tone was sharp.

"Well, what's this I don't know?"

"I'm taking her to your place, The Heights. She's startin' in the laundry."

Biddy's head came up now at the sound of Tol's voice that was bordering on a bark as he cried, "The laundry? She's startin' in the laundry? Biddy? No, you can't put her to that, Riah. And up there; it's slavery."

"She's got to earn her livin' and she has to start somewhere, and it's the only vacancy."

"Vacancy, be damned!" There was silence now before, his voice less sharp, he said, "I can't understand you, Riah. Never could and never will. Gee-up! there." He took his whip and flicked the horse, and this alone told Biddy that he was very angry.

They had walked some yards before Riah burst out,"He should mind his own damned business. What is it to him where I put you."

"He knows it isn't right, Ma."

They both stopped and faced each other, and Biddy dared to go on, her voice breaking as she said, "Only the scum go into laundries. I've heard you say that yourself."

"That was outside laundries, washhouses. This is different. This is a family, where you'll be in uniform. And what does he know about it anyway? He didn't come after the master died, did he?"

So that was it. She still hankered after him. But he had his woman, and she looked nice. That had incensed her ma. Here her mind jumped off at a tanget as she thought, I'm thinking like the master, using words in me mind like incensed.

"Him preaching to me what I should do when his whoring is the talk of the place."

Whoring. She had never heard her mother use that word before. It was a bad word. But the young woman hadn't looked bad, she had looked pleasant. She wondered why Tol didn't marry her. What did whoring really mean? She'd have to look that up. She should have brought the dictionary with her. Yes, that's the book she should have brought with her. She would get it next time when she got her leave.

The thought of leave brought her mind back to what lay before her and she tried to visualize not only the laundry, but the house and the people in it. She had no idea what to expect. Faintly she recalled the church service when gentry filed into their special seats that were set in a kind of gallery to the right of the pulpit. But they had been dim distant figures. She had seen the rows of servants who sat in the pews at the back, and one thing she remembered about them was that they were nearly all dressed alike. One of the village girls told her that her mother supplied the hot bricks for the gentry's feet, and that at one time they used to have a stove in the gallery, but the smoke from it made them cough, so now they only had hot bricks in velvet covers.

They had reached the main gates, and as if their coming had been announced the lodge-keeper Bert Johnson was throwing open the gates, and so Riah, going up to him, said, "We are making for the house, we've got to meet the housekeeper at half past nine."

"Get out of the way! Go on! outside." As he flung his arm wide they retreated hastily backwards. And now he cried at them, "Get out of sight!"

"Out of sight? Why?"

'Why?" He now came towards them, his face thrust out. "The coach is coming down the drive, that's why. It's the mistress. Move yourself!"

They backed into the main road and stood by the hedge, and presently there came through the gates a coach and pair. The coachman sat stiffly on his box. He wore a high hat, a dark brown overcoat, and he wielded a long whip.

As the carriage turned into the road both Riah and Biddy caught a glimpse of the brim of a hat at one window and the face of a young person at the other.

During the passing of the vehicle the lodge-keeper had stood as if to attention, and now, as he closed the gates, Riah approached him, saying, "Well, is it all right for us to go through now?"

"No, it isn't. Not this way. Along there." He thumbed in the direction from which they had come. "There's a little gate; it leads around the outside of the grounds, take that. You'll come into the yard by it."

So saying, he turned his back on them and went into the stone-built lodge that stood to the side of the drive.

Riah glared after him for a few seconds before she turned away, saying as she did so, "Come on."

They found the gate and started to walk between two high hedges, the path being wide enough to allow them to walk abreast; but it could not have taken a vehicle. It seemed to wind endlessly on and on. And then it rose steeply and they were brought to a halt by the sight of the house in the distance. A tree had been cut down here and part of the hedge taken away with it, and there, over a prim patchwork of lawns, beds, and paths bordered by hedges, Biddy first saw The Heights. It looked gigantic, like a whole street that had been lifted from a town, and not just one street, but three piled on top of one another. The early morning sun was warming its frontage which from this distance seemed to be hovering in the air. She made out a myriad of windows and the tops of two archways. She couldn't see the bays.

For a space they were both awed into silence; then simul-taneously they walked on together, and the path, still going upwards, began to twist and turn as if it was straining away from the house. Then suddenly they walked out of the dim border of trees and into bright light, and there before them was a high stone wall and in the middle of it, a wooden door.

Having passed through this the whole aspect changed and for a moment Riah thought that she was back in the pit row, for there to the left of her was mound after mound of ashes, and the smell that assailed her nose told her that they were near a cesspool. They rounded a clump of bushes and there it was.

Their noses wrinkling, they crossed a small bridge over a tiny runlet of water and, leading from the bridge, were three pathways. One, they saw, led to a gate in a field, but the other two were hedge-bordered, and, more to herself than to Biddy, Riah said, "What now?" And Biddy put in, "The left one, Ma" – she pointed – "'cos the house lies t'other way."

Without making any comment they took the left-hand path, and they walked almost a hundred yards before they knew they had arrived, because here the pathway widened considerably into a broad ash-strewn space. Beyond was an arch, and through it they glimpsed a yard.

Once in the yard, they both stood looking about them in amazement, because the yard was as long, if not longer, than the pit row and down one side of it were horse boxes; and there were the horses with their heads bobbing over the half-doors. Connected with the stables was a series of buildings and at the end, towering above them, was a big barn.

For the first time that morning her mother spoke pleasantly, and under her breath she said, "I may see Davey," she said quietly.

"What do you want?"

They both swung round to see a man in leather breeches and a leather jerkin looking at them.

"We've . . . I've got to see the housekeeper."

"Oh aye. Well, go along there" – he pointed to the end of the yard – "through that next arch and you'll come to the back of the house. You don't want the first door you come to but the second."

"Thank you." She had to put her hand on Biddy's shoulder to turn her around. She couldn't fathom the look on her daughter's face: it wasn't fear, because she didn't think the girl knew what fear was, yet . . . yet there was some kind of apprehension in her expression.

When they had passed through the second archway and entered another yard, which she saw at once was bordered completely to the left of them by the side of the house, she pulled Biddy to a momentary stop, hissing at her now, "Mind your manners when you go in there, and talk natural. Do you hear me? Talk natural. None of your fancy stuff, draggin' your words out, else I can see you'll be in trouble from the start."

Biddy shrugged herself from her mother's hold and walked a step ahead of her towards the second door, and there, after a moment's hesitation, Riah knocked upon it.

It was opened almost immediately by a boy of about nine years old, and he looked at them brightly, saying, "Aye?"

"I've come to see the housekeeper."

"Oh." He looked behind him, then pulled open the door, saying, "You should have gone in by the passage." He jerked his head to the side.

"We were told to come to this door."

He stood back and they entered a square room, two walls of which had long slat tables attached to them with racks above and below. One table was crowded with lamps, the other was covered with boots and shoes of every description. The boy now left the room through a doorless aperture, and they heard him say, "Kathy, go and tell cook to send word to Mrs Fulton that there's a wife here to see her and a lass along of her."

When the boy came back into the room, he looked at Biddy who was staring at the shelves and, his voice as bright as his face, he pointed to the boot rack, saying, "The first lot's gone up an hour since. These are the spares." Then jerking his thumb towards the other long shelf he said, "I've trimmed fifteen of them already this morning."

Both Biddy and Riah shook their heads; then Riah said gently, "You've been very busy."

"Aye, we're always busy."

Riah now looked at her daughter as much to say: There you are. This young lad must have been up all hours to get this work done and he looks happy enough. So what have you got to turn your nose up at, miss?

Biddy now saw a girl a little younger than herself standing in the opening. She stared at them both for a moment before she said, "You've got to come this way." Her voice was broad, her face was round, and her cheeks red. She was wearing a starched cap that covered her ears. She had on a blue print dress, the sleeves rolled up above the elbow and the rest almost enveloped in a coarse hessian overall. As they followed her through the next room Biddy saw the reason for the coarse apron, for the three tables were covered with pans, all fire-smoked, soot-bottomed iron pans, and at the end of one of the tables was a thing that looked like a square bath on stone stilts, and it was full of black scum-filled water.

They were in the next room now, which Biddy described to herself instantly as a huge scullery. A girl was at a stone sink washing dishes, and Biddy had never imagined there were so many dishes in the world as what she saw on those tables. Here, too, there were dirty pans, but these were copper ones.

And now they were in the kitchen, and this was the biggest surprise of all, both to Riah and Biddy. The kitchen in Moor House wasn't small, it was bigger than the living-room had been in the pit row, but this kitchen was almost as large as the entire middle floor of Moor House.

Biddy too, was overwhelmed, not only at the size of the place, but at the contents. One end of the long table had different iron gadgets screwed to it, part of one wall was hung with shining copper pans. Next to them was a row of brass-pronged forks, and the ovens appeared enormous. There was one each side of a large open fire, above which an enormous iron spit dangled; and there was a smaller fire with a round oven above that.

There were three people in the kitchen. The elderly, short fat woman, who was standing at one side of the long table, had a very pleasant face and her manner matched it. "She'll see you presently," she said; then she added, "You're Davey's mother, aren't you?"

"Yes. Yes, I am."

"And this is your lass?"

"Yes." Riah nodded now towards Biddy and the fat woman smiled at Biddy as she said brightly, "Oh, you'll fall into it. They all do. Takes time but they all do."

The second woman looked about thirty. She stood at the end of the table pushing handfuls of nuts into an iron cup, before turning a handle. From the effort she was using it appeared pretty hard work. There was also a girl of about sixteen, peeling vege- tables at a shallow trough sink. They all wore the same kind of uniform: a blue striped cotton dress with white apron. Only their caps were different. And Biddy had already taken in the fact that these must denote their rank in the household.

There appeared now, at the far end of the room, another servant. This one was in a grey dress and her cap was different again; also the broad apron straps were edged with a small frill. She beckoned to them; and now Riah, nodding towards the cook, as if in farewell, pressed Biddy before her towards the housemaid. This woman was tall. She looked a solid woman, almost, as Biddy thought, as old as her mother. She didn't speak but held the door open for them, and they passed through and into a broad passage, off which a number of rooms led. It was on the last door at the end of the corridor that the maid knocked, and when she was bidden to enter she pressed the door open and allowed them to pass in.

As Biddy passed her she turned her head and looked up at the woman and, the impish side of her forcing its way through her misery, she remarked to herself, This is one occasion when the master would have said I could use a colloquial expression such as, "Cat got your tongue?"

But when she stood side by side with her mother looking at the small figure sitting behind the oak desk, the impish smile vanished. The woman was about fifty years old, she guessed. She had dark hair and her features were prim, indicated mostly by her mouth, which was full lipped and which Biddy was quick to notice kept pursing itself as if she was sucking a sweet. When she spoke her voice matched the rest of her. "So this is the girl?" she said.

"Yes, ma'am."

"How old is she, did you say?"

"Fifteen last December, ma'am."

"And am I to understand this is her first time in service?"

"Yes, ma'am."

"Tut! Tut! She doesn't look very strong. She's very thin."

"She's quite strong, ma'am. She's been used to garden work for some years now."

"Garden work?" The neatly combed head with the goffered cap perched dead in the middle of it and from which two starched streamers fell down just behind the ears, seemed to lift slightly with surprise. "She doesn't look strong enough for garden work. Do you mean potato picking and such like?"

"No, ma'am. Real garden work, growin' vegetables and tendin' fruit bushes and diggin' and the like."

"Oh, well." The cap gave another little jump which seemed to bring the housekeeper up from her chair, and to Biddy's surprise, she saw that she was no bigger than herself. She came round the desk now and, addressing Biddy solely, she said, "You'll get a shilling a week. You arise at five in the morning. You finish at six in the evening. At eight o'clock you have twenty minutes for breakfast. At twelve you will stop for dinner and see to the cleaning of your room which you will share with another maid. You will attend church with the rest of the staff every Sunday, and every other Sunday you have leave time from two o'clock in the afternoon until seven in the evening in the summer, and from one o'clock till six in the winter. You will be allowed one candle a fortnight. Your room companion is allotted the same, so you have a candle a week. When you are working in the laundry you will come under Mrs Fitzsimmons, at other times you will be answerable to me. You address me as Mrs Fulton. At no time are you to go round to the front, back, or west side of the house. Should you at any time encounter any of the family, you will do your best to make yourself scarce. You understand?" She paused as if for breath.

Biddy made no answer, simply stared wide-eyed straight into the face of this little woman, seemingly fascinated by the constant pursing of her lips when she wasn't speaking. But now she had started again.

"You do not speak unless you are first spoken to, except with those on your own level, who are the three laundry maids and the lower kitchen staff. Do you understand what I'm saying, girl?" She cast her eyes towards Riah, and the look said, Is your daughter stupid? Then her cap jumped even higher as the new member of her staff spoke for the first time, saying, "I understand you perfectly, Mrs Fulton."

The housekeeper was so surprised at the tone that her lips stopped their pursing and spread themselves wide. Again she was looking at Riah, whose face was scarlet now. But when Riah offered her no explanation, the lips dropped together again and gave an extra purse before she said, "Say goodbye to your mother."

They looked at each other and in this moment Biddy wanted to throw herself into her mother's arms and cry, "Oh, Ma, take me back. I'll do anything, if you'll take me back." But the look on her mother's face silenced such a request and when she said, "Goodbye now, and behave yourself mind. Behave yourself," she felt she was being abandoned. Biddy watched the door close on her mother; then looked back at the little woman, as she thought of her; and the little woman looked at her.

Behave yourself. So we have a joker here, have we? were the little woman's words to herself. Well, I have a way of sorting jokers out.... I understand you perfectly, Mrs Fulton.... So part of her joking was to ape her betters, was it? Forward young brat! And not yet been sent out to work, and she on fifteen. Well, she'll soon learn to know her place here, and the hard way or else.

"Now, Miss Bridget" – the tone was heavy with sarcasm – "should I hear you aimin', however badly, to imitate your betters, then you will learn what it is to go without meals for a day, and also to lose your leave time for a month. An' these are only two of the minor ways you can be made to recognize your place in this establishment. Do you understand me?"

"Yes."

"*Yes what?*" The small body bristled.

"Mrs Fulton."

"Yes, Mrs Fulton. And never forget it. Now we will see to havin' you properly dressed. Follow me."

Biddy picked up her bundle and followed the housekeeper, through corridors, and through a maze of doors until she felt she must have come to the end of the house, the working part of it at any rate. In a long narrow room that had a peculiar smell, which she likened at first to moleskin, then to calico, she saw three women. They had all been seated, but they rose immediately on the housekeeper's entrance, and she, addressing the eldest woman, said, "This here is the new laundry maid. You know what she requires. See to it. And when you're finished, Julie here—" she turned to the youngest of the three, adding, "can take her and show her her room. She's sharing with Jean Bitton. Then to the laundry. I will, by then, have advised Mrs Fitzsimmons of her comin'." And with one hard look at Biddy she marched from the room. And no sooner had the door closed on her than the head seamstress, turning to the woman next to her, muttered, "We're in a tear this morning, aren't we?"

"Are we ever anything else? Hello there. What's your name?"

This woman was now addressing Biddy, and she said, "Bridget Millican."

"You Irish?"

Biddy hesitated a moment before she answered, "Not that I know of." And at this two of the women started to laugh.

"Well, come on." The head seamstress took up a tape measure and began to take Biddy's measurements, saying as she did so, "They won't be new stuff, just alterations from the last one. Poor thing. But her clothes have been washed, so you won't catch anything."

Catch anything? What had the girl had? Whatever she'd had she must have died of it.

182

"Where you from?" It was the woman the housekeeper had addressed as Julie who asked this question, and Biddy replied, "Moor House."

The three women looked at each other; then Julie repeated, "Moor House? That's over the church way, isn't it?"

"Well, we're about a mile from the church, yon side."

"Moor House," the second woman repeated now; then looking at the others, she said, "That's where the hermit man used to live. Well, I mean the one who spent all his time with books, so I heard. Is that the same place?"

"Yes." Biddy nodded at them.

"But" – the seamstress was now leaning towards her – "wasn't there something about him leaving the house to his housekeeper?"

"Yes. That's my mother."

Again they exchanged glances. Then it was Julie who made a statement: "And you're gona work in ... in the laundry?" she said. It was as if she was baffled by the situation, and Biddy answered her frankly, saying, "Yes, because he didn't leave any money."

They all stood staring at her for a moment, until the head seamstress exclaimed, "Well, let's get on with it."

The measurements taken, Julie now led Biddy from the sewing-room. But she didn't take her back towards the kitchen quarters; she led the way still further into the house along more passages, up more stairs, and then lastly to the garrets. And there Biddy saw what was to be her room. It was hardly larger than the store cupboard at the house. The two beds were merely wooden-based pallets with the bedclothes folded at the foot. There was a table with a jug and basin on it, and, except for some nails in the back of the door, nowhere to hang clothes.

"'Taint madam's bou ... doir," Julie said. "Worst of the lot. But there. . . . Well, put your bundle down an' come on."

After retracing their steps for some way they entered a yard by a side door, and there at the other side was a long low brick building. It was situated at the end of a number of outhouses. Biddy was quick to notice that this yard wasn't attached to the stable yard.

They were halfway across the yard when Julie paused for a moment and looking down on Biddy, she said, "You're going to find it hard in there, lass, mind. I better warn you, Jinny Fizsimmons is a real slave-driver. But I'll give you a tip. You stand up to her. And Sally Finch an' all, she's the first scrubber. You'll find Florrie McNulty, she's the assistant, she's all right. And so is Jean Bitton. She's the staff scrubber. But in any case, you're gona have your work cut out. And that's not just a sayin', it's a fact. You know" – she shook her head – "I can't understand your mother puttin' you into a situation like this after ... well, you being brought up in that house. You see, we've heard about him, the owner, through Mary Watts. Well, you wouldn't know this, but she's the first housemaid, and she's on speakin' terms with Miss Hobson, she's madam's lady's maid. You see, they've both been in service here over thirty years, so you see what I mean about speakin' terms like. An' Mary knows that Miss Hobson used to visit the owner of that house now and again because at one time she had worked there, Miss Hobson I mean. Do you follow me?" She smiled now, and Biddy said, "Yes, yes, I follow you." And then Julie ended, "Well, I'm only explaining that's how we know. I understand he was a very clever man."

"Yes, he was."

"Did ... did he ever talk to you?"

Biddy opened her eyes in surprise. "Talk to me? He ... he taught us, all of us."

"Oh aye, yes" – Julie nodded now – "of course, your brother's in the stables. 'Tis said he can read an' write. Can you read an' write?"

"Yes, I can read and write."

"My, my. Well" – she now bent towards Biddy, saying softly, "I wouldn't let on to anybody about that if I was you, 'cos it might get up to Mr Froggett. He's the butler, and he's been here a long time an' all, an' he's got the master's ear, an' the master doesn't hold with readin' an' writin'. I know that much. I bet he doesn't know that your brother can do it or he wouldn't reign long. You see, the gentry" – she jerked her thumb upwards now – "they look upon things like that as an aggravation. It makes people unsettled. And they're right, you know, in a way. ... Well, come on, else we'll starve to death out here." And she laughed; but Biddy didn't laugh.

They entered the laundry by way of a heavy door giving no hint of what was beyond it; but having passed through it she was immediately enveloped by the smell of washing. It was so strong that it stung her nostrils. She had a sensitive nose, and now she sneezed in the steaming atmosphere of soap-suds, hot irons and the peculiar stench that arises from water on hot ash.

Through the mist she made out four pairs of eyes directed towards her. The first pair were small and round, set in a large red face on top of a bulky body. This she guessed must be Mrs Fitzsimmons.

This woman was standing behind a table in the process of ironing some flimsy material; when she put her hand under it, it seemed to float away from her. The second pair of eyes were like slits in the thin face of a woman slightly younger. She was ironing aprons. The third pair were inserted in a round fat face above a plump body. The girl was standing in front of a bench that had a trough at the side, and she had been in the process of scrubbing some garment. She looked about sixteen or seventeen, and her face was running with sweat. The fourth pair of eyes just seemed to peep at her before vanishing.

The head laundress left her table and walked slowly towards a glowing round iron stove that was set on some stone slabs at the end of the room. The five platforms round it for different sized irons gave it the appearance of a pyramid. Biddy watched the woman put her iron into a space, then pick up another, turn it towards her face and spit on it before walking back to the table, where she rubbed it on what looked like a greasy looking pad before placing it on an iron slab; and then she emitted the word, "Well?"

"This is the new girl, Mrs Fitzsimmons. Mrs Fulton gave orders to bring her over. She's not properly uniformed yet, but she will be the morrow."

The big woman left her table now and stood in front of them, and concentrating her gaze down on Biddy, she said, "What's your name?"

"Bridget Millican."

"Bridget Millican. Well, forget it as long as you're inside here; you'll be Number Four from now on. Understand?"

Biddy made no reply to this, and the woman barked at her, "I was talking to ya!" And at this Biddy remarked sharply, "Yes, I understand." Again her tone had changed, but unconsciously this time, and the woman stared at her for a moment before glancing at the seamstress as if for explanation. Then she turned and called to the small girl, shouting, "You! Three." And when the small girl came running, she said, "Show her the ropes." At this Julie turned away and the small girl held her hand out in a beckoning motion towards Biddy.

The head laundress returned to her table and for a moment there was only the sound of the banging of the flat irons interspersed with the grating sound of the scrubbing brush.

The room was a long one, running lengthwise each side of the main door; but at one side it took on an 'L' shape and the young girl led Biddy round into this section, which was a separate washhouse and, like the rest of the laundry, stone floored; and there she turned to Biddy and whispered, "I'll show you everythin'. Don't worry; I'll show you everythin'."

Biddy nodded at her and waited, and the girl said, "Me name's Jean Bitton. Because you've come I've been moved up; I'm a staff scrubber now. You'll be doing what I used to do, so I'll show you." Her head was nodding again and she was smiling widely; then putting her face close to Biddy's, she said, "Don't worry. You get used to it."

She would never get used to it. For the first time she could remember she felt afraid, not so much of the people but of the work. It was all so strange. Whereas, she told herself, she could learn from books like lightning, she felt she'd never learn the things she had to do in this place.

"Look, first thing in the morning, you see to the stove. It's kept on all the time: you bank it up at night, but you've got to fill up first thing in the morning. It needs four buckets. Those are the buckets." She pointed to two large wooden buckets standing against a door which she now opened and, motioning with her head towards some doors at the far end of a yard, she said, "Them's the coalhouses and the netties." She closed the door again and then went on, "Well, your next job is here." She now led her to two large low tubs and, pointing down to them, she said, "You put the roughs in there to soak overnight and you wring them out first thing in the mornin' through the mangle. The water gets freezin' this time of the year, but you get used to it." She was nodding brightly all the time she was talking.

The mangle was the only recognizable piece of equipment in this whole place. It was like the one they had back home. She thought of the house she had left only a few hours ago as home, and always would. And on the thought it came to her again that the master would have been upset, very upset, had he known what work she was about to take on.

"And these" – the young girl was now pointing to a great pile of working trousers – "them moleskins and corduroy breeches," she said, "are from the stables. It's trouser week for them in the stables. These are mostly the lads' stuff. They get mucky, very mucky, and you've nearly always got to scrub the bottoms after soaking afore they go into the hot wash. Never boil." This last was accompanied by a vigorous shake of her head and she repeated, "Oh, never boil them. But these boil," she said, pointing to another heap. These were shirts, all blue striped.

She was moving on again, and now she was looking into one of three bins. "These," she said, "are the rough coloureds, petticoats and that, from the sewing-room, the kitchen staff, and ours in here; except Mrs Fitzsimmons, she has hers done with the middle staff lot, like the cook and the housemaids an' such." She now peered into Biddy's face and added, "You look flummoxed."

Biddy nodded as she repeated, "Aye, I am a bit. Yes, I am a bit."

"Oh, you'll soon come to it. Now this—" she pointed to a large poss tub already half full of hot water and clothes, and she laughed as she said, "You've seen one of them afore I bet."

"Yes, yes, I have."

"But I bet you haven't seen this kind of mangle." And she now took Biddy's arm and pulled her towards a box that looked like three big coffins placed together. It was six feet long and about four and a half feet wide and under the two top boxes were two rollers, and as if the great cumbersome thing was the young girl's own invention, she said proudly, "This is the presser. It's as good as an iron for some things, like the trousers and the rough shirts and things like that. Put them through when they're just off dry and they come out fine. Look." She now gripped a big handle attached to a wheel all of eighteen inches across, and it took all her strength to turn it, smiling broadly as she did so; and when she stopped she said, "You'll soon get the hang of it."

To this Biddy answered in a voice little above a whisper, "I don't think I ever shall."

"Oh, you will" – the smile left the girl's face – "you'll have to. An' you'll get out at times durin' the day an' all. I'll be goin' along of you, takin' the baskets back and collectin' the dirties." At this

Biddy pricked up her ears and said, "We take the washing back? Will we take it to the stables?"

"Eeh! no." The girl pushed her. "They're all left in the sortin' room over in the house an' the staff take it from there. Fancy you askin' that." And she pushed her again.

Her face straight, Biddy said, "Me brother's in the stables."

"Is he?" There was awe in the girl's voice. "What's he like?"

"He's fair, very fair."

"Oh, that one. Oh, aye, I've glimpsed him."

"Glimpsed him? How long have you been here?"

The girl now bowed her head and said, "Oh, six years coming on."

"*Six years?* Well, our Davey's been here over four."

"Oh aye. Yes, that could be." The girl was nodding at her solemnly now. "But you see we're not allowed to mix. In church we can see who's new an' that, and at half-year pay-day an' Christmas when they have the staff get-together. But then, up till last year, you see, I had to just look on."

"Why?"

"Well" – her head drooped again – "I'm from the house, the poorhouse."

"Oh."

The brown eyes were looking into hers now as she said, "An' there's two lads in the stables. They came at the same time as me. But, you see, we're not allowed privileges like the others."

"But why?"

"Well, 'cos we're taken out of charity, see."

The statement was made without bitterness. "And these are good jobs. I've been very lucky; so are the lads; 'cos they could have been sent for sweeps, an' I could have been put into a factory, and some of them are worse than the House of Correction they say. Oh, I'm very lucky. And you" – she now caught hold of Biddy's hand – "you'll get to like it. And the food's fine. An' you get your uniform and a present at Christmas an' leave every fortnight. But—" The brightness left her face as she added now, "we can't go anywhere on our leave, the lads and me, unless ... well, unless we're invited, you know like somebody takes us."

Terrible. Terrible. Terrible.

The word was yelling in Biddy's mind. Eeh! when she looked back she'd had the life of a lady and she hadn't known it.

"What do you two think you're up to? I thought you were told to show her the ropes."

The young girl almost left the ground, so quickly did she spring round, crying now, "I . . . I have. I . . . I am, Mrs Fitzsimmons, and she's taken it all in. She'll be all right. I have. I'll start her on."

"You do, an' quick, an' get back to that poss tub or I'll know the reason why."

Biddy made another mistake, she turned and looked fully at the woman; and now the bawl of the voice almost lifted her, too, from the ground as the laundress screamed, "Get your head down over that tub afore I duck you in it!" And as Biddy now turned towards the tub of wet clothes the voice came at her, yelling, "An' roll your sleeves up first, you idiot."

It was with great difficulty that she stopped herself from obeying the flash of anger that spiralled up through her body carrying with it such words as, Don't you call me an idiot. I'm no idiot. If there's an idiot round here I'm looking at her.

Eeh! she would never be able to stand this. She'd run away. But if she did, what then? She could only run back home, and there'd be another mouth to feed and no shilling a week coming in. And if her mother wanted to stay in the house, then they'd all have to work.

As she plunged her arms up to the elbows into the ice cold water and dragged out of it a heavy garment, there now rose in her a feeling of resentment that overshadowed that which she had for the laundress, and this feeling was against her mother.

2

For the first week, as she told herself, she didn't know where she was. The work in the laundry didn't seem to get easier with the days, but harder; and Mrs Fitzsimmons piled more and more work on her. She had been used to grubbing in the ground in the cold weather, she was no stranger to back-breaking work such as digging, but this, having to skitter from one job to another under the yelled orders of the laundress, had become a torture to her. For the first three nights she had cried herself to sleep. Her fingers were numb with wringing out heavy working clothes in cold water; her shoulders ached with possing and scrubbing; her nose wrinkled in distaste when she even thought of the garments she'd had to scrub. When, at night, she had muttered to Jean Bitton, "They must all be filthy," Jean had said, "They're no different, Biddy, from the house clothes and those of the gentry. Eeh! you wouldn't believe. I've seen some of them, an' they're changed every day you know."

"Every day?" She had widened her tear-dimmed eyes at this new friend and Jean had nodded vigorously as she whispered, "Oh, yes. The mistress and old madam change every day. And the master and Mr Stephen, they can go through three shirts a day sometimes. Then there's Mr Laurence. But you don't have much from him as he only comes home for the holidays. But from the two young rascals, Mr Paul and Miss Lucy, you can have three changes a day for them, especially if they're going visiting. And Miss May's as bad. But of course, she's a young lady."

It was only at the end of the first week that Biddy began to work out in her mind the household staff. She had learned that there were eight in the master's family, one of whom was old madam, who had all the west wing to herself and who very rarely appeared with the rest of the family. She had learned that the butler was one Thomas Froggett. He was fiftyish, thin, and had a wily look; he wore fancy clothes and had garters at the top of his stockings. And the first footman was James Simpson. He was younger, but taller and fatter. The second footman was one John Thompson. He was younger still, a small man and looked ordinary. Then there was somebody called Mr Buckley. He was the valet. But up till now she hadn't seen one of these men, and she had merely glimpsed the first and second housemaids, Mary Watts and June Cordell. They were grown women, as were the first and second chambermaids. The first chambermaid's name was Peggy Tile. She was older than the previous two, well into her forties. But the second chamber-maid was younger. Her name was Chrissy Moore. She had merely glimpsed people as she and the laundry staff filed into the servants' hall to have their one sit-down meal of the day. This was at half past six after the rest of the staff had eaten. They were accompanied by the lower kitchen staff. The cook, as did the head seamstress, ate with the upper household staff; the valet and the housekeeper and the governess ate in the latter's sitting-room.

It astounded her that it took twenty-one indoor staff to look after eight people, seven if you didn't count the one who was away most of the time. Then, as she reckoned from Jean's talk, there were thirteen outdoor staff, which included the laundry and the lodge-keeper and his wife. But this wasn't taking into account the home farm and the blacksmith and the three wall men. These, she understood, were a separate unit altogether and miles away at the other end of the estate.

What she had come to fully understand in this short time was that the laundry staff were the lowest in the hierarchy, and she herself was the lowest in that section; also that, in each section in the household there was someone who considered himself or herself superior to the rest. It even happened at the last table, as their meal was called, when Anna Smith, the assistant cook, took the head of it and directed when they could start to eat and when they were finished. She also dictated the time when talking was permissible.

The whole system was so bewildering that Biddy constantly told herself that she would never get used to it. Nor did she want to get used to it. Time and again during the last few days she had been for walking out, just like that. She had imagined herself walking up to the laundress and saying, "Well now, Mrs Fitzsimmons, you big loud-mouthed individual, there's the washing and if you want it done, get at it!'' She was continually forming such cutting sentences in her mind and imagining the ensuing look of utter amazement on the laundress's face.

Looking back over the week, Biddy could see that the laundress's manner towards her had from the first been rough, but on the second day after the housekeeper had made her daily inspection, the woman's attitude towards her had worsened. It was as if she had been told to find fault with everything she did.

It was on the third day she had said to Jean, "Do you think I could slip along to the stables to see our Davey during the dinner break?" This was a meal of cheese and bread and ale brought to them at twelve o'clock, and they were given forty-five minutes in which to eat it, clean their room, and attend to the wants of nature. It was during this latter period that Biddy thought she would have time to dash around to the stables, but Jean was horrified at the suggestion and warned her that if Mr Mottram or Mr Lowther or the bigger stable boys saw her they would split on her, because one of the lads had been dismissed for keeping company in secret with a girl in the kitchen. They had both been sent packing.

So it wasn't until Sunday when she was being packed into the back of a cart lined with wooden forms that she saw Davey. He was walking with two other young men towards the wagon that was the third in the procession and he turned and smiled at her, and it was a nice smile, a warming smile, and she answered it and nodded at him before she was pushed up into the cart and along the form.

She glimpsed him again as they filed into church, the male staff at one side, the females at the other. Not all the staff were present, but what there were made a good third of the congregation.

She was in the very back row seated between Jean Bitton and Julie Fenmore, and when, after some ten minutes, there was a stir at the front of the church towards the altar, it was Julie who, with her hand over her mouth, whispered, "The family's in."

Up till then she hadn't seen any member of the family. She had no idea what they were like and so, letting her imagination run riot, she saw them sitting in their gallery, stately superior, on a par with the gods and goddesses she had read so much about over the past years.

She was bored with the service. She had nothing to read. During the sermon Parson Weeks's voice almost sent her to sleep. She told herself she'd ask her mother for her father's Bible when next she went home. But taking in the rows of still figures, hands joined on laps, she wondered if it would be a wise thing to do, especially as reading was frowned upon.

The day was bright and frosty and as the cart travelled back along the road the girls chatted to each other; but she sat quiet, looking out through the wooden slats that boarded the sides, and again she was crying inside, If only I could go home.

Once they were down from the cart Jean explained the procedure: they were to go to their room and change into their working clothes, then have their bite, which was their midday meal, after which they'd collect the dirty laundry and sort it all up, soak it ready for the early start in the morning.

She had never worked so much on a Sunday even when they hadn't gone to church; her mother had considered it a day of rest. In the summer they had all gone down to the river and had games in the field. The tears came to her eyes when she thought of the wonderful life she had had in that house. She hadn't been aware of it at the time, she had taken it for granted, thinking it would go on forever. If only the master had lived, he would never have let her work in a laundry.

It was as they were later sorting the clothes that Jean said, "Would you read me a story the night, Biddy?"

"Yes. Oh yes." She was flattered at the request and she added, "I'd love to. What d'you like?"

"Oh, I don't know, anything; I just like to listen to people reading, like the parson this morning, about the comin' of the Lord an' things."

"Well, I haven't a Bible with me, but I'll bring it next time I go home. There're some lovely Bible stories. There are others though that are not so nice; they're all about killings and things. But I've got a book of tales with me, and I'll read you one of those."

"Oh, ta. Look." Jean leant towards her and in a conspiratorial whisper said, "We'll snuff the candle an' get undressed in the dark, an' that'll save it a bit, so you can read more."

"That's a good idea. Yes, we'll do that."

For the first time since coming into this strange world she felt the return of her old excited self. Somebody was interested in reading. Perhaps she might even be interested in learning to write.

Now it was her turn to whisper, "Would you like to write your name, Jean?"

"Me, write me name? Me own name?"

"Yes, yes."

"Oh, aye, that would be wonderful. Eeh! nobody can write their name here. Well, I expect the butler an' the housekeeper can likely. Oh aye, they'll likely be able to write their own names. And people like the lady's maid. An' of course Miss Collins, the governess. Oh, but fancy me being able to write me name." She now stopped her work and, gripping Biddy's cold wet hands, she said, "Eeh! I am glad you come, Biddy. Eeh! I am. I've never had a friend afore."

Biddy was both touched and flattered at this demonstration and, her thoughts jumping ahead, she said to herself, And I'll not only teach her to write her name, I'll teach her to read an' all, and anybody else that wants to. Aye, I will. And that'll show Mrs Fitzsimmons, because she doesn't know 'B' from a bull's foot. As the master might have said, she is proficient in ignorance.

At this she began to laugh as she told herself that that was a fancy bit of thinking. And Jean, looking at her, laughed too as she asked, "What you laughing at, Biddy?"

Lifting up a long white lawn nightdress by the arms, Biddy danced it up and down over the tub of cold water as she said, "I just thought of something funny."

"What kind of funny? Tell me."

What good would it be repeating a saying of the master's to Jean, and so, swinging the nightdress widely from one side to the other in the water, she said, "I was imaginin' this was Mrs Fitzsimmons and I was dooking her."

At this Jean put her head back and let out a high scream of a laugh in which Biddy now joined her; then their laughter was cut off and they clutched at each other in fright as a tap came on a window some distance down the room. Slowly they turned their heads towards it; then Biddy, springing away from Jean, ran to the window and, pushing it up, she said, "Oh, hello, Davey. Hello."

"Hello, Biddy." He put out his hand and touched hers, then said, "How's it goin'?"

It was some seconds before she answered, "Not very well. I don't like it."

"I didn't think you would. But you get used to these things.

Give yourself time. I'm ... I'm just on me way home. I'll tell me ma I saw you."

"Ta ... thanks, Davey. Oh, it's nice seeing you." Had she ever called him loutish? At this moment, to her he looked as he had done years ago, beautiful. "How did you get round here?" she asked.

"Oh, there's ways and means, an' I've got a couple of look-outs." He nodded to both sides of him.

"You won't get wrong?"

"No, no." He shook his head. "Anyway, you're me sister, and I'm surely allowed to see me sister." His eyes moved from her now to the girl standing some way behind her, and Biddy turned and said, "This is my friend Jean. We sleep together. She's been very good to me."

He inclined his head towards Jean and said, "Hello, Jean."

Jean made a muttering sound that could have been anything; then Davey said, "I'll have to be off. I'll see you now and again; an' I'll tell me ma you're all right." He was already moving from the window when she said, "Davey."

"Aye?"

"I wish I was coming with you. Do ... do you think you could ask me ma to ... well, take me back?"

After a long pause he said, "You know the situation as well as I do: she wants to stay on there, and she's got to be kept."

"Aye, yes." She nodded at him. "All right." Then smiling, she added, "By, I'm glad to see you, Davey."

"And me you." He backed from her now, then turned and disappeared into the shrubbery behind the coalhouses.

When she closed the window and looked at Jean, she noted that her friend's face was scarlet, and rather inanely she said, "That was our Davey."

"Yes." Jean nodded at her now and, her voice small, she said, "He's lovely. His hair's like those angels you see in the church painted on the windows."

Yes, she supposed he did look like that to other people, even though his face had changed. He had certainly looked like an angel four years ago. That's how the master must have seen him, like an angel, someone to adore. Of a sudden she felt sad. The laughter had gone from the washhouse. It was full of soiled clothes, dirty clothes, filthy clothes; and it came to her that it was because of that angel that had just disappeared into the shrubbery she was having to work among it all, because if he had never struck the master with the scythe, it was doubtful if the master's heart would have given out as soon as it did. Yet, could she blame Davey? Because it hadn't started with him, nor with her mother taking up the post at Moor House, it had started right back in the pit village when her da had died of cholera in that terrible year. Where then did blame start? The master could have answered it, at least explained if there was an answer to it at all.

That was another thing she was going to miss, was missing already, someone to talk to, discuss things with, explain things; someone to put her on the right path of thinking. But that would never happen now, for never again would she meet anyone like the master. From now on she'd have to think for herself. And she would do. Oh aye, she would do. As the master said, every available minute she got to herself, she must read. She wasn't going to grow up and be like this lot here. Oh, she liked Jean, and she would help her all she could, because she wasn't dull; but as for the rest, they were a lot of numskulls. Yes, yes, they were. But she would show them. And she surprised Jean by taking up a poss-stick and thumping a tub of linen into a soggy mass; then even more, by now drying her hands on her coarse apron and exclaiming loudly, "It's Sunday. We shouldn't be working on a Sunday. Come on over here in the corner and I'll tell you a story."

"But what if . . .?"

"We'll hear the latch lift. Come on, I'll tell you a story."

That story was the beginning of a chain of events of which even Biddy's fertile mind could not present her with the ultimate picture.

During the following week, Biddy not only told Jean a story but she read her a story. She also taught her to write the first three letters of the alphabet; and she promised her that before Christmas she'd be writing her name and spelling cat and dog.

On the Sunday morning, the day of her leave, she counted the minutes during the service and after it, and up till one o'clock, when she was free to start on her journey home. But before she could leave the house she had to go to the housekeeper's room for Mrs Fulton to look her over. Fault was found with her attire, from her hat to her boots. Her hat, Mrs Fulton said, should not be worn on the back of her head but well over her brow. As for her coat, it was creased. If it had been hung up it wouldn't have been like that. With regard to her boots, they lacked shine. She had, Mrs Fulton said, a good mind to make her go back to her room and polish them, but as this was her first Sunday on leave, she would overlook her slovenly attire. And she finished by saying, "You may go."

Biddy had all the trouble in the world to stop herself saying, "It's clarty outside, the roads'll be muddy, I could be up to me ankles in no time." Only the effect of that response on the housekeeper stopped her, for she knew the woman was quite capable of cancelling her whole leave. So once she had escaped through the back door and had walked sedately across the yard, as soon as she entered the long hedged path that bordered the grounds, she grabbed up her skirts and took to her heels and raced as if the devil were after her.

The coach road, as she had surmised, was very muddy, and in her running she had to skip and jump over the potholes; and she reckoned she had run almost half the distance to home when she had to stop and gasp for breath. She rested for a moment with her back against a tree at the side of the road before hurrying off again, not running now, yet not merely walking; her step was a trip as if she were about to go into a dance. And all the way along this road, on this Sunday, she hadn't seen a living soul until she came to the old turnpike, and there she saw Tol. He wasn't driving the wood cart today but walking and crossing from one side of the road to the other when she espied him and she cried, "Tol! Tol!"

He turned round and waited until she came breathlessly up to him, and, his face bright, he exclaimed, "Well! Well! Where are you running to with your face like a beetroot?"

"Home."

"Of course, home." He nodded at her. "Your first leave day?"

"Yes."

"Do you like it?"

The smile slid from her face and her mouth assumed a pout before she said, "No, Tol, I don't like it. I hate it."

"Aye" – his voice was soft – "I thought you would. I get word of your doings now and again through the lads in the stables. I bet you were pleased to see Davey that day."

"You know about that?"

"Oh, I know lots of things." He turned his head to the side while keeping his eyes on her. And now she smiled at him, saying, "You always did."

"What time have you got to be back? Sixish, isn't it?" he said.

"Yes."

"Well, I tell you what. I'll meet you here with my . . . what do you think?"

"The cart." She had poked her head up towards him. And now he shook his, saying, "No, not the old cart. Madam—" he assumed a pose before going on, "I have acquired a trap."

"You haven't, Tol! A trap?"

"Aye. I just got it last week. There was a sale at Brampton Hall, Fellburn way. I went over with the groom. He was looking out for harness and there was this old trap. Hadn't a lick of paint on it for years and spokes missing. And a little old pony. He looked on his last legs. But you should see them both now. Anyway, I'll be off duty around three the day and, madam" – he again assumed a pose – "I will await you on this very spot."

"Oh, Tol." She had a desire to throw her arms round him. She had the added desire to beg him now: "Come on back home with me." But all she did was press her face against his arm while he held her to his side for a moment before, without another word, she ran off, asking herself as she did so, why in real happy moments she should want to cry. . . .

Riah was waiting for her on the road outside the gate, and they both put their arms around each other and held tightly together, Riah knowing that she had missed the company of her daughter more than she would admit even to herself, and Biddy's feelings telling her that she loved her mother and she always would.

Johnny and Maggie came running across the yard and there followed more hugging and questions came at her from all sides: Did she like it up there? How long had she to work? What did she have to eat? Had she a nice bedroom? And she answered all their questions, not all truthfully, because she couldn't say to her mother as she had done to Tol that she hated the place; at least, not yet, not in front of the other two, because that would have spoiled the merry atmosphere. And it was merry . . . and yet sad, and the sadness was emphasized when she entered the library. And she was near to tears again as her fingers gently stroked the table where she had sat each morning in the week, year after year, as she sometimes imagined, since she was born, because she could not recall life before she had come under the master's teaching.

Over a tea of bread and jam and scones and apple pie, she had to describe to the two youngsters the duties of the different members of the staff. But when she was asked about the house and its occupants, she had to admit she hadn't seen any of them, which even surprised Riah, for she said, "You've never clapped eyes on the master or mistress yet?"

"No, Ma; and I don't suppose I will, not till half-pay day, and then Christmas. Jean, she's my friend that I told you about, has been there for years, and she only ever sees the mistress when she hands her her present at Christmas."

"You get a present?" Maggie was looking at her starry-eyed, and when Biddy nodded, saying, "Everybody gets one," both children shook their heads in wonder.

It wasn't until it was almost time to leave that Biddy was alone with her mother, and Riah then, straight-faced, asked, "How's it really going?"

And Biddy answered truthfully. "I don't like it, Ma," she said. "The work's awful, but ... but I could put up with that. It's the laundress. She's a nasty woman and she doesn't like me. And the housekeeper doesn't like me."

"You're imagining things."

"Oh, no I'm not, Ma. But of the two, Mrs Fitzsimmons is the worse, 'cos I'm with her all day. Still" – her face took on a little lightness – "you know what I'm doing, ma? I'm teaching Jean her letters and how to do her name and...."

"Now, now, lass. Now look. I'd be careful along those lines. Now I warned you about that." Riah was wagging her finger in Biddy's face. "They don't like it, not only gentry, but servants in such houses. You see, when people rise in that kind of service they get ideas about themselves. An' it's got nothing to do with reading and writing, it's the difference—" Her voice trailed away now because she found that she hadn't the words to explain thoughts in her mind with regard to underlings who had risen in a household and were still unable to read or write their own name. But deep within her she had the explanation, for although she herself

199

could read and write there were times when this young daughter of hers, who could rattle off quotations and talk like the master had done, aroused in her a feeling of inferiority, which, in its turn, bred animosity.

But Biddy reassured her now, saying, "It won't cause any trouble, Ma. And Jean won't let on. Ma ... Ma, would you mind if I bring her home on me next leave? She can never go out anywhere on her leave 'cos she has nobody belonging to her. She was from the poorhouse."

"Oh, poor bairn. Yes, yes, of course, you may bring her."

"Oh, thanks, Ma ... Ma—" She turned from Riah now and walked down the drawing-room and into the hall. Still with her back towards her mother, she said, "I saw Tol when I was coming. He was by himself, Ma." She didn't point out that Tol had a Sunday duty to do, too. "And Ma, he ... he asked after you."

"Did he?"

"Aye," she lied glibly. "He said to give you his regards. . . . You know what he's got, Ma?"

"No."

They were in the kitchen now, "He's got a trap, Ma, and a pony."

"Very nice for him."

"And he's going to meet me and take me back on it."

"Well, well, now, aren't you lucky?" They were standing in front of the fire and facing each other, and Riah said, "In that case, it's time you were going. Get your things on."

"Ma. . . ."

"Get your things on, Biddy."

Biddy got her things on.

The light was fast going as they crossed the drive and Biddy drew them to a halt as she turned and looked along the length of the house and quietly she said, "I love this house, Ma. I hope you never have to leave it."

Riah turned abruptly away and walked down the drive, her mind again in a turmoil. Why hadn't she told her daughter that if she died tomorrow the house would be hers, not Davey's, him being the eldest? And too, what was more significant still, if she was to marry she would have to leave, and then again the house would be Biddy's. Why hadn't she told her? Again her mind would not give her the truthful answer which would have been that buried deep within her was a live resentment against the man who had, first, taken her son from her, at least he had caused her son to leave this house, and then her daughter, by first educating her above her station, then by making her the real benefactor of his twisted generosity. And he had left herself what? A home that was hers as long as she remained a prisoner in it, with no company, no man to hold her. And oh God, how she longed to be held. At times she thought, to hell with the house, she'd go down to the cottage in the dip and offer herself to Tol, even as his next woman. And that, her mind had told her, could be a solution: she could be his woman and still have this house. So what was stopping her? What?

3

It was about one o'clock on Christmas Day that Mrs Diana Gull-mington leant forward, peered between the light of the small candelabra set at each corner of the dressing-table, and gently moved her fingers through her soft sparse white hair; then looking at the reflection of a woman that topped hers in the mirror, she said, "I look quite bright this morning, don't you think, Hobson?"

"Yes, madam. Extremely bright."

"I always do in cold weather. Suits me, cold weather. The boys broke me into it years ago, rolling me in the snow. Give me me hair."

When Jessie Hobson placed the wig carefully on her mistress's head the reflection in the mirror became transformed: the nut-brown hair piled high seemed to lift the sagging wrinkled skin upwards over the fine bones of the broad face and to take at least ten years off the eighty-two and bring the face more into keeping with the voice.

Once more the old lady looked at the face above hers saying, "Another Christmas ding-dong, Hobson. I didn't think to see it."

"You'll see many more, madam."

"Oh, don't take that note, Hobson. You know, you make me flaming mad when you feel you've got to say the right thing. And how many times have I told you that over the past years? Look, turn me round to the window; I expect the horde is about to arrive at any minute now."

Jessie Hobson turned the chair that was set on wheels and pushed it towards the long window; and there she pulled the velvet drapes still further back, saying as she did so, "It's starting to snow, madam."

"Yes, yes, I can see that. Pity it didn't come down in the night and block the road and they would have had to walk." She turned her head and there was an impish grin on her face as she looked at her maid, and Jessie Hobson, suppressing a smile, said, "Oh, madam."

"Well, all that damn ceremony. It makes me blood boil, not only today but every Sunday. And that woman has as much Christianity in her as a boa constrictor. What was she wearing this morning?"

"Mrs Gullmington was wearing a blue velvet outfit, madam."

"Blue velvet. That must be new."

Now the old lady turned and looked at the woman who had been her maid and confidante for more than thirty years and she said, "You've heard this question before, Hobson, and you can't answer it I know, but I still ask it, and of myself: why had my son, a fellow like he was that could have got any woman from any county in this country, to go and pick a little dark mean-eyed sanctimonious shrew like that? I never liked little women you know, Hobson."

"I'm a little woman, madam."

"Oh, Hobson" – a thin blue-veined hand flapped towards the maid – "you know what I mean. There are little women and little women and this one is as narrow in her mind as in her body. And what would she have been if she hadn't married my Anthony, eh? Tell me that. An old maid likely, in a manor, in a very minor manor, in the backwoods of Northumberland. Why—" The face was screwed up now and again she repeated, "Why on earth had he to take her? Now if it had been her cousin Emily, Laurence's mother, I could have understood it, because, as you remember, she was a bit of a beauty. Did Laurence go with them today, do you know?"

"I espied him on the drive talking to Miss May earlier on."

"You mean you espied him on the drive being talked at by Miss May. She's brazen is May. Holy like her mother, but brazen."

They both laughed softly together now and the old lady exclaimed, "Ah, here they come, the chariots." Then she leant forward to watch the two coaches and three open carts drive past the west wing, which was her private portion of the house, towards the front entrance where the two coaches stopped, while the three carts continued on to the stable yard. Grunting in her throat, she said, "Now for the pantomime. Get me ready, Hobson. Give me the lot today, tiara an' all. That's the only vanity I have left, to outshine that little shrew."

When Jessie Hobson went to get the jewel box from the Chinese bureau that stood at the end of the room, her mistress called to her, "You're walking worse today, Hobson. Are your feet worse?"

It wasn't until Jessie Hobson returned with the box and placed it on the dressing-table that she replied, quietly, "They've been hurting a lot of late, madam."

"Why didn't you say, woman?"

Jessie smiled to herself. This dominant woman who could be kind and thoughtful in so many ways, could at the same time be as blind as a bat when to open her eyes would lessen her own comfort.

"You should soak them in brine."

"I did so, madam."

"I'll get Pritchard to look at them again."

"It would be no use, madam, he said he can't do anything. It's the insteps you know, they've dropped."

"My insteps never dropped."

Jessie again smiled to herself. No, her insteps had never dropped because she had never to stand for hour after hour attending to someone's wants; nor had she had to be continually taking messages to one of the family and in doing so had to traverse a gallery before entering the main house, then along another gallery and down a great curving staircase. And this could happen ten times a day, and had done for years past, until three years ago when they had acquired a house boy, whose job now was to run errands to other parts of the house. . . .

It was about twenty minutes later that Mrs Gullmington again looked in the mirror and, ridiculing herself, said, "Ridiculous! I look as if I'm dressed up for a ball. Nevertheless, that's how it's going to be. I'm ready."

On this Jessie Hobson went to the door and gave directions to the small green-liveried boy standing there. Then leaving the door open, she went behind her mistress's chair and pushed it along the broad corridor, to the first gallery that opened out into quite a large hall, from which stairs led downwards; but she passed these, then through a pair of grey-painted communicating doors, held open now by two footmen, and along the second gallery and towards the head of the main staircase. Here, the two footmen took their positions at each side of the chair and, lifting it, walked crab-wise down the winding staircase to the hall below.

The men having set the chair down, Jessie Hobson once more took up her position behind it. But she did not immediately push it forward because her mistress was surveying the double line of servants arrayed across the hall. They stretched from the green-baized doors leading into the kitchen quarters, to within a yard of the drawing-room, and as she surveyed them the female knees bobbed and the men touched their forelocks.

The double doors of the drawing-room had been pushed wide and there, in the middle of the room, facing the fireplace, but set well back, was the Christmas tree. And standing to one side of it was the old lady's son, Anthony, a man of about forty-eight, tall, heavily built, with fair hair and blue eyes. And to his side sat his wife Grace. She was older than him by two years. She was small, she had dark hair and grey eyes which were set deep in a round face that at one time could perhaps have been termed pretty.

Standing next to his father was Stephen Gullmington. He was twenty-two years old and in appearance very like his father, but he differed strongly in character. Next to him was his sister May. She was nineteen years old. She was tall, fair and thin, being quite unlike her mother in looks. Her face wore a bored haughty expression.

At the other side of the tree was an empty chair and next to it the young man who was known as Laurence Gullmington and whom most people took to be the brother of Stephen and May and the two youngest children. But he was the son of Grace Gullmington's cousin, and the reason why he had been brought up in this house and to believe for years that he was a Gullmington was entirely the work of the woman he called grandmama. He was of medium height, thin, and of a dark complexion, with deep brown eyes, a straight nose and a wide mouth.

Next to him stood Paul Gullmington. He was sixteen years old and had red hair. Why this should be, the whole family questioned. No Gullmington had ever had red hair; only Grace Gullmington's narrow-minded attitude to all things, and people, saved her from suspicion in this matter.

His sister was the last in line. She was fifteen. Her name was Lucy. In looks she was like her mother might have been at her age. Being the last child, she had been spoiled and pampered.

They and the various guests all watched the old lady being pushed gently towards the empty chair; and now her son and first grandson stepped forward and assisted her to her feet, where she stood for a moment shaking down her voluminous skirts. Then swivelling slowly round, she was assisted into the great black oak carved chair, the arms of which ended in dragon's heads. Her thin bony bejewelled fingers covered these heads as she looked slowly about her.

Then she spoke. Coming straight to the point, she looked at her son and said, "This year we'll make a change. We'll delay the wine and chat and not keep them standing out there waiting. It's more sensible, because they have the meal to see to, and we can be enjoying our exchanges while they get on with it. Should have done this years ago."

She now brought her eyes round to her daughter-in-law whose face had become so tight that her cheek-bones were showing white, but Diana Gullmington smiled at her as if the shrew, as she always thought of her, was conceding her proposal cheerfully.

And now she lifted her hand and pointed towards the double doors as she looked at her son, and Anthony Gullmington, without glancing towards his wife, went to the fireplace and pulled on the bell-rope summoning the staff to its presentation ceremony.

The first one to enter the room was Anthony Gullmington's valet. He walked slowly across the open space towards the family, bowed to the old lady, then stepped towards Grace Gullmington, and after receiving his present he inclined his head towards her, saying, "Thank you, ma'am," then took six steps backwards before turning and leaving the room. He was followed by Miss Nichols, Grace Gullmington's maid. Then came Miss Collins the governess; Mrs Fulton the housekeeper; Thomas Froggett the butler; James Simpson the first footman. These were the cream of the staff, and had not headed the queue outside but had awaited their call in a side room.

They were followed by John Thompson the second footman; Kate Pillett the cook; Mary Watts the first housemaid; June Cordell the second housemaid; Peggy Tile the first chambermaid; and Chrissy Moore the second chambermaid; and Mrs Morrison the head seamstress.

There followed a break in the proceedings and an arrangement of the presents before the sewing-room maids came in. First, Mary Carson; then Julie Fenmore. Then came the kitchen maids; Anna Smith the assistant cook; Daisy Blunt the vegetable maid; Polly Neill the scullery maid; and Kathy Ward the second scullery maid.

Tagged on to these two were Billy Kelly the pantry boy, and Harry West the boot and lamp boy.

There was another pause before the appearance of the outdoor staff, when Bill Mottram, the coachman, stumped slowly in. On his departure there was a giggle from the young daughter of the house because he always had difficulty in walking backwards. She seemed to have been waiting for this. Peter Lowther, the groom, followed. Then came the five stable boys, Ben Fuller; Rob Stornaway; Micky Taggart; Tot Felton; and David Millican. This boy too, like his outside master, seemed to have trouble in walking backwards. And again the young daughter of the house giggled audibly before being silenced by a look from her grandmother.

The lodge-keeper and his wife followed.

In the order of position, the farmer and his wife and the farm hands and the blacksmith should have been squeezed in somewhere along the line, but it was the custom for their presents to be taken to them by the young members of the family first thing on Christmas morning.

So it showed in what low esteem the laundry staff was held when they came last in the long procession. Mrs Fitzsimmons, walking with mincing steps, assumed a dignity that bordered on the comic. Florrie McNulty came next. This thirty-four years old woman, one could see, was deeply impressed at the honour that was bestowed on her for she not only bent her knee, but almost touched the ground with it. Sally Finch aimed to follow suit; then came Jean Bitton, nervous, eyes cast downward as befitted a creature from the workhouse. Last of all, came the new hand Biddy Millican.

Although Biddy was tired of standing and tired of listening to the whispered Oohs and Ahs of the present gatherers, her mind was bemused by the beauty around her. For the first time she was seeing the interior of the house, and its magnificence amazed her. The hall, with its marble statuary, its beautiful carpets, the dazzling colours of the pictures lining the open gallery above the staircase, brought to life the palaces the gods had dwelt in in the stories that the master had sometimes read aloud to them. By the time she reached the drawing-room door she was quite unconscious of the bustle about her, the to-and-froing of the servants, the whispered directions, so much so that, standing on the threshold awaiting her turn to enter, which Jean's passing her on coming out would signal, she had to be nudged forward into the galaxy of beauty.

Slowly she walked up the space towards the great lighted Christmas tree, and unlike Jean's and those of many of the others, her eyes were not downcast, nor her head held on a downward tilt, as she had been bidden, but it was back gazing at the angel at the top of the tree. She managed to bring her gaze downwards before she approached the half circle of people seemingly awaiting her. She took them in with one sweep of her eyes. She knew she had to approach the lady seated to the left of the Christmas tree with the gentleman standing next to her – they were her master and mistress whom she was seeing for the first time – but her sweeping glance returned to the old lady seated in the big black wooden chair. Her attention was drawn to her because she seemed to be sparkling all over: her hair was covered with jewels, as were her chest and her hands; she looked like a queen.

She was aware of a noise being made in someone's throat. She came to a halt opposite the mistress of the house and when she was handed a small parcel she dipped her knee and inclined her head and said in a clear voice, "Thank you very much, ma'am." She thought it was better to add the 'very much', nobody told her not to.

Instead of walking backwards for six steps, she again glanced along the family row and she smiled at them. Then, with great dignity and as if she was acting in a play, she took three steps backwards, paused and let her smile cover them again, before turning and walking from the room, not with eyes front, but with head moving from side to side, even dropping backwards as she took in the colours of the ceiling.

But no sooner had she reached the hall, and the doors were closed behind her than she was almost lifted from the floor by the first footman who gripped her by the collar of her dress and whispered fiercely, "Little smarty, aren't you? *Get!*" And at that he almost pushed her on to her face.

When she regained her balance, she turned round, her mouth open and about to tell him what she thought, but there, also staring at her, was the magnificently dressed butler.

Mary Watts, the first housemaid, came at her now, saying, "Get yourself away, girl. You're a ruction raiser, if ever there was one, grinning like an idiot at the family. We'll hear more of this."

She could have heard more of this if she had been in the drawing-room at that moment, for Lucy was doing an imitation of the laundry maid. Curtseying now to her mother, she said, "Thank you, *very much*, ma'am." Then she did the backward walk and was about to flounce round to conclude her pantomime when she was brought to an abrupt halt by her grandmother saying, "Girl! Behave yourself. Stop acting like a little slut. If the servants don't know their manners, they have little chance of learning from you.... Well now." She looked around her family, then with her usual forthright approach, she went on, "Come on, let me have that drink, and then to the presents. Yours are scattered around there." She pointed to the tables at the far end of the room. "Hobson has marked them plainly. No mix-up this year."

As each of them put a present on her knee, he or she bent forward and kissed her cheek. Even her daughter-in-law did this, saying as she did so, "I had it especially made for you, Mother-in-law."

"Well, what is it?" As the stiff old fingers fumbled at the parcel, Laurence Gullmington assisted them to reveal a very fine cashmere shawl and when it was held up for her inspection he said, "It's beautiful, Grandmama." And she nodded and said, "Yes, it is. Thank you, Grace. Very kind. Very kind. Now what have you got me, Anthony?"

Her son brought his present to her and hovering over her, he said with a laugh, "Well, Mama, mine's a very small present, but knowing you haven't much jewellery, I thought I'd get you these." When the box was opened to disclose a pair of jewelled ear-rings her eyes gleamed and she said, "Nice, nice. Thank you, Anthony." She lifted her face for his kiss.

And so the present giving went on, and two hours later a dinner followed. Then they all had a rest while the staff enjoyed their Christmas meal in the servants' hall, for once in the year sitting down all together, but at four separate tables, the diners at the bottom table waiting on their superiors.

But the dinner was only the beginning of the staff festivities for, after clearing away, the tables and chairs were pushed back, as were also two partitions that divided the room from that part which was used for storing dried goods. Once a year this was cleared to make space for the party.

It was a custom to invite the master and mistress and household to join the party, but it had never been known for the mistress to accept the invitation. The master had sometimes popped in for five minutes or so, but the duty, and it was considered a duty, fell to the eldest son and any other member of the family who would like to join him. But even these did not stay long, knowing that their presence acted as a restraint on the hilarity.

It was said, among the staff, that before the old master died when madam had ruled here, which in reality she did to this very day, she and the master had come in to the party and hadn't been above joining the dancing. But that had all stopped twelve years ago after the old master had died and Mr Anthony had brought his wife and family here, as was his right. . . .

It was half past eight when the party began. Sally Finch, Jean and Biddy were sitting on a wooden form near the dividing doors. They were all agog with excitement. Jean was describing how the party had been set off last year, and the year before, and likely would be tonight: James Simpson, the first footman, could play the fiddle and Peter Lowther, the groom, could do wonders with the flute, and they generally played the Sir Roger De Coverley. But just the older ones danced that; it would be the young ones' turn when the games started.

It was as Jean predicted: the party got going with the Sir Roger De Coverley, danced only by the upper hierarchy of the staff. And now the first game was about to start, a game which embraced everybody: a large circle was formed, with one player being delegated to run round the outside and to tap a member of the circle on the shoulder, this one to chase the first player, trying to catch him before reaching the open space. If he couldn't, then he had to do some kind of forfeit before he could take his turn tapping someone else on the shoulder. It was at this point that the door opened and some of the family entered.

Leaving the ring, Thomas Froggett went hastily towards them and conducted them to seats that had been set apart at the end of the room. The visiting party consisted of Mr Stephen, Mr Laurence, young Master Paul, and Miss Lucy. Miss May, like her mother, never put in an appearance on these occasions.

Once the guests were seated, the game started in earnest. There was no feeling of restraint among the staff, this was their night. Shoulders were tapped and the runners encouraged by shouts for one of them to fill the gap. Then the cry would go up: "Song, dance, or rhyme?" Nearly always the choice was dance, because it was the easiest.

When one of the stable boys tapped Jean, she was so surprised to be chosen that for a moment she didn't run and there were cries of, "Go on! Go on!"

She, too, chose to dance, and when her feet tried to imitate a clog dance, she nearly fell over, causing great laughter around the ring. Now it was her turn to choose, and she tapped Davey on the shoulder and he beat her to the gap; but they closed it to him and opened it further along and pulled Jean in. And so he had to choose.

He stood for a moment, his eyelids blinking, his fair skin red, while Biddy willed him to do something good. Recite, she said to herself. Recite. Recite, man. He had learned a lot of rhymes and poetry during his lessons. But he too chose to dance, and he was pushed into the middle of the ring, only to surprise them all and make Biddy feel proud of him as, imitating a gentleman, he placed his left hand on his hip, extended his right hand to the side, his fingers spread, and then proceeded to lead an invisible partner forward in a dance, bringing forth shouts and clapping from the others.

Biddy swelled with pride at her brother's achievement. She realized from where he had taken the dance steps. There was a big book in the library with drawings showing ladies and gentlemen dancing, and he had mimicked them.

When he tapped her on the shoulder she went off like a hare, but he beat her to the gap and there she was, pushed into the centre of the ring with the cries coming at her: "Song, dance, or rhyme?" And she had no hesitation in saying, "Rhyme." And she heard some voices repeating, "Rhyme."

Part of her mind was in a high state of turmoil, another part was quite calm, for she imagined the master to be standing near the gentry and he was looking at her and she knew she must do him proud. Some of the last poetry he had made her read had been from the poet called Shelley. So she stood straight, her head up as he had taught her, her mouth set with her tongue tucked behind her lower teeth, and as he had taught her to read so she spoke:

"I fear thy kisses, gentle maiden,
Thou needest not fear mine;
My spirit is too deeply laden
Ever to burthen thine."

She paused here for a moment, her eyes looking straight ahead; then went on,

> "I fear thy mien, thy tones, thy motion,
> Thou needest not fear mine;
> Innocent is the heart's devotion
> With which I worship thine."

There wasn't a movement in the room. If she had blasphemed, spewed out obscene words, she could not have stunned the majority of the audience more than she had done. After a moment there was a smothered giggle here and there from the younger ones, but all the adults in the room fixed her with their eyes, and the brightness that had shone from her face as she recited faded away as she looked back at them. Her head turned slowly. What was the matter with them? It was a lovely poem. She didn't understand it all but she liked it, the sound of it, the feel of the words, and the master had said it was a thing of beauty. Then into the stillness came the sound of a single clap, a hard definite clap, and all the eyes were turned on to the visitors and to Mr Laurence, then to Mr Stephen, who had joined him. The two younger ones were not clapping; but now, as if given a lead, here and there a servant, thinking best to take a cue, joined his hands together and clapped. But they were mostly male hands that did the clapping, except those of Jean and the seamstress, Mrs Morrison, and Julie Fenmore, her second assistant.

Biddy had no need to be told that by reciting the beautiful poem she had stored up trouble for herself, and that in a way she had brought the game to an end, for now the housekeeper had motioned to the butler who motioned to his second-in-command, and the music struck up again.

As Biddy moved down the room to join Jean in the corner, she had to pass the visitors, and it was as she did so a hand came out and touched the sleeve of her dress, drawing her to a halt, and she turned and faced the two gentlemen of the house. It was the one she now understood to be Mr Laurence who spoke to her. "You recited that very nicely," he said.

"Thank you, sir." Her voice was a mere whisper.

"Who taught you to read?"

"The master, sir. I mean Mr Miller from Moor House."

"Oh." He nodded at her, then cast his glance at Stephen, and Stephen, bending down, asked her kindly now, "And what else did he teach you?"

"Oh, lots of things, sir."

"Lots of things?"

"Yes." She nodded at him.

"Such as what?" It was Mr Laurence speaking to her again, and from where he sat her eyes were on a level with his and she looked straight into them as she said, "Reading and writing. But I could do that afore I went there. Then Latin and some French." She watched the eyes narrow as they continued to stare at her and she knew that the young man was finding it hard to believe her. She didn't like being thought a liar by anybody, and so her tone lost its quiet, even subservient note and took on an edge as she said, "'Tis the truth, sir. He taught me for five years, and my brothers and sister. My brother is over there" – she turned and pointed now – "the fair one."

The two men continued to look at her in a dumbfounded way, as did the younger boy and girl, but the expression on their faces represented in this moment exactly that which would have been on their mother's face had she listened to such audacity coming out of a servant's mouth, and not an ordinary servant either, but a creature who was the lowest of the low in the household. As if of one mind, the brother and sister were about to rise and walk away when Laurence's voice stilled them. He hadn't turned towards them, nor yet seemed to be aware that they were about to leave, but he said quietly, "Stay where you are; you might learn some more for your good."

Now looking over Biddy's head, he noticed that although some of them were dancing while others sat around the walls, nevertheless all were aware that this child was being taken notice of.

He had always considered there were too many servants in this house and that there was a form of snobbery among them that outdid even that of their superiors. He hadn't taken much notice of such things until he had gone to Oxford two years ago, but in that city, at least within the confines of the university, one naturally had servants, and some of them were servile individuals. Yet he doubted if their attitude to each other would be the same as that of the servants in this household, and in others round about at which he stayed, and he doubted very much if his father, unlike

Lord Chesterfield, would remember any servant in his will, nor say of them: "They are my equals in nature and only my inferiors in fortune." And he was sure in his mind that Chesterfield must have been thinking of someone with an intelligence such as this child here possessed when he wrote those words, for was she not surprising, quoting Shelley and saying that she could read Latin and French. It was utterly unbelievable. But he hoped, for her own sake, that this news didn't reach Mama, a title he had always given to Grace Gullmington, although they were but second cousins, for of all the minds in the household he knew that his adopted mama possessed the narrowest. So he would have to see that these two rips by his side kept their mouths shut. Stephen was speaking to the child again, saying, "Let us hear another rhyme."

Stephen was a good fellow, one of the best. He couldn't have loved Stephen more if he had been his brother, and they were as close as brothers, yet he knew that what Stephen knew about poetry or literature of any kind was minimal. Now had it been horses. Well, that would have been different. Like his father, if it had been possible he would have eaten and slept on his horse. But here he was, unthinking as usual of the consequences of anything he might say or do, urging the child to repeat her performance and by doing so picking her out from the rest of the company. Yet he had himself to blame for that; it had been an irresistible urge that had prompted him to put out his hand and draw her attention.

His voice quiet, while his elbow gently nudged Stephen, he said, "I think the young miss would like to join the party. You must remember we are just onlookers."

"Oh, yes, yes, all right. Away with you!" And Stephen made an exaggerated gesture of shooing her off.

She turned from him without further words and went and joined Jean, who was sitting open-mouthed and wide-eyed in the corner near the dividing doors. But when Biddy took her seat beside her neither of them spoke; they watched the visitors rise now and, attended by the housekeeper and the butler, move down the room towards the far door, Miss Lucy muttering, "Oh, aren't I a clever girl. . . . They'll skin her for that."

In the hall Laurence caught hold of Lucy's shoulder and as he did so he also laid a hand on Paul's arm and, drawing them together, he bent his head down towards them, saying, "Stephen

214

and I here" – he glanced at the taller young man who was standing grinning now – "we think it best if you don't mention this episode to Mama or Papa."

The girl and boy stared back at Laurence; then the boy said surlily. "Papa doesn't hold with the lower classes learning."

"Now who told you that?" Stephen gripped his younger brother by the shoulder and walked him across the hall, saying, "Papa's go-ahead, he wouldn't mind."

"I think he would. Paul's right."

Stephen now turned and looked at Laurence and his eyebrows went up as he said, "You really think he would, Laurence?"

"Yes, yes, I think he would."

"Oh well, yes, I suppose you're right."

They had reached the drawing-room door when Laurence spoke once more to Paul and Lucy. In a quiet slow tone he said, "Mama would be greatly disturbed if she knew of two people who take jaunts on a Sunday and upset the stable lads and the laundry girls; especially would she be annoyed with you, Lucy."

The brother and sister exchanged glances; then Paul, his tone sulky, said, "We've got the gist, but why should you worry about what happens to a laundry skivvy?"

"Perhaps just because she is a laundry skivvy, and the lowest of all of them back there." He jerked his head towards the servants' hall. "And they can be even more deadly and spiteful than you two when they get going." He now grinned, and they grinned back at him; then Lucy, putting her head on one side, said quietly, "You would split on us, wouldn't you, Laurence, if we disclosed that that person could read and write?" And he nodded solemnly at her, saying, "Yes, without a moment's hesitation."

Then both Laurence and Stephen, and even Paul, were surprised at the girl's next words for, her lip curling, she said, "It only goes to prove that you are not our real brother." And on this she flounced from the door and made for the stairs, leaving the three males looking after her.

It was Stephen who, disturbed now out of his usual tolerant and slightly absent-minded manner, said, "I'm sorry, Laurence. That's unpardonable, really unpardonable. Why, you're more than one of us than . . . than" – he pointed to his younger brother – "than Paul there. I'll go up there this minute and shake her guts up, see if I don't." But as he made to dive off Laurence caught hold of his arm, laughing now and saying, "No, no, don't be silly, Stephen. Let it pass. I know Lucy. She'll be all over me in the morning."

Stephen puffed and blew for a moment, but only for a moment for he was quite willing to let it pass; he hated disturbances of any kind. Yet he was certain of one thing, his feeling for Laurence was that of a brother, a beloved brother at that.

He turned now and said to Laurence, who was moving away, "Where are you off to? Aren't you going to join Father for a drink?"

"I'll be with you shortly," Laurence called back; "I'm going to say good-night to Grandmama before she settles down."

"Oh, right. Tell her I'll be up in the morning. Doesn't want too much company at one go. Been a long day for her." ...

When Laurence entered the old lady's room, she was propped up in bed, and all except her head and neck seemed to be swallowed in the huge four-poster bed. He did not take a chair at the bedside but hoisted himself up on to the coverlet, cupping one knee in his joined hands. There he sat looking at the wizened face under the pink silk ruffled cap for a moment before he said, "Another one over."

"What are they doing down there now?"

"I'm not quite sure except that Mama and Papa and May are in the drawing-room, and Stephen and Paul have just joined them."

"Did you look in on the party?"

"Oh, yes, yes." His face twisted into a tight smile as he added, "And some party it was tonight."

"What happened? You look as if you'd enjoyed it. Don't tell me you danced with Collins or Nichols, or Mrs Amy Fulton, she of no body and less brain."

"No." He shook his head. "Something much more exciting than that."

"What could be more exciting than that?" Her lips screwed themselves into a smile, and he said, "I know one thing, you would have enjoyed it if you had been down there and witnessed what I did."

"Well, what did you witness?" Her voice rose. "Go on, tell me."

"Well, I won't be able to give you any real impression of the incident, and I'm sure you won't believe what I'm going to tell you. First of all, let me ask you a question. How do you view your laundry maids? Because they still are *your* laundry maids, the two older ones are anyway. I remember them from I was a boy. But there are three younger ones now, and the youngest of the lot ... oh, she can't be more than fourteen I think ... and yet I don't know, there's a kind of age in her eyes.... Can you recall the present giving?"

"Can I recall the present giving?" Her nose twitched. "What do you think I am, a bundle of old bones in her dotage? Of course, I can recall the present giving. What about it?"

"Well" – he laughed – "the very last one to come in was this young girl. She added a couple of extra words to her thanks, then her departure was slow as she viewed the room."

"Yes, yes." The old head nodded. "Yes, I remember the child. And I knew what would happen to her when she once got through those doors and was collared by Mrs Fulton, likely got her ears boxed."

"Well, that was she. She had to do a forfeit in a round game and she stood up there in the front of the whole lot of them and she quoted a verse from Shelley."

"Shelley? Who's he?"

"Oh, he's a poet. He died some time ago. His work is quite controversial at the moment."

"And she was *quoting* him, that girl?"

"Yes, and beautifully."

"How did that come about, a laundry maid quoting a poet?"

"Well, from what I can gather she came under the patronage of the late owner of Moor House, you remember, Mr Miller."

"Percy Miller? Oh, yes, yes. Hobson's hero."

"What?" He leant towards her and she repeated, softly "Hobson's hero." She nodded towards the end of the room where Jessie Hobson was putting clothes back into the wardrobe. "She used to work for the Millers, and apparently was in at that fellow's birth. Visited him until he died.... Didn't you, Hobson?" Her voice now rose and Jessie Hobson turned round and said quietly, "Yes, that's so, madam."

"You heard what was being said then?"

"Yes, I overheard, madam."

"Well, what do you know about this girl?"

"She's the daughter of the housekeeper who has four children, and Mr Miller taught them for so many hours a day, so I understand."

The old lady now looked with widened eyes at Laurence as she said, "Did you hear that? God in heaven, what'll be happening next? And she's in this household?"

"Yes, she's in this household. Well, in the laundry."

The muscles of the old face moved, making a pattern like water flowing over ridged sand, and then the bedclothes began to jerk up and down as the old lady's whole body shook with her mirth. And when she spluttered she grabbed at a lace-edged handkerchief lying on the silk coverlet and dabbed her mouth and then her eyes before she said, "Imagine what will happen when Lady Grace gets wind of this, a little scholar in her laundry. Not that she would recognize one laundry maid from another if they were pushed under her nose."

"That's not all." Laurence was now joining in her glee and he leant a hand on each side of her shaking body as he went on, "She says she can speak French and knows Latin into the bargain."

The old lady's laughter ceased and she said quietly now, "You're joking?"

"No, Grandmama, truly I'm not joking."

"Then all I can say, 'tis a great pity for the creature, for where does she think that will get her, only into serious trouble, as her head will be telling her she's too clever to use her hands. I've never gone along with any ideas of your father's, you know that" – she too alluded to her son being Laurence's father – "but I've always been with him in this business against the education of the lower classes, because where is it going to get them? Nowhere, except where they are at present, serving in one way or another and, in the main, yes, happy." She inclined her head in a deep obeisance now, giving her words authority as she repeated, "In the main, yes happy, because they are satisfied with their lot; but teach them to hold a pen and to read from a page, then you are dropping seeds of discontent into their otherwise contented lives. What is more, you know my ideas on God and His supposed directions for the human family. There are many things on which I disagree with Him. One such as you know is the superiority of man, which is rubbish. But with regards to His placing of human beings in certain positions, whereby a servant is subject to his master and in return the master has a duty to his servant inasmuch as he should see that he is fed and clothed in return for his labour, I'm in wholehearted accordance. So with regard to this little genius in our midst I would say that it's a pity she is here. No good will come

218

of it for the child, for as you only too well know once the mind begins to work it gropes at reason, and reasoning has no place in the life of a servant. You would agree with me, would you?"

"No, Grandmama, no, I wouldn't."

"You wouldn't?" The head came up abruptly from the pillow and the lace frills fell aside, exposing the bony shoulders, and again she said, "You wouldn't?"

And once more he replied, "No, I wouldn't. I'm for people using their minds, and whether we like it or not, more and more are doing it. There are great stirrings in the world outside our little domain, Grandmama. You wouldn't believe. Here" – he swept his arm wide as if taking in the whole domain – "in these two thousand acres is a world behind the times. Outside there are great rumblings below, and there are eruptions bursting to the surface here and there in strikes and murders. You did hear about the gibbeting at Jarrow, didn't you, of the miner who killed the deputy? And that's not all. They are bringing soldiers into towns to quell riots, and the navy into ports to guard the merchant ships. And as for reading and writing, men are defying their masters here and there and doing just that."

"*Nonsense. Nonsense.*"

"No, Grandmama, it isn't nonsense, it's common sense. It's got to come sometime."

"What has got to come sometime, equality?"

"Well, since you've said it, perhaps."

"Oh, *go away. Go away.*" She slumped down into the bed again. "Jack will be equal to his master when Christ makes a second coming and as, to my mind, He hasn't made the first yet, there's your answer. Go away; you tire me."

"I don't tire you." He was leaning over her again. "I annoy you by stimulating your mind. You know I do. I set you thinking. You said yourself, remember, I'm the only one in this establishment who can set you thinking. And ten to one this time next year you'll be using my tactics on someone else."

She didn't come back at him with, "Never! Never!" but surprisingly and in a small voice, she said, "I may not be here this time next year, Laurence. Sometimes I know I won't be here; other times I'm frightened that I won't be here. Death is a very frightening thing, Laurence, and I'm not prepared for it, I'm still too much alive up here." She now pointed to her frilled cap. "And as my mind tells me that there's no heaven and no hell, only a great nothingness, I'm afraid to go into it." Her hands now clutched at Laurence's, and he brought them together and stroked them as he said softly, "There may not be a heaven or hell, Grandmama, but there is surely a something. There is no great void, no great nothingness; that thing that's alive up there" – he nodded towards her head – "will go on."

"How do you know?" Her voice was a mere whisper now and that of an old woman, and as quietly he answered back, "I do know. I feel it, and I'm not the only one. There's new thought running through the world. The old ideas are dying; people are laughing at penance and purgatory. There are men who are performing miracles as Christ did, just by touch, and they are not charlatans, no more than He was. All right, all right" – he shook the hands he was holding – "He may not have been God, or the Son of God, but He was a great man with a great mind, and a greater spirit. So just think on that. Just think that that great mind of yours cannot die. Your body, yes, it will rot, but nothing can destroy thought. It cannot be touched, or seen, or held, yet it tells us everything. . . . Go to sleep now, dear, and remember one more thing: I need you, if it is only to argue with."

He bent now and kissed her wrinkled cheek; then he slid from the bed and walked out of the bedroom and into the dressing-room, where Jessie Hobson was arranging a complete change of her mistress's underwear for the morrow, and, stopping by her side, he said, "She'll sleep now, Jessie."

The woman turned to him and, her face solemn, she said, "You always do her good, Master Laurence, and she's always better when you're at home, but she's very fractious at other times."

"Yes, I know." He patted her arm. "She's not easy. . . . You look tired."

"I am a bit, Master Laurence."

"You should have help."

"I've put that to madam, but she won't hear of it."

He was on the point of wishing her a good-night when he turned and looked at her and said, "This child in the laundry, what do you know of her other than what you've said?"

"Only that she's very bright an' that Mr Miller thought highly of her. I'm sure he'd be disturbed if he knew that her mother had sent her into a laundry."

220

"Why did she?"

"Oh, well, as far as I can gather, from what little I know, she hasn't any money, and although Mr Miller left her the house...."

"He left her the house?"

"Oh, yes, sir, he left her the house, but no money to keep it up, and so she put the girl out to work, as her brother has been for the past few years. I think she hopes that she and her other children will be able to survive in that way, although I can't say how long she'll last with the small wage they both get. Oh, I'm sorry, sir. I know it's enough, because of their uniform and...."

"It's all right, it's all right, Jessie. I know what you mean.... Life's an odd mixture, isn't it?"

She paused before nodding and saying, "It is. It is, Master Laurence."

"Good-night, Jessie."

"Good-night, Master Laurence." And watching him leave the room, she thought, He's nice, but he's strange. Fancy talking like that about God. It's a wonder he wasn't afraid. And for a moment she felt afraid for him, because she had seen what happened to people who questioned the Divinity of the Creator.

In the far, far end of the house, in the last room that was ten feet by eight and at this minute deathly cold, Biddy too was thinking that life was very strange, so strange that it was making her cry. She was sitting on the edge of the pallet bed hugging her knees as she stared into the black darkness. Her outdoor coat was draped round her shoulders over her nightgown, and her day clothes were laid over the foot of the bed for extra warmth.

Jean had been asleep this past hour, tired with the excitement of the day and the joy of possessing a pair of mittens given her by her mistress, and a blue hair-ribbon which she had received from Biddy herself.

Biddy too had received a pair of mittens, but she thought nothing of them, she had knitted better ones herself. The whole day had held little joy for her except that she had been amazed at the beauty of the house. As for the party, she would know the result of that tomorrow morning, because after it had broken up the housekeeper had waylaid her and commanded, "Come to my office at nine o'clock in the morning." And then as she had passed the butler and the footman, they had looked down on her as if she was some strange creature, and the butler said, "My, my! it's comin' to something, it is that."

Oh, she wished she could go home.... Yet, there had been one bright spot in the day. The two young masters had spoken to her so nicely, and the one called Mr Laurence reminded her in some way of her old master, and he seemed to know about poetry. She thought she could like him, but not the two younger ones. She knew spite when she saw it in people's eyes and the young miss had really turned her nose up at her, as had her brother.

There were a lot of strange people in this house. She had felt lonely at times for people back in Moor House, but here there were too many people, and all of them, it seemed, at one another's throats by what she could make out from the bits of gossip she overheard. So she supposed she wasn't the only one that was going through it.

Oh, he wished she was home. If she did something awful she would be sent home. But then what would her mother say? Perhaps not very much, but she would think all the more, losing two pounds twelve shillings a year, and having to feed her. But surely there were other jobs she could get. But what kind of jobs? What was she fitted for? All she could do was housework, or digging, weeding, and planting, and now, of course, laundry work. Oh, that place. She ground her teeth, then flounced round and into the bed and pulled the covers over her head. If she ever got sent away from this place it would be for going for that Mrs Fitzsimmons.

But the following morning at nine o'clock as she stood before Mrs Fulton's desk in her box-like office, the housekeeper almost took the laundress's place in Biddy's mind as a means of being dismissed, for she kept ranting on at her, as if last night she had committed a crime in saying her poetry. Dirty, she called it. A young girl like her reciting about kissing. And now she seemed to be almost frothing at the mouth as she said, "And you had the affrontry to stop and speak to the young masters."

"I didn't. One of them pulled me to. . . ."

"Don't you dare answer me back! Don't you dare speak until I give you permission. All you had to do was to dip your knee and listen, then walk away."

"I'm not dumb."

"How dare you!" This last was a bellow that brought the woman to her feet, crying, "If it wasn't that Finch has gone sick with stuffing herself, leaving Mrs Fitzsimmons short-handed, I would send you packin' this very minute."

Biddy watched the housekeeper's chest move up and down. It reminded her of the bellows back home in the kitchen. And now after one long breath the housekeeper said, "I have asked you before, I'll ask you again, what did the young master say to you?"

When this question had been put to her before she had answered nonchalantly, "He just talked," fearing that if she had repeated what he had said it would have aroused the woman's wrath. But now, throwing caution to the wind, she put it in a nutshell by saying in no small voice, "He asked me how I'd become educated?"

It wouldn't have surprised Biddy if the housekeeper had collapsed on the floor at that moment; but what she did do was turn her head to the side and then move it in a half circle while her eyes appeared to follow an imaginary object. But when once more they were glaring at Biddy she became speechless for a moment; then, her words struggling out of her small puckered lips, she said, "Girl, you have no place in this household, and I'm going to make it my business to see you leave it at the earliest possible time. Do you understand me?"

Biddy's whole body was trembling, part with injustice and part was a dry sobbing that was racking her chest. When now the housekeeper's arm was thrust out and her finger pointed, like a stick of lead, towards the door, Biddy turned and stumbled out. No sooner had she reached the passage than the tears forced themselves over the lump in her throat and flowed down her face, and blindly now she continued down the passage instead of taking a turning that would lead to the yard door, and so entered the kitchen, and for a moment she quelled the laughter round the table where Kate Pillett was enjoying a joke with Mr Laurence.

Laurence had always been a favourite of the cook's since he was a small boy and when he was at home it wasn't unusual to find him sitting on the edge of the table munching one of her pies.

Anna Smith had her head back laughing loudly, as had Daisy Blunt who was peeling vegetables at the sink, but Daisy kept her back turned which proved she was concentrating on her work and not taking advantage of the young master's visits.

The laughter ceased and they all looked at the girl hurrying down the room and rubbing one cheek after the other with the back of her hand. And she paused for a moment near the table and looked at the cook before running out of the kitchen and into the boot room and so into the yard. She had appeared oblivious that one of the young masters was in the kitchen and she had passed him without dipping her knee.

Laurence now looked enquiringly towards the boot room and then at the cook, and she answered his look by saying, "Oh, she's been getting it in the neck from Mrs Fulton. It's about last night, sir."

"What did she do last night?"

"Oh, well." The cook now rolled out some very thin pastry before she said, "She made a bit of a show of herself saying those rhymes like that, though meself, I thought it was funny. But coming from such a youngster, well . . . anyway, she's not the type that will reign long here. Mrs Fulton was only looking for an excuse to get rid of her, and this'll be it. Anyway, laundry maids are ten a penny. Would you like another pie, sir?"

"No thanks, cook. No thanks." He smiled at her now, adding, "As usual they spoil my appetite for my meal."

"Go on with you, sir. If I remember rightly, you used to be able to eat six at one go and come back for more."

"I was filling out then. I've got to think of my digestion these days. But thank you; as usual your pastry is excellent."

Again the cook said, "Oh, go away with you, sir." Then both she and her assistant dipped a knee as he nodded to them before making his way up the kitchen.

Once he had gained the house he stood for a moment considering. It was no business of his, and yet in a way it was. He had stopped the child and talked to her and therefore he knew he had put her in a position of envy, and the little lady Fulton was showing her powers. He paused a moment, then with a quick right about turn he went once more behind the screen, through the green-baized door and into the corridor. And there he knocked on the housekeeper's door, and when he was told to enter the woman was so surprised she popped up from her seat, saying brightly, "Well, Mr Laurence, what can I do for you?"

"I've come after a position."

"Oh, Mr Laurence, you're always a tease." Her voice and manner were coy, and he smiled at her as he said, "Well, Mrs Fulton, what I've really come about is to apologize."

"Apologize, sir? What on earth have you got to apologize for?"

"Well, it's about that incident last night, Mrs Fulton. You know, that child." He paused as if it was difficult to remember the incident, then went on, "I think now I was very remiss in talking to her. Looking back on it, it seemed as if I was singling her out, and it was never my intention to do so. But at the same time she seems a very bright little girl. Don't you think so, Mrs Fulton?"

"Well, sir, I . . . I find her . . . well, rather forward." The coyness was slipping now.

"Yes, yes, I . . . I agree with you, but . . . but merely in a scholastic way, which is very unusual I suppose in the position she holds. But perhaps you'll take her under your wing, you're so used to seeing to young girls like her. And—" He smiled broadly now, even laughed a little as he added, "I was telling madam about the incident last night and she was most interested in the fact that a child like her should be quoting Shelley . . . you know, Shelley the poet."

"Er, oh yes, yes, sir." The tone was flat now.

"Well, I thought I would just apologize for what was really my fault and for what, on her part, might have appeared unseemly behaviour. But I knew you would understand. You must make allowances for me: it was Christmas Day and I'd imbibed a great deal of wine. Well, they are waiting for me in the stables and I must go and shake up an appetite." He smiled again at her, adding now, "You have put on a splendid table for us these last few days, Mrs Fulton. It's a credit to you. Goodbye."

"Goodbye, sir."

In the main hall once more he stopped, closed his eyes for a second and said to himself, How could you? Talk about being smarmy. Then chuckling inside, he answered himself, saying, All in the furtherance of education. Isn't that what I aim to do? As he hurried now towards the front door he cast his eyes around him as he answered his own question by saying, Yes, but not here or in these parts. By God no. Oxford or no place.

4

Laurence Gullmington would have been both interested and amused if he had witnessed the course education was taking in the very end room of the north wing of The Heights most nights of the week when four heads were bent over a solitary candle.

It happened that Florrie McNulty had learned of Biddy and Jean's midnight vigil, not only of learning letters but of story reading. She had risen one night from her bed next door and come into the little room to tell them to stop talking, as she couldn't get to sleep for the muttering. Florrie McNulty was thirty-four years old and when she saw what the fifteen-year-old Jean had already learned from the newcomer, she was both amazed and intrigued, and in a hesitant way had asked Biddy if she would teach her to write her name. Of course Biddy was only too pleased to have another pupil, but there was a snag. Florrie shared a room with Sally Finch and Sally Finch always sucked up to Mrs Fitzsimmons, and what the three of them were sure of was Mrs Fitzsimmons would never submit herself to being taught anything by Number Four, or the runabout, as Biddy was known. And, as Biddy pointed out, Sally would go and split on them, but Florrie McNulty said, Oh no, she wouldn't, because she had something on Sally that would keep her mouth shut, and even persuade her to join the classes.

So it was that they now had two whole candles a week ... and not only two, for part of Florrie's position in the laundry was being in charge of the candles there, and she was able to save all the butts. What was more, Florrie had the knack of making candles from the melted wax and string.

The lessons had begun in the New Year, and by Easter three laundry maids could not only write their names, but many single syllable words and almost as many two-syllable words. Moreover,

Jean and Florrie McNulty could count up to fifty, and Sally Finch to twelve. Sally Finch did not grasp things as easily as the others, yet because she was learning she had, in a way, become a different kind of person.

They all knew at times that Mrs Fitzsimmons was puzzled by their attitudes towards each other: there was no bickering among them, and when they could, without making it too obvious, they would help each other. The laundress wasn't used to a happy atmosphere. She was a bully by nature and she thrived on discord, but her shouting and yelling seemed to be having little effect on her staff these days, and when she came to think about it, it was all since that smarty miss had come into the laundry. There was something about that one that she didn't trust. And it was said in the house that Mrs Fulton had been on the point of packing her off but had been warned not to from above. Now why was that? Something about old madam having an interest in the girl. Yet to her knowledge, old madam had never sent for her, nor clapped eyes on her, except at Christmas, when, once again, she had made a show of herself.

Every leave day now Biddy took Jean home with her and they would bring back a different book with them. Biddy had taken her little stock of books back home because during one of her weekly examinations of the rooms, Mrs Fulton had seen Biddy's books on the window sill, and having picked up one after the other as if she was able to read them, she had informed Biddy to get that rubbish out of her room or else it would find itself in the fire.

There was a plentiful supply of paper and pencils in the library at Moor House, but she only took a few sheets back with her, and each girl hid her work under her mattress.

Jean being with her on her visits home meant that Biddy had little private talk with her mother, but even so she sensed that she was very lonely, and at times she would say to her, "I saw Tol, and he was by himself." And only last week she dared to say, "Ma, you know something?" And when her mother had said, "What?" she had added, "Tol hasn't got a woman now. He's living by himself." And her mother's stiff reaction was, "How do you know that? Did he tell you?" to which she had answered, "No, not really, but I know it's true. It came in a roundabout way. It appears that the mistress got wind of it and he was warned, so the story goes, because the mistress is very pious."

It was at this stage that her mother almost turned on her, saying, "And he put up with it, sent her packing? He's gutless. That's what he is, gutless. What business is it of theirs up there what a man does after his working hours? They want to look to their own men if I'm to believe all that Fanny says. Pious indeed!"

Biddy had returned to the house thinking that at times she couldn't understand her mother. She knew for a fact that she wasn't for Tol having a woman, and yet she was blaming him for giving her the push. There were lots of things that she couldn't really get to the bottom of. She had learned a lot about life from her reading, yet it seemed a different kind of life to that which went on under her nose. Real life wasn't so nice or so easy, nor yet, at times, so terrifying as the life she had soaked up from her books, but she knew that the book life was the life the master had led, and it was something apart.

But you couldn't live apart in the house, nor could you be unaware of the intrigues that went on, not only whispered but things seen with her own eyes, like what she had come across up the woodland path between James Simpson the first footman and Mary Watts the first housemaid. She was walking up the pathway on the soft snow and they hadn't heard her, and there they were, standing by the tree in the deep twilight, locked so tightly together as if they were fighting. It must have been Mary Watts's leave day, because she had her hat and coat on. But the footman was still in his bright uniform. He was very bossy, was the footman, and you had always to give him his place and say Mr Simpson to him. As for Mary Watts, she was haughty, almost as haughty as Miss May. And yet they had been doing that. Life was very strange.

But Easter was coming and her mother was making her a new frock from some beautiful material out of the attic trunks. What was pleasing her more than anything was, their Davey seemed to be taking a liking for Jean, and Jean was over the moon. He'd often come to the laundry window on a Sunday and talk to Jean as much as he did to her. He had changed, had their Davey, not only in his looks but in his ways. He hadn't been very ready with his tongue when he was at home, but now he was, and he made jokes. Only one thing he wasn't happy about, that she was teaching the others to read and write. He had warned her, saying, "That could get you into trouble. Deep trouble. They're funny about that here. For meself, I never let on I can write, I sign me name by a cross." And she had turned on him and exclaimed, "Oh! our Davey, after all the learning you got." And to this he had answered, "Well, that doesn't stand you in any stead in a house like this. Do your work, know your place, eat your grub, and be thankful. That's what I say, and you'll be wise if you follow the same line."

She would never follow the same line, for she knew there was something inside her that would urge her to protest, no matter what the consequences. At times she wished she didn't feel like this, and once or twice she'd had to curb the feeling, as when the young master and mistress were out for a game and would come rampaging through the laundry kicking at the bundles of washing and grabbing up ladlesful of dirty frothy water and throwing it over the girls, the while Mrs Fitzsimmons laughed her head off at what she called their pranks.

Today was her and Jean's Sunday on. Mrs Fitzsimmons, Florrie, and Sally, were all on leave. It was a beautiful bright day, and near four o'clock in the afternoon, and they had just finished putting the staff underwear into a sawn-off tub of cold water and the men's underwear into a similar tub standing nearby.

Drying her arms on a piece of coarse sacking, Jean said, "Doesn't look as if Davey's gona make it the day, does it, Biddy? Perhaps they've made him change his day again 'cos the masters are joining the riders."

"Oh, there's plenty of time yet, up till six o'clock."

"Yes, but he's nearly always here afore now."

Biddy turned to her companion, "Well, if he doesn't come," she said, laughing, "I'll march straight along into the stables and say to Mr Mottram, 'Where's me brother? Why hasn't he come along to see us this afternoon? Now answer me. Quick. Come on now. I'm not having him sent to that Lord Milton's place with the horses, they can find their own way.'"

She was mimicking Mrs Fulton, and as Jean doubled up with laughter there came a sharp tap on the window.

Both girls ran to it. Thrusting it open, they looked bright-eyed at Davey. But Davey wasn't smiling today. "I can't stop," he said immediately; "I've just come to warn you to look out, Miss Lucy and Paul are on the rampage, carrying on like two kids. They've been in the harness room and messed things up, dabbed things with blacking. Mr Lowther's furious. He told Mr Paul that he would see the master. And Mr Paul called him a stupid old pig. I think you'd better scoot across to the house as soon as possible."

"We can't do that, Davey; we're here till six and there's quite a bit more to do. If we went across there afore that time and ran into Mrs Fulton, that would be worse than meeting up with Mr Paul and Miss Lucy." She smiled now, and he replied, "I don't know so much." Then looking at Jean, he paused before saying softly, "Hello, there." And she replied as softly, "Hello, Davey."

"Well, I'd better be goin'." He nodded from one to the other and then slid out of sight. And the girls closed the window and walked back to the middle of the room where Jean asked, "What'll we do if they come in here and start playing up?"

"Well" – Biddy wagged her head – "if they mess up the sorting like they usually do, I'm going to leave it like that until the morrow morning, and if Mrs Fitzsimmons says anything I'll tell her that the young master and mistress were in here working yesterday and this is the result."

"You won't."

"Oh, yes I will."

And from the look on Biddy's face and the sound of her voice Jean knew that this mentor of hers would do exactly as she said. Her admiration for Biddy was boundless. She had never met anyone so brave and so clever. Each day she told herself that she loved her.

It was almost an hour later when the girls let the big wooden-slatted drying-horse down from the ceiling. It was a heavy cumbersome affair, especially when as now the five rails were laden with the rough ironing, which had been done last thing the previous night, and consisted of all manner of towels.

Biddy had just secured the rope around the iron staple in the wall when the laundry door burst open and in marched Paul Gullmington and his sister Lucy. They were both in riding-habit, each carrying a small whip, and as if they were still on their horses they galloped down the length of the long room making whooping noises, until they came to a standstill opposite the two girls.

"Well now! Well now! What have we here? Two foxes?" Paul looked at his sister. His eyes were bright, his mouth wide with laughter. Her eyes too were bright, but her mouth wasn't wide with laughter, she was concentrating her gaze on the skivvy whom Laurence had favoured on Christmas night, and whose face over the past weeks had intruded into her vision more than once, as would have done any face that Laurence favoured. Laurence was her favourite and, she had imagined, she had always been his. She had decided that she would marry Laurence when she grew up, that's if May didn't get him beforehand, because he wasn't her brother. Yet this skivvy here had dared to hold his attention.

"What do we do with foxes?" She looked at her brother, and he replied, "Chase. Chase!" And now they both started to do a standing gallop, smacking their sides with their whips, and at this Jean turned and ran.

They did not, however, pursue her but cried at Biddy, "Run! fox. Run!"

When, ashen-faced, she remained standing still, the boy grabbed her by the shoulder and pushed her forward; and when she stumbled he pushed her again.

Jean was now standing at the far end of the wash-house pressed tight against the wall, and Biddy was being pushed towards it when suddenly she turned round and faced her tormentors, crying at them, "Stop it! both of you. You're acting like idiots."

They stopped abruptly, and their expressions changing, they glanced at each other and the boy said, "She called us idiots."

"Well, she would, she's very learned. She can write her name and speak French and Latin. Didn't you know?" And she now went into French, saying, "Que je suis une fille habile." And now he, throwing his head back and looking upwards to the ceiling and lifting his hand high in blessing, exclaimed loudly, "Gloria in excelsis Deo."

The charade might have ended here if Biddy had been able to stay her tongue, but her face scarlet with temper, she cried at them, "And both your accents are provincial."

This is what the master had continually said to her over the years: "Don't talk like a provincial. This is not patois; you are speaking the French language as you would your north-country English."

The effect of her words on the two young people opposite her was to take the grins from their faces. The very fact that this lackey could use the word provincial, and was applying it to them, enraged them both.

What followed happened so quickly that it brought screams from both Jean and Biddy, for when Lucy Gullmington's whip came across Biddy's ear and the side of her face, the echo of it hadn't died away when she felt herself thrust backwards; and then she was toppling, and for a moment she lay stunned, oblivious of the cold water soaking her clothes, for her head had come in contact with one side of the tub and the backs of her knees with the other. But the ice-cold water did one thing for her, it revived her anger to such an extent that she struggled to rise; but did so only with the help of Jean's hands. Then she was standing dripping in front of her tormentors and as quick as her young mistress had attacked her she reciprocated, for she almost sprang on her now and, twisting her around, she thrust her against the other tub of men's underwear and into it. It was all done so quickly that the boy had no power to prevent it happening.

The strange thing about it was that Lucy Gullmington didn't scream; but the sounds she was making were like throttled groans, and when her brother pulled her out, her riding-habit smeared with the scum from the dirty water, she stood shivering, for the water had penetrated to her skin. Then thrusting her brother's protective hands from her, she growled, "Get her!" before her eyes, darting from one end of the laundry to the other, came to rest on the lowered drying-horse.

Biddy was now struggling with the young master, wreathing and twisting in an effort to get free from his arms which were tight around her. But she was no match for him. Between her gasping she was aware of two voices, Miss Lucy's giving orders and Jean's crying, "Oh, don't! Please! don't. Don't!"

She knew a moment of terror when, lying flat on the stone floor now, the young master sitting on her legs while pinning her arms together, she saw the girl sweep the linen from the two lower rails; but her mind still didn't tell her what was in store for her, not even when she heard linen being ripped. Then her arms were dragged above her head and her wrists tied together so tightly that she cried; and her ankles, too, were tied, but not close together.

She screamed out, "Jean! Jean!" but heard only the young master's voice growling, "You make a move and you'll be next."

When they hoisted her to her feet she would have fallen had she not been held up roughly by the back of the collar of her dress. The next thing she was aware of was the creaking of the pulley that lifted the drying-horse; then the girl's voice said, "Just there." Now she was being dragged under the bottom rail of the horse and her joined hands were tied to it with strips of linen. But still she couldn't imagine the ultimate until she felt her arms were being wrenched from their sockets and only her toes were touching the ground. Her screams deafened her; then they jerked the pulley rope and she stopped. In the strange silence that enveloped her she looked down at the two faces staring up at her and she imagined she was looking at devils and the last thought she was conscious of was that they had done this before, they knew exactly how to do it, and they were crucifying her like Jesus on the Cross.

So intent had the two young fiends been about their business that they hadn't noticed that Jean had escaped by the back door and into the yard; and now she was flying helter-skelter towards the stables, crying, "Oh dear God! Oh dear God! Oh dear God!" as she went.

So intent was she in her rushing and so blinded with her own tears that she bumped into two men. One of them had to put his hand out to save her from falling backwards. And now she was looking up into the faces of Mr Stephen and Mr Laurence. They were both in their riding-habits, and she cried at them, "They've got her strung up. Please come. Come on. Please, come. They've got her strung up."

"What are you talking about, girl?" Stephen shook her shoulder, and she gulped and the saliva ran out of her mouth before she could say, "In the wash-house. Master Paul and Miss Lucy, they've strung her up."

The two young men turned and looked at each other and it was Laurence, his face twisting, who said, "Strung who up?"

"Biddy. They've strung her up . . . on the drying-horse."

Again the men looked at each other. Then turning, they ran together down the stable yard, round the corner of the coach house, and into the laundry yard. But when they entered the laundry they both came to a dead halt at the sight of their brother and sister standing below a girl who was hanging by her arms from the bottom of the drying-horse.

It seemed that Stephen took only two strides before he reached them, and what he did was instantaneous. With doubled fist he felled Paul to the ground, then with open hand he brought it hard across Lucy's face, causing her to cry out and to stagger back into Laurence's arms. But Laurence thrust her aside as if his hands had been stung, and then reached up to take the weight of the limp figure in his arms as Stephen lowered the drying-horse and then untied the knotted linen. When he pulled it away from the rail, so Biddy's dead-weight limp body slumped through Laurence's arms to the floor.

As the two young men stared apprehensively down on her Stephen said, "Oh, my God, no! Try her heart."

Laurence put his hand inside the collar of her dress. At first he could feel no beat until his fingers moved; and then he nodded and, looking at Jean, who was kneeling on the floor opposite him, he comanded, "Go and get the housekeeper, quickly." Then he looked to where Stephen was standing over his younger brother, growling now, "By God, I'll take it out of your skin for this, young 'un. And wait till I tell our father. If you want to sport, sport with those that can strike back."

Paul was holding his jaw and he looked defiantly at his brother as he said, "She pushed Lucy into a butt."

"There must have been a reason for it. There's a reason why you two are in here. What brought you? As for you—" He turned and looked to where Lucy was standing staring towards Laurence as he knelt on the ground by the side of the hated girl, and he said, "This will put the final stamp on it, miss. Mama won't be able to save you now. You had a warning last time: one more escapade and it's away to school with you, where they might knock some manners into you. But as regards manners" – he was glaring at Paul now – "school doesn't seem to have done much for you. For two pins I've a mind to kick your bare arse till you can't sit on it."

"Look here." Laurence was beckoning to Stephen now and gently he turned Biddy's face to the side to show a red weal rising from the middle of her ear down to the side of her chin. "What does that signify?" he asked, and Stephen, now glaring at his sister, was almost made speechless when Lucy, staring back at him, said, "And I'll do it again."

"By God, you will, miss!" He strode to her now and, swivelling her around as if she were a bundle of straw, he almost lifted her from her feet as he hopped her up the laundry and thrust her out of the door. But when Paul made to follow her, he said, "You stay where you are, laddie. There'll be work for you to do if I know anything."

Mrs Fulton came hurrying into the laundry, only to stop and look aghast for a moment at the scene before her. Then, as she stood above Biddy's prostrate form, she muttered, "That girl again. She's always in trouble."

"And whose fault is that?"

The little prim face became tight as she said, "No one's but her own, sir, I would say."

"And would you say there was any reason for her to be strung up to that contraption?" Laurence thrust his arm back. "What if she had died from shock?"

"Well, it certainly wouldn't have been my fault, sir, as I had no hand in the business."

No, she was right; she'd had no hand in the business. The hand or hands had come from her betters. He looked at the little woman with dislike as he now said, "Get someone to carry her to the house and put her to bed, and see that she's attended to."

As she turned away, Stephen cried, "No need to get someone, Mrs Fulton, my brother here will be only too pleased to carry his victim to the house. Won't you, Paul?"

"I'll do no such thing."

"You won't? But, by God you will!" The heavy boot caught the young fellow in the buttocks and nearly lifted him from the ground, and his face red with anger, he cried, "How many more of those will I have to give you before you do what I tell you? Pick her up."

"I could never carry her; she's too heavy."

"She wasn't all that heavy when you strung her up, was she? Now get at it, or do you want another?"

The boy's teeth were clenched, his face almost as red as his hair, and as if he were being forced to touch something unclean, he bent and slipped one arm underneath Biddy's thighs and the other under her shoulders. But he could not have got to his feet with her except for Laurence's help. Then he was staggering up the laundry with his burden, and would surely have dropped her had not Laurence taken the girl from him, crying, "Open the door," as he did so.

Paul stumbled forward and thrust open the doors and stood aside and watched the man, whom for years he had thought of as his brother and whom he had never liked, stumble out and across the yard under the gaping mouth and wide eyes of a number of the staff, and into the house through the boot room.

Paul now walked out of the laundry and into the house by the main door; then made his way up to his sister's room. He went in without knocking, and as he looked at her he was surprised to see that she was crying. He put an arm around her shoulders and said, "Don't you worry. We'll get our own back on that creature one way or another. It might take time, but you'll see, we'll do it. You'll do it your way and I'll do it mine. Oh yes, I'll do it mine."

5

❧❧

There was a feeling of excitement running through the staff, and none so high as in the laundry, for tomorrow was the thirty-first of July.

The laundry staff had always been aware of their status in the household. No one could get lower than the laundry staff except the cesspool cleaners, but they came from outside and weren't even allowed anywhere near the house. The nearest they got to any of the staff was when they delivered their loads to the farm and this only happened three times a year. So the combined efforts of the laundry staff – with the exception of course of Mrs Fitzsimmons – was to show them.

It just might have been possible that Biddy would have taken notice of Davey's warning with regard to the signing of names had it not been for the incident in the laundry. It had left a deep mark on her that she could have been subjected to such torment through, in the first place, no fault of her own, except for being audacious enough to answer the young master and mistress back, but to be held responsible for what had happened by those in charge, including both the butler and the valet besides the house-keeper, had incensed her.

What had happened, Mrs Fulton had informed her, had happened because she was what she was, a troublemaker, a harbinger of ill fortune. Nothing, Mrs Fulton said, had been the same since she entered the household, for, before that, who would have thought of Mr Laurence and Mr Stephen going for Master Paul and Miss Lucy, especially when, as everybody knew, she doted on Mr Laurence. All right, they had strung the girl up. She hadn't been the first one that had been strung up; and, too, she had got off lightly because she hadn't been flogged. If it had been in the days of the old master she would have been, and she wouldn't have dared open her mouth. Well, Mrs Fulton had informed her, the matter had gone before the master and mistress and they had agreed that she was to have another chance. If it had lain with her, she knew what chance she would have given her. And poor Miss Lucy being sent off to school when everybody knew Miss Lucy hated school. She would hardly attend to Miss Collins's lessons, all she wanted to do was ride. And what was wrong with that for a young lady? As for Master Paul, his allowance had been cut. What did she think about that? Couldn't she see that she was a troublemaker.

Biddy had lain in her bed for three days, and for the first day she had hardly known where she was. Her mind played tricks with her, taking her into the fanciful stories she had read. She had seen herself gambolling through forests, sailing over seas that were beyond imagination, and, strangest of all, being wooed by a prince. She had hung on to that part of her delirium. They had called the doctor into her the second day and he greeted her with, "Well, well! the lively pupil." He had examined her and found her unhurt except for the weal down the side of her face, which, he had said, would fade with time.

How the news of the incident had spread to her mother, she didn't know, but she came on the third day and said she was going to take her home; and in spite of this being her dearest wish and then her hope, she had refused to go. The reason for her change of mind escaped her at the time, but shortly afterwards she knew that the reason was to do with defiance, for she meant to show them. She meant to show that she was different from the lot of them: she was learned. She was determined not only to read more, but to carry on studying her French and Latin. This she knew might be difficult without guidance, but she was going to try.

But now the excitement that ran through the staff section of the house would reach its highest point tomorrow at the end of the corridor of the north wing, for the four laundry girls were going to sign their names when they received their half-pay.

The procedure of pay-day was similar in a way to that of the present receiving on Christmas morning. The only difference was, they went one after another into the library where, at the head of the long table that ran down the middle of the room, sat the master, while standing to one side of him on this day was his new steward, Mr Daniel Yarrow, and to the other side of him, his butler Thomas Froggett.

As each member of the staff approached his name was called out by the butler and the steward checked it from a long list and stated the amount to be paid; then the master counted it out before handing it to the butler, who handed it to the recipient, then said, "Sign," which meant in every case a mere cross.

The head of each department had preceded its underlings; and now at the end of the long list Mrs Jinny Fitzsimmons sidled into the room, subservience oozing out of every pore of her large body. When she received her six pounds ten shillings, she dipped her knee, looked at the master and said, "Thank you, sir," to which he did not reply with a movement either of the eye or head, but sighed as he continued to look down on the long list of wages he was being forced to meet. When the steward now read from the list saying, "Florrie McNulty, assistant laundress, three pounds nine shillings," Mr Gullmington counted the money out, handed it to the butler who then, handing it to Florrie, said, "Sign."

And Florrie signed. Slowly, in copperplate writing, she wrote, "Florrie McNulty."

A cross takes but a second to make, but fourteen copperplate letters took over forty seconds and brought three pairs of male eyes on her. When she had finished she straightened her back, smiled, dipped her knee, and said, "Thank you, sir," backed two steps from the table and marched out. And march is the descriptive word.

The three men now looked at each other but said nothing.

Then there entered Sally Finch, and the steward read out, "Sally Finch, staff scrubber laundress, two pounds twelve shillings." The master handed the money to the butler and the butler handed it to Sally, saying after a slight hesitation, "Sign." He pointed to the paper, and Sally, before signing, looked up at him and smiled. She had only ten letters to her name, but it took her almost as long to sign as it had Florrie.

After she had dipped her knee and said, "Thank you, sir," and departed, the master looked at his butler and said, "What is this, Froggett?" And Froggett, after a slight gulp, said, "I . . . I wasn't aware that they . . . could write, sir."

The steward was now saying, "Jean Bitton, scrubber laundress, one pound sixteen and threepence."

Jean looked nervous. She was remembering what Davey had said: unlike Biddy and the rest, if she got the push she had nowhere to go, only back to the poorhouse. But nevertheless, she wrote the name that had been given to her when at the age of six months she had been placed in the care of the poorhouse authorities, Jean Bitton.

There was silence among the three men now as they waited for the last laundry assistant to enter, and at least two of them knew who was the instigator of this insurrection. The butler had no doubt whatever in his mind; and the master had heard of the poem reading on Christmas night, but more so, there was in his mind now the incident when this girl entering the room now had so enraged his daughter and son by ridiculing their French pronunciation that they had strung her up, and in doing so had created a division in the family, which was apparent to this very minute.

Anthony George Gullmington considered himself an easygoing man. He did not demand much from life, so he told himself: a good table, good wine, his body needs satisfied, but most of all some good horseflesh between his legs. That's all he asked. For the rest, he paid a large staff to see to the running of his house. By God! he did pay too. Look at the money that had passed through his fingers this morning, besides which he had to pay to clothe them from head to foot and allow them to eat their heads off, and drink his wine. Oh yes, he knew what went on all right, he was no fool. But as long as they kept their place he closed his eyes to lots of things. That was the main thing though, they keeping their place. He was not a religious person, not like his wife, at least he was no fanatic, but he did believe that God had ordered a certain way of life for different beings and that way could not be carried out unless the lower classes were kept in their place and accepted their place; and their place was to work with their hands and only to use their heads as much as was necessary to achieve the best results of their labour. So far and no further. But once a man started reading and writing, then you had trouble. He had an example of it among his own. Well, not exactly his own. Stephen was no scholar and Paul was going to follow suit, but Laurence preferred a book to a horse. And that wasn't natural for a gentleman, except he intended to turn into a crank, like that one who had died recently over at Moor House. *Yes. Oh yes.* And this was the result of his crankiness coming towards him now. How old was she? She was tall; she looked sixteen or more, and good-looking. She'd be a beauty in a year or two's time, with a figure to go with it. Well, if she was wise there were uses for that figure. But he doubted if this one would be wise, for she had already got a taste of the power of the pen and she had sent three examples in before her. My God! He felt an anger rising in him. Here was the kind of person who instigated trouble and upheavals. If she had been a man there was no knowing what she would have caused. Anyway, she had already caused enough in this household, but she'd cause no more.

The steward called out, "Bridget Millican, laundry" – he paused on the next word – "runabout". Apparently he had not heard of such a title before. "One pound six shillings."

Anthony Gullmington counted the money out, handed it to the butler, and the butler, pushing it across the table to Biddy, pointed to the paper and in a voice that sounded like the knell of doom said, "Sign."

Biddy looked from one to the other of the men; then she signed her name. It did not take her many seconds and she did it with a flourish. When she went to dip her knee and say, "Thank you, sir," the master looked at her and he said, "Since when have you been given authority to teach my staff to write?"

The response of Biddy Millican from the pit row might have been, "What ... what do you mean, sir?" But Bridget Millican, who had come under Percival Miller's tuition, said, "I did not think I needed permission, sir; I did it in my spare time."

"You knew that it was forbidden."

"No, I did not, sir."

"Well, miss, let me tell you, it is forbidden. You are here to work. You have been assigned to a certain position. That is all that is required of you. If I wished my staff to be educated, I would give the order for it. Do you understand me?"

"Yes, sir." The big brown eyes showed no fear of him. There was a strange quietness in their depth that, for a moment, made him want to retaliate, just as his son and daughter had. Who was this girl anyway? What was she? How dare she! What were things coming to! The platitudes raced through his mind. Now turning his glaring gaze on the butler, he said, "Fetch me the house-keeper." Then to Biddy, "As for you, wait outside."

Biddy might have appeared calm, but it was only on the surface for inside she was trembling, and she felt sick. There was a slight commotion in the hall, a bustling of servants, some of them looking up the stairs. The butler now passed her with the house-keeper and if she had any doubts that her time here was short, their looks confirmed it.

They had no sooner entered the library than the master's voice could be heard bawling at them, and as he preceded them from the room still bawling, two footmen carried Madam Gullmington's chair down the last of the stairs and placed it in the hall.

It was her custom on a fine day to be wheeled around the garden, and this was a fine day, a soft windless day, but the old lady gauged immediately there was a high wind of temper blowing through the house, and as she saw her son approaching her, she stopped him, saying, "What's all this?"

"What's all this?" he repeated. "Defied in my own household." He pointed to where Biddy stood waiting with downcast eyes. "That individual has been running a tutoring under my very nose, under the nose of this entire staff presumably. Four sluts from the laundry signing their names in full. How many staff have we here, Mama? You tell me. Have any of them been able to read or write? Oh . . . Fulton" – he waved his hand to the side – "she can write her name and count, and that's about all, because she has to. But for the rest. . . ."

"Be quiet." She was staring fixedly at her son. Then she ordered Jessie Hobson now, "Take me to the drawing-room," and Jessie, obeying, pushed the wheelchair into the drawing-room, and as she turned to leave, Grace Gullmington entered.

She was dressed for the carriage in a voluptuous skirted blue taffeta gown over which was a cream lace coat, its skirt kept up balloon-wise by the dress. Her hat was of cream straw. It was a tall hat, its crown bedecked with flowers, its intent to give height to its wearer, but it achieved only the opposite effect. She had the appearance of an overdressed doll. But her voice was by no means doll-like as she demanded, "What may I ask, is this narration about?"

"You may ask, woman." Her husband was bawling at her now. "If you saw to this staff as you should do, the present occurrence would never have happened: nor would that incident three months ago have taken place. You haven't any idea how to bring your family up, madam. If you stopped praying and did a little more saying, this household would run more smoothly. We never had anything like this in Mama's time, did we?"

His face was almost ruby red as he addressed his mother, and her reply was, "Shut up, Tony, and sit down and calm yourself, and tell me what this is about."

As if he was still a young boy, her son immediately sat down and after drawing in a number of hissing breaths he said, "It's that young skit who apparently was given a little knowledge by that mad bloke down at Moor House, and she has passed it on to the rest of the laundry staff, except the top one. They all came in there this morning" – he thumbed towards the fireplace – "and signed their names, brazen as brass. Rows and rows of crosses, and there were these three scum signing their names. And all through that miss, who also prides herself that she can speak French. Did you ever hear of any such thing?"

"She'll have to go."

Anthony Gullmington now glared at his wife as he shouted "Of course she'll have to go. She should have gone long before now."

Then the attention of both was drawn again towards the old woman in the chair for she had laid her head back against the leather cushion and was staring upwards, her eyes wide in her face that looked like a mask, so thickly was it powdered. And now she began to talk: "Yes," she said, "send her packing. And the others with her if you like. Yes, do that, and it will be all over the county that Gullmington couldn't bear any of his staff to write their names." Her head came forward now as she went on, "Not that I'm for the lower classes writing their names or being educated in any way, no, I'm with you there, Tony, but what I'm thinking about is, you've decided that Stephen must try for Parliament next year. Now as far as I can gather from both Laurence and Stephen there are men up there who are making themselves felt calling for certain liberties for the lower classes, and causing contention in this house at the present moment, trying to get bills through to establish schools for the education of the poor in every parish in this country. Now of course they can push all the bills through the Commons that they like, but it's getting them through the Lords. That is the crucial point; and I think there is as much chance of getting education for all the poor through the Lords as that child who has caused a rumpus becoming Queen of England. But that isn't the point" – she now looked at her son – "the point at the moment is, education for the lower class is a platform from which young men may spring quickly into prominence, young men like Stephen who have never been heard of outside this county." She drew a long breath before going on, "Now Tony" – she nodded slowly at her son – "it is your dearest wish, isn't it, that Stephen will some day take his seat in the House? Well, can you tell me what his policy is going to be? Is he going to shout for the status quo as ninety per cent of the landowners in the country are doing, or join the other ten per cent, some of them, I understand, factory owners in the Midlands who have cut as much as an hour off their employees' day; and moreover, besides their free Sunday they allow them to finish at four o'clock on a Saturday. Eh? Eh?"

"Now all this you should have learned from your son and Laurence over the past weeks, for quite candidly I have become weary of the conversations that have flowed back and forward over my chair, and even over my bed at night, between them. And I can tell you this, and it's not going to please you, particularly you, Grace." She was looking at her daughter-in-law. "If anyone should stand for Parliament it should be Laurence, because his cause seems to be, again this controversial word, education, and if Stephen ever does take his seat up there, he'll have Laurence to thank for stuffing some facts into his head and giving him a purpose, because he would never have found it on his own, being too much like his father." And she riveted her gaze on her son. "All you have ever thought about, Tony, from the time you could crawl, has been horses. There may have been one or two other things that have alighted on your horizon, but they've taken second and third places. Horses. Horses. Horses. And Stephen is no better. Oh, I'm not saying" – she moved her head from side to side – "I'm not saying that Stephen is not a decent enough fellow. I'm very very fond of Stephen, and I will prove it if he carries out this idea, for to be a member doesn't so much require brains as money; it will take large sums to pave the way and buy him in. And you, Tony, no longer have any large sums to play around with, have you? I could say, you could of course pave his way with the money you spend on horseflesh, but that would be asking too much, wouldn't it?"

"*Oh, Mother.*"

"Don't say, 'Oh, Mother,' like that to me; you know I am

speaking the truth. But let's get back to the point. If you dismiss this girl and the reason for it spreads, Stephen will have to find another crutch on which to help him limp to London, because education was going to be one of the flags he was going to fly to attract the attention of his peers. Of course" – she pursed her wrinkled lips – "there's always the other side of it, he could take the opposite course and sit unnoticed among the old fogies up there until his beard touches his knees."

She watched her son now lumber to his feet and heard his teeth grind against each other before he said, "I'm against it, Mother. You know I'm against that kind of education."

Her voice was soft as she replied, "Yes, I know you are, Tony, as I am, and as is Stephen at bottom, but do you know anybody who has ever furthered himself politically by coming out into the open and standing up for what he knows to be right? You tell me of one. Parliament to my mind is a rookery: everyone of them cawing, cawing, cawing, in order to stay on their bit of the branch. And they all caw the same tune. If they changed it, the rest of the flock would attack them." She now turned and with a grin on her face, she nodded at her daughter-in-law, saying, "A very good simile that. And when I'm on about birds, compare the number of eagles with rooks. They are few and far between, but by God, don't they stand out. And some of them even come to believe in the noises that they're making. Not that I think Stephen has the makings of an eagle, but he could come in under one of their wings, to be noticed. Well, what about it?"

"What do you want me to do?" Her son's voice was quiet now. "We can't keep that girl on after this. The staff wouldn't tolerate her."

"Who's master in this house, you, or Fulton and Froggett? Anyway—" she now bounced her head towards first one then the other, clasped her thin white lace mittened hands together before stating, "I'll take the girl."

"*You'll what?*"

"You're not deaf, Tony; you heard what I said. And this business seems to have come about at an opportune time, because Hobson's feet won't carry her much longer, and this girl can be trained to fetch an' carry. And I shall certainly see that she has no opportunity for furthering her education as long as she's in my house. It's a solution, as I see it, that will benefit everyone in the

245

long run. She can come off your wage sheet, I'll see to that; the staff will be glad to get rid of her; and what's more, your name won't be bandied about for dismissing a poor little mite because she could write her own name. I can just see it. I can just see it. ..."

"I don't see this matter your way, Mother-in-law." Grace Gullmington's voice cut in deceptively quiet. "No, I don't. I think she should be dismissed, and I'm sure our neighbours and the people who matter will agree with Anthony's" – she inclined her head towards her husband – "decision. No one could blame him in the least, in fact I'm sure he would be hailed. ..."

"Don't try to be more stupid than God made you, woman."

The insult brought a scarlet flush to Grace Gullmington's face and a reproving, "Now, now, Mother," from Anthony, and she turned on them both, her eyes flashing now. "You are a pair of nit-wits," she cried. "Always have been and always will. And of the two, you are the bigger, madam." The saliva actually spurted from her lips on the last word. "And let me remind both of you, I may keep to my own end of this establishment but what should be evident to you is, I still rule it, because if I were to decide to move myself to another estate, and I could do, my legs may be weak but my head is far from it, I take my money with me." She now let her blazing gaze rest on her son as she ended, "And how long would you survive on your two thousand a year? This house is yours by inheritance, but it needs one hell of a lot of money to keep it up. You would, I foretell, be living in a dower house within months. So think on it. As for you, madam" – once more she was looking at her daughter-in-law – "don't you dare say to me that you will not have such and such happen here. How you ever came to be mistress of this place will always be a mystery to me. Now if it had been your despised cousin, Laurence's mother, I could have understood it, because besides beauty, she had brains. And that's why you hated her, wasn't it? Why, if it hadn't been for me, you would have rejected her plea for a home for her child. In fact, you did reject it, didn't you? Although she had been deserted and was dying, you hadn't it in your mean little heart to give her succour and. ..."

"Mama! Mama!"

"Don't you mama me. You will not stop my tongue at this stage; this is always something that I've wanted to say. Now ring that bell for Hobson." She flung her arm out towards the bell-pull hanging by the fireplace. "And let me say this finally, if I hear one more aggravating word I will do as I threatened a moment earlier. As you both know, Buxley Manor is up for sale and I've always liked that establishment. I would be doing Lord Milton a service in buying it, for he has run out of money for his gambling up in London. ..."

The door opened and when the butler appeared, the old lady cried at him one single name, "Hobson."

Jessie now came hurrying into the room as quick as her painful feet would allow and as she turned the chair round and went to wheel it into the hall, the old lady cried, "That girl, the one that has caused the uproar, where is she?"

"In the hall, Madam."

"Send her up into my house and tell her to stay there. I will see her on my return. *Now*." She cried the word at the two footmen, and they once again lifted the chair and carried it out through the front door on to the wide drive.

As this was taking place Jessie Hobson hurried across to Biddy where she was standing in the shadow of the stairs, and said to her, "Go to the west wing, madam's house."

Biddy was unable to speak for a moment and she gulped and sniffed before she could say, "I ... I don't know which way.... And why?"

"*Never mind why, girl.*" Jessie now turned and, beckoning June Cordell towards her, she said, "Take this girl up to madam's house. Put her in my sitting-room." And the woman said, "Yes, miss;" then beckoning to Biddy, she took her past the foot of the main staircase, across the hall, through a side door, along a passage, and up two flights of narrow stairs, then through another door; and now Biddy found herself in the gallery of the house for the first time. The maid hurried her along it, then pushed open one side of a heavily embossed cream enamel double door, after which she put out her hand and pulled Biddy inside and into the hall that opened out of the west wing gallery. There were a number of doors leading from the hall, also two passages. At the end of one passage the maid thrust open a door and, pointing, she said, "Stay there." But instead of turning immediately away and scurrying back as she had scurried here, she looked at Biddy through narrowed eyes, saying, "Eeh, the things you get up to. It's as they say, there's never been a one like you here afore. Why do you do it?"

She waited for an answer, but Biddy remained silent. She was too bemused to even think of a reply. In the ordinary scheme of things, she should be on her way out with her bundle after that commotion in the drawing-room, for it had just sounded exactly like a row in the pit row on a Saturday night when some of the men had come home rolling drunk. It was impossible to believe that the gentry could raise their voices like that. Young ones, like the two that had attacked her, oh, yes, them, but not when they were grown up and held positions. Why had she been sent up here? Suddenly she sat down on the nearest chair which was a rocking-chair and to the amazement of the housemaid she began rocking herself.

As June Cordell was to say in the staff room later on that day, the sight of the girl sitting there rocking herself and not saying a word, as cool as a cucumber like, gave her quite a turn. She agreed whole-heartedly with the rest of them that there was something odd about her. And fancy finding all that stuff in her mattress, and that book that the housekeeper said was a foreign one, besides the one with poems. And that wasn't all. Look what they had found in the other laundry maids' mattresses, practically the same, except they hadn't any foreign books. It was right, there was something weird about her, and things had never been the same in the house since she came. And remember what the parson had said last week about evil spirits. Well, there was something in that. But then look where she had landed? Up in the choice part of the house. Anyone of them would have given their eyeballs to be promoted up there permanent like, because it was a sure thing that Miss Hobson's feet wouldn't hold her up much longer, and now it could be possible that she would train that one to take her place. Eeh! it was incredible.

Everyone around the table agreed that it was incredible.

But this was to be at seven o'clock that evening.

Upstairs, sitting on the rocking-chair, Biddy did not put the word incredible to her situation, for she was unable to think clearly about it all. She did not know what was going to happen to her, nor why she had been sent up here. There was only one thing sure, she would soon find out.

It was over an hour later when she found out. Jessie Hobson, coming into the room, brought her to her feet, and the older woman, wagging a finger at her, said, "Now Biddy, listen to me. I haven't much time to prime you, all I can say is there's a chance in a lifetime staring you in the face. It's up to you how you behave, whether you get it or not. Do you understand what I'm saying to you?"

"Not . . . not quite."

Jessie closed her eyes for a moment, then said, "Well, it's like this. Madam has saved you from being thrown out. Why, I really can't tell you." Her voice sank. "She's a contrary character; she could have just done it to spite the mistress, but for what reason doesn't matter. You're up here and your job will be to run, and fetch, and carry. Do all the menial jobs, but at the same time watch me and all the things I have to do for madam; then if you can fit in, who knows, she might take to you or she might not. If she takes to you, she'll give you a rough time; if she doesn't take to you, you won't be here to have a rough time. Now, do you understand me?"

"Yes, Miss Hobson."

"Well, come along now. But there's one thing I'll tell you before you start: you've got everybody in this house, except" – she pulled a long face now – "your pupils, agen you, and I'm not only meaning the staff, but them up top an' all. So if you want to remain here, you've got a battle on your hands."

She didn't want to remain here. But then what was she thinking? One day she could become a lady's maid. The glory of the sudden realization lifted her chin and straightened her shoulders, and now she followed Jessie Hobson out of the room, along the wide corridor, past four doors, then stopped with her before another set of double doors.

Jessie tapped lightly on one door, then pushed it open, at the same time taking Biddy by the hand, and then slowly led her to where the old lady was sitting in a blue velvet-padded chair near the window.

Biddy had never seen the old lady close up before. She looked terribly old to her. She thought she had never seen anybody look as old, not even the very old women in the hamlets, because even if their skin was wrinkled, it still looked like skin, whereas this face was so painted and powdered it looked like one of the china dolls she had seen the one and only time she had visited Gateshead Fell Fair.

"Well! Well! So this is the creator of all the trouble."

The voice had no connection with the face for it was strong and vibrant.

"So you can read and write, miss. You have also touched on French and Latin, so I understand. Well! Well! How learned you must be."

Biddy felt her face growing scarlet. She was being made fun of.

"Speak to me in French."

When Biddy remained silent the voice barked at her, "Do you hear me, girl? I said, speak to me in French."

Her mind was going at a gallop trying to form a sentence. Then the words threw themselves at her; they jumped into her mouth and from her lips and she said, "Bon jour, madame. J'espère que vous êtes en bonne santé."

"My God!" The old lady was looking up at Jessie Hobson now, and she cried, "She can! She can do it. And you know what she said to me, Hobson? No, of course you wouldn't. She said—" She turned her head now towards Biddy and commanded, "Tell her what you said in English."

Biddy wetted her lips, swallowed, then said, "I wouldn't be so bold, Madam."

"Do you hear that? Do you hear that, Hobson? What are things coming to, eh? A laundry slut, only one above the sewage cleaners in status, speaks to me in French, then disobeys my order."

Her manner changing, and her rouged and powdered face seeming to crack as it was screwed up and thrust towards Biddy, she cried, "Well, let that be the last evidence of your learning I am to hear. Do you understand me? There'll be no more French up here, and no more reading and writing. Speak girl. Do you understand me?"

Yes, Biddy understood all right, but she couldn't answer, or she wouldn't answer, and so Jessie put in hastily, "I'll see that she doesn't, mad...."

"Shut up! Hobson. Let her answer for herself. Do you understand me, girl?"

"Yes, madam. I understand you perfectly."

The words were spoken in a way that Percival Miller would have approved of, and they caused the old lady to sit back on her chair and to close her eyes for a moment. When she opened them again she stared at the flushed face before her, the brown eyes looking straight into hers, and her voice was deceptively soft as she said, "You understand me; that's good. But do you mean to obey me?"

A large section of Biddy's mind cried at her: Say yes. Say yes. But when she heard herself say quietly, "I cannot promise faithfully, madam, to obey you on that point," some part of her shrank down inside and buried its head, waiting for the onslaught, while she continued to stare into the small faded blue eyes that were glaring into hers. She watched the head turn slowly and look up at her maid, and she listened to her saying, "We can understand now, can't we, Hobson, why the whole household is up in arms?"

"Yes, madam." Jessie's voice was small, her face was wearing a pained look, and she cast her eyes towards the girl she hoped would be her charge but whom she could now see haring out the back gates with her bundle.

"Do you think she realizes that she has set this whole household agog today, and, from what I can gather, not only today? Do you think she knows that she's got all the staff against her?"

"Yes, yes, I think she does, madam."

"You think she does?" The head was turned towards Biddy again, and now the question was put to her: "Do you know, girl, that you have got all the staff against you? And for whatever time you stay in this house, long or short, their feelings towards you, if I know anything about that class, will remain the same, if not intensify. Do you know that, girl?"

What had she to lose? She was for the road in any case. Yet, of a sudden, she didn't want to be for the road; she somehow felt that she would like to work for this old woman. Why? She didn't know, because she could be a holy terror, she could see that. A small section of her mind asked her how the master would have answered in this case; and then he was in her mind, pushing the words through her throat, into her mouth, and they came out as she said, "I know fine well, madam, how I am looked upon by the staff, but I would be willing to put up with that if I could be employed in your service, and although I cannot promise you truthfully I shall never read or write again, I can promise that I shall work well for you and give you my loyalty for as long as you need me, that is, if Miss Hobson—" She now glanced at Jessie Hobson, whose face seemed to have stretched the other way, as she ended, "if she will guide me to know your wants."

It was then that the most surprising thing happened, surprising not only to Biddy, or to the lady's maid, but to Diana Gullmington herself, for she put her head back and she laughed. She laughed heartily for the first time for many a long day, for she found that she was being both amused and interested by this creature from below stairs, well below stairs.

When the water from her eyes made rivulets down through the powder and rouge, Jessie grabbed at a fine lawn handkerchief from a box on the table to the side of her and as she handed it to her mistress she smiled at her. "Take her away and get her decently clothed," the old lady said.

6

During the time the domestic upheaval was taking place Stephen and Laurence were touring France; May was with a distant cousin enjoying for the first time the London season; Paul was staying with a school-friend in Durham; and Lucy had only on that particular morning taken coach to Doncaster where she was to spend some weeks of her summer holiday with the family of her father's cousin. She had travelled chaperoned by the family's children's governess who had been sent to escort her. This was the second year she had holidayed with this family; the first time she enjoyed it immensely as there were three sons all older than her, besides two who were younger, and to all she had been able to show off her prowess as a horsewoman.

So it was that only when each of them returned at different times during the next weeks did they learn of the uproar that the laundry maid had caused yet once again; and their reactions were all different.

Stephen had said, "She isn't up there? Not on you life!" May had said, "It's disgraceful. How could you allow it, Mama?" And her mama had answered her with one word, "Grandmama," which told all. Lucy Gullmington had actually stamped her foot and declared that if she should cross her path, she would slap her face for her, to which Laurence had replied quietly, "I shouldn't do that if I were you for in some curious way that child has a habit of winning." To which Lucy had replied, "Child, indeed! She's no child; if she's a child I'm a child. She's an upstart skivvy, and I'll never be able to understand you taking her part." And May had put in at this stage, "He does it just to vex you ... and me. Don't you, Laurence?" And Laurence had said, "Don't be ridiculous."

The only person who didn't make any comment at all was Paul, and Laurence took note of this and didn't like what it signified. ...

He had only been in the house a few hours when he paid a visit to the west wing to be greeted by Diana Gullmington holding her arms out to him and crying whole-heartedly, "Oh, I am glad to see you back. Do you know I have been very worried, especially when I learned there were summer storms at sea."

"Oh, Grandmama—" He kissed her on both cheeks, then took his seat beside her as he said, "The crossing was the proverbial millpond. Of course it had to be; I ordered the waters to be still. However strong Stephen's stomach is on land, it becomes a weak thing when it is set upon water. He had a fearful time going over."

"Did you enjoy your trip? Tell me, tell me all about it."

"Oh, yes, we enjoyed it thoroughly. Paris I found very civilized at the moment."

"Really!" the old lady cut in now. "Civilized you say? Which Napoleon is it who's trying to scare the world now? Candidly Laurie" – she put her hand upon his knee – "I've been worried all the time you and Stephen have been over there. Civilized, you say?"

"Well, in Paris that is, but as one travels through the country there's a great deal of poverty, but it's a different kind of poverty from here."

"Poverty!" She stressed the word. "You didn't go to France to seek out poverty."

"But if it's staring you in the face, Grandmama, you can't help but see it, and smell it."

"Oh!" She wagged her hand in front of his face and her nose twitched as if she was already experiencing the stink as she said, "Thank God you're not going in for politics, although at one time I used to think you should, because the trouble with you, unlike Stephen, you would be voicing your own opinions and that would never do in Parliament."

He wasn't aware of the door opening or that anyone had entered the room until she looked beyond him, saying, "What is it, girl?" And now he turned in his chair and saw a young person, tall and slim. She was wearing a pale blue cotton dress edged at the neck by a small white collar and white cuffs at her wrists. On her auburn hair was a small cap which in no way covered her head, but was perched like a crown in the centre of it. The face underneath the cap was cream-skinned, the cheeks flushed slightly pink; the eyes were deep brown and long-lashed; the eyebrows followed the bone formation; the mouth was large but well-shaped; the nose was small and the chin firm. The girl was the same, yet not the same as the one he had lifted down from the laundry dryer. That face had appeared like one on the point of death, this face emphasized glowing life. He thought he had never seen a face that expressed life so vividly, yet in what way he found it hard to define, for she wasn't smiling; her expression, he would say, was neutral.

"I have brought your milk, madam." Biddy set the small tray with a glass of milk on the side table, and the old lady said, "My goodness, is it time for that again?" Then looking at Laurence, she added, "That old fool Pritchard has stopped my afternoon wine. He says it's going to my legs. I told him not to be an ass; good wine never drops below the chest." She gurgled at her own joke; and Laurence joined her, then asked, "How are they?" And she, looking down at her blue taffeta skirt said, "Still there I suppose, but sometimes I don't know what use they are. Why should this happen to me? I ask you. I've lived a moderate life; I've never exceeded three glasses at dinner, never; I like my afternoon nip, but what's that, I ask you . . . Girl!" She was now yelling at Biddy, and Biddy half-way to the door turned about, and the old woman, still yelling, cried, "What have I told you about waiting to be dismissed?"

"I thought madam having company. . . ."

"You're not here to think. I've also told you that. Away with you."

Once the door closed she asked of Laurence, "What do you make of that, eh? Did you ever see the likes, how she answers back?" Then thrusting her face towards him, and her eyes twinkling and her lips pursed, she said, "I'll let you into a secret. I enjoy her in a way. You know why?"

"No, Grandmama."

"She's not afraid of me. Now isn't that strange? She's not afraid of me. Old Hobson was scared out of her wits for the first year or so, and she's been with me now all of thirty years and at times she's still scared. But that one, with her reading and writing which I've forbidden her to continue, she's of a new generation, don't you think?"

"Yes, I do think so, Grandmama."

She leant back, surveying him through narrowed eyes as she said, "I suppose you've heard all about the rumpus and the reason why I brought her up here?"

"Yes." He nodded his head slowly at her. "I've heard one version of the reason, diplomacy with regards to Stephen and Parliament. But that wasn't the real reason, was it?"

She grinned at him now as she said, "It's the only satisfaction I get out of life, opposing her. I'm very loyal in my likes and dislikes, Laurence, and I've never forgiven Tony for landing me with a daughter-in-law like her. Why should he pick such a mealy-mouthed, pious piece, I ask you? He was a rake and was off with this hussy and that, and I'd rather have had any one of them any day of the week than that one." She thumbed towards the bedhead. "And he became a different character once she got him. He's almost as mealy-mouthed now as she is. Do you know he was the means of two servants being sent packing with their bellies full in his young days? Did you know that?"

He hadn't known that and he didn't smile at the new knowledge.

"Of course he couldn't hold a candle to his father. As for his grandfather, whose exploits Harold regaled me with on our wedding night during the time he had breath—" she pulled a face now before going on, "it would appear that if any male servant wished to marry a female one, he had to get his leave, and his price was to test the qualities of the future bride." She now stopped, her eyes narrowing still further as she said, "You're not amused, are you, Laurence?"

"No, Grandmama, I can't say I am."

"You're not against women, are you?" The question was serious and he answered her seriously, "No, Grandmama, I'm not against them, not at all."

"How many have you had so far?"

He rose slowly from the bed, saying now, "That is my business and mine only."

"Oh" – she flapped her hand at him – "don't you start being mealy-mouthed, else that'll be the end of me. Go on, get yourself away."

He didn't obey her, but smiling low, he leant towards her, saying softly, "You know what you are? You are a wicked old woman."

She stared back into his face for a moment before replying, "Wicked I may be, but old I'm not, except from here." And now she brought her hand across her eyebrows, then added, "Admitted from here downwards, but above that, I am no more than thirty."

He laughed out aloud now, saying, "You're right, perfectly right."

"Laurence" – her voice was low now – "have you thought of marrying?"

"Yes. Yes, I've thought of marrying, but that's in the future."

"Anyone in your eye?"

He cocked his head as if considering, then looking back at her, he said, "No, no one in particular."

"Have you ever thought of May?"

The question brought him ramrod straight, and now he drew his chin into his cravat before repeating, "May! You mean as a wife?"

"Yes, I mean as a wife."

"Oh, Grandmama, you must be joking. She's . . . she's. . . ."

"She's not, she's no blood connection with you whatever. Well, if there is any there it's such a thin line it wouldn't help to make a spider's web."

"That may be so, but she is my sister in all other ways."

"She is not your sister in all other ways, and she's got you lined up."

"Oh, Grandmama" – he gave a slight laugh now – "this is sheer imagination."

Her manner changing abruptly, she said, "Don't tell me that I imagine such things. I am versed in the ways of both women and men. I can interpret a look half a mile away, so to speak. May is fond of you, more than fond of you."

"Well, if that is the case, Grandmama, she's going to be very disappointed, because I don't, and never have, and never will, consider May as anything but a sister."

"You're a fool then. Next to Stephen, she could be very well off when I go. As for you, do I have to remind you that you haven't got a penny?"

"No, you don't have to remind me, and I am very conscious that I owe my upbringing to you, but as for not having a penny, I understand that I shall come into a little money when I am twenty-five, and in the meantime, if I had to, I could earn my living by teaching. In any case, I mean to teach, and this will bring me in enough to live on."

"Money when you're twenty-five, and what will that be? A measly three hundred pounds a year. It wouldn't keep you in cigars."

"Then I won't have to smoke cigars. Goodbye, Grandmama. I'll see you later." As he turned abruptly from her, she called after him, "Pighead. Stupid, short-sighted pighead." And after he had closed the door her voice still came at him.

As he was passing down the hallway Jessie came out of the adjoining room, and he paused for a moment and after exchanging glances with her he shook his head before hurrying along the gallery and to the double doors. As he neared them, one opened and Biddy came through, and she side-stepped quickly and held it back so that he could pass. And he had gone through without a word to her and she was about to close it when, swinging round, he took a step backwards and, stabbing his finger towards her chest, he muttered, "Don't let her stop you reading. Do you understand? Do it on the quiet, on the sly, but don't stop."

Her eyes wide, she moved her head once as she said, "I won't, sir;" then added, "I haven't."

"You haven't?"

"No, sir, I haven't, I mean stopped reading."

He stared at her for a moment longer, his face still expressing his annoyance; then, he gave a shaky laugh before saying, "Good. Good. Keep it up," then turned from her.

Jessie was waiting for her at the dressing-room door and immediately she said, "You shouldn't have told him that. What if he lets it out downstairs?" She pointed towards the carpet, and to this Biddy answered, "He won't."

"How do you know?"

"I . . . I can't tell, but somehow I don't feel he would give me away."

"You know, girl," Jessie said, "sometimes I think you take too much on yourself, and one of these days it will trip you up. And where will you be then? Flat on your face. Go on" – she gave her a slight push – "get the bath ready. And I'm warning you, be prepared for squalls because she's got to take it out on somebody, and I know who that'll be tonight." She nodded and smiled grimly, and Biddy, looking at the kindly woman over her shoulder, said, "Yes, and I do an' all."

7

❦❦

Biddy's leave day had been altered, but Jean would still continue to go to the house. Davey would now accompany her, and this, Biddy guessed, would add to the pleasure of her visit because, as had been evident for a long time, she had definitely cottoned on to Davey. However, Biddy wasn't sure that the feeling was returned in that way by her brother. Somehow you could never be sure how their Davey really felt.

And not only had her leave day changed but she had been deprived of one by way of punishment, and so it was a month before she saw her mother and Johnny and Maggie again.

Riah, of course, had been given all the news from Davey and Jean, but she knew nothing about the workings in the domain in the west wing. And now, sitting on the bank of the stream while the two younger children splashed in the water, Biddy regaled her with the daily routine in madam's household. And at this point, Riah exclaimed in amazement, "You've got to bathe her?"

"Aha, every inch of her." Biddy now spluttered and put her hand over her mouth. "The first time I helped Miss Hobson I thought I would have died. I did, Ma, I thought I would have died. All the stuff had to be taken off her face with grease."

"And you had to do that?"

"Well, not for the first week or so, but now I do it."

"And bathe her?"

"Well, yes, I help. Oh, and Ma, oh" – she closed her eyes and shook her head – "you wouldn't believe it, because she looks so grand, regal, like an old queen when she's sitting up all dressed, even in bed she looks like that, but in the bath, you know what I likened her to in me own mind? A long piece of wrinkled clay with four sticks attached."

"Oh, lass." Riah was now flapping her hand at Biddy while she rocked herself backwards and forwards.

Biddy, in her element now, went on to describe the preparation. "Imagine that's the bath." She pointed to two rocks sticking out of the bank. "Well, at the top end, on the outside of course" – she bobbed her head now – "there's two hooks and on these goes a special towel, and it covers the whole top of the bath, and madam sits on this, I mean she's lowered on to it so that none of the spelks stick in her." She swallowed and muttered. "You know what? The funny thing is the towel keeps floating up between her legs and it's all I can do at times not to burst out laughing. That is until she starts on us if the water's not warm enough, or it's too warm, or the soap slips and we have a job to find it. Eeh! Ma" – her face became serious now – "I just don't know how Miss Hobson managed on her own. No wonder she can hardly walk on her feet 'cos even with the both of us we're running all day to her bidding ... madam's bidding, but—" Her expression changed again and, laughing once more, she said, "But when we get her out of the bath she has to be powdered all over, you know like you used to put Fuller's Earth all round Maggie. Well, it's just like that except this is very scented powder. Oh, it has a lovely smell. And she has cream put on her face every night, and then last thing a kind of a strap under her chin. I'm not joking, Ma. Listen ... stop laughing, it's the truth."

They now fell against each other and during the seconds they remained so, Biddy knew a happiness that she hadn't experienced for some time.

When they were sitting straight again, Riah said thoughtfully, "You know, when our Davey came back and told me what happened I couldn't believe me ears. I mean, to be lifted out of the laundry and into a position like that. But it was right what our Davey said."

"What did he say, Ma?"

"Well" – Riah plucked at some blades of grass before going on, "He said, in a way he wasn't surprised because things always happened to you; you made them happen, and always would." She smiled now as she added, "He said he'd never be surprised at anything you did. And he had Jean doubled up in the kitchen when he said, if the King came riding through The Heights and said, 'Where is Miss Bridget Millican? I want to take her up to London,' he said you wouldn't turn a hair, you'd say, 'Thank you very much, sir. Just wait a tick till I get me bundle an' I'll be with you.' It isn't often our Davey's funny or cracks a joke, but that Sunday I laughed more than I'd laughed for a long time. Except just now about that bathing business."

Biddy was looking into the stream to where the children were splashing each other and her voice was quiet and serious sounding now as she said, "He's not right, Ma, I mean about me not turning a hair, because I get very frightened at times. And it's odd, but when I do it makes me do things as if I wasn't frightened. You know what I mean, Ma?" She turned and looked at Riah, and Riah, answering truthfully, said, "No, not really, lass; I don't think I'll ever know exactly all you mean. But ... but oh, I'll tell you this, I am glad you're out of the laundry. I did feel guilty for pushing you in there, because I knew you were worth something better than that. But I felt you had to start somewhere, and ... well, you knew how I was fixed."

There was silence between them for a moment until Biddy asked tentatively, "Are you very lonely, Ma?"

"At times. Yes I am at times."

Impulsively now, Biddy screwed round on the grass and said, "Why don't you let Tol come and see you again?"

"He has been."

"He has?" Biddy's voice was high.

But Riah's tone was flat as she answered, "Yes, he has."

"And ... everything's going to be all right?"

Riah now began pulling the grass up by handfuls as she said, "Not as you mean it."

"Why?"

"Well, it's very ... well, sort of complicated. I'll ... I'll tell you the whole of it someday, but ... well, I can't marry him, or anybody else."

"He asked you to marry him?"

"Yes, he did." Riah brought her head forward to emphasize her words.

"But what's stopping you, Ma?"

"A number of things, which would take a lot of explaining. So ... so don't ask me any more. Don't probe. Everything's all right. I've got a good home, a beautiful home, and I might as well tell you I love the house and I never thought to see the day when I'd own a place like it. *Never. Never.* What's more, you're all set to rise in the world. And that's all I'm gona say for the present, so don't keep on, just let things settle."

"Will he be coming back, I mean calling ... Tol?"

"That's up to him."

"Oh, Ma, why can't you have him? He could do so much here about the place. And it would be lovely, and. . . ."

"I'll say two things more and then we won't talk about it for a long, long time. He wouldn't come here, that's one thing. The other thing is, I wouldn't go there, not to his place. Now that's my last word on the subject at present. Come on." She jumped up from the green. "Let's go back and get some tea. . . . Come on, you two. Stop messing about and come on if you want anything to eat." She turned away now and walked up the meadow; and Biddy stood looking after her, oblivious of the children sitting now on the bank chatting up at her. She couldn't imagine her mother turning away the love of a man like Tol just because she wanted to live in this big house. Her mother had changed.

For the little while they had been sitting on the bank here and during that moment when they held each other, her mother was the woman she had known during the first months in this place. But during the last few minutes she had reverted back to the other person, still her ma, but not the tender loving creature she seemed to remember from years ago; no, she was someone who was so changed that she was now weighing up the house and its possessions against the love and comfort and companionship of a man, and of such a one as Tol. And the odd thing about it was, she knew her mother loved Tol. Yet, as she had already learned, there were all kinds of love, some outweighing others. And the house had outweighed Tol.

The sun had gone from the afternoon. . . .

An hour later she had taken two slim volumes from the library, slim, because she wanted to put them in the pockets of her petticoat, pockets that she had made for this very purpose. Now she was ready to go, and she was giving herself plenty of time because the day was hot and she didn't want to hurry.

They all set her to the gate, but when Riah held her close for a moment the joy of the previous embrace was lacking. Johnny and Maggie insisted on walking a little way along the road with her. Unlike herself and Davey they both seemed to have stood still with the years and she looked upon them as young children, although Johnny was now fourteen and Maggie thirteen. Then Johnny demonstrated his age when, out of earshot of his mother, he said quietly, "Biddy, do you think you could speak for me to be set on with our Davey?"

Immediately she turned on him, saying angrily now, "No, I can't. And you're not going there. Who's going to look after the garden here? And Ma's lonely enough without you going. Now get that out of your head. And you don't know what it's like up there. There's no positions like assistant lady's maid down in the stables, I can tell you that; you're knocked from dog to devil. Our Davey had to go through it. It's a wonder he stayed. If he hadn't been mad on horses he wouldn't."

"I'm fourteen, Biddy."

"Aye, you might be" – her voice softened now – "but wait a while."

"I'm not gona stay here forever."

"No, I don't suppose you are. But stay put for the time being, and don't upset me ma any more than she's been upset lately."

"She should have married Tol; he wants her."

She actually stopped and looked down on her sister now, and Maggie, from the wisdom of her thirteen years, said, "We're not blind, Biddy. We know what's going on."

"All right." She drew in a deep breath, before adding, "If you know what's going on, then have a little patience and a little thought for Ma. She's not happy at all."

"Neither are we. We never see anybody from one week's end to the other."

Biddy stared at Maggie. She was small and slight for her years, but she was pretty. Her eyes were green and her hair was brown and her skin was clear. She understood how she felt about not seeing anyone, because she herself, at times, felt lonely up in the west wing, not that she ever wished herself back in the laundry, but she did wish she could see a few more people, people that she could talk to. The only talking that Miss Hobson did was to instruct her into what a lady's maid did and did not do. She missed the company of Jean at night; she missed the chatter; and so she knew how her sister felt; and her brother also. Her voice much softer now, she said, "Hang on a little longer. You never know, things might change."

"Pigs might fly."

She gently cuffed her brother's ears as she said, "Go on, Mam's waiting. She'll be wondering what we're talking about. Try to be content. Go on with you."

"Ta-ra," they said. And she answered, "Ta-ra."

As she made her way along the road she felt disturbed, not only about her mother now, but about the two youngsters. Maggie would have to stay put, but Johnny, being a lad and lively, would, if he took it into his head, go off at any time. There were always young lads running away to sea or joining the army.

Having enough time at her disposal, she did not keep to the main road but went out of her way to take the side road leading to the little fall.

The little fall was just what it said, a sheet of water tumbling over rocks not more than eight feet high. At different times during the past summers she had taken Sunday walks here and sat on the bank below the fall. She had never taken the others with her on these walks, it had been too far anyway for the young ones' legs, and Davey, even in those days, saw little beauty in nature, except the sight of horses galloping across fields.

She now took off her hat and short grey coat that her mother had made her to go with her best dress; then taking one of the books from her petticoat pocket, she told herself that she would have five mintues. She hadn't got to be in till seven and she could tell the time from where the sun was. She looked down on the book for a moment before opening it. It was the last one that the master had dealt with. It was a translation from the French and although it was plainly written, there were lots of things she couldn't understand about it but which she wished she could, because one or two phrases had caught her eye and stirred her mind. She told herself she would have to start at the beginning of it again, although the master had taken her almost half-way through it. She flicked at the pages, glancing here and there, reading a line or a sentence, for her mind wasn't really on it; she was disturbed about conditions back home and about feelings that were new and strange and exciting inside herself. She could, in a way, translate these feelings, and in defence of them, she told herself that it wasn't because she hadn't a lad that she was feeling this way, although it would have been nice to have somebody of her own age to talk to, a lad, that is. Yet, where would she find one whom she could talk to about the things that interested her? The lads nearest to her were in the stables, and not one of them could read except Davey, and their Davey was the last person who would talk books.

Would she always be like this, on her own, and end up like Miss Hobson, a spinster lady? Oh no, she wouldn't like to be a spinster lady. She sighed, then looked down at the book and began to read. It was about this rich man in France called Helvétius. She could never pronounce that name right for the master. What she understood about him was that although he was rich, he wanted the poor people to have land and, of all things, to work less hours. He seemed a very good man, as wise as Voltaire. Yet, as the master had pointed out, Voltaire had different ideas altogether from Helvétius.

She became engrossed in her reading. The sun was hot on her neck. She seemed to be back in the library, the table strewn with books and papers, and she could hear his voice crying, "You are not in England now, you are in France, and Frenchmen don't speak like Englishmen, or women." She seemed to be in a half-dream world until something intruded into it. She still continued to read, but the words came slow, until they finally stopped. And then she was afraid to turn round, and when she did, she jerked, not only her head but her body, and brought her knees up under her as if about to rise. But when she saw who it was that was standing looking at her, she let out a long slow breath, and when he said, "I'm sorry if I startled you," she made no reply.

It was Mr Laurence, and he was leading his horse, and the reason why she hadn't heard him was, they were on the grass and not on the bridle-path. By way of explanation he said, "My horse has cast a shoe; I was keeping him off the rough road as much as possible. ... Don't get up. Don't get up." He put his hand out to stop her, and then when the horse lowered its head and began to munch the grass, he left go of the reins and walked towards her. And he looked down on her for a moment before turning his gaze on to the fall.

"It's a beautiful little spot, isn't it?" he said softly.

"Yes. Yes ... sir." She had almost forgotten the 'sir'.

"Do you often come here?"

"Not often now, sir, but when I was at home I used to take the opportunity whenever I could."

"It's a good place to read." He nodded down to her book. And now she put her hand on it as if to cover it. Then remembering that he was for her reading, she dropped her hand to the side and said, "Yes, yes, it is a good place to read, sir."

"What are you reading?"

She was hesitant in showing him the book, and he said, "Poems?"

"No, sir, it's French philosophy. Well, I mean, it's translated."

"French philosophy." She watched his eyes grow bright; she watched his lips fall together and his head move from side to side; and then he said, "You know, Biddy. That is your name, isn't it ... Biddy?"

"Yes, sir."

"Well, you know, Biddy, you are a remarkable person."

"I don't feel remarkable, sir, anything but." She turned her head from him now and looked into the tumbling water before she added in an ordinary tone as if speaking to one of her own kind, "I only know one thing, wherever I seem to land there's always a disturbance."

"That's the same name for being remarkable, being a disturber. May I?" He pointed to the bank, and her mouth fell into a slight gape as she stammered, "Ye ... yes, sir, yes." And at that he glanced back at the horse to see if it was still munching, then sat down on the edge of the bank, his legs dangling over it.

Holding out his hand, he indicated that he wanted to see the book, and when she handed it to him he looked at it for a number of minutes before he said, "Helvétius. My God!" Then as if apologizing, he added, "What I mean is, I've merely touched on this man and his theories. You know—" he turned and looked fully into her face now as he said, "you were very fortunate to come under the care of Mr Miller. I didn't know him. I saw him at odd times and I think I spoke to him twice, but now I wish, I wish dearly, that I had been braver and gone to visit him, although, I understand, he didn't welcome visitors."

"I think he would have welcomed you, sir. He welcomed anyone with an open mind, or, like myself and my brothers and sisters who had minds that needed opening. But I must say" – she pulled a little face at herself now – "he had to use force at times to get through." She laughed openly now as she went on, "He once said that he was competing with a hammer and chisel and that he was losing."

He laughed with her as he put in, "Not a bit of it, he was joking.

266

By the way, do you still read Shelley?" There was a twist to the corner of his mouth as he asked the question, and she nodded at him before she answered, "Yes, sir." Then the smile going from her own face, she said, "Shelley wasn't a bad man, was he, sir?"

"Shelley bad? No, of course not. What makes you ask that?"

"Well, it was" – again she stumbled – "well, the reaction of the staff the night I said his piece of poetry. They said it was—" She couldn't utter the word dirty, but added, "Not quite right."

"What do you yourself think about his poetry?"

"I . . . I think it's beautiful. There are bits that I apply to different things, like the water there," she pointed to the fall, and he asked, "What is that?"

"Oh, just a few lines, sir."

"Go on, tell me. Say them."

"They will sound silly when I say them, sir. It isn't like reading them."

"Leave me to be the judge of that. Let me hear them."

She wetted her lips, wiped the perspiration from each side of her mouth with her middle finger, then said,

> "My soul is an enchanted boat,
> Which, like a sleeping swan, doth float
> Upon the silver waves of thy sweet singing;
> And thine doth like an angel sit
> Beside the helm conducting it,"

Her head drooped slightly as she finished. There was silence between them until he murmured, "That was beautifully said. Never be afraid to quote aloud. . . . Do you know anything about Shelley?"

"Nothing much, sir." She was glancing at him now.

"Well, he died just a short while ago. Oh, what would it be? Seventeen years gone, and he was only thirty."

The master had told her this, but she pretended that it was news to her and said, "Really! Poor soul."

No, not poor soul, Biddy, pure soul. Do you know where those lines are from?"

"Well, I know in my mind, sir, but I can never pronounce the name."

"*Prometheus*. I can hardly get my tongue round it either."

267

"Do you like poetry, sir?"

"Some . . . some, not all."

Again there was silence between them. And now they were looking at each other straight in the eyes when he broke the silence by asking, "What do you want to do with your life, Biddy?"

"I don't know, sir."

"Marry? Have children?"

Her gaze slanted downwards before she answered, "Yes, I suppose so, sir. But . . . but there's a problem there." Again they were silent, until she turned her head and looked at the sun; then, slowly rising to her feet, she said, "I've got to be on my way, sir, or else I'll be late in."

He looked up at her but made no attempt to rise, but said, "Yes. Yes, I understand. And I must apologize for intruding into your solitude."

"Oh, no sir, no." Her face was unsmiling as she looked down on him. "I . . . I never get the chance to talk to anyone like this. And . . . and this is a time I'll always remember." He didn't move but held her gaze for a moment longer; then he said, "I also, Biddy. I also shall remember this time."

"Goodbye, sir."

"Goodbye, Biddy."

He watched her walk across the sward to the bridle path. And she knew he was watching her, and not until she was out of his sight did she seem to draw breath. Then she closed her eyes, for she knew in that past short time she had met *the lad*, the only one that would suit her, and that this being so, her future was writ in large letters, she would end up like Miss Hobson.

8

❧❧

It was the first week in December and the day following her birthday that Biddy overheard a conversation that was to affect her future and also explained the real reason why her mother had refused Tol, and the reason gave birth to resentment.

It should happen that madam had caught a chill. Over the past months, she had been attended at odd times by Doctor Pritchard, and on these occasions Miss Hobson had waited on the doctor. But when the doctor arrived this particular morning, Jessie Hobson was downstairs in conference with the housekeeper, and so it was Biddy who showed him into the room; and recognizing her, he said, "Well, well; so this is where you are, girl?" And she had answered simply, "Yes, Doctor."

She followed the same procedure as Miss Hobson: she brought in a bowl of warm water and fresh towels; then returned into the adjoining room, which was both closet and linen room. And it was from there that she heard the doctor say, "Well, well; so you've got the Millican girl at your beck and call now, madam."

And the reply that came made Biddy close her eyes for a moment as the voice said, "I don't know about beck and call: servants don't scurry as they used to do in my young days; things have changed out of all recognition; they not only take their time, but they speak before they are spoken to."

"Oh, well, as you are employing an heiress, in a way that's to be expected. Now let me have a look at your chest."

"What did you say?"

"I said, let me have a look at your chest."

"No. About an heiress. What did you mean?"

"Oh, that was an exaggeration, but only in a way. Now breathe in."

"I'll not breathe in. Take that thing away. What do you mean by an heiress, an exaggeration?"

"Well, it's common knowledge that Miller left the house to his housekeeper or mistress or whatever she was, but on condition that if she remarries she has to move out and it reverts to the girl, lock stock and barrel. In any case it'll come to her when the mother dies, and not to the boy. That was specified."

"Is this a fact?"

"Of course it's a fact. I was there when the will was read out."

The result of the imparting of this information had caused Biddy to lean back against the linen rack, her eyes like saucers, her mouth open. Her mother had never told her, had never let on. That's why she wouldn't leave to marry Tol, because if she did the house would come to her. What was more, she had imagined that if her mother were to die the house would pass, naturally, to Davey. The eldest son always got everything. Oh, her ma had been devious. That was the word, devious. She'd rather stay in the house and give up Tol than let her have it. Yet how would she herself have been able to keep up the house? But that wasn't the point. Her mother had kept it from her that the house would be hers one day. And she hadn't given it a thought that the doctor or solicitor would blab.

"*Girl!*" The voice brought her upright and into the bedroom, and there was the old lady looking at her steadily for a moment before saying, "Show the doctor out."

She showed the doctor out as far as the double doors, and he said no word to her, nor she to him, he did not even thank her for holding the heavy door open for him.

She had hardly got back into the room before the voice came at her again, "You, girl!"

When she reached the foot of the bed she said, "Yes, madam?"

"Why didn't you tell me about this property you're coming into?"

Should she say she didn't know? If she did, this would put her mother in a bad light. What she said was, "I didn't think it would be of any interest to you, madam. In any case from what I gather it won't be mine for many a long year."

"Nevertheless, if your mother was to die tomorrow it would be yours, wouldn't it?"

"Yes, madam."

"And then you'd walk out of here, wouldn't you?"

"That would depend, madam."

"On what?"

"I'm ... I'm not quite sure ... circumstances, money to keep the house up."

"Yes, yes, a house needs money to survive. But you could sell the house. It would bring a decent sum that place. I remember it well. ... Was your mother his mistress?"

"*No, she was not, madam.*"

"Be careful. Be careful. Don't use that tone to me."

She cast her eyes downwards and she was aware that her face had turned scarlet, and the voice came at her, saying, "Don't show any temper here, miss, or you'll soon find out your mistake. Where's Hobson?"

She was about to answer, "With the housekeeper, madam," when the door opened and in walked the younger daughter of the house, and the old lady exclaimed in an entirely different tone, "Ah Lucy, my dear, when did you get in?"

"About half an hour ago, Grandmama."

The girl came to the bed, leant over and kissed her grandmother; then she straightened up and looked at Biddy, and for a moment Biddy thought she was going to smile at her. She stared at the girl. She had only been away at the boarding school a matter of months, yet she seemed completely changed. She was much taller, and her manner was quieter. She couldn't imagine that this was the same person who had helped to string her up to the clothes horse on that awful Sunday. On her first visit home from the school she had looked surly; now, her expression was different, as was her manner, she had lost her boisterousness. That school was certainly having an effect, and for the better, if she knew anything.

"Well, well, now. Sit down and tell me, tell me all your news. How are things at this school? I hear nothing these days. May gallivanting, Stephen up in London, Laurence in Oxford, Paul in Newcastle. By the way, Laurence should be here tomorrow."

"I'm afraid he'll not, Grandmama; I've just heard he's changed his plans."

"What?" The wigged head was lifted from the bed. "What did you say? Since when?"

"Mother received a letter this morning, so I hear. He's ... he's going straight on to France to his friend's for the holidays and may not be back."

"Well, I'll be damned. He can't do that. Do you hear, Lucy? He can't do that."

"Grandmama—" Lucy Gullmington took the wrinkled hand and patted it as she said, "Laurence, fortunately for him, is a free agent, he can do what he likes."

"What are you talking about, free agent? Doing what he likes. He's to come home for the holidays. You go down and tell your mother to write immediately and say I forbid him to go to France."

"He's already gone, Grandmama."

"My God!" The head flopped back on the pillow. Then the eyes were turned on her granddaughter and the voice was quiet now as she said, "He's gone to France before, but he's always come home first."

"He likely wants to avoid May, Grandmama."

"How do you know anything about May?"

"We all know, Grandmama, although I don't think he need worry so much now as I understand she's being escorted by a title."

"Titles are two a penny and they've got no money. . . . And you, girl—" The old lady suddenly paused for breath as, now pointing towards Biddy, she gabbled, "get about your business and close your ears to anything you hear in this room – you understand? – or it will be worse for you."

Biddy retreated to the toilet room and through it into the box-like room that served as her bedroom, and there she sat on the bed for a moment. The news had saddened her: she wouldn't now see Mr Laurence until the Easter vacation. Since that magical afternoon by the fall she had seen him a number of times, but always in the house, and he had spoken to her but once. That was one time when madam had gone for her harshly in his presence; and when afterwards he met her in the corridor he had stopped her and said, "Don't mind her tongue, it is her only pastime. And you know, I think, in a way, she is rather fond of you. She only bawls at those she's fond of; to the people that she doesn't like, her manner is polite and cool." He had smiled at her and she had said not a word, but as he turned away she had said to herself, Why couldn't you say something?

She knew that she had been looking forward to his being here for Christmas. She had been reading hard, sometimes well into the night with the aid of candle ends – and there were plenty of them to be had on this floor – and always towards one purpose, to astound him again perhaps with her knowledge. She was once more reading *Candide*. She liked the idea of the innocent man, young yet who had a fund of reason in his head. She loved to follow his adventures through the army, through shipwreck, all in search of a new world. Of course, she realized it was all fairy tale, yet at the same time threaded with common sense. And she longed to discuss it with someone, as Candide himself did, and learn through discussion.

Had she hoped that she might talk with Mr Laurence again? But where could this have taken place? Certainly not inside the house, and apparently not outside either, because she had stopped by the fall on every leave day, even when it was raining and blustery, but no one had even passed by.

When the door burst open and Miss Hobson demanded, "What do you think you're doing, girl, sitting there?" she answered, "I . . . I was feeling a bit sick." And to this Miss Hobson replied, "You'll be sicker before the day's out. Madam's in a right tear, and if I know anything, it won't fade with the light. Master Laurence is not coming home for the holidays. I think it's very bad of him. He knows how she looks forward to his company more than that of any of the others. But I know what it is, it's that Miss May. She follows him about like a lapdog, hanging on his arm shamefully, and he's not for her. I know he's not. I've heard him say as much to madam. Madam's for it, left, right, and centre. . . . What's the matter with you? You're not sickening for anything are you?" Jessie Hobson leant towards Biddy and Biddy, answering perkily now, said, "Sickening? Me? Of course not. What would I be sickening for?"

"Well, you look peaky. By the way, what did the doctor say?"

Yes. What did the doctor say? She had forgotten about that. That was another thing. Oh, she was fed up. For two pins she would walk out, go straight home and say to her mother, "Well now, so this is to be my house when you die, or if you should marry. Why didn't you tell me?" But she couldn't do that . . . she wouldn't let on she knew anything about it. She'd play the same game as her mother, but for different reasons.

She answered Jessie by saying, "I don't know. He never opened his mouth to me."

It was a colloquial answer. She would have to watch herself, she was dropping back more and more into them these days. What she should have said was, I don't know. He didn't inform me.

Oh, anyway, what did it matter – learning or anything else? – for she was mad, mad, stark staring mad. She must be to harbour the thoughts that came into her head.

Christmas passed and Biddy wasn't sorry, for she felt she was the only one in the house who hadn't in some way enjoyed herself. She hadn't gone to the servants' party. When she had mentioned it to Jessie Hobson, Jessie had said, "You won't be going this year, Biddy; and neither am I. Anyway, I don't have to tell you that there is a feeling against you downstairs, and it isn't because it's you with your funny ways, it would have been against anybody who had risen from a place like the laundry to the top floor."

To this Biddy had answered, "It doesn't matter; I don't want to go."

She had a brief word with Jean. Things were still apparently the same in the laundry. But in spite of this Jean was happy because Davey was continuing to show an interest in her.

She had not even stood in line with the rest of the staff for her Christmas present, because, as Jessie had pointed out to her, hers was a different household. She would get her present from madam.

And she did get a present from madam, and the quality of it had surprised her, and had caused her to express her pleasure quite verbally which had seemed to please the old lady, and for once, she hadn't been barked at for talking. The present was a small silk shoulder shawl, with a yellow pattern on it and hand-worked lace around the edge. Of course, it had been used before, but what did it matter? And she also received six lawn handkerchiefs of good quality; and she knew these hadn't been used before because they hadn't any initial on.

On her leave day before Christmas her mother had said, "What's wrong with you? There's something on your mind. Is there some trouble up there?" And she had answered, "Not more than usual." And Riah had said, "What do you mean by that?" And she had replied, "Oh, I always seem to be in hot water. I was having a word

274

with our Davey in the yard before I came away and Mr Froggett, the butler, happened to be passing and said he would report me. I said I was only talking to my brother, and he went for me for daring to answer him back. Who does he think he is anyway?"

The encounter with the butler hadn't really disturbed her because it wasn't the first time that one or other of the upper staff had tried to get at her, but she found this as good an excuse to give to her mother as any other for her attitude, for she had found it impossible to be natural.

Before leaving to return to The Heights she had walked from room to room, and she had looked at the furniture with different eyes. In the drawing-room there were two small writing desks in reddish wood. The master had called them *bonheur-du-jours*. She realized they were beautiful. There were sets of small tables, and chests of drawers inlaid with different woods. And she had thought, If I live long enough, all these will be mine. She hadn't said to herself, when my mother dies, because she didn't want her to die. All she wanted for her was to be happy, and for the old feeling she'd had for her to come back.

But at that moment she couldn't find it in her heart to love her. And she had wondered if their Davey knew about the real circumstances, because if he didn't he would be under the impression that one day it would all be his. And this did seem to be the real state of affairs because he no longer minded coming into the house, which attitude, she thought, didn't say much for his character, after all the fuss he had made and what he had done to the master. She often pondered on that situation, and would ask herself what in the name of goodness would make a man love anybody like their Davey, even when he had been bonny. It was odd, and she had to admit, not quite right. Still, she didn't blame the master, she blamed their Davey for being mad about the pony he couldn't have.

Life was strange. She had thought she was very knowledgeable, but the more she read and the more she tried to learn, the more she knew how ignorant she was. And just lately she had read words to this effect that one of the philosophers in Greece had said years and years ago. There were so many things she didn't understand and she kept wishing she had someone to talk to.

9

It had been a bitter winter and now it was a cold Easter. All the family were home for the Easter holidays. There were lots of comings and goings and a great deal of bustle down below. A big party had been held for Miss May's twenty-first birthday, and this had been preceded by a dispute in madam's drawing-room when May declared that she was going to become engaged to Lord Milton's son, and her grandmother had screamed at her, "He's an imbecile, like his father. There's insanity in the family."

Then later, madam had gone for Mr Laurence, again calling him pigheaded and a fool.

Mr Laurence hadn't come upstairs for over a week after this, and when he did, he mostly talked politics and about the bills in Parliament. Day after day, they would appear to her to be like two strangers discussing a subject on which they had opposite opinions. It was mostly to do with the contention of how long a child should work in the factories. Some of them it seemed had been known to work eighteen hours at a stretch when the regulated factory hours had been thirteen to fifteen hours a day, but that was all past, madam had defended, while Mr Laurence had said, only in some cases, for children were known to be working from five in the morning till six at night, and dropping on their feet.

Well, she had thought after listening in to this, did he not know that the laundry workers in this very house started at five in the morning and went on till six at night, sometimes seven? Had she not almost dropped on her feet when she had first come here? Funny that people couldn't see what was under their noses. As for the bill he was talking about that had been passed in thirty-one, which prohibited children from doing night work and only thirteen hours a day at most, what about when she and Miss

Hobson had to get up and attend to madam in the middle of the night because she wanted a hot drink or her pillow straightening, or some such?

And Mr Laurence had reasoned that the factory owners were taking little heed of the bill, for children were still being exploited. You had to go no further than Newcastle, he said, to see them ragged, verminous, and hungry. As for London, once you passed through some quarters there, you were never the same again, that is, if you possessed a conscience.

And madam had again told him he should go in for Parliament.

During the three weeks of his vacation that he had so far spent at home he had spoken to her no more than the greeting of the day: "Good-morning, Biddy. Good-evening, Biddy." That was all. And she wondered at it. It was as if she had done something wrong. She looked back to the day by the falls. Had she been forward? Yes, perhaps she had. He being a gentleman, he had spoken to her kindly and she had taken advantage.

Well, if that was so, that was so. She must keep her head on her shoulders and think for the future. She wasn't going to stay here forever: another year's training and she would apply for the post of lady's maid somewhere else, and start a new life.

And she was to start a new life in a new post, which, when she looked back on it, came about with a strangeness that was comparable with the mythology the master had made her learn.

It happened in the second week in July. She had taken her half-yearly pay home to her mother and Riah had given her back three shillings; she had also surprised her with a dress and matching coat that she had made out of the still plentiful material from the boxes in the attic. And she had insisted that she put them on and carry her Sunday dress and jacket with her.

She had been delighted with her appearance. Her mother was very good with the needle: her stitches were small and her ruching so fine as to appear to have been done by an expert at such work. She had kissed Riah tenderly and forgotten for the moment the animosity she bore her for withholding what she felt now were her rights in the future.

She had no hopes that Mr Laurence would come riding by and have a word with her for he had been at home over a month now and she'd had two leave days during that period, and on both she had sat by the fall, and no one had disturbed her.

And now here she was sitting on the bank again. She had opened her bundle and spread her Sunday dress on the grass so that her new one would not be marked in any way. She had taken off her hat, and the wind, which was fresh, was lifting her hair from her brow and ears.

Perhaps it was the wind that smothered the sound of the horse's hooves until they were just behind her on the bridle path. And now she swung round, a half-smile of welcome on her face which stayed for only a second before fading at the sight of the horseman. It was Mr Paul.

As she watched him dismount, she got hurriedly to her feet and, picking up her dress, she stuffed it into the bundle.

She had told herself repeatedly during the time she had been at The Heights that she wasn't afraid of any of them; but there was one exception, and she admitted it to herself, she was afraid of young Mr Paul, because since the day he had manhandled her in the laundry he had never once spoken to her or acknowledged her presence when he was visiting his grandmother, even though she was all the while conscious that he was watching her. And strangely, she imagined that each time he returned from boarding school he had aged in years, not in months. Now, as he approached her she seemed to see him as a man, fully grown, not someone around eighteen. She didn't know whether he was coming up to eighteen or past it, she only knew that he didn't at this moment look like a youth.

His voice was civil as he said, "Hello there."

It was a second or so before she answered in stiff politeness, "Good-afternoon, Mr Paul."

He was standing an arm's length from her now, and she noticed that his hair seemed to be the same colour as his polished riding boots. Her eyes had been drawn down to his boots because, as on that memorable Sunday, he was tapping the upper part of his leg with his riding crop.

"I've disturbed you?" he said.

"No, I was just about to go."

"Sit down," he said.

"I've told you, Mr Paul, I'm just about to go. I've got to get back."

"Sit down," he said. And now his hand came out and pushed her gently, and she stumbled a step backwards to where the gnarled stump of a tree grew out of the bank, and she turned and looked at it, then side-stepped it.

Grabbing her arm, but his voice still quiet, he said, "Sit down."

"Leave go of my arm." Her words were slow and as yet there was no tremble in her voice.

"When I'm ready."

With a quick wrench she was free; but only for a moment, for now he grabbed her by the shoulders and swung her around and, bringing his boot viciously against the back of her knees, he lifted her feet from the ground, and the next thing she knew she was on her back and clawing at his face until he had spreadeagled her arms and was lying over her. His nose almost pressing hers, he growled at her now, "I've thought about this for a long, long time, you laundry slut, and I'm going to make you pay for that bloody school I'm now at. I hate it, do you hear? I hate every minute of it, but not as much as I hate you for having me kept there. I'm going to leave some marks on you, miss, that you won't forget in a hurry." And at this, he brought his face to the side of her and buried his teeth in the lobe of her ear. And when she screamed, he said, "Shout as much as you like, there's no one comes round this way very often. I've seen to that. I've followed you twice."

Now he raised himself from her a little and swung her arms upwards until he was gripping both her wrists in one hand; with the other he ripped the buttons from the front of her dress and, thrusting his hand down her bodice, he gripped her breast. Fruitlessly she kicked at his shins, and when she screamed he put his mouth on hers. Now gathering all the strength of which she was capable she managed to bring up her knees, and when she saw his body lift and roll to the side she imagined her effort had accomplished this, but as she lay gasping she saw another figure, and it

279

was bending over him and beating him with a riding crop. It was some seconds before she herself rolled on to her side, and to her amazement she saw that her rescuer was no other than Miss Lucy and that she was laying about her brother as she had once laid about herself.

Managing to stumble to his feet, he cried at her, "Give over! What the hell do you think you're at?"

"I'll tell you what I'm at, and more, when we get back to the house."

"Have you gone mad? Do you see who that is?" He was pointing down towards Biddy now. "Remember what you did to her? She was the means of sending you off and getting my allowance cut."

"I know what she did, and I know what we did. It was our fault."

"God Almighty! What's come over you? Is that school a bloody convent you've fallen into? You haven't been the same since you've been there. Mine is hell, but be damned if I would let it change me."

"No, you won't let it change you; you'll do as father did, and grandfather did, and Stephen is doing."

Biddy had struggled to her feet and was trying to arrange her clothes, and she watched the brother and sister glaring at each other. He was now dabbing at the blood running down the side of his cheek where her nails had torn the skin away. She watched him turn abruptly and walk to his horse, and the girl follow him, and to her amazement, she listened to her say, "What . . . what if she'd had a child?" And as he put his foot into the stirrup he said, "Well, what if she had? It's the lambing season around Easter for her and her type. And anyway, in two months time, I'll be in the army, and she could name one of the stable lads she rolls with."

As he dug his heels into the horse's flanks she felt a great weakness coming over her – it was the same feeling as the last time he'd had his hands on her – but she didn't want to faint, so she sat down abruptly again and bowed her head forward until the mist cleared from her eyes. And when she looked up, there was Miss Lucy standing looking down at her.

"Are you all right?"

"A bit dizzy, miss."

"I'm sorry."

She was amazed to hear this, and she didn't answer but kept her eyes on the girl. As her brother had altered, so had she. And she recalled now that during the past two weeks she had been visiting her grandmother almost every day, which was unusual, and most times she had looked at her as if wanting to speak; at least, so she had fancied. But she had told herself to remember what this young lady was really like.

Here she was, though, looking down on her, and in a quite kindly fashion. Then she was further surprised when she saw her young mistress lower herself onto the grass, pick up a tiny pebble and throw it gently into the water. And she couldn't quite believe her ears when the young girl said, "Do you mind if I talk to you?"

"No, miss, not if you wish to."

Lucy Gullmington now turned fully round and looked at Biddy as she said slowly, "You are very intelligent. I disliked you for it; in fact, hated you at one time for it. You know much more than I do; apart from Grandmama and Laurence, I think you know much more than anyone else in the house, high or low."

"No, miss," Biddy shook her head; "I don't really. I'm very ignorant. I read a lot, or when I can, and this tells me how ignorant I am. When I first came to the house, I ... I thought I knew everything, because of what the master ... Mr Miller had taught me, but I know it was just surface stuff. And he knew it, he told me so."

"Biddy. May I call you, Biddy?"

Biddy shook her head. She couldn't understand the attitude of this young lady. What was more, her head was splitting, her breast was paining, and her ear was bleeding.

"You ... you can call me what you like, miss."

"Oh" – the girl now gave an impatient shake of her head – "don't be humble, it isn't in your nature. You're not like that with Grandmama, and if you can stand up to her you can stand up to anybody."

At another time Biddy would have smiled at this, but what she did was to hold her head to one side and put her handkerchief to her ear; and when she took it away and looked at the bloodstain, Lucy said, "He did that, he bit you?"

"Yes."

"He's a cruel swine. All men are cruel."

Biddy's eyes stretched slightly. There was something here she

281

couldn't understand. And she was further puzzled; in fact, she was absolutely amazed when Miss Lucy's hand came on hers and in a low voice she said, "I . . . I wonder if you would be my friend. I . . . I have no one I can turn to."

A thought passing through Biddy's mind like a streak of lightning cleared it for a moment, but she repudiated the words it printed, saying, No, impossible. Nevertheless, she looked at the girl and said, "Are you in trouble, miss?"

Lucy's head was drooped now. There was no resemblance between this girl and the proud, haughty, bossy, even cruel young miss seen by all the staff as well as herself.

She listened now to a muttered voice saying, "When I saw Paul attacking you like that, it brought back . . . it reminded me—" She lifted her head now and ended, "You see, I knew how you felt, because I . . . I have experience of a similar situation."

"No! miss."

"Yes."

"You mean, miss?"

"Yes, yes, I think so."

"*Oh, my God, miss.*"

"That's what I said when I knew. Oh, my God, I said. And I have kept begging Him not to make it so, but He hasn't listened."

"You . . . you were attacked, miss?"

Lucy now turned her head away, saying, "No, I wasn't attacked. Well, not really. I . . . I was teasing. I . . . I didn't realize what the outcome would be. I was in love, at least that's what I thought. Then from teasing and playing . . . well, something happened. I didn't want it to happen, I think I was as frightened as you were, but it happened, and then happened again."

"Can . . . can you not be married, miss?"

The head moved slowly. "He is married and has children. He . . . he was the father of my friend." She turned quickly now, her hand over her mouth, and saying, "But, you'll never repeat that. Promise me you'll never repeat that."

"I don't need to promise, miss, you needn't worry. But . . . but what are you going to do?"

"I don't know. I only know I had to tell someone. You see, back there" – her head nodded in the direction of the house – "the men can do what they like. They can have their mistresses, they can go whoring as often as they like, and not a word said against them, but the womenfolk, they must be like the hymn, as pure as the driven snow. No word of scandal must touch a Gullmington woman. I know now what May has been going through, because she wanted Laurence and Laurence didn't want her in any way. And so, she's going to marry this stupid man because she can't wait any longer. We are made in a dreadful way, don't you think, Biddy?"

Biddy thought for a moment and then she nodded her head slowly in agreement. "Yes, I think we are made in a dreadful way," she said. "It's worse because we mustn't speak of it, mustn't show our feelings."

And then there were the feelings of the moment with which she had to contend, and these were making her feel sick, and her ear was paining, so were her arms.

"What am I to do, Biddy?"

"You must tell madam."

"I've thought of that, but I haven't the courage."

"Well, she's the only one in your family that I think could stand it, I mean, the shock."

"I've ... I've thought of running away, but I could only run to friends, and all they would do would be to bring me back home. They would be very kind and thoughtful but they'd be shocked too."

"Are you going back to school?"

"*No. No, never.*"

"Well then, you've only got just over a fortnight, haven't you? You'll have to do something, miss."

"Yes, yes, I'll have to do something. But I don't seem to be able to think."

"How far have you gone, miss?"

"It is past the second month. I ... I didn't know what was happening at first. I was very ignorant about such things. Mother is not the kind of person you can talk to, at least about private matters, except to say ...." She now looked upwards to the sky and her voice was bitter as she ended, "Purity ... keep oneself pure. I should have asked her how one went about it, shouldn't I?"

Biddy got to her feet now, saying, "I have to get back. My time's almost up. Will I walk with you, miss?" while at the same time hoping the young mistress would say no, for she wanted to run back to the house and get cleaned up and see to her ear, and perhaps lie in the bed and cry about her lovely dress being spoiled and the fright she had got and ... oh, everything.

Lucy was on her feet too now and she said, "My horse is just round the bushes there. Yes, please walk with me."

Along the road they remained silent for quite some way and only the clop-clop of the horse's hooves and the wind swaying the trees that bordered the road disturbed Biddy's thoughts. It was Lucy who broke the silence between them when she said, "Grandmama has taken to you."

And Biddy was bold enough to answer, "So I've been told before, but she has a very funny way of showing it."

"You know what she told me about you?"

"No, miss."

"She said she had told you to stop reading but that she knew you still kept it up."

"She told you that?" Biddy smiled a little, and Lucy answered, "Yes; and that was only last week. Now if it had been last year she had told me that I would have wanted to scratch your eyes out. Isn't it strange how one can change?" She turned and looked fully at Biddy again and now she said, "Could you, do you think ... could you break it to her in some way? Pave the way for me? I'm so afraid that if I tell her, she'll have one of her screaming fits. And not only Hobson would hear her, but any of the maids who happened to be passing. But ... but if you could do it last thing at night when ... when Hobson is in bed and everything is quiet. ... Would you?"

For a moment there flashed into Biddy's mind a picture of the reception the breaking of this news would receive; but then perhaps not last thing at night when the old lady would be lying down and vulnerable without her wig, her teeth, and her face devoid of all plaster, for from experience she knew that, in this state, the old lady was always more amenable; still demanding, but her demands couched in quieter terms, more as requests. Yet she was surprised when she heard herself say, "Yes, all right, I'll try."

"Oh, thank you, thank you. You see, she's ... well, she's had experience with this kind of thing before, when my father mis-behaved and there were results, if not on the doorstep, pretty near it. And then she had a dreadful time with my grandfather, so I've gathered from servants' chatter and such."

The way she had said servants' chatter made Biddy, for a moment, imagine she herself had been excluded from that category; but then she was brought back to reality when they neared the gates and Lucy, pulling the horse to a stop, said, "We cannot go any further together, but I will come up in the morning, early. Perhaps you will meet me, say around nine o'clock in the gallery, and ... and let me know what has transpired. Will you do that?"

"Yes, miss. Yes, I'll do that."

"Thank you. Thank you very much."

"Goodbye, miss."

"Goodbye, Biddy."

As if she was emerging from a dream, she walked slowly up the long narrow path that skirted the grounds. Had all this happened to her since she had left home not an hour and a half gone, attacked by that devil? And what would he have done if Miss Lucy hadn't come on the scene? ... Miss Lucy. Eeh! dear God, what a predicament to be in. And it could have happened to her. Yes, it could, because she couldn't have fought him off much longer.

She made her way quietly through the side door, keeping the edge of her loose coat pulled together over the now buttonless bodice of her new frock and she had also tugged her hat to one side in order to cover her ear. But she met no one until, at the foot of the stairs that gave on to the gallery, she came face to face with Mrs Fulton. The housekeeper, deliberately blocking her way, looked her up and down before she said scornfully, "My, my! we are dressed to kill, aren't we? You certainly didn't go out wearing those clothes, did you, Miss Millican?"

"No, I didn't, Mrs Fulton. I acquired them when I reached home."

"Oh, you did, you did. And you have taken to wearing your hat on the side, I see. Straighten it!"

"I like it on the side, Mrs Fulton."

"I said, straighten it, girl!" The small face showed fury as her hand came out to push the hat straight on Biddy's head. And Biddy, lifting her hand to prevent her, let go of her coat and it fell open to disclose the ripped bodice, which in turn showed the top of her petticoat.

The housekeeper's face stretched as if it was being pulled from all sides and she emitted the word, "*Well!*" and it said everything. And Biddy, now almost slapping the hand from her head,

repeated, "Yes, well, Mrs Fulton. I was attacked on my way here.
I must tell you about it sometime when I have nothing better to
do." And on this she actually thrust the older woman to the side.
And when no protest was flung at her for this daring action, she
knew that her torn and bedraggled appearance had, for the
moment, raised such a question mark in the housekeeper's mind
that she had become speechless.

Upstairs, she was greeted by Jessie saying, "Thank God you've
come. I'm nearly mad with toothache and madam is in one of her
moods, nothing can please her, and she's asked for you twice. She
said you were late, but you're not. What's the matter?"

It had taken some seconds for Jessie to realize something was
not quite right with her assistant, and when Biddy pulled open her
coat, then lifted the hair from her ear and stood silent, Jessie said,
"My God! What happened to you, girl?" And Biddy replied
simply, "Mr Paul. He attacked me."

"No!"

"Aye, yes. *Oh, yes.*"

"Did he . . .?"

"No, but it wasn't his fault that he didn't; Miss Lucy came along
and beat him off."

"*Miss Lucy*, beat him off?" For a moment Jessie forgot her
toothache and her face screwed up in amazement as she repeated,
"Beat her brother off?"

"Yes, yes, she did."

"Well, well. But I must say, there's a change in that girl since
she was sent away to school. She's much better mannered, lost all
her devilment. They must have knocked it out of her there."

"Yes, I think they have. Now . . . now I'll go and change." She
was about to turn away, then stopped and said, "Me mother made
me this dress and coat. It . . . it was lovely when I left the house."

"Oh, what a shame, lass. But it's still lovely. We'll fix the front.
. . . But Master Paul. Eeh! If the master . . . No. But if Mr Stephen
or Mr Laurence knew about it, by! my, they would skin him alive."

"Yet, from what I understand they are not above doing such
things themselves, only in . . . well, a more licensed way." There
was a touch of tartness in her tone now, and Jessie replied, "Aye,
well, that's the way of all gentlemen. But I can tell you, they
wouldn't stand for what's been done to you, an' by one of their
family." Then shaking her head, she added sadly, "It's funny, girl,

how things always seem to happen to you. I've never known anyone like you for creating...." Instead of trouble, she added, "things. And I wouldn't say you were to blame all the time. It's just that, somehow—" She shrugged her shoulders, then cupped her cheek with her hand and grimaced as pain stabbed at her again before adding, "Go on, get changed and go into her, because I'm not going to be long out of me bed."

"Take some laudanum; it might ease it and put you to sleep."

"Yes, yes, I will. I thought of that last night, but was afraid I wouldn't waken when she shouted. I seem to forget at times that you're here and capable. It's surprising how she's taken to you and let's you talk. She never did it with me. She still doesn't. Go on. Go on now."

Biddy went, but she was slow to change into her uniform because she was experiencing reaction to the struggle she'd had earlier on. And as she sat on the side of her bed, she thought, I'll have to try to get me mind clear and think what I'm going to say, and how I'm gona say it. And I'll have to keep awake until Miss Hobson's asleep. And on this thought she felt guilty, because she knew that Jessie was a person who knew how to keep her tongue still; she must be because who else in the house besides herself knew that at intervals Mr Mottram the coachman came up to madam to report on her son and his doings in Newcastle. Madam had brought Mr Mottram with her when she first came into this family, and it was well known in the house that he was madam's man, but what was not equally known was that he was madam's spy and had been for years, so she understood.

This was a queer household. Nothing she had read, she told herself, could hold a candle to it for its goings on. And now, she herself this night was to create more goings on, and she was afraid of the outcome.

Twice she had to get out of bed and sit on the edge of it to prevent herself falling into a deep sleep.

At nine o'clock they had settled madam for the night and the old lady had been impatient with Miss Hobson because she complained of her toothache. "Go down to the stables, woman," she had said, "and they'll put a bit of wire around it and one good tug and you'll have no more aches and pains. Have them all out. That's the best way. I did. Do as I bid you and I'll have a set made for you. Oh, go to bed, woman!" she had cried at last. And Jessie had gone to bed, after taking a dose of laudanum. It was some time, however, before her snores told Biddy that she was well away, yet it was still not ten o'clock and there would be movement in the house down below – the gentlemen played billiards at night, or cards, and it was sometimes near twelve o'clock before they settled into bed. She doubted if she could keep awake till then.

At one point she put on a dressing-gown that had been passed on to her from Jessie, and, creeping into the hallway, went along the gallery towards the folding doors. The last window in the gallery overlooked part of the front of the house and when she saw there was no reflection from the lamps outside the front door, she knew that the servants had retired. The butler and the valet might still be up; they couldn't go to bed until the last member of the household was in his room, but she doubted if there was any chance of anyone coming to this end of the house now, and so she crept back and entered the dressing-room, where she stood for a long moment with eyes closed before she gently opened the door and entered madam's bedroom.

Through the light from the turned down lamp on the bedside table, she was surprised to see the old lady, not only awake, but sitting propped up in bed. When she had last left her she had been tucked down into her pillows. But Biddy was quick to note that the pillows were re-arranged, which proved that madam wasn't as helpless as she sometimes made out to be.

"Girl, what is it?" The voice came to her soft, as it usually did in the night.

Slowly Biddy approached the bed, and she drew in a long and deep breath as she stood looking into the wizened face before she said, "Madam, may I talk to you?"

"Talk to me, girl, at this time of night?"

"It's very important, madam."

"What's important about you that won't wait until the morning?"

"I don't wish to talk about myself. It's about ... about one of the household ... the family. I ... I have been asked ... I mean —"

The thin body moved in the bed and Biddy for a moment imagined she could hear the aged skin crackling.

"What you getting at, girl?"

"It's ... it's about Miss Lucy, madam."

"Miss Lucy? What about Miss Lucy?"

"I ... I have something to tell you."

"About Miss Lucy?"

"Yes, madam."

"Carrying tales?" The voice had lost its softness.

And Biddy's tone also changed when she answered, "No, madam, I'm not carrying tales. I never carry tales. Miss Lucy asked me to ... well, the fact is, madam" – she now nodded her head – "she's frightened, terrified to tell you herself."

She watched the old lady press herself back into her pillows and move her head slowly from side to side as if to get a better view of her, and when she said, "Go on," Biddy said, "I don't know how to tell you, madam, because it's going to be a bit of a shock."

"Girl, I'm used to shocks. My life has been made up of shocks. What is it you have to tell me that Miss Lucy is afraid to tell me herself?"

Again Biddy gulped, but she didn't take her eyes off the old lady, and her hands wavered in front of her as if ready to throttle any yell she might give, for from experience she knew that madam's voice had a great carrying quality.

"She ... she's going to have a baby, madam."

The body seemed to be possessed of a new life, a young life, for when madam sat suddenly bolt upright in the bed, Biddy's hands actually did go out. But they only touched her shoulders and she was appealing to her now, "Madam. Madam. Don't say anything. Don't shout."

Her hands were shrugged away and the voice hissed at her, "Who's going to shout? What do you mean, girl, shout? And don't stand there. Bring a chair and sit down."

Biddy brought a chair and sat down, and the old lady now commanded her, "Talk."

"Well, Madam, I happened to come across Miss Lucy when I was returning from my leave. I was sitting by the river. Miss ... Miss Lucy seemed distressed. She ... she seemed changed, different, and then she told me."

The small mouth was puckered until the lips parted and demanded, "Why you?"

Yes, why her?

She said, "She hadn't anyone else, madam. I mean, she was afraid to tell the master and mistress."

"Damn well she might be afraid to tell them. Yes, damn well she might be. My God in heaven! For this to happen and at this time. Her mother would go mad." Then characteristically she added, "Not that that would matter very much. All right. All right, girl, she was frightened to tell them. But why couldn't she come to me herself?"

"Because, madam, she thought that you would go for her as . . . as you sometimes. . . ."

"Yes? Go on, go on. Don't stop now."

"Well, as you sometimes do in the daytime." Biddy's head was nodding defiantly now, while part of her stood aside amazed to witness this happening. "And she was afraid that some member of the household would hear."

"And so she asked you to do her dirty work?"

"No, it's not dirty work. She's very much afraid. And . . . and you're always quieter at night and. . . ."

She closed her eyes tightly and there was a silence between them now. Then the old woman's voice low and with a tremble in it, she said, "Go on, girl, tell me what you know. Who is responsible? Some weak-kneed, fumbling schoolboy?"

"It . . . I think it is the father of her friend."

"What!" The body was brought from the pillows again. "Her friend? That must be the one she has spoken of. He's a teacher in the school, and if I'm not mistaken, has a large family; well, four or five, or something like that. God in heaven! God in heaven!" Her hands were clasped now and she was beating them on her chest as she cried, "He'll pay for this. He'll certainly pay for this."

"Madam."

"Yes, girl?" She was giving Biddy her attention again.

"If . . . if you do that, I mean, accuse him, the . . . the whole thing will be made public, and then . . . well, she might as well have gone and told her mother in the first place. I think she imagines you will come up with . . . well, what I mean is" – her head was moving again from side to side – "some sort of scheme to . . . to prevent it being made public."

"What does she mean, some kind of scheme? You can't prevent the birth of a child. You can't cover up the birth of a child. Oh my God!" Now she had her hand on top of her nightcap and as she screwed it round on her head the wisps of white hair fell across her brow and she muttered to herself, "I've got to think, and think hard." And turning her eyes on Biddy, she added, "If this came to light it would clamp the lid on so many things: my daughter-in-law's standing in the county, and the fact that her uncle is to be made bishop. My God!" She rocked her head on the pillow. "I can see the effect it would have on her. It would even turn her guts white. Then there is Stephen, and Parliament. And we musn't forget May who is about to marry that idiot out of pique, or perhaps the allure of one day being called Lady So-and-So. Life has its compensations. Oh yes, but what compensation is it going to have for that stupid little young idiot? When did this happen? How long has she carried?"

"Over two months, I think, madam."

"Oh my God! I've got to think. I've got to think." She was muttering to herself now, and when Biddy moved uneasily in the chair, for she was feeling weary and far from her healthy self at the moment, the old lady said, "Fetch a blanket. I ... I want you to stay with me. I want to think, and we must talk. I've got to reach a solution before the morning when that stupid girl comes hoping I'll have a miracle ready for her. Well, she'll find out I can't perform miracles."

She was still muttering to herself while Biddy went into the dressing-room and returned with a blanket.

Sitting down to the side of the bed again, Biddy draped the blanket round her knees and her waist while she half turned to face the old lady who, looking at her pointedly now, said, "She's got to get away from here. That's evident. That's the first thing. But *where? Where?* Friends are out. If you want a secret spread from here to Land's End, tell it to a friend. I have kept my own counsel all my life, that's why my head is clear today. ... Don't fall asleep, girl. We've got to think."

"Yes, madam."

"Are you warm enough? It gets very cold in the night, even in the summer."

For a moment the thoughtfulness caught Biddy off her guard

and she could make no reply till the voice, muffled but still harsh, came at her, saying, "Well, are you?"

"Yes, madam. Thank you, madam."

"Well now, sit back. Think what you would do in her place, and don't be afraid to tell me what you think. They always say two heads are better than one. Now if this was happening to you, what would you do?"

What would she do if this was happening to her? Go home to her mother and be rated for a fool, then have the child and live under the stigma for the rest of her life, and alone, for no man would take her after that. Take her to use her, yes, but not marry her. But it wouldn't happen to her. It wouldn't happen to her. For she'd never marry. Never marry. Never marry. To the chant in her head sleep overcame her. . . .

She awoke feeling that her whole body had become permanently twisted; her cheek was pressed against the wooden edge of the chair, one hand was on the bed and the other was clutching the blanket up to her neck. Slowly she blinked and tried to rise quickly as she realized that she had fallen asleep, but the effort brought a groan from her and the voice to her side said, "It's all right, girl. Take it slowly."

She took it slowly, and when she was sitting up straight she blinked and murmured, "I'm sorry, madam. I . . . I didn't mean to fall asleep."

"Nor did I, girl. Nor did I, but we both couldn't keep awake all night. However, it's now five o'clock."

"Five o'clock!" Biddy went to rise, but the cramp in her legs caused her face to screw up with pain and she repeated again, "Five o'clock! I've . . . I've been asleep all night, madam?"

"Yes, you've been asleep all night, girl."

"Have you slept, madam?"

"On and off. On and off. Now I would like a cup of tea. The house will be astir in a little while and then I want you to go and get into your clothes as quickly as possible."

Biddy made the cup of tea for the old lady, watched her drink it, poured her out another, then retired to the little kitchen and drank two cups herself before going to her room to get dressed.

When she again returned to the bedroom the first thing madam said to her was, "Well, have you any ideas in your head, girl, concerning this matter?"

"Only one, madam."

"Then let me hear it."

"It's . . . It's just occurred to me that wherever Miss Lucy went in England, there might be somebody who knew of her. It's amazing how things pass around. So if . . . well, I thought, if she could go abroad for . . . like a long holiday. . . ."

"Huh!" It sounded like a stifled laugh, but the countenance remained grim as she said, "Under other circumstances you would have likely made something of yourself, girl, because that is the idea that has struck me too, abroad, but not for a long holiday. Young girls like Miss Lucy don't go for extended holidays. For whatever length she's got to be abroad there's got to be a purpose in it, and I've thought of the purpose. But I must have help, and the only one who can help in this case is Laurence. He will take her across to France to school. She will purportedly stay with friends of his. He's got very good friends in France, so he tells me, and they have young daughters and sons. She can supposedly board with them while going to school, but she's got to have a maid, and that maid will be you."

"*Me, madam?*" Now Biddy thrust her hand over her mouth because the exclamation could have been heard down the corridor, and at this the old lady cried, "Who's bawling their head off now? Yes, you girl. You, I understand, have bragged about your ability to speak French. Well, this will be an opportunity to learn how the French speak French. And don't tell me, you can't go, because I'm going to tell you something: you, my dear girl, are at the bottom of this trouble."

Biddy put her hand flat on her chest and was for saying again, "Me, madam?" But the "Me!" she brought out was in the nature of a squeak, and madam replied quickly, "Yes, you. If it hadn't been for that affray in the laundry, Lucy would never have been sent to that school. Her mother was against it." Madam did not add at this point that she herself was for Lucy's departure from under the wing of an inadequate governess and her psalm-singing mother.

"Now, don't stand there gaping, girl; I want you to go downstairs and see one of the men. Froggett is a lazy beggar, he will not be up yet, but Thompson will likely be about. Tell him to go and wake Mr Laurence and inform him that I wish to see him as soon as possible, and that means before breakfast. Make that point clear."

"Yes, madam." Biddy went out of the room and had reached the communicating doors without realizing she had moved a step: there was a feeling as if she was walking on air; for a moment she had forgotten about Miss Lucy's predicament, she could only think, I'm going to France. I'm going to France. And to this she added, Oh, Mr Miller. For it was as if he was standing by her side saying, "Now, what did I tell you."

It was John Thompson she saw when she descended the main staircase. This man had been more kindly disposed towards her than any of the other male staff. And now he greeted her quietly, saying, "What is it, lass? I've never seen you down here afore at this time, or at any other time for that matter, not in this part of the house." He smiled, and she said, "I've got a message from madam. She wishes you to wake Mr Laurence and tell him she wants to see him immediately . . . before breakfast."

He leant his face towards her, saying, "Something up?"

"No." She shook her head; then again, on a higher note, "No, except" – she made herself smile now – "she's had a sleepless night and she wants to take it out on somebody. Miss Hobson and me are not enough."

He laughed now, saying, "By, she's a tartar. But we still know who rules the roost, don't we?" He pulled a face at her and she answered, "Yes, we still know who rules the roost. Will you give the message, Mr Thompson?"

"Yes, I will, lass. Here, just a minute." He touched her arm as she turned away, and now he looked from his right to his left before quietly saying, "I'm glad you bested them," and he jerked his head towards the servants corridor. "By! you did that, especially Ma Fulton. Keep at it, lass."

"Thank you, Mr Thompson. I'll try." With quiet dignity she turned about and went up the main staircase knowing that he was watching her. As she made her way back to the west wing, she thought, Wait till the news breaks and they know I'm accompanying Miss Lucy abroad. It'll burn some of them up. And for a moment she felt a wave of satisfaction pass over her.

What she did next was to go into Jessie Hobson's room. Jessie was still sound asleep, and so she left her, but she thought as she did so, She's got to know. Yet why should she? Miss Lucy could really be going to school in France, finishing, they called it, like when the young men went away on world tours to finish. But finish what? She didn't know, she only knew one thing, that poor Miss Hobson was going to find things hard having to run, fetch and carry all on her own again. But likely she would get help; there were plenty downstairs who would jump into the position, given the chance. . . .

It was not more than fifteen minutes later when she saw Mr Laurence coming towards her from the gallery. She could see that he had donned his trousers, but was still wearing his bedroom slippers and a brown corded dressing-gown. She also noticed that he must have sluiced his face, likely to waken himself up, because the front of his hair was wet.

He asked of her immediately, "What is it? Is there something wrong?" And she answered hesitantly, "Yes, in a way, sir. Yes."

"She's ill?"

"No. Nothing like that, sir, but she'll . . . madam will tell you. Would . . . would you like a cup of tea, sir?"

He had moved from her towards the bedroom door, but turned his head and said, "Yes. Yes, I would, Biddy. That would be nice." Then he went into the room.

She did not hurry with the tea-making; she wanted to give madam time to tell him all she knew and what she intended to do about it.

When she eventually tapped on the door while balancing a small silver tray on one hand and entered the room, she was surprised by the lack of discussion taking place. Mr Laurence was sitting in the chair she had vacated earlier, madam was propped up in bed, and they were both looking towards her.

She put the tray on a small table and placed it at his side, and he looked at her and muttered, "Thank you," the while he continued to stare at her.

Now madam spoke to her, saying, "Mr Laurence agrees with what I told you earlier. But the matter must be dealt with slowly. He will go across to France with you both and see you settled in with the family."

"No, Grandmama." He was looking at her. "I told you, it can't be with that family. They have too many connections in London, and. . . ."

"All right. All right. It's all right." She had closed her eyes tightly and her bony hand was flapping in a protesting movement as she said, "Yes, yes, you've told me. But I still think it's a pity. They'll need supervision, both of them."

"Well, I'll see that they get that, Grandmama. But the centre of Paris is no place to settle them. Anyway, I'll think of something."

"You do that. You do that. And" – her face brightened a little – "you could put it to them that you are going across to France to settle the matter. What I mean is, to make arrangements for her supposed school et cetera. And ... and I think it would be a good idea if you did go across beforehand, and make sure of their apartments. Then take them over just before you return to Oxford. What do you say?"

Biddy watched him nip on his lower lip. She watched his eyelids blink. Then he almost jumped, as she did, when madam barked with her usual daytime voice, "It's got to look natural." And she lay back and put her hand to her head as she muttered, "Why should I have this at my time of life? It isn't right." Now she was glaring at him. "It isn't, is it, Laurence?"

"No, Grandmama."

"But you can see the result of what exposure would mean? She would be ruined for life, the stupid little fool. But what will be much more important to her mother and father is that they would never be able to live this down."

"Don't worry." He put his hand soothingly on hers and patted it and said again, "Don't worry. I'll see to things."

She looked at him, her expression showing pain now as she said, "Don't worry. You say, don't worry. My worry's only starting. I'll be worrying about her all the time she's over there, and having her child in a strange country when the experiencing of such an event should occur with her family about her. And to think" – she poked her face up now from the pillow – "it'll be their first grandchild. Oh, it isn't to be tolerated. Don't worry, you say. Then there's those Frenchmen. I know what they are like. ..."

"Biddy here, will be with her, and" – he turned and looked at Biddy – "I think she'll be able to manage most Frenchmen. What do you say, Biddy?"

Biddy stared back at him. Only yesterday she hadn't been able to manage a young Englishman. What she said was, "Shall I pour your tea, sir?" And he answered, "Yes, please."

She poured out the tea and was about to turn away and leave

296

the room when madam's voice checked her, saying, "And I'll be losing her an' all, and Hobson is dying on her feet."

"You'll have to have someone else to take her place, Grandmama."

"Who? One of the dudheads from downstairs?"

Biddy had reached the door when madam's voice halted her yet again, saying, "A moment, girl." When she turned and looked across the room towards her, the old lady exclaimed, "You have a sister, haven't you? How old is she?"

"Fourteen, madam."

"Fourteen. Is she bright?"

"She's as I was at her age. She can read and write."

"Never mind about reading and writing, is she bright in other ways?"

"Yes, madam. But ... but she helps my mother."

"From what I understand of your mother's situation, she's in need of money. You will go home presently and tell her that your sister will take your place for the next few months and she will be paid well. She will begin on three shillings a week and I shall see it is paid to her every fortnight. As for you, while you are acting as companion, five shillings per week will be paid to your mother for you."

"Thank you, madam." A minute later, standing in the kitchen, she repeated, "Five shillings a week and three shillings a week, and everything found for Maggie, and in her own case, the means of travelling to a new world. It didn't seem real. Nothing seemed real.

She was standing at the small sink looking out through the window beyond that gave a view of the side gardens when the door opened and she turned expecting to see Miss Hobson. But it was Laurence who stood there, and he didn't speak until he had crossed the small room and stood by her side. Then looking down into her face, he said softly, "When ... when is the child expected?"

"I'm not sure, sir."

"It is sad, very sad, and, if I may say so, strange that she should confide in you."

"I thought so too, sir, yet ... yet she seems changed."

"Yes, I had noticed that, particularly these last few weeks. She must have been very worried."

"She was, sir. She is."

"They say good comes out of evil. I would have dismissed that until this moment, because I think this is a wonderful opportunity for you. There's nothing expands the mind like travel, and you were interested in French, weren't you?"

"Yes, sir. But I must say that I would rather not have had my education extended at such a cost to Miss Lucy."

He didn't answer for a moment, and then he said softly, "No. No, you are right, Biddy, the cost is high. Yet I must tell you that once you have been abroad, you'll never feel the same again; I doubt if you will be content to take up this kind of duty." His hand made a wavering motion which took in not only the room but the whole house. "And as I see it, there'll be no reason why you should, because I should think you would be qualified to teach. There is a movement ahead to provide schools for poor children, but apart from that, you could go as governess. Would you like that?"

"I would, sir, very much." He was looking into her face now and she into his and her eyes became misted and for a moment she imagined his face moved closer to hers; but the mist cleared and he was standing exactly as he had been before, only now his hand came up and rested gently against her cheek, and it was with the greatest of efforts that she stopped her own fingers from covering his. Then his voice little above a whisper, he said, "You are a remarkable girl, Biddy."

His fingers left her face. He looked at her a moment longer, then he went out. And she turned and leant against the sink and her hands gripped its stone edge until her nails hurt.

10

The commotion in the house was worse, Jessie said, than when Mr Riddle brought his small tribe of chimney-sweeping boys.

The family always went away in September so that the servants could deal with the soot that even the best of Mr Riddle's team brought down in scuttlefuls. The only one who seemed to enjoy the invasion by the tiny boys, aged from seven to ten, was madam. Often she would be wheeled to the gallery window to watch their scurrying backwards and forwards across the yard with the bags of soot. And once, it was said, she had gone into the laundry yard to watch them being washed after they had finished their week's work. It was known that Mr Riddle's boys liked coming to The Heights, for they were always fed well, and each had a sixpenny piece given to him before he left. It was also known that the same boys never came more than twice: they had either died or grown too big for the chimneys.

So the sweep week, as it was known, was a week of commotion. As were the following three in getting the place shipshape again to receive the family back. Yet this didn't happen until September. But here they were only part way through July and the whole house in a buzz, all because Miss Lucy had absolutely refused to go back to her own school and madam had decided that she should be finished off in France. And so she was going to stay with Master Laurence's friends and be educated with the young members of the family.

But what was causing the biggest verbal commotion downstairs was the fact that madam had insisted that *that one*, that laundry slut, should accompany Miss Lucy as maid. Did you ever in all your life hear of anything like it?

When it first came to Mrs Fulton's ears, they said she had almost collapsed, and she had asked for an audience, not with the mistress, but with madam, because she was only too well aware who ruled the house, and she felt that madam should know that the girl she was having trained as a lady's maid was of questionable character. And she had explained the proof she had of this.

No one knew what madam had said to her, except that she had been told to come back within the hour.

The result of Mrs Fulton's visit was that madam asked Biddy the meaning of her torn clothes, and Biddy unhesitatingly answered, "I was attacked by Mr Paul, madam, and Miss Lucy beat him off. It was following this she gave me her confidence because she saw I could have been placed in a similar predicament to herself."

No one knew what madam had said to Mrs Fulton on her second visit, only that that lady descended to her own quarters with a very white face and had not been approachable for some time. . . .

Riah had taken Biddy's news in dumb silence. She had always known that this child of hers was different and that one day she would achieve something. Yet still, she couldn't believe that she was going across the sea to that place where they had revolutions and people's heads were chopped off. In the ordinary way it was a place where only the gentry were able to go but her daughter was going; true, as maid to a young lady, but nevertheless she was going. And what was more, she was losing her other daughter, at least for the time being, she was told.

At first she had protested at Maggie's going to the house, but Maggie had cried and begged to be given the chance. And, as she pointed out, there was the three shillings a week and not having her to feed or clothe.

Biddy had told her she was to get five shillings a week. It was all too good to be true, or would have been if she herself was happy, for now she'd be left alone in this house with only Johnny, and he so restless that she wouldn't be surprised to find him gone one morning.

And so came the morning of departure. The luggage was packed in the coach that was to take them to where the boat sailed for

France. Biddy's mind was in such a whirl that at times, even up till an hour ago, she had closed her eyes tightly and asked herself if she was awake and not dreaming.

She kissed Maggie goodbye and, looking down at her, she said, "Do everything you're told, and don't be afraid of madam. She shouts a lot, as you've heard, but you'll get used to her."

Then in Jessie's sitting-room, when she held out her hand to the old woman, Jessie had put her arms around her and kissed her, and there were tears in her eyes as she said, "Take care of yourself, lass." And leaning close to Biddy she had whispered under her breath, "I don't know what it's really all about but I'm no fool. Anyway, take care of her, because you've got a head on your shoulders. Goodbye, lass, and God go with you."

Her own eyes were wet when she went into the bedroom and stood before the figure in the chair sitting near the window.

Madam stared at her; then extending her hand, she clutched at Biddy's, saying, "Take care of her now, and when it is born bring her back. Laurence will see about an adoption. I'm relying on you to see that all goes smoothly. Do you understand me?"

"Yes, madam."

"You won't lose by this, girl, I promise you."

"I want nothing more, madam."

"A girl in your position will always need more if she means to rise to the top of her station. Goodbye now. Keep me informed."

"I will, madam." She bent her knee and turned and walked hurriedly out of the room.

On this occasion she did not go down the back stairs. The coach was waiting at the front door, and she walked with straight back and head up towards the communicating doors, then on to the long gallery where she surprised a number of the servants standing at the windows. But they all turned from watching Mr Laurence helping Miss Lucy up into the carriage to look at the Millican chit walking towards the main staircase as if, as they said later, she owned the place. But she wouldn't have dared to do that if the family had been at home. It was a pity they had to leave for London yesterday to attend Miss May's engagement party. And it was also a pity that Miss Lucy wasn't going along with them. There had been ructions between the master and mistress because old madam had got this idea into her head about her granddaughter's education. But they all knew who would win; like in every other way

301

of life, it was the one who held the purse-strings that called the tune. But oh, the mistress had been upset. She had even called in Parson Weeks to speak to madam. But what had happened there nobody knew except that the poor man came downstairs with a face like a beetroot.

When Biddy reached the foot of the stairs Thomas Froggett turned from the front doors and, his mouth agape, he watched her walk towards him, then pass him without a glance in his direction, and the sound he made was something between a hiss and a choking cough.

The two footmen were standing near the carriage, and John Thompson would have helped her into it, but Mr Laurence, his hand on her elbow, assisted her up the steps; then he himself followed. James Simpson closed the door. Bill Mottram on the box shouted, "Gee up! there." And then they were off, leaving behind a mostly indignant and wondering staff.

Even Davey, who had watched the performance from a stable door while standing the chaff of the other boys about his sister rising in the world, felt indignant that their Biddy was once again doing something that brought her to the fore and made her more disliked than she already was.

In the carriage, Lucy sat in silence beside Laurence, with Biddy sitting opposite to them until the coach was passing through the gates when she looked out of the window to where the lodge-keeper was raising his hat to her, and she said, "I don't care if I never ride through these gates again." And Laurence, catching hold of her hand, said, "Oh, now, now, Lucy, don't say that." And she turned her gaze on him as she said, quietly, "It's true, Laurence." Then looking at Biddy, she asked her, "Would you like to stop and say goodbye to your mother?" And Biddy answered, "Yes, if you don't mind, miss, I would."

"It's been arranged already. Mottram knows when to stop." Laurence smiled from one to the other.

"You know, you're like Grandmama, Laurence, you think of everything."

He answered her jokingly, saying, "I'm not like Grandmama, Lucy; I could never get up to her pitch if I tried. Moreover, her cosmetics wouldn't suit my complexion."

While Lucy smiled faintly at this, Biddy thought, He is like her. She's not his grandmother, but he is like her.

When the coach stopped, Biddy alighted, saying, "I won't be more than a minute or so." And Laurence answered, "You needn't hurry, we've got time and to spare."

Riah was waiting for her at the front door and she went straight into her arms, muttering, "Don't cry, Ma. Don't cry, Ma."

"I feel awful, lass."

"Yes, I know. You're bound to. You'll be lonely."

"Oh" – Riah shook her wet face – "it isn't that. I've got to tell you, an' I've left it to the last minute. I should have told you long afore. It's about this." She raised her eyes and her hand, indicating the house. "You see, the master didn't leave it to me, not really. He said, I could stay here, in his will, as long as I didn't get married. But somehow he felt that I would, and anyway, whether I married or died, the house was to be yours, and I've kept it back from you for various reasons."

"It's all right, Ma." Biddy's face too was streaming now. "It's all right. I know. I know."

Riah rubbed the tears from her eyes with the back of her hand as she exclaimed, "You know? How do you know? I mean...."

"Oh, it doesn't matter. I've known for a long time. And, Ma, I hope I never come into it until I'm a very old woman." She smiled now through her tears.

"Aw, lass, lass." Again they were holding each other close; then Biddy muttered, "I've got to go; they're waiting."

"I can't believe it. I can't believe it. All this happening. You goin' to France, of all places in the world. And he learned you the language. It's strange. It's strange."

"Yes, it is, Ma.... Are you coming to the gate?"

"No, lass, no. I ... I'd only make a fool of meself. And look at me, in me house things, I'm not much to be proud of. Go on."

"I'll always be proud of you, Ma." Their hands held tightly for a minute, then their fingers drew apart, and Biddy turned and ran down the drive.

She was nearing the gate when through her blurred vision she saw beyond the back of the coach a well-known figure crossing the field at the other side of the road, and when she reached Laurence, who was holding the door open for her now, she looked at him and, a plea in her voice, she said, "Could ... is there ... I mean, is there a minute to spare? There's a friend of mine." She pointed. "I'd like to say goodbye to him."

Laurence glanced at his watch. "It's all right," he said. "Yes, barring accidents" – he smiled – "we'll be in Newcastle in good time."

"Thank you." Her glance darted from him to the figure sitting inside the coach before she turned away and hurried to the dry-stone wall bordering the field.

When Tol caught hold of her hands across the wall, he muttered thickly, "All set then, lass?"

"Yes, Tol."

"Good luck, then." He nodded at her; then his voice dropping, he added, "Don't worry about things at this end."

"Me ma's lonely. She's lost. We've all gone now except Johnny, and I'm worried about him an' all. I feel he could scoot at any time. He's restless."

"Don't you worry your head, I'll have a talk with him. And . . . and I'm going to see your ma."

"When?"

"When you get yourself away off the road and on your journey and I can get past you." His joking reply filled her throat and she leant impulsively forward and kissed him.

Lucy had been watching the meeting from her side of the coach, and now she turned and, looking to where Laurence was standing once again glancing at his watch, she said, "It's odd how she can create love and hate, isn't it?" And he replied, "Yes, as you say, Lucy, it's odd."

The next minute he had his hand on Biddy's elbow and was helping her up into the coach. Then with a word to Mottram, he climbed after her and banged the door, and as it closed they all knew, in different ways, that a period of their lives had ended and what lay before them were many difficult problems.

Tol watched the coach until it had rolled out of sight, then slowly he went up the drive and knocked on the kitchen door. Receiving no reply, he entered the room and found it empty. He now knocked on the communicating hall door before passing through, but he could see no sign of Riah. He crossed the hall and gently pushed open the drawing-room door; and there she was sitting huddled on the couch. She was sobbing so deeply that she wasn't aware of his presence until his hand came on her shoulder, and she started with a cry that ended in a gasp. Then she straightened up and lay against the back of the couch, her face awash with tears and her breath coming in gasps.

Taking a seat beside her, he took hold of her hand, saying, "Come on now. Come on. It isn't as bad as that. She's taking a chance in a lifetime. She'll be somebody in the end, will Biddy. She's somebody now; in fact, she always has been. But you'll be proud of her, you'll see."

"Tol." Her voice was small.

"Yes?"

"They've" – she gulped in her throat – "all gone, except Johnny, and ... and he's threatening to run off. They've all left me."

"But they're all alive, and doing well. You should be proud of them."

She lifted the bottom of her apron and rubbed it round her face, then muttered, "Yes, yes, I suppose I should, but I can feel nothing except" – she swallowed again – "lost. It was ... it is as if I'd never borne them. I'm lost." She turned her face fully to him now and muttered, "I'm lost, Tol."

"Well—" his voice came low and deep as he said, "there's a remedy for that, you know, Riah, any day of the week, or any minute of the day. And I'll say this, I'm not asking you to marry me now. If you want to stay in this house, I can understand that, but there was nothing in the will to say you couldn't love me, and me you. Now was there?"

He watched her screw up her eyes tightly; he watched fresh tears stream from beneath the closed lids; he watched her head droop on to her chest; and then he put his arms about her and drew her gently to him and, stroking her hair, he murmured, "You need me, Riah. You can't go on fighting it off forever, and I need you. Oh, how I need you, because I've loved you from that first time I saw you standing with the bairns in the yard of Rowan Cottage."

He brought her face round to his now and his eyes held hers for a moment before he kissed her. Then he said, "For well or ill, Riah, that's a seal as good as any marriage certificate to me. Come on, now, cheer up; everything's going to be bright from now on.

And look" – he shook her gently by the shoulders – "I want a cup of tea made afore I get back to me work. I'm a working man you know, and—" The smile left his face and, his voice quiet and low, he ended, "and like a working man I'll come home to you tonight." And at this she closed her eyes and fell against him.

The following day was Sunday, and Davey paid his usual visit accompanied by Jean.

Both of them regaled her with the talk that was going on up in The Heights. And Davey said that it was a good job Maggie was safe in madam's part of the house because such was the feeling, he understood, in the servants' hall that they might have pulled her hair out. They thought it was most unfair that not one of them from the house had been given the chance to assist Miss Hobson.

It was while Jean was helping Johnny to pick fruit from the orchard that Riah had Davey to herself. And although he wasn't of a perceptive nature he couldn't help but notice that there was a change in his mother; and he said so immediately, "You look bright," he said, "as if our Biddy had come home instead of gone off." And then he added, "How did you leave her anyway yesterday?"

"Oh, we were . . . well, a bit upset, me more than her I think, because . . . well, I had to explain something to her that I should have done a long time ago after the master died. It's about this house."

"What explaining had you to do to her? It's yours."

"No, not really."

"*What!*" He had been sitting at one side of the kitchen table and he half rose now, and again he said, "What? . . . But he left it to you."

"Just on conditions."

"What conditions?"

"Well, that I didn't get married again. If I did, well—" She paused now and he waited, and then she said, "If I did I'd have to move out and the house would go to Biddy."

"*To our Biddy?*" His big face was screwed up. "But it can't. Look, Ma, I'm your son and the eldest. What you own should come to me."

"Not in this case."

His mouth opened and closed twice before he said, "What . . . what if you died?"

"It goes straight to her."

"No, be damned!" He was on his feet now, and she too, and she yelled at him, "Yes, yes, be damned, Davey. And what are you making such a fuss about anyway? It's only recently you've come back to the house; you wouldn't come near it for years."

"No, not as long as he was in it."

"But it is still his house, and you're in it."

"It isn't his house, he's dead."

"He may be but his influence is still here, and you must be thick-skinned if you can't feel it."

"Feel his influence? He's a spiteful bugger, that's what he is, or was. God!" He flung himself round, punching one fist into his other palm as he said, "I had it all fixed in me mind. I was going to leave up there now that you've got more money from our Biddy and Maggie, and I could turn this into a home garden, like vegetables and fruit to sell to the market. Some people make a mint taking fresh stuff into the market at the week-ends. I had it all worked out."

"Well, you can damn well get it unworked out. The place'll never be yours."

"It's not right, after what he did to me."

She turned now, her face scarlet, her voice ringing: "He did nothing to you, it's what you did to him," she said; "you crippled him and brought on his end quicker than it should have been. He did nothing to you."

"He tried."

"He did not."

He had his hands flat on the table now leaning towards her as he yelled back at her, "He had a damn good try."

"He didn't. He didn't. Not the way you put it. His mistake was in caring for you. Aye. Aye, he loved you and he mentioned the word and I didn't understand it at the time no more than you did, but I know now he would never have harmed you, not in the way you're making out."

"He's harmed me now all right, hasn't he? Spitting at me from the grave 'cos I would have none of him."

"You can think what you like, but I know one thing, he would have always seen to Biddy in some way or other, because he admired her having a mind of her own and a brain."

"Brain be damned! All she is is brazen. And I'll tell you something about her that you don't know, she's been up to tricks on her own, because it's going round the place that she came back from her leave all bedraggled and the front of her dress open down to the waist, and her hat on one side as if she was drunk. And she cheeked the housekeeper when she wanted to know how she got like that. You didn't know that, did you?"

No, she didn't know that. She remembered now that Biddy had had a cut on her ear. She'd said she had tripped against some wire. But Biddy wouldn't be up to anything like that; she had more sense.

"That's surprised you, hasn't it, about your brainy miss?"

"Well, all I can say to that, Davey is, whatever happened wasn't of her doing. Somebody likely tried it on; and they would get as much as they sent if I know her."

"Yes, she's such a clever bugger, isn't she?"

"Don't you use that language here."

"Oh, shut up!" As he turned from her she screamed back at him, "And don't you tell me to shut up. By God! it's coming to something."

"Aye, it is." He had rounded on her once again. "And when we're talking plain, I'm going to tell you this. I'm not tipping up anything more: it's everybody for themselves; I can see that."

"Very well. You're entitled to keep what you earn. Thank God now I've no need of it. All I can hope is when you and Jean marry and start a family. . . ."

"Who said anything about marrying Jean?" His face was stretched.

"Well, aren't you? You're courting her."

"I'm damn well not, nor ever had any intention."

"Then why do you bring her here on a Sunday?"

"I don't bring her, she walks along of me. Remember, it was your wonderful daughter that brought her."

"But . . . but the lass understands . . . ."

"That's her mistake then, isn't it?"

308

"She's a nice lass. A good lass." Riah's voice showed her bewilderment, and he said, "Yes, she might be, on top, but where did she come from? She's from the poorhouse; nobody knows about her people. I wouldn't be marrying anybody like that."

Riah's voice was scarcely audible now, but there was a hiss in it as she said, "Then you better make it plain to her, hadn't you?"

"I've nothing to make plain. If she's got those ideas, it's her fault. And if there's any explaining to do, I'll leave it to you, because I'm off back now, and I don't care if I never come back home again."

As he made for the door, she called, "Davey!" And when he turned towards her, she said, "Those are my sentiments an' all. I don't care either."

He stared at her, his eyes widening slightly; then he went out and banged the door behind him.

The world had gone topsy-turvy. Yesterday morning she had been in despair with the thought of the loneliness that stretched ahead, then last night she had experienced loving like she had never imagined it, for it had never happened that way with Seth. She had woken this morning and held the pillow to her that had cradled Tol's head until the early hours of the morning, and when she had got up, it was as if the years had rolled off her and she was a young girl again, and this was her first love. And it was her first love. Yes, her first real love. And all morning she had floated around the house, her feet not seeming to touch the ground. Then she had baked and made a fine tea for Davey and Jean coming. And Davey and Jean had come, and Davey had gone, and she couldn't recognize the nature of him. From where had he inherited such traits? Not from her. And oh no, not from Seth, because Seth had been a good honest man. But why was she searching for a match to his nature, because she could now hear her own mother speaking through him. He had the looks of his grandfather but the complete nature of his grandmother. Although she hadn't recognized it then, she realized now it had shown on the day he took the pip because the master had been unable to buy him the pony. Everything was all right as long as it went his way, but if it didn't, then there were sparks flying. That had been her mother's way too.

Well, Biddy was gone across the seas. Maggie was in service.

309

They had both gone from her, but she hadn't lost them. And she hadn't lost Johnny as yet. But she knew that irrevocably she had lost her eldest.

Why was it that happiness was always bought through a heavy price?

PART FOUR

The Outcome

1

Madame Arnaud's house was situated outside the small village some distance south of Paris. It had once been a farmhouse and consisted of eight rooms all on the same floor. Madame Arnaud was living on a small pension and was pleased to let part of her house to supplement her income. What had been the farmyard proper now formed a terrace, on to which her visitors could walk from their sitting-room, which was very pleasant in the summer but which formed a wind tunnel in the winter.

Her present guests had been with her for some months now. They were Madame Lucille Millican and her sister-in-law, Mademoiselle Bridget Millican. Madame Lucille was a young widow, a tragic case really, so the villagers understood. She had married beneath her and the young husband had died, but her family would still not forgive her mistake. That was the English, they knew nothing about love.

But apparently there remained one member of her family who still had a heart and understanding, for her brother came out at intervals from England to see her. And, as Madame Arnaud had told the butcher, he was expected this very day and she hoped there had been saved the plumpest goose for her. And the butcher assured her that she would have the plumpest. And the grocer assured her that the sweetmeats and the crystallized fruits that she had ordered were all ready to be sent to the house.

The whole village knew how generous Madame Millican's brother was: his purse flowed with francs, and he was such a nice gentleman, everyone was out to please him.

A little whisper had stirred through the village that perhaps Madame Millican was not quite a widow and her brother not quite a brother; but be that as it may, that was the way of the world and nobody was going to question it, not here in France. Of course, if such was the case, it would explain why the young person was having her baby in France instead of England, because the English were such hypocrites: a man could be found in his short clothes and a woman in her shift and yet they would both deny knowledge of each other; they were in that state merely to discuss the English weather, which, like their lying, was unbelievable. . . .

Back in the farmhouse, sitting at either side of a roaring fire, the two girls were knitting. Biddy had taught Lucy how to knit, and in return Lucy had taught Biddy embroidery. Over the months they had read together, studied French and tested it on madame and the villagers, whose French apparently wasn't Parisian French but a patois, and caused both parties some fun during the exchanges.

Altogether the days passed pleasantly, at least for Biddy, but for Lucy there were periods when she went into depression so deep that Biddy became worried. It was at these times she talked herself silly, as she put it. She told Lucy about her early life in the pit village, about the master, and went as far in an attempt to stir her interest as to relate his liking for Davey, and the result of it. This last instance had the desired effect and brought the question from Lucy, "He actually cut him down with the scythe?"

But today Lucy was bright because Laurence was coming. Her hands stopped plying the needles, she rested the shawl she was knitting on the mound of her stomach and she looked into the fire as she said, "I wonder what the reaction will be to my not going home for the holidays? Do you think they will believe that I've been invited by the family to join them for Christmas in their country house?"

"Oh, yes, yes. Mr Laurence could explain that away."

Biddy felt a quickening beneath her ribs now as Lucy, looking at her, said, "You know that Laurence is of no blood relation to the family, except very distantly, being the son of Mama's second cousin?"

"Yes. Yes, I understood something like that."

"May was in love with him you know. She was quite brazen about it. I used to hate her because of that, I mean, being in love with him, because I loved him too." She paused now and, her eyes tight on Biddy, she said, "I still do. Yet there was a time when I imagined I was in love with——" After a quick shake of her head she added, "It's dreadful to be of our age, isn't it? All your values are mixed up: you don't know what you want, but yet you do; your

314

body burns for what you want while you tell yourself it's a sin. I was brought up on sin. Until I was eight I never saw my mother more than five minutes a day, and then there would be days, weeks even, when I didn't see her at all, when she would be on holiday and I was left with Miss Collins, who had been instructed to instruct us, both Paul and me, in all the things that came under the heading of sin, and this included asking for second helpings ... greed, bathing oneself without a cover on the bath ... impurity, letting one's mind drift at night ... bad thoughts. On, on, and on."

"Really?"

"Yes, really. Did you have anything like that to put up with?"

"No, never. The only thing I can remember is dropping to sleep while my father read from the Bible. After a twelve-hour day at the farm I wasn't very interested in what Moses had to say, although I sometimes got my fingers rapped to make me pay attention." She smiled now, and Lucy said, "Do you know, you were lucky. Servants and such always envy those above them, and they imagine they know all that goes on in the household. They don't, at least not in the minds of their masters. ... Biddy."

"Yes, miss?"

"Nothing much escapes you, does it?"

"Oh, I wouldn't say that, miss."

"Oh, don't be coy."

"I'm not." The protest was made as if to an equal. "Only your saying that nothing much escapes me makes me feel that I'm sort of nosey and I'm not."

"I wasn't meaning it that way. But as Grandmama would say, you've got a head on your shoulders. And now I'm going to ask you something. Do you think Laurence likes me ... I mean, still likes me, in spite of this?" She patted her stomach.

It was a moment before Biddy could answer, "I ... I'm sure he does, miss. He's always liked you."

"What I'm getting at Biddy is, do you think he more than likes me? Do you think he would marry me?"

Biddy put down her knitting and, leaning over, she picked up the poker and pushed a gnarled root into place in the open grate, and now she muttered, "I ... I couldn't say that, miss. I've got no idea."

"You could probe and ... and ask him ... I mean, not outright, but just gauge his feelings."

315

"No, no, I couldn't, miss." She was standing now looking down on Lucy and she repeated, "No, I couldn't do that. It isn't my place."

"Oh, don't keep on about place, Biddy." Lucy tossed her head impatiently. "We've been thrown together for months. There's no position between us now, and never could be again. I . . . I've been turned into a woman before my time, and somehow you were already a woman, in your mind anyway." She paused, then asked, "Why won't you do this for me?"

"Because I couldn't."

"You talk to him. You talk to him a lot and he to you. On his last visit you walked miles with him, alone. You must know how to bring a conversation round to any subject that you like."

"That is a personal subject, miss; there should be ways and means of you tackling it yourself."

"Like this?" Lucy again patted her stomach but harder now. "I'm . . . I'm thinking about when it's all over. I'll . . . I'll need someone. I don't feel I can carry on alone, not even with you, although you've been marvellous." She now put her hand gently on Biddy's arm as she added, "I don't dare to think what would have happened to me if I hadn't come across you that Sunday. Oh, yes I do." Now she was nodding her head. "If I'd told Mother I would have been packed off somewhere, into a convent likely. Look Biddy, please. You . . . you needn't put it bluntly. Well I know you wouldn't, but just . . . well, sound him. Will you? Please. Because I . . . I need him. I can't go back home again. Not to that kind of life. I'd die, or do something."

"You won't die, or do something." Biddy's voice was harsh now. "You'll have a baby to see to, and love. . . ."

"*I won't. I won't.*"

Biddy was thrust aside now as Lucy pulled herself to her feet and, seeming to forget that she had dismissed the difference in their positions just a moment earlier, she cried at her, "I've told you before. I'm not keeping the child. You with your plebeian outlook. Use your head, how can I? Even if I wanted to. And I don't want to; all I want to do is get rid of it." She now brought her two hands over the sides of her stomach as if she was actually throwing the child from her, and Biddy, also forgetting her position for the moment, said, "All right. All right. I know what you've said before, but I put it to you, you needn't cast it off

316

altogether. You can have it fostered and go and see it from time to time."

"*Shut up! Shut up.* I want none of it. Do you hear? I want none of it. Oh, my God." She turned away, her hands now holding her head, crying, "I might as well have stayed back home."

In the small hallway Madame Arnaud listened to the raised voices coming from her guests' apartments. She couldn't understand a word of English, but a verbal battle is understandable in any language. So when she answered the knock on the door and saw the gentleman standing there, she exclaimed, "Ah Monsieur. Monsieur. Welcome. Welcome. You are just in time to stop the altercation." And pointing towards the far door, she added, "When the weather is bad, tempers are short. No one quarrels in the summer."

As she helped him off with his overcoat he listened to the exchange of voices, both high and angry, and he thought, Oh, dear me, dear me. What now?

But before he opened the door the voices had ceased and when he stood in the doorway and looked at them both staring at him, he said, "Well, well! No welcome?"

Then Lucy ran towards him, and he took her in his arms and kissed her; and she kissed him, and she leant her head on his shoulder until he gently pressed her aside and walked to where Biddy was standing in front of the fire. Holding out his hands, he took hers and pressed them warmly while looking into her face and saying, "Hello, there." And she answered, "Hello." She omitted the Mr Laurence, but said, "We didn't expect you until this evening."

"I got an earlier coach and I walked from the village. Well now, what have you girls been up to?" He turned and held out an arm to Lucy. And she came to him and, again leaning her head on his shoulder, she looked towards Biddy as she said, "We've been quarrelling, and it's over you. She said you weren't at all good-looking and your French left a lot to be desired."

He was looking at Biddy now – her face had turned scarlet, her mouth was open – and he said softly, "Well, she was right in both cases." And when Biddy said, "Oh, miss," he didn't need confirmation that the quarrel had been of a more serious nature. As for Biddy, she left the room saying, "I must see madame about the meal."

She did not, however, go to madame's quarters but went along the narrow corridor and into her own bedroom, and there, standing with her hands pressed tight together, she muttered to herself, "Equality." That last little scene recalled shades of the girl who had taken the whip across her face on that particular Sunday.

For the first time in all the months she had been here, she wished she were home because what lay before her was two weeks of his presence in the house; and what was more, she had, in some way, to find out how deep were his affections towards Lucy.

And she was to find out on New Year's morning, 1841.

2

❦❦

The holiday had not been without its gaiety. They had all walked together and laughed together; they had played cards; they had even sung together old Christmas songs accompanied by madame on her spinet. And then had come New Year's Eve.

Lucy had not been feeling well for some days, and on New Year's Eve she had kept to her bed. The doctor from the next village had been called in and he said it was but a slight malaise. This often happened in the eighth month, all she had to do was rest. So when the church bells chimed from the villages, Biddy, Laurence, and Madame Arnaud, stood round Lucy's bed and drank her health.

After Madame Arnaud left the three of them sat and chatted for a time until Laurence took his leave after kissing Lucy and saying, "It's going to be a good New Year, Lucy. Just you wait and see." Then he said good-night to Biddy and went out.

Biddy now set about settling Lucy for the night and when she had finished, Lucy took her hand and asked softly, "Have you talked to him?"

"No . . . no, not yet."

"You will do? Because he goes back the day after tomorrow."

"The opportunity hasn't arisen," Biddy said.

"You've had him on your own most of today. Why . . . why didn't you speak then?"

"It's a very difficult subject to raise."

"It shouldn't be for you, Biddy, your wits are sharp. Try. I must know before he goes back."

"I'll try. Good-night."

"Good-night, Biddy. And a happy New Year."

"And the same to you, miss. Yes, the same to you."

To her surprise Laurence was waiting for her in the hall and he beckoned her silently towards the sitting-room door. Once inside the room he took her hand and drew her to where the lamp, by the side of the fireplace, was still burning, and standing square in front of her, he put his hands on her shoulders and said, "A happy New Year, Biddy."

She was trembling from head to foot, and the words stuck in her throat before she could say, "And ... and to you, sir."

"Don't call me sir any more, Biddy. Do you hear?"

She remained quiet.

"My name is Laurie. And ... and you know what I'm going to say, don't you?" She made a slight movement with her head, and he shook her now, saying, "Biddy Millican of the straightforward tongue, don't lie."

"I'm not ... I'm not lying."

His face became straight and he said, "No, you're not lying. You have never guessed then how I really feel about you?"

Again she made a small movement with her head before muttering, "No, only the other way about."

"The other way about?" His voice was a mere whisper, and she repeated in no louder a tone, "The other way about."

"Oh, Biddy." He went to pull her into an embrace, but she stiffened and said, "Mr Laurence."

And at this he put in, "I've told you, no more Mr Laurence."

"It'll have to be."

"Why?"

"You know as well as I do. This ... this isn't right; it can lead nowhere. And you've just suggested I talk straight. Well" – she gulped in her throat – "I'll do it now. I ... well, no matter what I feel, I want no hole and corner affair; I don't want to end up, in fact I won't end up like Miss Lucy. So there."

His hands dropped from her shoulders, his head bowed; then he said, "You think my intention is to use you in that way?"

She dared to answer, "What other way is there between us two?"

"The proper way." His chin jerked upwards. "I love you, Biddy. Do you understand that?" Again he was holding her by her forearms and his grip was tight. "I think I've loved you from the moment I saw you and heard you pouring Shelley into the deaf ears of that thick-headed crowd. Yes, right from that very moment. Don't you know why I haven't stayed at home for the holidays lately as long as I usually did? Because then I would think, as you are thinking now, this cannot be, this cannot come about. Now I know it can, and it will, even if it means our emigrating going to another country. I needn't ask you if you would be afraid to share poverty with me, because you know what that's like. I don't. You'll have to teach me how to handle it, because I'll have to earn my own living from now on by teaching. That's the only thing I can do. I . . . I love you, Biddy. I . . . I cannot get you out of my mind. When you are in a room, I cannot take my eyes off you. I became more attentive to Grandmama because I knew I would see you."

She brought out now on a shuddering breath the word, "Madam!"

"Oh . . . madam. Oh yes, she'll yell her head off. But after all, what can she do? What can any of them do? I don't belong to them, although I must admit I owe them a great deal. Well, at least, I owe Grandmama, because if it had rested with the woman I call mama, and even her husband, I might have been a workhouse brat. My mother was of good family, poor, but with a name. And then there is this disease that mama suffers from, religion and prejudice. My father, I understand, was a very ordinary man, and a bit of a scoundrel. He abandoned my mother just before I was born. That's how I landed up at The Heights. I understand he died abroad when I was six years old, here in France as a matter of fact. I know nothing of his people; and my grandparents, too, are dead. They left me a small sum but I don't come into that until I am twenty-five. So, may I ask if you will starve with me, Biddy, until that time?"

"*Oh! Oh!*" It was as if the exclamations were easing a pain; and then she fell against him and put her arms about him, and he pressed her to him as if he would never let her go.

When their lips parted, their faces flushed, they looked into each other's eyes and smiled, and he whispered, "Oh, Biddy, Biddy. Oh, my dear. You know you are the most wonderful person I have ever met in my life. Yes, yes, you are," he emphasized, pressing her hard to him with each of the last four words as if to stifle any protest from her. And now her head drooping, she muttered his name for the first time, "Laurie," she said, and to this he said, "Yes, my dear one?" And she answered, "I feel like a traitor."

He pressed her slightly from him and, peering into her face, he said, "A traitor. You? Why?"

"Lucy."

"What about Lucy?"

She turned her eyes to the side and gazed down into the embers of the dying fire before she said, "She's . . . she's in love with you. She . . . she wants to marry you. She hopes that you will feel the same."

"Lucy?" The incredulity came over in his voice. "*She what?*"

"She's in earnest, so very much in earnest. And . . . and she needs some one."

"Oh, nonsense, nonsense. This is because of her condition. Now, if it had been" – he pulled a slight face – "if it had been May, I . . . I could have believed it, but not Lucy."

"Yes, yes, Laurie. She is banking on it."

"Then she'll just have to unbank."

He now took her hand and pulled her down on to the couch beside him, and becoming serious again, he said, "It's preposterous. I've never acted other than as a brother towards her."

"Yes, but she knows you're not her brother."

"You mean to say, knowing her condition and after being with that man who is already the father of children, she would expect me to . . .? Oh, my goodness me. Never! Never!"

For a moment she thought, Men . . . their outlook; even if he had been in love with Lucy, as things were he wouldn't have considered marrying her. She dared to say, "What if it had happened to me?"

"Happen to you? It wouldn't have."

"It could have, if she hadn't intervened when I was attacked."

"But that would have been different, that was against your will. By what I can gather, this was of her own doing. She wasn't raped, she flirted with a middle-aged man. And young girls seem to have an attraction for middle-aged men. Undoubtedly they don't need much encouragement, but nevertheless, what was needed she supplied. The case is different altogether."

"But you are so caring of her."

"Yes, yes, I am, because no one else in the family would be, except Grandmama. If the matter had rested with her I am sure she would have commanded Lucy to have the child there. But she knew the result of such an action on every member of the family. What I've done, I've done in part for Grandmama. She's an old dragon, yes, admittedly, but I'm very fond of her. And, you know, there's one thing in our future favour" – he drew her into his arms again – "she's very fond of you."

"Yes," she said, "as a servant."

"Well, perhaps," he admitted now; "but, she'll change her tune."

"Knowing madam, she never will."

"Well, that will be a pity, because nothing, Biddy, do you hear me? nothing is going to come between you and me, ever."

"Oh, Laurie. Laurie." As she leant her head against him he said, "How old are you, really?"

"Eighteen just gone."

"Nearly too old for marriage," he said, and they both started to laugh. Then his voice becoming serious, he said, "What are you going to tell her?"

"Nothing. Oh" – the word was high – "oh, nothing yet, not until the baby is born, because she has bouts of depression now...."

"But you must, you must give her some inkling that my affections are placed elsewhere. You mustn't let her go on hoping."

"Please. Please, Laurie, let us do nothing until the baby comes and she is back home. She's determined to have nothing to do with the child."

"Well, I can understand that."

"I can't."

He touched her cheek gently as she went on, "I'll be thinking about it all the time, being brought up in some small foreign home when its rightful place is back in England in that house, having all the attention in the world."

"Well, that can never be. You know that. Just imagine the shock of her landing back there with a baby in her arms, even if she wanted to."

She looked at him steadily for a moment. "That shock wouldn't be half as great as the shock of Mr Laurence announcing the fact that he wishes to marry Biddy Millican, who once slaved in the laundry and was considered the lowest of the low," she said.

He pursed his lips and smiled now and, taking her face between his two hands, he said, "And who has more brains in her little finger than the rest of that community put together? And who among them can converse, not just talk but converse? Biddy

Millican. And it is she I mean to marry, even if the shock paralyzes all at The Heights."

"And it might do just that, and also close the gates on you forever."

"No, that won't happen, not as long as Grandmama is ruling that roost. No, I'm not afraid of that, for I don't think there is anything I could do that would turn her against me. Perhaps that sounds conceited, but there it is. I pride myself I know her inside out."

Biddy could make no reply to this, because she couldn't see madam through his eyes, and there was a section of her mind that was worried, not for herself, but for him.

And all she could say to herself, and in her old idiom, was, "Oh, dear God, let things pan out."

3

Lucy's baby was born on a Wednesday in the third week of January, 1841. It was a very bad delivery, her labour having lasted over a period of three days. It was a girl child, and after it was washed it looked so beautiful that Biddy cried over it.

There was a great deal of bustle in the house. A midwife and Madame Arnaud had delivered the baby and now both were anxious as to the condition of the mother for after some hours the afterbirth had not appeared.

The doctor had been long in coming as the roads were in a bad state, and when he saw the condition of the young mother, he shook his head and tut-tutted and gave her a strong dose of laudanum as well as a concoction from a green bottle before proceeding to perform a minor operation on her.

When she screamed, Madame and Biddy held her down. And Biddy seemed to go on holding her for the next twenty-four hours, because every time she neared the bed Lucy would put her arms out and beg, "Hold me, Biddy. Hold me."

A fortnight ago she had sent a letter to Laurence in Oxford. It wasn't only a love letter, it was also telling of her concern for Lucy's condition. Now, three days after the baby's birth she wrote again and sent the letter by special coach to Dieppe, hoping that it would catch the mail-boat, and then the train, and reach him within two to three days. There were no words of love in this last letter, only the fact that the doctor had his grave doubts that Lucy would survive, and would he please come at once.

Two days later, around five o'clock in the morning, Lucy died, her head resting on Biddy's arm. Time and again she had asked, "Will Laurie come?" And Biddy had assured her, "Yes, yes. He should be here any time now," knowing that the letter would probably not yet have reached him.

Repeatedly she had tried to get Lucy to look at her child, hoping that it might, in some strange way, give her an incentive to live. But she had always refused; she even became agitated when the baby was mentioned.

Biddy could not believe that the young girl was dead until Madame Arnaud lifted the head from her arm. She had become so stiff she found it impossible to move for a moment or so; then when realization dawned on her she cried aloud, reverting to her old vocabulary, saying, "Eeh, no! No! Eeh no!"

"'Tis God's will." Madame covered the still white face with the sheet and led Biddy from the room.

The unreality of the situation stayed with her for the next five days, when the doctor said that the body must be buried; it would no longer be safe to leave it exposed.

Almost at her wits' end now, Biddy didn't know what to do. By this time, either she should have had a letter or Laurie himself should have appeared, because on the morning Lucy died she had sent word straightaway to him, telling him the news, and that he must inform her parents.

She had just enough money to pay for the funeral expenses and the extra meals that madame provided for the mourners who consisted of most of the villagers. The coffin had been borne on a cart to the little graveyard that was sheltered by a wood. The only flowers on it were some bunches of snowdrops and aconites. And as she stood at the graveside and watched the earth being shovelled on to the plain wooden box, she kept telling herself that this wasn't happening. It was a dream. All these past months had been a dream. Laurie was part of the dream too, and all these strange people were part of the dream. The only thing that was certain was the baby lying in the farmhouse in its little crib. And she had to keep her thoughts on it because it was the only evidence she had of reality.

Having had no reply from Laurence to her two letters, the dread increased that something had happened to him. If that were so, what would happen to her and the child? Nobody was going to take the baby, unless they were paid for it. But the very thought of passing it over into strange hands was now almost unbearable. From the first moment she had held it it had bred in her a love, a new love, and when she put the pap bags to its mouth and watched it sucking while it gripped her finger with one of its tiny hands, she told herself it would be impossible to part with it, unless it was into very good hands. And the only hands she could think of were those of its own people back in England, in The Heights. It should go back there no matter what. Its mother was no longer here to bear the disgrace, so surely they would find it in their hearts now to forgive her and care for her child. . . .

The following day she was proved wrong, for not only did Laurie arrive, but also Anthony Gullmington and Stephen. It should happen that the two letters had definitely been delivered to Laurie's quarters in the university but he had taken leave to go to London to attend a course of lectures. When he returned and found both letters he went straight back to The Heights and presented his adoptive father, mother, and brother with the facts, and had been amazed when Anthony Gullmington had at first refused point-blank to make the journey: "She's dead? Then she's dead," he had said.

It was only when Laurence had pointed out to him that the child still survived and that if nothing was done Miss Biddy Millican would undoubtedly bring it back and present the family with it that he was persuaded to come.

Yet, Anthony Gullmington had put it to Laurence that, seeing he had managed the whole affair so far, he could see to the rest of it. But Laurence would have none of this. His daughter, he reminded Gullmington, was dead, and in a foreign country. They could and would presumably say that she had died of a fever. And so what would people think if he didn't have her body brought back?

Madam had seen the sense of this and she had made her wishes known to her son, and so here they all were entering the sitting-room of the farmhouse and looking towards Biddy. That was, until Laurence, going quickly to her side and taking her hand, said, "Oh, my dear, when did it happen? And how?"

She looked from him to the two tall men gazing at her, no doubt amazed at Laurence's attitude towards her and she said, "Will you, please, be seated."

They stared at her for a moment longer before, together, they both sat side by side on the couch.

But when she said, "Can I get you some refreshment?" Anthony Gullmington growled, "*No! girl*. We don't want any refreshment." And Laurence put in quietly, "We had a meal in the hotel back in Paris. Tell us what happened."

327

And in a few words she told them; then added, "I had no instructions and the doctor said she must be buried. So two days ago they buried her in the cemetery" – she pointed towards the window – "a little beyond the village." Then she added, "The child is very healthy, sir, and . . . . "

"I don't want to hear anything about the child."

"She's your granddaughter, sir."

"Don't you dare take that tone with me. Remember your position."

"I do remember my position, sir, and I am not in your employ."

"*What.*" He was about to rise when Stephen put his hand firmly on his father's arm, saying placatingly now, "What she means, Father, is that Grandmama employs her."

"I know what she damn well means, and she's insolent."

"I have no intention of being insolent, sir. I'm only stating a fact. And I can add to it by saying that I have stayed with your daughter these many months and cared for her, and I care for her child and wish to see the best done for it."

"God Almighty!" He turned and glared at Laurence now. "Who does this one think she is?"

"Well" – Laurence put his head back on his shoulders for a moment – "this is not the time or the place to tell you, but since you ask, she is someone who has become very dear to me."

"*Good God! Good God Almighty! What is this?* Have you lost your senses, man? This . . . this slut who has caused more. . . . "

Both Biddy and Laurence spoke together, Biddy's voice almost as loud as his as she cried, "Don't you call me a slut! I'm no slut," and Laurence saying, "If she is a slut then she is the least of the sluts in your household, sir, for in intelligence she is above any of your offspring."

Father and son now looked at each other, not believing what they were hearing; then together they both rose to their feet, and it was Stephen who said, in a quieter tone but with a stiffness to it now, "We could talk about this, Laurie."

"There is nothing to talk about regarding my affairs."

"I forbid you the house as long as you continue to associate with this. . . ."

"That will certainly be no hardship to me. But forget about me for a moment. What you have come here to discuss is what is to be done with your . . . your granddaughter."

"She is not *my granddaughter*. I have *no granddaughter*."

"When the child is deposited on your front doorstep, as is the rule I think in such cases, then you will have some explaining to do."

"You wouldn't dare! Neither of you would dare."

"Father." Stephen was speaking again and the mind of the future member of Parliament was evidently getting to work because what he said was, "There is a way out. We could take the responsibility of the child, Father, and have her fostered. There are plenty of places in this country."

"Oh no, you don't." Laurence's voice was quiet as he broke in. "I know what you would do, both of you, you would dump her, and in the lowest possible place. If she is to be fostered it is to be in England and with suitable foster parents."

Anthony Gullmington's eyes narrowed to slits now as, looking from Laurence to Biddy, he said, "You have both emphasized that she is my granddaughter, then as such I have claim to her, and I can do what I like with her."

"Not if I know it. You ... you attempt to place her anywhere without my knowledge and, to put it plainly, I shall cry this affair from the house tops of every one of your friends in Durham and Northumberland."

"My God!" The words came deep, yet on a whisper. "I just cannot believe it. After all the care and consideration you have been shown in my house over the years, you turn like a viper on me in this my hour of need."

"*Your* hour of need! Your daughter had an hour of need but she was so afraid of your hypocrisy and that of my so-called mama, that she begged a servant, as Biddy here once was, to break the news to Grandmama, because she was terrified to do it herself."

Looking at her late master, Biddy imagined for a moment that he was going to have a seizure. Then he growled at her, "Leave us," and as she went to walk away he spoke to Laurence, saying, "You too."

Laurence paused a moment, then followed Biddy. In the hall he took her hand and said, "Don't worry. Things are bound to come out right."

They were joined in a moment by Madame Arnaud who asked, "Would the gentlemen like some refreshment? I have pie and fresh bread, and. . . ."

"No, thank you, madame." Laurence inclined his head towards her. "We ate back at the hotel."

She looked at Biddy and said, "I shall be very sorry to lose you; you have been such good company. And the baby, she is so beautiful. And your visits, sir. Oh, I'll miss your visits." She paused and turned to look at Anthony Gullmington and Stephen emerge from the room. Then returning her attention to Laurence, she went on, "Monsieur will be having a stone put up at the head of his daughter's grave? There's a good stone-mason in the next village. Pierre burnt the name in the wooden plaque, and he had difficulty because it was so long, and he's not very good, is Pierre. But Jean Lacousse, he is a good mason. He charges but his work is good. And it would be good to see Madame Millican's name in stone, and it's such a nice name: Lucille Beatrice Millican. The villagers and me, we would look after the grave well...."

"What did she say?" Anthony Gullmington was looking at Laurence, and after a moment's hesitation Laurence said, "She was talking about a headstone."

"She mentioned a name, Lucille Beatrice...."

"Yes." Laurence inclined his head; then added slowly, "She was known as Mrs Millican. Biddy was supposed to be her sister-in-law."

The father and son looked at each other.

"And she was buried under that name?"

"Yes."

"What about the certificate ... baptism, the child's?"

"It" – Laurence glanced at Biddy – "it too bears the name of Millican. She was christened Louise Grace Millican."

Almost in horror now Biddy watched a slow smile spread over Anthony Gullmington's face. Then he looked at his son. Stephen wasn't smiling, but he was looking at Laurence, and Laurence said, "That won't get you out of this."

"No?" Anthony Gullmington pursed his lips for a moment before repeating, "No? Well, it will go a damn long way, I should say, for who's to prove that a child called Millican was born of my daughter? My daughter died of a fever, as we were to infer. I had that placed in the Newcastle papers before we left." He now turned to Biddy. "You have dug your own grave, miss."

"I have done no such thing, sir. I can prove that I've had no child."

"And who would believe it? Who will believe you? Mud sticks. Well now, I shall leave you and your charge, and you too, Laurence." And all sarcasm leaving his voice now and bitterness filling it, he said, "You ungrateful swine, you!" And with this he marched out.

Stephen did not immediately follow his father, but he stood looking from one to the other; and then he said, "I'm sorry, Laurie. Believe this, will you? I'm sorry."

"I believe you, Stephen. But you believe that it was her child, don't you?"

Stephen cast his glance downwards, paused a moment, turned, and then followed his father.

Biddy and Laurence stood looking at each other. The expressions on their faces were similar: they looked like two fighters who had been told they had lost the battle which they felt they had previously won.

4

Riah looked at Tol standing opposite her in the drawing-room, and she said, "First thing in the morning I'm goin' to the Justices. My girl's in that foreign country. She went with their daughter. I want to know what's happened to her. Have you heard nothing more?"

"Nothing, except that Miss Lucy died of a fever. But there is more. Everybody knows it up there, but what it is they can't fathom."

"Has Mr Laurence not returned either?"

"No. And that's another funny thing. They were supposed to be with his friends, I mean Miss Lucy and Biddy. That ... that seemed to be the whole idea, that Miss Lucy's education was to be furthered with the young people of the French family."

"Ma! Ma!" The door burst open, and Johnny stood there, his hand still on the knob as he cried, "They're comin' up the road. I saw them from the rise."

"Who is?" They both moved towards him now.

"Our Biddy. And it looks like she's got a man with her."

"No, no. You must be mistaken. You couldn't make her out in this light." She glanced towards the window to see that the twilight was deepening into dark, and the boy cried at her, "It is! It is! She glimpsed me and waved me from the road. They should be at the gate now. Come on! Come on!"

And Riah and Tol went out, running now, out of the front door and on to the drive, to see coming towards them Biddy, who was carrying what looked like a child in her arms, and a man by her side weighed down with two heavy cases.

As Riah went to put her arms about Biddy, crying, "Oh! lass. Oh! hinny," she stopped and peered down on what she now saw was indeed a baby, and her mouth remained agape as Biddy said wearily, "Let's get inside, Ma, we're tired. We had to walk from the crossroads. Oh ... this is Mr Laurence."

Riah turned her head to the side and looked at the man who smiled at her and said, "Good evening, Mrs Millican."

"Let me have those, sir." Tol picked up the cases that Laurence had placed on the ground. "Thanks, Tol," said Laurence, and they all moved across the drive and through the front door and into the hall; and there, Biddy, handing the baby to her mother, said, "Hold her a minute till I get my things off." And Riah taking the child, looked down on it as she thought, Not our Biddy; no, no! Anyway, who to? And thinking thus, bustled them into the drawing-room.

"You have every reason to look amazed, Mrs Millican," Laurence said. "But you are no more amazed than both Biddy and I are to find ourselves in our present situation. We ... we have a lot to tell you, a lot of explaining to do, which will no doubt amaze you further. But" – he smiled warmly at her now – "would it be possible for Biddy to have a warm drink, and perhaps some milk for the baby? Both suffered on yesterday's boat crossing. Neither of them, I'm afraid, enjoy the sea, and the train and coach journey has been long and arduous. We thought to stay in Newcastle for the night, but there was a coach leaving nearby, so we took the opportunity...."

Trying to regain her senses, Riah muttered quickly, "Oh, yes, yes of course. I'll get you all something, yes. Will you give me a hand, Tol?"

"Aye. Yes, of course, Riah."

"And you, you come on with you." Riah caught hold of Johnny's arm and pulled him from his staring, not at Biddy, but at her companion, because he knew who he was, he had seen him out riding with the other masters.

Biddy sat back in the corner of the couch and looked to where the child was lying asleep at the other end. Then her eyes travelled towards Laurence, and she said softly, "It's going to be difficult to explain things because you know what she thought when she saw me with the child?"

"Yes, I've got a good idea."

"Well, if she thinks that, others will think the same."

"Oh no, they won't." His voice was firm. "Not after tomorrow morning when we present the evidence in Grandmama's boudoir."

"What if she were to deny it?"

333

He rose now from his seat by the fire and, sitting on the edge of the sofa, he said, "She couldn't. I have letters from Lucy. Moreover, there's the French doctor and Madame Arnaud. I'd go to the lengths of bringing them across if she tried. Oh, I'm not worried. When we present the child to her it will be a fait accompli. And as her word is law in that household, she'll see that justice is done."

Once more Biddy didn't answer, but to herself she said, I wonder.

It was close on midnight. A great deal of talking had been done, mostly by Biddy and Laurence.

That Riah had been astounded at the sight of her daughter bringing home a baby was nothing to what she felt when this man, this gentleman, told her he wished to marry her daughter, and went on to say that he had no money, at least not for another year, and even then his income would be small, being merely three hundred pounds a year, which to her sounded like a fortune, but to him hardly represented boot-blacking money.

What he proposed to do, he told her, was to teach; in fact, they would both teach. Their idea was to start a school. Where, they hadn't decided yet, but if he could find rooms in Oxford they would soon get going. "But Biddy has a house here," Riah said. "Yes, when you have no further use for it." And taking Biddy's hand, Laurence went on, "And we both hope that that won't be for many, many a long day." And Biddy nodded her head confirming his statement with a smile on her face.

Riah looked at Tol, and Tol's eyes were speaking plainly to her, and what she said next brought Biddy up from the couch: "Tol and me are going to be married, and you know the conditions about the house, so there it is. This is yours now and it's big enough for any school."

Biddy turned her gaze on Laurence, but her face didn't show any enthusiasm as she said, "But you wouldn't want to stay here, live here, so close to . . .?"

"Oh, that wouldn't affect me. They have already thrown me off

334

and I them. I ... I would be delighted at the idea." Laurence looked round the room, got up and walked across to Riah and, taking her hand, he said, "Now are you sure of this?" But before she could answer, Tol put in, "I am, sir, and it should have happened a long, long time ago."

And so it was settled. The only thing there remained to do was to take the baby to madam, then return here and prepare for a wedding, and start a new and exciting life together.

They both knew it wasn't any use approaching the house by the main gate because, as Riah had said, she had already tried to get in to speak to Mr Gullmington, but the lodge-keeper had his orders and wouldn't let her through the gates.

So after Tol had dropped them from the cart, they took the servants' path, but only after climbing the wall, because the gate here, too, was locked, which it had never been before. Laurence had climbed the dry stone wall to the side, which at this point was five feet high; Biddy handed him the child, then adeptly she climbed it herself, and when they were both standing on the narrow path, they looked at each other and grinned like two errant children before quickly making their way to the house.

They had both agreed to take the side entrance that led to the west wing. And this they did without being observed until they reached the gallery, and there, coming towards them, was the first footman, James Simpson. His walk was stately, his countenance set in the usual unsmiling mould as befitted his station ... until he saw them. Then his composure was completely shattered, and he stammered, "Sir ... I think, sir."

"Get about your business, Simpson." Laurence's voice was a command and he waved the man to one side. Then taking Biddy's elbow, he led her towards the ornate double doors and through them towards madam's apartments, there to be confronted by Peggy Tile, the first chambermaid, part of whose duty was to see to the cleaning of the kitchen and the staff quarters on this floor. Standing next to her was Maggie, and at the sight of her sister, Maggie cried, "Eeh! Biddy. Our Biddy!"

When Maggie rushed towards her, Biddy gently pressed her aside with one hand while she cradled the baby with the other, and she said, "Where is Miss Hobson?"

"She's with madam."

"Is madam still in bed?"

"Yes. Oh yes. Eeh! Biddy." Maggie looked towards the baby; then she added, "Will . . . will I tell madam or Miss . . .?"

"No, don't bother. We'll announce ourselves." Biddy glanced quickly at Laurence, and he, stepping forward, thrust open the bedroom door, allowing Biddy to pass, then closed it quickly behind him. And there they both stood for a moment looking to where, devoid now of her nightcap, madam was sitting bolt upright, staring at them as if she didn't believe her eyes.

Laurence led Biddy towards the foot of the bed before speaking, and then he said to the old lady, "Good-morning." He had not given her his usual title of Grandmama. And he added, "We are sorry to disturb you at this early hour, but we thought you would be eager to see your great-grandchild."

They both watched the old face quivering, with what emotion they couldn't tell. When she did speak, it wasn't to them, but without taking her eyes from them she pointed to Jessie Hobson, saying one word, "Out!" And Jessie shuffled away from the bed after glancing apprehensively at the two figures standing there.

When the communicating door had been closed, and not until then, madam spoke again. "What do you expect to gain by this, eh?" she demanded.

"Now, now." Laurence came round the side of the bed and stood looking down at her. "Don't let us mince words. You sent your granddaughter away because she was going to have a child. Well, she had that child, and she died, and we've brought the child to you, because your son won't recognize she is the daughter of his daughter. Surely—" he now screwed up his eyes as if to see her better, and paused for a moment before adding, "it isn't possible that you're going along with him? No, no. You wouldn't, would you? I know it is a bit of a shock, having your plans go awry. . . ."

She cut in now, her voice extraordinarily vibrant and bitter as she said, "My plans going awry, you said? It was to avoid what this person and you here" – she now looked towards Biddy – "have accomplished that my plan was put into operation in the first place. What does she expect to gain from it? Marriage into the family? Blackmail? Never. Never. Not while I have a breath in me. ... You are a slut, girl ... a slut."

"Don't you dare call Biddy a slut! She has served you and yours without thought of herself. And you'd better know right away, Grand—" he stopped himself from adding the mama and inserted, "Madam, that I wish to make this girl my wife."

In the silence that ensued the child coughed, but that was the only sound in the room, and as Laurence looked into the wizened face he knew that this news had come as no surprise to her, she must have already been informed of his intentions in this matter.

When she did speak, her voice was no longer loud, but each word was spat at him as she said, "You are in a dream, and dreams are made up of irrationalities, and you are bound to wake to reason in a very short time. You have been brought up as a gentleman, and you were originally from good stock, but to demean yourself by marrying—" she paused now and held her long, veined hand out flat in Biddy's direction, before she went on, "*this*, which perhaps you have not considered will mean associating with her class. If you want her so much, take her as a mistress. I will condone that, but marriage ... no, never! And don't" – her voice rose again as she stared into his blazing countenance – "don't speak until I have finished. Now I am going to address her."

The bloodshot eyes, like pin-points of red fire, concentrated now on Biddy, whose face had lost every vestige of colour and whose lips were pressed tight, but ready to spring apart at any moment, and she waited for what this old tyrant, as she thought of her now, had to say to her. And what madam said was, "The child, I understand, was christened in your name, also its mother bears your name on her gravestone so the child to all intents and purposes is yours. Now I shall make a bargain with you, miss. I shall settle on you the sum of five hundred pounds, this to be paid immediately. I shall also pay for the child's upbringing with any respectable family you care to leave it with, if you will promise me to have nothing to do with this young man whom, sorrowfully I say now, I have always looked upon as my grandson. Should you not agree to these terms, then I am afraid you will bring disrepute not only on yourself but on him."

"She will never bring disrepute on me."

Madam turned her face with its furious expression towards

Laurence now, crying, "No? You marry her; she has a child; who gave her that child? You. Your name would be mud in the county, not because you gave her the child, no, but because you are imbecile enough to act as any local yokel would, and pay for his pleasure. You would be the laughing-stock of the county."

"You think so?" Laurence's face was also white except where the stubble on his chin stood out like a dark shadow. And in a quiet voice that seemed to enrage the old lady even more, he said, "I had never imagined you to be naïve ... wily and machiavellian even, capable of extremely low cunning, but never naïve. Take one thing at a time with regard to your granddaughter. First; why, if she died in France, wasn't her body brought over and placed in the family vault in the churchyard? There'll be questions asked about that, surely. Secondly, the small fact that she didn't return for the holidays. Of course, these are not proof that she bore a child, but what is proof she stated in her own handwriting in the letters she sent to me in Oxford."

They stared at each other for what seemed an interminable time. When she next spoke her voice was quiet too. "Do you know I had never imagined anything could happen in life that could make me say that I never want to set eyes on you again. Yes, indeed, you may look sorrowful ... and I may add, you will never inherit a penny of mine, you have lost yourself a fortune, for the bulk of all I possess was to go to you."

He put in harshly now, "Only if I had married May?" And at this she shook her head saying, with a touch of sorrow, "No, no. I got over that. But now you will be a penniless nothing all your life."

His face hardening again, he said, "Not so. My mind will provide my livelihood. I won't need to spend my days like your son and your grandson, wondering what to do to get through them."

"That may be so, but you'll spend your days being shunned by your own kind."

She turned her head slowly from him now and looked at Biddy, and, her teeth wobbling in her mouth, she muttered, "I curse the day, girl, that you came into this room. I go further back to the time when you first came into service here, a washhouse drab, the lowest of the low."

As Biddy saw Laurence about to protest she put her hand out

to him, while hitching the child further up her arm; then looking at her late mistress, she said, "In position, yes, madam, but mentally, even at that age, I felt superior to any member of your staff. And not only the members of your staff, because your granddaughter, although I came to have an affection for her, had very little intelligence. As for her brother, he had no mind at all, stables would have been a fitting place for him. I won't go on to name the rest of your family, madam, you have your own opinion of them which I have listened to you voicing often, so, as you have saddled me with your great-grandchild, I accept the responsibility. She bears my name, yes, and doubtless, you and your family will do your best to prove by gossip that she is mine. And so she shall be, until she reaches the age of reason, and then I shall tell her who she really is, and where her rightful place is. And her adoptive father" – she turned and looked at Laurence – "will show her the letters from her mother. Madam, I am sorry for you. Remember that, will you? I am sorry for you."

On this she turned and walked out of the room. And Laurence paused a moment, and, looking at the figure of the old woman who seemed to have swelled to twice her size with an indignation that prevented her speaking, he said softly, "I am sorry for you too, Grandmama, but in a different way. The child will be brought up well. I can only promise you this, that we shall wait some time after she reaches her age of reason before we tell her the truth, because rejection at any age is difficult to bear. I can only hope her training will sustain her. Goodbye, Grandmama."

His jaws were tight when he reached the hallway, there to see Biddy commanding her sister, saying, "Do as I tell you, get your things, you're coming home."

The girl looked from Biddy to Jessie, and Jessie said softly, "It's all right. Get your things."

When Maggie scurried away, Jessie, staring at the child, said, "So that was it?" And Biddy answered tersely, "Yes, Miss Hobson, that was it. Miss Lucy was sent away to have her child because the disgrace would have been too much for the family to bear. And now the child is too much for the family to bear. They are going to put the onus on me. But you know and I know whom she belongs to."

"Aye, lass. I guessed it from the first, and when she didn't come back at Christmas. Yes" – she nodded – "I know, but you'll be hard put to make them" – she thumbed to the floor – "believe this, especially with the tale that's going round."

"What tale?"

Jessie now looked towards Mr Laurence and he said, "It's no tale, Hobson."

"I . . . I just heard a whisper, sir . . ."

"Well, the whisper will grow into a shout shortly, and everyone will put two and two together, won't they?"

"Yes, likely, sir. 'Tis the way of the world. I'm sorry, sir."

"Oh, don't be sorry for us, Hobson, at least don't be sorry for me. I might as well tell you, I had no intention of staying here. I had plans to move to Oxford and make that my permanent residence, but now I'll be living practically on the doorstep, and that will be confusion confounded."

Jessie looked at Biddy, and Biddy said briefly, "The house is mine. Mother is marrying Mr Briston. We are to set up a school there."

"Good Go. . . ."

She didn't finish 'God' but added, "I . . . I'm sorry." Then she smiled wanly as she went on, "You were always a surprise, lass, right from the very beginning. Things always seemed to happen where you were. I think I said that to you once."

"Yes, you did. Well, here's Maggie; we must be off. And, I'd just like to say, Jessie" – she said the name softly – "thank you for your training. It'll stand me in good stead in the future." She leant forward now and kissed the old woman on the cheek; then turned about and walked through the hall towards the double doors, and there Laurence opened them for her and Maggie, and they passed through and on to the gallery where a number of servants were busily doing nothing and stared in silence at the small party making for the door leading to the back stairs. Then as of one accord they gave an audible gasp as they looked towards the far end of the gallery from where their master was striding towards the intruders who had now stopped and were awaiting his approach.

Anthony Gullmington was not alone. His wife was on one side of him, his son on the other, and they were both remonstrating softly with him. When his wife caught hold of his arm he thrust her off, then bawled at the servants, "Out of the way!" before coming to a halt a few yards from where Laurence, Biddy and Maggie stood, the latter visibly shaking.

It was evident to all that rage was preventing the master of the house from speaking for the moment. When eventually the words came the spittle dripped from his mouth with them.

"How ... how dare you, sir, enter my house without my permission and ... and bring that ... that slut with you! I could have you both horse-whipped and thrown out bodily ... bodily. I have only to ... to say the word."

"Why don't you? Most of the servants are within earshot."

"You ... you damned upstart! I'll ... I'll—" As he made to spring forward Stephen caught hold of him by both arms, saying, "Father. Father, enough!"

"Enough, you say. Enough, after all I've done for him? He's an ungrateful swine."

His countenance showing an almost equal anger, Laurence cried, "Ungrateful, never! And what I'll have you understand, sir, is, it was in gratitude that I protected your daughter and tried to spare your family the disgrace it wouldn't have been able to bear. Granted it was on the suggestion of madam, but I carried it out. And this" – he pointed to the child that Biddy was pressing tightly to her – "is the result. She is...."

Two things at the moment stopped his flow: the look of entreaty on the face of the woman who had been his adoptive mother, and whom he had never liked, as she implored, "Please. Please, Laurence;" the other, the blow that caught him on the shoulder and sent him reeling back towards the staircase door.

The blow had been intended for his head, but so quickly had Anthony Gullmington wrenched himself from his son's hold that he himself had over-balanced as his arm had thrust itself out to strike and now he was half crouched against the wall and within an arm's length of Laurence who had righted himself and was standing with clenched fists, but these tightly pressed against his sides.

It was Stephen who spoke now, saying, "Go, Laurie, please." And he pulled open the stair door, but Laurence still stood glaring at the man who had now straightened himself up but remained leaning against the wall and returning his look with equal vehemence.

"Come, Laurence." Biddy spoke the name quietly, yet it would appear she had shouted it for it widened the eyes of the servants and brought a quiver to Grace Gullmington's face.

Slowly Laurence turned about, but he did not precede Biddy to the stairs. Putting his hand on her arm, he pushed her gently forward, and as he passed Stephen he looked him straight in the eyes and felt a pang attack his chest as he found no bitterness in the look that met his, if anything the message they sent to him was one of sorrow and understanding.

When they reached the yard they stopped for a moment, and her voice trembling, Biddy asked, "Are you hurt?"

"No, no." He tried to smile at her as he said, "The answer might have been different if the blow had landed where he intended it should."

"Look, there's Jean." Maggie tugged at Biddy's sleeve, and Biddy looked to where Jean was crossing the yard holding one end of a large linen basket.

Turning towards Laurence, she said, "Would you mind? I won't be a moment. I might not see her again." And hurrying now she went to where Jean stood open-mouthed, staring at her, and she drew her to one side, saying hastily, "There's no time to talk, and I mightn't see you again, but I thought, would you like to come and work for us?"

"What do you mean, Biddy? At the house? Your house?"

"Yes. There won't be much money but it will be better than here. You could come over next leave day and we'll talk about it."

"Oh, thanks, Biddy. Ta. Is . . . is that the baby?"

"Yes, this is the baby."

"'Tis . . . 'tisn't yours?" It was a whisper.

"No, it isn't mine, but nobody will believe it."

"Oh, Biddy."

"Never mind. See you soon."

"Aye, Biddy. Aye. Ta. Thanks."

Quickly now, she rejoined Laurence and Maggie, but as she made to go towards the side path Laurence took her arm, and none too gently, saying, "No, not that way. We will go by the main drive." She stared at him for a moment, then lowered her head over the child and did as he bid without any protest as to the advisability of it.

As they crossed the stable yard, Biddy glanced about her, hoping that she might see Davey, but she seemed to see every stable hand except him. He had likely got word of their presence and was ashamed of the scandal. In a way she felt hurt. But what did it matter? Nothing could add to the hurt she was feeling at this moment. That awful scene Laurence had had to endure, and that old woman up there who had talked to her as if she was something crawling on the ground. Yet she knew that as she listened to her she had seen herself through her eyes as someone of such a low degree that even the thought of marrying Laurence would be presumptuous.

They were walking on the drive in front of the house now. There was no one to be seen, not outside, but both she and Laurence were aware the house was very much alive behind the windows.

It was an amazed lodge-keeper who opened the gates for them but he raised his cap and his voice was very civil as he said, "Good-morning, Mr Laurence." And Laurence said to him, "Goodbye, Mr Johnson."

They walked over a mile before being met by Tol. He was driving the wood cart. It was half filled with logs and Maggie had to climb among them while Biddy and Laurence squeezed on to the driving seat.

Tol, seeing the look on their faces, remarked briefly, "Had it rough, sir?" And Laurence replied, "Sort of, Tol."

There was no further discussion until Tol dropped them at the gate, when Laurence said to him, "If they find out what you've been doing this morning, you will very likely be out of work."

"That wouldn't worry me, sir." Tol smiled at him. "Anyway, I'm sure you'd set me on. I've always thought that would be good for market produce." He nodded towards the wall before adding, "And I'm not the only one who thinks that way."

"Thank you, Tol, for the ride." Biddy's voice was low, her face unsmiling, and he replied, "It's a pleasure, Biddy. It's a pleasure. And may I say this to both of you." He looked from one to the other. "I only hope you're as happy, leastwise in the future, as your mother has made me."

Biddy turned away, almost at a run, hugging the child to her, for there was an emotion rising in her that she had to quell until she got into the house. But when once she reached the kitchen where, on seeing Maggie, her mother exclaimed, "Why, what are you doing here?" Biddy for answer thrust the child into her arms, saying, "Take her for a minute, and . . . and leave me be, just for a minute or so." And with this she ran out of the kitchen and across the hall and into the library, and there, flinging herself into the leather chair which had for so long been used by the master, she gave rein to her pent-up feelings.

After a while her crying subsided and she sat quietly looking about her, and she seemed to sense the master's presence near her saying, "This is where life begins for you. You are still very ignorant, but you will learn as you teach." That's what he had once said to her: One learns as one teaches. And sometimes one learns that the pupil is more intelligent than the master.

She hadn't heard the door open, nor was she aware of Laurence's entry until he stood in front of her and drew her up into his arms, and there, holding her close, he said softly, "I'm sorry, my dear, I'm sorry to the heart you've had to suffer all this through no fault of yours. Are you willing to bring her up as our own? You know, I could do as I said, and bring over the doctor and Madame Arnaud and take the matter to court. Letters would prove...."

"No, no." She lifted her head from his shoulder. "I ... I want to keep her. Somehow it's strange, but ... but from the moment she was born I felt ... I can't understand it." She blinked the moisture from her eyes and swallowed deeply before going on, "It was just as if she were mine. To tell you the truth I would have hated to leave her up there. I'm ... I'm not crying about her, it's the things that madam said to me, of me. They made me wonder what ... what I'd be doing to you if we marry."

He held her gently away from him, his chin pulled into his neck, his eyes narrowed, and he repeated, "If we married? There's no if about it, we are getting married. I love you. When I say, you are the only woman ... and I mean woman, that I have ever loved or am likely to love, I would add that many in the same position might say the same things to you, knowing that nothing remains stationary in this life, not even emotions, and that some day they would forget these words or, if not forget them, repeat them to someone else. But with me, Biddy, I can swear to you that that will not be so, because as I have already told you, I have known from the very first that you were for me, and I for you, although, truthfully, I tried to evade the question, even for a time thinking as madam does, that the solution would be to take you for my mistress. Yet, I knew that you would never countenance that." He pulled a slight face at her now before going on "When I stayed away it was because I imagined any union between us would be impossible to bring about because of the insurmountable problems. But life being what it is, I know now that there is no problem that I wouldn't surmount to get you, to marry you, to make you my wife. And" – his smile widened – "you are getting no bargain. My worldly possessions, at least for the next year, amount to eighty-seven pounds in the bank, a few sets of gold cufflinks and studs, and two gold watches, while here I am, not only proposing to a most beautiful, highly intelligent young woman, but she is giving me a home, a lovely home in which to start a dream of mine, a school for young men."

"No. No." He was amazed at the strength of the push that forced him backwards from her as she cried at him now, "For young men and young women. Definitely, *young women.*"

She watched him close his eyes while his head drooped, and now he muttered, "Yes, ma'am, young women. They will certainly be admitted to our school."

"In even numbers, sir."

"Yes, ma'am" He was gazing at her, his eyes bright and twinkling. "In equal numbers."

"And with equal attention."

"And with equal attention, ma'am." His head nodded with each word.

"In all subjects."

"As you say, ma'am, in all subjects. I agree with everything you say; in fact, I will put it in writing on the day you first sign your name as Mrs Laurence Frederick Carmichael."

Her eyes sprung wide. "Is that your name, Carmichael?"

"Yes, that's my real name, Carmichael."

"Oh, Laurie, Laurie. What a lovely name. Thank you for offering it to me." Slowly she went into his arms now, adding, "I will love and honour it and you all my days."

On a windy day at the end of March they were married in the village church, reluctantly it would seem, by Parson Weeks. The bride's stepfather, Mr Tol Briston gave the bride away. There was one member missing from the family party. Davey had left The Heights the day after Biddy's visit. He had not gone back to the house, but had given Tol a message for his mother, saying he wasn't going to wait to be thrown out, and that, anyway, he had been half promised a job at a farrier's in Gateshead Fell. It transpired that the farrier had a good business and also a daughter of marriageable age whom he met when stabling the coach and horses in the town.

The bride was attended by her sister and her friend Jean. The groom was supported by two friends who had come up from Oxford.

The combined number should have hardly filled the two front pews of the church, yet it was packed to the door, because it wasn't every day that a gentleman from a place like The Heights married a servant, even one with a head on her shoulders, but who had arrived back home from across the seas with a bairn. Now that was a mystery: was it? or wasn't it? Some said it wasn't hers. Then if it wasn't hers, why was he marrying her? There was more than a whisper that it was Miss Lucy Gullmington's. Now that was a thing to say, wasn't it? But then it was a fact that the housekeeper had seen the bride there all rumpled from her rolling in the grass the day the bairn was conceived. All right, it hadn't run nine months, but there were plenty of people alive today who had been born at seven months, weren't there? Anyway, there she was, at the altar, looking as beautiful as any bride who had ever knelt there, and him looking like a dog with two tails. Well, all they could say for sure was, from the looks of them, they'd like to bet that another bairn would join the present one, seven months or nine months, and it likely wouldn't stop there.

And to think all this had come about because Mr Miller had taken her, her brothers and sister, and her mother in off the road not eight years gone. It just showed you that people should be careful before they do a kindness.